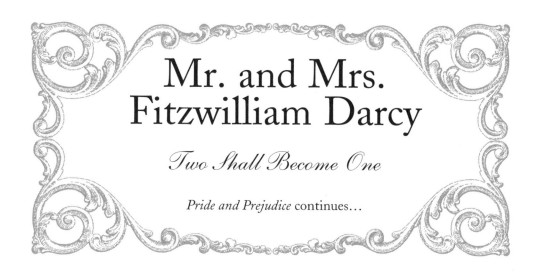

Mr. and Mrs. Fitzwilliam Darcy

Two Shall Become One

Pride and Prejudice continues…

Sharon Lathan

SOURCEBOOKS LANDMARK™
AN IMPRINT OF SOURCEBOOKS, INC.®
NAPERVILLE, ILLINOIS

Published by Sourcebooks Landmark, an imprint of Sourcebooks, Inc.
P.O. Box 4410, Naperville, Illinois 60567-4410
(630) 961-3900
FAX: (630) 961-2168
www.sourcebooks.com

Library of Congress Cataloging-in-Publication Data

Lathan, Sharon.
  Mr. and Mrs. Fitzwilliam Darcy: Two shall become one: Pride and prejudice
continues / Sharon Lathan.
     p. cm.
1. Darcy, Fitzwilliam (Fictitious character)--Fiction. 2. Bennet, Elizabeth
(Fictitious character)--Fiction. 3. England--Social life and customs--19th
century--Fiction. 4. Domestic fiction. I. Austen, Jane, 1775-1817. Pride and
prejudice. II. Title.
  PS3612.A869T86 2009
  813'.6--dc22
                2008037085

Printed and bound in the United States of America
VP 10 9 8 7 6 5 4 3 2 1

Table of Contents

Foreword

OVER THANKSGIVING WEEKEND OF 2005, I entered a movie theater with my best girlfriend and teenage daughter to watch *Pride & Prejudice* starring Keira Knightley and Matthew Macfadyen. My only expectation was to enjoy a sappy chick flick with two of my dearest women friends. I had never read the classic novel by Jane Austen, nor had I seen any of the previous adaptations.

To my stunned amazement, I walked out of that theater sporting a heart swelling with romantic sentiment and warm fuzzy feelings running amok, and I was soon to embark on a pathway that would change my life. Within two months, I had joined the ranks of fan fiction writers from all over the world who have adored this timeless tale of true love. I have since read the novel and seen a few of the previous adaptations, but my heart remains enamored with the recent movie and the incredible actors and actresses who brought these delightful characters to life.

My personal quest was to delve realistically into the Regency/Late Georgian Era of England in the early 1800s while exploring the future of the Darcys. It began as a lark, but in true Mr. Darcy fashion, I was well into the middle of it before I recognized what I had begun. Quite before I turned around, I had my own website and was reaching the one-year anniversary of their wedding with fifty-plus chapters under my belt. Yes, it is an obsession!

What I have strived to recount is a marriage in its purest embodiment: a union based on commitment, equality, passion, friendship, honesty, and love. I wanted to answer the timeless questions regarding happily-ever-after and how two individual people meld into one soul. Along the way there are humor, drama, friends, family, and life events to experience with the lovers.

The Darcy Saga, in its entirety, is about how two people who are bonded and committed to each other move through life. That is the plot, the theme, and the essence of the story. They are not the same people once they have each other.

This first novel deals with the initial days into weeks, ending with five months of wedded bliss as the family prepares for the Season in London. I do not rush, as I want the reader to share in the joy of new love as it blooms and alters and strengthens William and Elizabeth. Subsequent novels will travel further along the timeline of life.

Welcome to Pemberley, and thank you for taking this journey with me.

Sincerely,

Sharon Lathan

Cast of Characters

Mr. Fitzwilliam Darcy: Master of Pemberley in Derbyshire; 29 years of age, born November 10, 1787; parents James and Lady Anne Darcy, both deceased; married Elizabeth Bennet on November 28, 1816

Elizabeth Darcy: Mistress of Pemberley; 21 years of age, born May 28, 1795; second Bennet daughter

Miss Georgiana Darcy: 17 years of age; sister of Mr. Darcy with guardianship shared by her brother and cousin, Col. Fitzwilliam; companion is Mrs. Annesley

Col. Richard Fitzwilliam: 31 years of age; cousin and dear friend to Mr. Darcy; second son of Lord and Lady Matlock; stationed with a regiment in London

Lord Matlock, the Earl of Matlock: Darcy's Uncle Malcolm, brother to Lady Anne Darcy; ancestral estate is Rivallain in Matlock, Derbyshire

Lady Matlock, the Countess of Matlock: Darcy's Aunt Madeline; wife to Lord Matlock, mother of Jonathan, Annabella, and Richard

Mr. Jonathan Fitzwilliam: Heir to the Matlock earldom, eldest Fitzwilliam son; wife is *Priscilla*

Mr. Charles Bingley: 25 years of age; longtime friend of Mr. Darcy;

resides at Netherfield Hall in Hertfordshire; married Jane Bennet on November 28, 1816

Jane Bingley: elder sister of Elizabeth and oldest Bennet daughter; wife of Mr. Bingley

Miss Caroline Bingley: sister of Charles Bingley

Mr. and Mrs. Bennet: Elizabeth's parents; reside at Longbourn in Hertfordshire with two middle daughters, *Mary* and *Kitty*

Edward and Violet Gardiner: uncle and aunt of Elizabeth; reside in Cheapside, London

Stephen Lathrop: Cambridge friend of Mr. Darcy; resides at Stonecrest Hall in Leicestershire; wife is *Amelia*

Henry Vernor: family friend of the Darcys; residence is Sanburl Hall near Lambton, Derbyshire; wife is *Mary*, daughter is *Bertha*

Gerald Vernor: son of Henry Vernor; childhood friend of Mr. Darcy; wife is *Harriet*; resides at Sanburl Hall

Albert Hughes: childhood friend of Mr. Darcy; wife is *Marilyn*

Rory Sitwell: Cambridge friend of Mr. Darcy; wife is *Julia*

George and Alison Fitzherbert: Derbyshire residents

Clifton and Chloe Drury: Derbyshire residents

Mrs. Reynolds: Pemberley housekeeper

Mr. Taylor: Pemberley butler

Mr. Keith: Mr. Darcy's steward

Mr. Samuel Oliver: Mr. Darcy's valet

Miss Marguerite Charbonneau: Mrs. Darcy's maid

Phillips, Watson, Tillson, Georges, Rothchilde: Pemberley footmen

Mr. Clark: Pemberley Head groundskeeper

Mr. Thurber: Pemberley Head groomsman

Mrs. Langton: Pemberley cook

Reverend Bertram: Rector of Pemberley Chapel

Madame du Loire: Modiste in Lambton

Marquis de Orman: Derbyshire resident

CHAPTER ONE

Mr. and Mrs. Fitzwilliam Darcy

THANK GOODNESS IT IS *finally over*, Fitzwilliam Darcy thought with a heavy sigh.

He realized that he probably should not entertain such a thought, but it could not be helped. The past eight weeks of his engagement had held many wonderful moments and all in all had been delightful, but also exceedingly trying. Daily he wanted nothing more than to spend time with his beloved Elizabeth. However, the constant pressures of wedding plans, visits from a seemingly inexhaustible quantity of friends and family, constraints of propriety, and business interests that had taken him from Hertfordshire on several occasions all had conspired to separate him from her far too often. Add to that his own uneasiness with all the social engagements, not to mention his continued distaste for Mrs. Bennet, and the weeks had seemed interminable.

Nonetheless, he thought while gazing lovingly upon his sleeping wife… *my wife!… There certainly were some marvelous times to be remembered.* In truth, he and Elizabeth had managed to pass numerous satisfying hours together alone, or at least almost alone, yet it never was sufficient as far as Darcy was concerned. She had teased him on occasion for acting like a petulant child whose favorite toy had been taken away. Initially, he had been a bit offended, but then he realized she was correct and had to laugh at himself. Yet he could not deny how bereft he felt without her by his side and how he had treasured every moment that they were together, even if it was brief.

They discovered, much to their mutual joy, that the trials of the previous months, during which each had suffered tremendously, had brought them to a place of complete understanding and honesty. The conversations they now shared were open, deeply profound, intimate, and blessedly free of all artifice and misunderstanding. He had revealed himself to her as he never had to any living soul, not even to his sister or dear Cousin Richard. She had done the same.

They had strived to learn as much as possible about each other. The resulting adoration and respect had only grown deeper with each passing day. And all this before they were married! Now they were truly husband and wife, and Darcy could only imagine their love and communion growing stronger.

He rested his head back against the rocking carriage wall, tightened his arm around Elizabeth, and closed his eyes as his thoughts continued to drift. The ceremony itself had been lovely. The women had triumphed in every aspect of the arrangements. Frankly, Darcy could not have cared less about the decorations as long as his precious Elizabeth became his wife. However, he understood the importance of these things to the ladies and had to admit that the Meryton church and the reception hall at Netherfield were stupendously adorned with flowers in profusion, ribbons and bows, candles and more.

Darcy merely gave it all a cursory glance, eyes riveted to the door. Once Elizabeth entered on the arm of her proud father, Darcy saw or heard very little else. She simply stole away his breath and all conscious thought! How he managed to recite his vows was a mystery. Elizabeth was wearing a simple but lovely white gown of silk with lace along the edges and a golden sash. She had styled her hair in an elaborate design of curls and braids with thin gold ribbon and buds of baby's breath and lavender intertwined. She wore the strand of sapphires he had given her as an engagement gift around her slender neck. Her fine eyes sparkled, her cheeks were rosy, and that special smile only for him highlighted her luscious lips. It was a picture imprinted on his mind's eye and would remain there flawlessly rendered for all of his life.

The lovely and ancient church in Meryton, where the Bennet family had worshipped for years, was perfectly suited for the ceremony. In truth, Darcy had always imagined marrying in the chapel at Pemberley and was mildly saddened initially at the natural choice to marry where both Bennet daughters had grown up. However, he quickly recognized the logic to the decision and realized that he honestly did not care as long as they were married with the sanction of the Church, religion being a vital part of his life.

The elderly vicar performed the traditional ceremony impeccably, his strong voice reciting the vows and quoting Holy Scripture with firm conviction. When Darcy slipped the slim, etched-in-jewels gold band onto Elizabeth's finger, nestling it alongside the sapphire and diamond engagement ring that had been his mother's, it was far and away the most profoundly moving moment in his life.

Elizabeth stirred slightly and he pressed her closer to his side, kissing her gently on the top of her head. He pulled the blanket further over her body and tucked it in. Once he was sure she still slept, he rested his cheek on her head and went back to his daydreams.

The reception at Netherfield was joyous, filled with all of their respective friends and relatives. The food was superb, the musicians exceptional, and the wine of the best vintage. Darcy had an extremely difficult time tearing his eyes away from his bride, but he did manage to congratulate Charles and Jane on their nuptials as well, realizing with a start that Jane looked quite beautiful herself. He was embarrassed to admit that he had not even noticed her presence at the church's altar alongside Elizabeth!

He and Lizzy had previously agreed that they would make their escape as soon as good manners would allow. Darcy had secured lodging at the White Stag Inn near Bedford. He had discovered this superb establishment years earlier while still at Cambridge. Located only a few miles off the main thoroughfare to London—on the turnpike to Cambridge, in fact—it was secluded enough to fulfill his preference for quiet while traveling, but also popular enough as a halting place for those journeying to Newmarket for the races, or on to Suffolk for the sea, so that it was well maintained.

It was also the perfect resting point for the two-day ride between London and Pemberley, a trek he had completed more times that he could remember. He had stayed at the White Stag so frequently over the years that the owners, a pleasant couple named Hamilton, knew him well. They had been ecstatic at the idea of hosting him and his new bride for the initial days of their married life.

All arrangements had been made in advance and, to ensure their privacy, he had rented out the entire second story. Luckily, the late time of year meant the road would be lightly traveled, with hired coaches rarely passing and passengers minimal. Even the pub would see few customers, although it would not matter greatly, as their suite was to the rear of the sturdy red-brick building and well away from the public rooms.

Their luggage had been sent ahead earlier in the day, so all would be ready upon their arrival. Darcy was breathless in anticipation of this night! Not just for the obvious reasons of their promised intimacy and consummation of their marriage, but for the peace and relief from the hustle and bustle of the past two months. Just to be alone with his beloved! Never in his life had any evening been so tremendously and lovingly contemplated.

The carriage pulled off the main road, and Darcy knew they were close to their destination. "Elizabeth," he whispered softly, "wake up, my love; we are almost there."

She moaned softly and wriggled closer to his side, wrapping her arms tighter around his waist. "Much too comfortable here," she murmured sleepily. "Do not want to move."

Darcy chuckled. "Well, imagine your heightened comfort in our room, and perhaps that will help you wake up."

She leaned her head back, safe and warm within the circle of his embrace, gazed into his brilliant eyes, and smiled. "You make an excellent point, Mr. Darcy, most excellent indeed!"

They stared for a long moment with their arms remaining tightly wound about each other. Finally Elizabeth could stand it no longer and exclaimed with breathless impertinence, "Are you going to kiss me, husband, or do I need to beg?"

He smiled impishly. "Perhaps I should have you beg. That might be interesting to watch. The proud Miss Bennet begging."

"Ah, but I am no longer Miss Bennet and since you hold the monopoly on pride, William, I daresay I would not be very amusing at all!" Her eyes were twinkling as they always did when she teased him.

He feigned deep consideration and seriousness while lowering his face to hers slowly. "Now it appears it is your turn to make an excellent point, Mrs. Darcy." He kissed her gently at first, then deeply as she responded in kind. Cupping one cheek and caressing tenderly, Darcy murmured, "I love you, Elizabeth, my wife." Allowing no opportunity for her to reply, he reclaimed her lips. Who knows how far the kisses may have gone, but, alas, they were interrupted by the carriage stopping with a jolt. Darcy released his wife with a lingering caress and regretful sigh.

They were greeted at the courtyard door of the inn by Mr. Hamilton. He welcomed them both as they alighted from the carriage and hurried them into the warm and inviting reception room. A servant took their coats and gloves.

Darcy spoke to Mr. Hamilton, assuring that all arrangements had been carried out, while Elizabeth looked around the room. The pub was to the left through an archway of polished oak and gray stone. Two men in farmer's garb sat at the edge of the bar, ale mugs in hand, as they attended to an unseen minstrel whose strains of violin music could be faintly heard.

The reception area was a quaint and cozy room warmed by a roaring fire in a huge fireplace located to the right; numerous chairs and couches were positioned around the heat source. An older gentleman sat in one chair, newspaper in hand, attending avidly to the words. A middle-aged couple sat upon a settee, lifting smiling faces to the Darcys, and nodding politely. There were rooms and hallways branching off from the main chamber, including a public dining area and what appeared to be a tiny library. Lizzy's attention was diverted to a stout woman with a sunny face who appeared from around a large desk.

"Welcome, welcome!" she sang. "Mr. and Mrs. Darcy! How delightful! Newlyweds! How precious it is to have you spending your first days with us!" Mr. Hamilton turned and introduced his wife to Lizzy.

Mrs. Hamilton continued in her breathless, singsong way of talking, "Mr. Darcy has been our guest so very often! And now he is married! What a blessing it is! A private parlor is set up for dining, Mr. Darcy, just as you requested! Dinner will be ready momentarily! All the dishes you asked for, Mr. Darcy! Very private!"

She took Elizabeth's hands and guided her toward a far room, all the while prattling on, "You look absolutely radiant, my dear! Stunning gown! And your hair! Beautiful!"

As Mrs. Hamilton continued, Lizzy glanced back to see Darcy grinning as he followed the two women down a short corridor to a small parlor overlooking the moonlit meadow outside the paned windows. Mrs. Hamilton seated them at a small table close to the fire, bustling about and rattling on, until Mr. Hamilton coaxed her out of the room with a promise that they would be left as unaccompanied as possible. Once alone, Darcy and Lizzy could not resist laughing.

"Are you pleased, dearest?" Darcy asked, scooting his chair nearer until their knees were touching.

"Oh yes, William, it is all so very wonderful." She reached over and took his hand, squeezing it gently. "You have gone to so much trouble for me, and I do so appreciate it."

"It was no trouble at all, my love, and I must confess I was not only thinking of you," he replied with a laugh, kissing her fingers. "As we have established, I am a rather selfish man and I want you all to myself, far away from Bennets and Bingleys or anyone else!"

"Well, now you have me, for better or worse. I hope I do not disappoint," she said with a sly look from under her lashes and a firm squeeze to his knee.

Suddenly Darcy had a difficult time catching his breath. "Oh no, Elizabeth. I am positive that it would be impossible for you to disappoint me in any situation." He placed his free hand over the dainty one resting on his knee, leaning instinctively toward her.

Sadly, before any further action could be taken, a maid entered with the first course. Darcy jerked backward with a ready blush, Lizzy laughing. The dinner was excellent, all of Elizabeth's favorite dishes, but neither of them were hungry. Odd, considering they had not eaten much all day, what with wedding jitters and endless socializing. The fact that this finally was their wedding night seemed to occur to them both at the same time. Anxiousness, underlying passion, and hints of nervousness dissolved any appetite.

Finally the courses had been served and taken away barely eaten. With scarcely concealed enthusiasm and a faint rosiness to her cheeks, Elizabeth announced that she would retire to her dressing room to change. Darcy nearly choked on his wine, but managed to maintain a calm demeanor as she rose from the table and leaned over to give him a brief kiss of passionate promise.

"Will it suit you if I am ready in half an hour?" she asked softly, to which he could only nod. With a tender caress to his cheek, she turned and left the room.

Never had thirty minutes lasted so long! Darcy truly thought he would lose his mind. He wandered into the small library and pulled a book off a shelf at random. Any attempt to actually read it was ludicrous to the extreme, but he made a show of it, employing all his well-perfected composure.

After twenty minutes he could stand it no longer and briskly strode to his dressing room. The house's manservant was awaiting him and assisted Darcy with his toilette. Darcy again found himself calling upon every ounce of his strength of will not to rush through the agonizingly slow procedures. Common sense did prevail, thankfully, since he did not reckon his new wife would appreciate her new husband arriving with a bleeding face!

Eventually all was done and he nervously entered the bedchamber, only to find it empty of his wife. He wandered around the room, pleased with the décor and the attention to detail Mr. and Mrs. Hamilton had ensured. There were several vases of flowers about the room, a bottle of chilled champagne, a platter of fruits and sweets and breads, a sofa, and an enormous bearskin rug with several cushions before the blazing fire. The spacious four-poster bed was turned down invitingly, plump pillows waiting. Darcy went to the window and gazed out at the moonlit lake behind the house, breathing deeply to calm his nerves and halt his trembling. Nothing to do but wait.

～～

Lizzy finished her preparations and dismissed her maid. The allotted thirty minutes had passed, but she remained seated at her vanity absently brushing her hair as she stared into the mirror, lost in memory.

Lizzy was no longer afraid of the intimacy to take place this night. In fact, she was actually highly excited, as scandalous as that may be in the opinion of some, such as her mother. However, it had taken some time for her to come to her current level of anticipation. She was a maiden, of course, but she understood the concept of the mating process. She had grown up on a working farm after all! However, understanding the mechanics of the sexual act in animals was far different than comprehending all the nuances inherent in the activity between people. The truth was that she had given the matter absolutely no thought.

Until William.

Upon her engagement, especially with the first tender kisses and touches of her betrothed, she found herself unable *not* to consider the realities. In fact, there were times when her mind could not focus on any topic except the intimate relationship between a man and woman, or more specifically between her and her fiancé. Usually, these times occurred when Darcy was near, but even visualizing him elicited the musings. Also, there were her dreams. The feelings and sensations his very presence engendered, not to mention when he touched or kissed her, were strong and incredibly pleasant.

As the weeks progressed, she found herself vacillating among excitement, shyness, desire, fear, happiness, anxiety, and every other emotion possible. That she desired Darcy was not a shock; it was the depth of her desire and the most obvious depth of his passion for her that left her stunned and breathless. He was so much more worldly than she! Would she be able to live up to his expectations? Would she know what to do when the time came? Would he be disappointed?

She smiled at the remembrance of her fears, easily conjuring up the uncertainty she had felt in those days not so very long ago and how Darcy had erased all of them. *My amazing William*, she thought, closing her eyes, *how perfect he is and how I love him.*

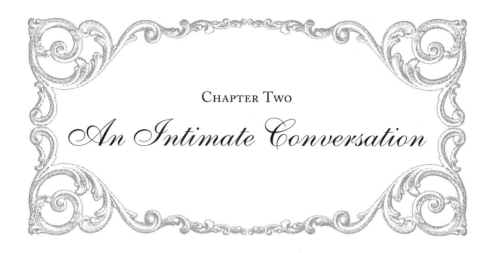

CHAPTER TWO

An Intimate Conversation

Three days before the wedding

L IZZY AWOKE WITH A start and a gasp. She was breathing heavily, as if having run for miles uphill. Her body trembled and sweat beaded on her brow. This was the fourth morning in a row she had awoken in such a state.

She looked over at Jane sleeping peacefully by her side. Jane, luckily, slept like the dead and never seemed anxious or perturbed about anything. Rather annoying actually and Lizzy peevishly wanted to pinch her, but she resisted the urge. The glow of the sunrise was barely peeking through the drawn curtains. It could not be but six o'clock, if that. Lizzy knew it useless to attempt returning to sleep, nor did she want to.

That might make the nightmare return.

With a shudder she carefully left the bed, not that Jane would wake up even if she jumped up and down several times! Lizzy pulled on her robe and curled up in the plump chair by the window.

William, where are you? He had been away for a week and she missed him desperately. The ache was actually physical. He had traveled, again, to London to finalize his business interests and settle various unresolved issues. He was sacrificing this time, he explained to her, so that his affairs would not need his immediate attention during the first weeks of their marriage. His greatest desire was to be alone with her at Pemberley with minimal intrusions, business or otherwise. She appreciated what he was suffering on her behalf, but it still was grim to be separated from him. His letters, arriving once—sometimes twice—each day, comforted her. In clear language he poured into each sentence his own grief at their sundering and his enduring love.

His return had been expected yesterday. A sudden and violent storm had erupted, however. She had sat by the window all day and long into the evening, wishing urgently to see him yet also panic stricken at the thought of him venturing into the fury of the lightning and unrelentingly lashing rain. Finally, very late, she had tumbled into bed exhausted. Her sleep, when it did overtake her, had been troubled. Then came the nightmare.

Each night the same… She was in a bedchamber unknown to her. There were no furnishings except for a ridiculously huge bed that filled the room and reduced her to the size of the dwarves she had seen once when the circus came to Meryton. At first she was alone and wearing a diaphanous dressing gown from her trousseau with her hair free about her shoulders. Then Darcy was there exactly as she had seen him when he proposed: hair windblown, loose shirt open at the neck, and no concealing waistcoat or tight jacket. Altogether fetching.

Initially it was the perfect dream. He held her, kissed her, and caressed her body as she had hitherto only imagined. The subtle sensations she experienced in her waking life when he touched her were, in her dream, magnified tenfold and felt in areas of her body she did not even know existed. It was heaven!

Then abruptly it would change. She would panic; fear would rise in her throat, threatening to choke her. She would struggle and beg him to let her go, but he would refuse. Gone was the William she knew and loved, his beautiful face altered into the proud, arrogant mien that he had displayed at the Meryton Assembly. Then he would look at her with disgust and anger and hurt, as he had when she rejected him at Rosings. At the last, he would turn from her and vanish. It was then that she would startle awake, gasping for air, his name on her lips.

Lizzy knew why she was having this nightmare. She was afraid. As simple as that. Her wedding was just three days away and she wanted to marry Mr. Darcy with all her soul, but she was dreadfully terrified of disappointing him and unsure of his expectations.

The tender liberties partaken during these past weeks of their engagement had revealed a side of her fiancé that Lizzy would not have initially suspected.

Reserved, disciplined, shy Mr. Darcy hid a deeply passionate nature. He was always the gentleman, always strictly conscious of propriety, and severely respectful of Lizzy's reputation.

Yet, on more than a few occasions his resolve and constraint had been dangerously close to being lost. On a handful of those occasions they had crossed minor lines that would be considered improper by most, but he had harshly and agonizingly controlled himself. She could clearly sense when he teetered on the edge in his ardor for her. If ever the term "violently in love" applied to a person, it aptly described her William.

She would not be truthful if she denied that his zeal for her was flattering and more than a little bit welcome. As evidenced by the first part of her dream, sensations and desires were coursing through her with every touch and kiss. Merely thinking about him, hearing his lush voice, or seeing his smile would send rivers of electricity up her spine. Innocent little Lizzy Bennet was more than a tiny bit affected by the presence, touch, and kiss of her betrothed!

She, too, had experienced her moments of urgently wanting more and wishing desperately that he was not always so controlled. Yet, as they had come to know each other better, spending hours in conversation, the comprehension of his maturity and worldliness had struck her forcibly. The scope of how her life was to change as Mrs. Darcy, Mistress of Pemberley and wife to this complex man with intense bridled passions and taut emotions, was overwhelming.

Thankfully, she had shared her concerns and emotions with her Aunt Gardiner. The wiser woman had spoken with both girls at length, allaying many of their fears and answering the pointed questions Lizzy had. Her aunt was an earthy woman, forthright and blunt. The clinical details of the art of lovemaking were candidly illuminated. Jane had scurried from the room halfway through the conversation, never to return. Lizzy brazenly remained and cataloged each piece of information. She had been tremendously relieved afterwards and looked upon Darcy with new eyes, causing her to blush profusely more than once, to his puzzlement.

Unfortunately, her mother broached the subject several times, much to her and Jane's dismay. Her parent's opinion was the diametrical opposite of Aunt Gardiner's. There was absolutely no doubt how her mother viewed the marriage bed. Her mother and father had an easy familiarity, and Lizzy supposed they cared for each other, but it assuredly was not a marriage of passion.

Mrs. Bennet clearly spoke of the sexual act as a trial to be endured with no evidence of pleasure to be gleaned. She confidentially and with pride imparted such pearls of wisdom as how to use their monthly woman's cycle to stave off unwanted advances, the vital necessity of separate bedchambers with stout locking mechanisms, and the crowning gem: the headache.

"It works every time," she confidently declared. "Of course, what proper lady would not suffer with a headache at the very idea of a man's advances?"

As embarrassing as her mother's well-meaning tirades were, she and Jane usually could find the humor in them. Lizzy knew her mother's faults well and could shrug off her assertions in this regard. She was confident that her aunt's advice was superior to her mother's.

No, the disquiet did not come from this but from the personal assaults on Mr. Darcy that her mother had made. It had happened a week ago, on the very afternoon that Mr. Darcy left for Town. They were in the parlor and Mrs. Bennet had launched into a conversation about wifely expectations, again. Jane rolled her eyes at Lizzy, and Lizzy had to bite her inner lip to keep from laughing. Mary and Kitty surreptitiously slipped from the room. Initially it was innocuous enough but then her tone altered. Lizzy could still recall every single word.

"The important thing to remember, girls," Mrs. Bennet said, fan fluttering, "is to be firm with your husbands. Naturally, you must submit when necessary; however, there are ways to avoid this, as I have revealed to you both. Jane should have no problems in this regard as her Mr. Bingley is so amiable and gentlemanly. He would never force himself on you, dear Jane. It is you, my Lizzy, who I fear for."

Lizzy's attention was caught by her mother's last words, but she was puzzled. "Whatever do you mean, Mother?" she asked.

"Oh, Lizzy!" her mother responded with a catch in her voice, as if what she was to say grieved her. "Mr. Darcy is so proud and arrogant! He is a gentleman to be sure, but also a man of substance, accustomed to having others abide by his orders and being in control. You will learn, I dread, that his demands on your person may be tremendous!" She dabbed at her eyes with her handkerchief.

Lizzy was stunned. She knew in her heart that her mother's accusations were unfounded and she wanted to defend her betrothed, but she was shocked speechless.

Mrs. Bennet mistook Lizzy's expression and continued in what she thought was reassurance. "Do not fret overly, Lizzy. I am confident you shall not have to worry once you have provided him with an heir. That is what is most important to men of his station. Pray, child, that you birth a boy first;

then all will be well. Men with social requirements such as Mr. Darcy cannot afford to allow their wives to be indisposed by frequent confinement. These great men always have mistresses to take care of their baser needs, leaving the wife free to fulfill her duties. Quite probably he has already established an arrangement of this nature so..."

"Mama!" It was Jane who surprisingly first found her voice and stayed Mrs. Bennet's words. Lizzy was frozen with shock and horror. Her head was spinning, and it was as if a dark curtain was being pulled over her eyes. *I am going to faint!* She screamed in the hollow recesses of her mind, *I need air!* She jerked up from her chair, swaying dangerously, and stumbled frantically from the room. She could faintly hear Jane saying something in an uncharacteristically sharp tone, and then she was safely beyond the room, reeling through the front door.

Jane found her shortly thereafter and comforted her as best she could. Jane's common sense and placid nature soothed Lizzy, and in time she reached a semblance of calm. Over and over she told herself that she knew Mr. Darcy was not that kind of man, that his love and respect for her was genuine and deeply felt. Even so, her mother had raised questions and new terrors in her mind. With this added to the maidenly forebodings that persisted despite her knowledge of the intimacies between the sexes, the nightmares had began.

As Lizzy sat in her chair watching the sun rise in the now cloud-free late November sky, her troubled musings clarified in her mind and she acknowledged the proper course to tread. She must discuss these issues with William. They had promised each other that they would never repeat the mistakes of the past, and the only way to ensure that vow was to be totally and completely forthright in every way. She needed to know the truth. More than anything, she needed the comfort that she instinctively knew he would give her.

A burden was lifted with a decision made, and Lizzy reckoned it was a good idea to clear her head further with a long walk in the brisk autumn air. Then she would prepare herself physically, dressing carefully, for certainly her beloved would return this afternoon and she wanted to look her best.

❧

By eight o'clock Lizzy had completed her walk and was dressed for the day. She had no clue how she would proceed in broaching such a delicate subject with her betrothed; however, she refused to worry over it any further.

While breakfasting, she and her family were surprised by the arrival of Mr. Bingley's carriage. Jane had planned to join Mr. Bingley for luncheon at Netherfield, so the carriage arriving so early was unexpected. Mr. Hill announced the carriage's arrival and accompanied his announcement with a letter for Jane and, even more surprising, a letter for Lizzy. It was from William! Lizzy's hands shook so terribly she could hardly open it.

My Dearest, Precious Elizabeth,

Please accept my humble apologies for greeting you, my beloved, in this impersonal manner. Rest assured that as soon as humanly possible I shall be greeting you with my arms tightly around you and my lips on your sweet lips, as they were created to be. My most fervent prayer is to allay any fears you may have regarding my well-being. I am safe at Netherfield, having arrived quite late last night. Bingley nearly was required to physically restrain me from rushing back out the door and into your arms. Reason prevailed but only when Bingley pointed out that, as the hour was well past midnight and you would surely be long abed, rushing into your arms might raise a few eyebrows! Frankly, his words fleetingly had the opposite effect as the vision of you abed was more than slightly appealing. Nonetheless, as you have probably surmised, being my clever Lizzy, I did stay here at Netherfield, dreaming sweet dreams of you.

Now I impatiently await your presence to assuage my aching heart. I wished to ride to Longbourn at first light, but, again, Bingley's rationale prevailed. As it is, this missive is undoubtedly disturbing your breakfast, but I can wait no longer! The carriage is for you, dearest, and Jane naturally as well. If your desire to see me is even half as profound as my need to see you, then you are probably already racing to the door! Hurry, my love.

Yours forever,

Fitzwilliam Darcy

Lizzy had not yet started racing to the door, but she had arisen from the table, breakfast completely forgotten. "Jane, how soon can you be ready to leave?" she asked, her impatience evident.

Mr. Bennet chuckled and grinned. "Why Lizzy, whatever is the rush?"

Lizzy did not deign to answer but continued to look at Jane questioningly. "Very well, Lizzy," Jane calmly stated. "We shall leave as soon as you are ready."

Lizzy fairly flew up the stairs and in record time was pacing the foyer, waiting on Jane.

～✥～

"Darcy! For pity's sake, man, please sit down!" Bingley laughingly said to his friend.

Darcy had been pacing as well, wearing a literal hole, Bingley feared, in the carpet before the window that faced the front drive. Darcy ignored his friend and went on about his business. "What could possibly be taking her... them... so long?" he mumbled to himself.

Mr. Bingley continued to be amazed at the change that had come over his dear friend since his engagement. Darcy would forever be intent and serious, uncomfortable with strangers and in social milieus, but now there was lightness to his bearing, a softening that was altogether fresh. The most obvious differences were his ever-present smile and ready laugh. It perhaps was not perfectly apt, but one could almost say he was giddy! As Bingley observed Darcy's face, he had a sudden epiphany: it was peace that he saw there. A deep contentment that had previously not been an aspect of his mien.

Bingley smiled in happiness and amusement. "Really, Darcy, be patient. The carriage left here barely an hour ago."

Darcy turned, a ready retort on his lips, but his attention was captured by movement outside. An expression that could only be described as unfettered joy diffused his face, and without a word, he dashed from the room. Bingley had no need to ask, and with a chuckle he followed.

Darcy took the steps two at a time and practically danced in impatience. The carriage had not completed its stop before he was at the door opening it with such force that Bingley winced, sure the hinges would shatter. Elizabeth was already rising, her face suffused with the identical expression worn by her betrothed. With nary a thought toward the appropriateness or propriety of his actions, Darcy encircled Elizabeth's waist with his strong hands and lifted her clear of the carriage. Her toes barely brushed the ground before he crushed her in his arms and twirled her about, each of them laughing hysterically. With supreme restraint Darcy refrained from kissing her passionately right there in front of God and everyone. He compromised by cupping her face with both hands and whispering a heartfelt, "I love you, Elizabeth!"

"Why, Mr. Darcy," Elizabeth breathlessly teased, "I do believe you missed me just a little."

They made their way inside, Lizzy's hand securely tucked into the crook of Darcy's arm.

Darcy had been far too anxious to break his fast that morning, and suspecting that the ladies breakfast may have been interrupted, the gentlemen had instructed Cook to prepare a repast for when their fiancées arrived. In short order the happy quartet was seated at one end of the long table. Darcy had managed to steal a few brief kisses on the way in and yearned to be alone with Elizabeth, but for now was content simply to have her by his side.

At one point Elizabeth leaned close to Darcy and softly spoke into his ear, "William, I am elated that you are back! I missed you so. Nonetheless, it is requisite that I scold you for venturing out into the storm yesterday. You could have been injured, and then where would I be three days hence with no groom to wed me?"

He squeezed her hand under the table. "I am prostrate with guilt, my love, for causing you pain. Please forgive me?"

"Of course I forgive you," she said with a laugh, "although I should not. I should be cruel and allow you to suffer as I suffered all day!" She removed her hand from his and affected an angry pout.

"You cut me to the quick, Miss Elizabeth! My torment at your disfavor is acute. I have no choice but to fall to your feet in abject humility and beg the indulgence of your forgiveness." With that proclamation he precipitously scooted his chair back and began to drop to his knees.

Lizzy arrested his movement by hastily grabbing his arms. "Ridiculous man!" she laughed. "Return to your seat this second! I forgive you." She proved her forgiveness by giving him a kiss. "I am still curious as to how you made it here at all and why you arrived so late. You appear hale enough so I must assume you were unharmed."

"My intent was to ride Parsifal from Town," he explained, "knowing I could traverse the distance quickly, the sooner to see your face, my love. The ominous clouds and the urging of Mrs. Smyth induced me to take the carriage. That decision, naturally, meant waiting longer to depart. I was hoping to beat the storm but, alas, I was still on the outskirts of London when the torrent began. The roads were muddied within minutes. My coachman persevered for quite some miles, but eventually we had to hole up at a pub in Mayfield.

"We were not the only travelers foolish enough to be caught in the storm, so the establishment was lively and offered a pleasant diversion for the afternoon. Surely not as pleasant as being with you, but, as I had no real option, I made the best of it. Finally I could stand the wait no longer and we pushed on. It was slow going, and foolhardy I expect, but in the end we arrived none the worse for wear except for being drenched and mud splattered."

All throughout brunch, even with Darcy's infectious delight, Elizabeth could not cease ruminating on how she was to proceed with veering a conversation toward the topic of her nightmare. She was deliriously happy to be with Mr. Darcy and, in light of his obvious pleasure to be with her, she found her mother's accusations and her own apprehensions did not carry as much weight. Even so, the questions needed to be answered and the small knot of disquiet in her gut must be alleviated.

Upon the completion of the meal, when all were satisfied, Jane and Mr. Bingley announced that they were to take a walk about the grounds. Lizzy was game for this, thinking that it would afford her the privacy she needed. Darcy surprised her, though, by saying that he had something to show her in the library first. Bingley seemed bewildered but he did not comment.

Darcy kept the library door ajar, naturally, but guided Elizabeth to a far corner. He took her in his arms, kissed her waiting lips with restrained ardor and taking the time to rain several kisses along her neck. All too soon, though, he released her and sat her on a sofa, sitting close beside and taking her hands in his.

He peered into her eyes with an intensity she had come to recognize, and said, "Very well, Elizabeth. Tell me what is troubling you."

She was momentarily struck dumb and then stammered, "What do you mean?"

"Do not play coy with me, beloved. I can feel when something is amiss in your heart. You have not been quite your lively self. Several opportunities to laugh at and tease me mercilessly passed you right by! That would never occur if all was well." He tenderly stroked her cheek. "Please enlighten me to your distress. Allow me to comfort you." He spoke softly and with tremendous love.

She knew this was the opportunity she had been waiting for, yet found herself unsure how to proceed. He waited patiently while she struggled within, never once letting go of her hands or ceasing his gentle caress or removing his eyes from her face.

"You are correct, William; I am troubled. We need to speak of a delicate subject. Or rather I need to speak of it. You must bear with me for this is exceedingly uncomfortable." She tentatively met his eyes and saw only devotion there. She took a deep breath and launched into her tale. "You must promise me, William, that you will not interrupt. This is quite difficult for me and I cannot lose my nerve or train of thought. Do you promise?"

For the first time Darcy was beginning to feel alarm. He had imagined some wedding issue that she was concerned about, but now he perceived it was more serious. Still, his trust in her was absolute so he promised without hesitation.

She began by haltingly describing her anxieties about their wedding night, her maidenly qualms of the unknown as well as her fears of disappointing him. He relaxed as she spoke. He understood her completely on this subject because he harbored the same emotions, but he was utterly confident that their love would triumph beautifully. She told him about her conversation with Mrs. Gardiner, and he had to smile. He greatly respected Lizzy's aunt; he found her a delightful woman of superior common sense.

Lizzy described her nightmare, which he thought rather humorous except for how she depicted his reactions and the memories of the past that were conjured up. He thought they had thoroughly discussed their horrible miscomprehensions and had agreed to pardon each other. Of course, dreams could not be controlled.

She paused momentarily, then arose from the sofa. He watched her carefully and felt his alarm again increasing. She walked several feet away, keeping her eyes averted. After a huge swallow, she resumed. She told him about Mrs. Bennet's "advice." He saw no humor in it at all, and his countenance darkened further with each passing word. He frowned at the very notion that he would seek to "control" his Elizabeth as her mother intimated. His eyes blazed at the implication that he would ever force himself on her against her will. By the time she repeated the "producing an heir" statement, his fists were clenched and his mouth a thin line of anger.

He was rigid on the sofa, stunned beyond coherent thought, aching for Elizabeth having to endure such torture. He was livid and intensely offended. It was fortuitous that Lizzy had turned away from him, or she never would have told him the rest. When she did, Darcy reached the end of his forbearance.

"No!" he roared and jerked up from his seat, causing Elizabeth to start violently. "This is unconscionable! How could she accuse me of such a malicious falsehood! It is not to be borne!" Darcy was beside himself with wrath. "Elizabeth, you surely do not lend any credence to this... this... filth?"

Lizzy was terrified. She had rarely witnessed Darcy so furious. "William... I..."

Something in her face brought him up short and he looked at her in horror. Suddenly bereft of the air necessary for speech, he could only gasp, "You do!"

He turned away from her, and it was her nightmare coming true. She had to think! She approached him slowly and placed her hand gently on his arm, feeling his tension. "William, you must listen to me." She spoke very softly. "I know you are not the man my mother says you are. I know you love me and would never hurt me. Ours is a relationship and a love far superior to my parents'. I am confident in this."

She could perceive a slight easing of his rigidity as she spoke, although he still had not looked at her. She went on, her voice breaking, "You must appreciate that there is so much I do not know about your world—or about you for that matter. You must help me to understand, William, please!"

He sighed deeply and finally relaxed, running his hand over his face. He turned to her then and took her face into his hands, wiping her tears. "Forgive me for my outburst, beloved. It was inexcusable."

He kissed her tenderly and held her close to his chest until their trembling ceased. "You are absolutely correct, dearest. I must help you to understand. This will be painful for me, and awkward, so now it is my turn to beg your patience and ask you listen uninterrupted. Can you do this?"

"You do not even need to ask, my love. Of course I will."

They returned to the sofa. Darcy leaned forward, elbows resting on his knees, and was silent for a long while. Lizzy waited patiently. Slowly he began to speak.

"My earliest childhood memories of my parents are of love." His deep voice was soft, barely above a whisper. "Love toward me and later for Georgiana, naturally. Love for their families and friends. Love for Pemberley and Derbyshire and all the many people whose lives depend on us."

He paused briefly and sighed deeply. "Mostly, though, it is their love for each other that is etched into my mind. When I was very young I took it for granted, did not recognize it for the special emotion it was. All I knew is that they somehow were happier when they were together. Each of their faces would light up when the other entered a room. They were forever touching each other.

Not inappropriately, mind you, but in little ways. Doors, which should have been open during the daylight hours, would be inexplicably locked. Sometimes in the middle of the day, they would both simply disappear to return later with a glow on their faces."

He blushed slightly as he revealed these private events. "Naturally I did not understand any of it until much, much later. Once, when I was perhaps nine or ten, I entered the parlor to see my mother sitting on my father's lap and they were kissing in a way I had never seen before. They did not see me and I left abruptly. I went directly to Mrs. Reynolds and told her what I had witnessed. I was not disturbed by it but simply curious. She laughed and told me it was perfectly natural and that someday I would understand." He smiled. "Then she said, 'In the future, Master Fitzwilliam, you would be wise to knock before entering a room,' and I always did."

Darcy's smile left his face and he swallowed before continuing. "When I was almost twelve, Georgiana was born. My mother had been ill throughout her confinement and Georgiana's birth was a difficult one. My mother almost died and, in fact, was close to death for several weeks afterward. My father was beside himself.

"I had come to rely on his temperate nature, implacable steadfastness, and seriousness. He was the type of man who could handle any crisis with wisdom and incredible patience. This is not merely a child's hero worship, Elizabeth; everyone declared this about him. He could not handle this, though. I do not think he slept more than a few hours at a time for weeks. I saw something in his face I had never seen before: fear. Fear of losing my mother."

Elizabeth knew she had promised not to interrupt, but she could not resist moving a bit closer and taking his hand. He squeezed her hand gratefully and met her eyes, smiling slightly.

"My mother did recover, and life, for the most part, returned to how it had been. She was weaker, more fragile than previously. My father hovered over her and, if possible, was extra attentive. Over the next years I puzzled over their relationship. I was still young but, always precocious, demanded knowledge on subjects that were often beyond my comprehension. My father encouraged this thirst for education on my part. My mother and Mrs. Reynolds endeavored, in vain, to make me laugh more, not to be so serious all the time."

He looked at Elizabeth with a twinkle in his eyes. "At Netherfield, when you teased me about being proud and said how you dearly loved to laugh, it was as if my mother were in the room putting the words on your lips. You are very like her, Elizabeth. Your wit is perhaps more caustic and sharp, but she found humor in the smallest things, as you do." He took a moment to caress her cheek and gave a brief kiss.

"I digress, however. As I said, I was curious. I observed the behaviors of the other married couples we knew. Some, like my uncle, Lord Matlock, and my aunt, obviously cared for and respected each other. Others, especially my Aunt Catherine and Uncle Louis, quite clearly despised each other. People marry for many reasons: security, position, lust, furtherance of the line. None of these reasons bring true happiness, as my parents possessed.

"All through my life, I have been inquisitive on this subject, and many others, truth be told. Mrs. Reynolds will delight in telling you stories, I am sure." He smiled wryly. "Rarely have I found a marriage like my parents were blessed with. In each case it has been a wonder to behold. Even when I was far too young to comprehend it all, I vowed that I would have a marriage as my parents did."

Again he paused and seemed to gather his strength and thoughts. He leaned his head back against the wall and closed his eyes. Still holding Elizabeth's hand, he continued, "When I was seventeen, my mother died. After the funeral, my father retreated to his room, and we did not see him for a month.

"When he emerged he was a changed man. Gone were the light in his eyes and the quick smile. He had aged overnight. He never fully recovered and only Georgiana could reach him. A sensible man would doubtless regard my father's grief as vindication for avoiding such an all-consuming love. I suppose that means I am not a sensible man, because it only heightened my resolve."

He arose and walked to the window, peering outside but not actually seeing. "I left Pemberley for Cambridge when I was eighteen. There I was exposed to an entirely different world. The education I relished and embraced. Learning is like breathing to me, and I loved every moment. Socially, I was a wreck."

He laughed and smiled at Elizabeth. "I am quite positive you are not astounded by this confession!" She laughed as well and shook her head.

"I was incredibly naïve, my love. My existence until then had been a sheltered one. Pemberley is isolated and Lambton small. My parents did not care for Town and my mother was frequently too ill to travel, so I had minimal exposure to society. Now I was thrust into it and I was overwhelmed. To this day, I do not make friends easily, nor do I enjoy a number of the entertainments that the college crowd engaged in, especially drinking and carousing. Many young men, Mr. Wickham for example, deem such pastimes as the primary purpose for attending University. I did not. I was there for an education, and my leisure was spent in quieter pursuits, such as billiards, chess, fencing, and, as always, riding. I gravitated toward gentlemen who were of like mind. My cousin Richard, Colonel Fitzwilliam as he would later become, was my primary companion."

"As for the ladies…" Darcy paused, and Elizabeth could discern how uncomfortable he was with the topic, so she said nothing. In time he continued, but refused to look at her. "I would be lying, Elizabeth, if I claim to have consciously made a vow of chastity. I did not. I was a young man with long-ings that I wished to gratify, but I refused to selfishly slake my appetites in a demeaning manner. My father had raised me to be a better man than that, and the excellent example of my parents' relationship was never far from my thoughts. I do not know what I thought the 'acceptable' situation would be outside of the sanctity of marriage, but it never occurred. I will not say it was easy, Elizabeth, but this is the truth of it."

"Also, I was appalled at the attitude of some men, Wickham and his ilk. They bragged about their sexual exploits and were lewd, crass, and ungentle-manly. There was nary a hint of affection or regard for the women involved. They justified their actions, naturally, by pointing out that the women were of low station or immoral. It made no sense to me. Were not they as immoral and low if they partook in such base activity? Also, many of the women were not those who were for hire. It became a game among some to hunt down and seduce certain ladies, servants and the like, and then to boast of the conquest. I was disgusted and refused to be party to it."

"My years at Cambridge passed, and I was extraordinarily happy there. By the time I left, still virtuous, I had for the most part mastered the forbearance and temperance that is innate in my character, which I inherited from my father."

Darcy began pacing, head bent as he spoke further. "I returned to Pemberley. Not two months later my father collapsed. It was totally unexpected. His heart, the physicians said. One week later he had died and I, at two and twenty and utterly unprepared, was Master of Pemberley and guardian to a grieving eleven-year-old sister."

"There truly is not a word in the King's English to describe how over-whelming my life became for the next year or so. Mrs. Reynolds completely took over the management of the household staff and upkeep. My father's steward, Mr. Wickham the elder, was a remarkable man. Without them, I believe Pemberley would have folded. Tragically, Mr. Wickham also passed a scant six months later. Fortunately, I had been an apt pupil. My uncle, Lord Matlock, assisted me tremendously and aided me in replacing Mr. Wickham with my current steward, Mr. Keith. Eventually I was able to breathe again and believed I could actually succeed in my new position.

"Then London Society came calling." His voice held a tone of disgust and bitterness. "New demands were placed on my shoulders, demands I wanted no part of, yet knew I had to accept. Elizabeth, I judge you do not yet appreciate what an agony it is for me. I am fully aware that interacting with society is my responsibility, but I so despise it. It is not just my own shyness and lack of proper social skills, although that certainly is a major part of it. It is the insincerity, the deceitfulness, the affected friendliness of the ton that repulses me. Few pure souls can be found and the women are the worst.

"London is replete with Caroline Bingleys. Women who held me in high favor because of who I was: the perfect 'catch' worth 10,000 a year. I am not a fool. I knew that none of them cared for me but only for my wealth and position. Married women, in the boredom and loneliness of empty marriages, offered themselves to me as a diversion. I was revolted.

"With each passing year, as I knew it was expected of me to marry, I despaired of ever finding a woman who would give me what I so urgently wanted and needed. I trusted none of them, even the few who piqued my interest. I began to believe that I would never have what my parents had, and I grew so bitter and so very weary of the search.

"Yet, at the same time, it hardened my resolve. If I could not find what I wanted, then I would not marry at all. I am a profoundly obstinate man, my love, if you have not realized that already! Once I set a course, I am loyal to it. If I was so fortunate and blessed to find love, then I would be devoted, faithful, and enduringly thankful until the day I died."

He stopped pacing and looked at Elizabeth. For a long time he gazed upon her beloved face and she tenderly gazed back. She hoped that her love for him, her pleasure in all that he had shared with her, was visible on her countenance. Finally, he returned and knelt before her, taking her hands in his firm grip.

"My dearest, precious Elizabeth. I have saved myself for you, even before I knew who you were. As trite as that sounds, it is the truth, and I do not merely mean in the intimate realm of our relationship. My principles, my pride perhaps, would not allow me to consider giving myself to anyone less than the woman I would love and marry. Even in my despair of ever finding you, I still clung to the idea that you existed. You had to exist! I simply needed to be patient. Call me a hopeless romantic!"

He chuckled softly and gently touched her cheek as she beheld him with absolute love and dedication. "My decision to wait for you, physically and emotionally and spiritually, was a worthy one. I know that we will be wonderful together, in every possible way, as husband and wife. I will never, ever want anything or anyone more than I want you! Elizabeth, my heart, you must know that and believe me."

She smiled at him and gently stroked his hands. Tears were coursing down her cheeks, and she could hardly speak. "I do, William. Thank you for sharing your life with me, past, present, and future. Thank you for waiting for me."

"You also must know, beloved, that I would never force myself upon you in any way. Your wishes, needs, and desires are of paramount importance to me. I sincerely hope that our relationship will never come to a point where we do not desire each other's company, but you must understand that I will always respect you and would never want to cause you harm or pain in any way. Elizabeth…"

She stopped his words with her fingers then leaned forward to place a gentle, chaste kiss upon his lips. "My darling William. I wish to please you as much as you wish to please me. Your words have eased my heart completely. I have no fears now, only the overwhelming need to show you how much I love you. Our wedding day cannot come soon enough for me!"

CHAPTER THREE

The Wedding Night

LIZZY TOOK ONE LAST look in the mirror and then entered the bed-chamber with a happy smile and wildly beating heart. The room was lit only by the fire, two oil lamps, the filtered moonlight, and a wall sconce on either side of the bed. For a moment she thought the room empty but then she noticed her husband standing by a window with his back to her. She caught her breath at the sight before her. He was standing as she had so often seen him stand, with spine perfectly straight, feet firmly planted, and one arm bent with his hand resting on his waist. He was wearing a long maroon robe with a black sash, and every detail of his physique was evident through its folds. She found the view enchanting, and her heart began to race crazily.

"William," she whispered.

He turned quickly at her voice and it was his turn to catch his breath. His carefully regulated control slipped instantaneously and his groin responded alarmingly. Several deep breaths were necessary to maintain his equilibrium. For a long moment they stood paralyzed, drinking in each other with their eyes. Darcy was the first to break the spell as he moved to meet her in the middle of the room. He longed to grab her and enfold her in his arms, yet at the same time, he wished to study her beauty, memorizing every line and curve of the vision before him.

He stopped a short distance from her and took her outstretched hands, halting her forward movement. She looked at him quizzically. "Elizabeth," he said huskily, "may I simply adore you for a moment?"

She smiled and matched his boldness. "Only, sir, if I may do the same!"

Elizabeth had picked a nightgown of sheer satin, pale yellow with tiny bows down the bodice, narrow strap sleeves, a deeply scooped neckline, and pleated gathers just under her bosom. Her hair was loose down her back and shoulders in a chestnut veil of soft curls. Darcy had seen her hair down on a couple of occasions, but never in such an intimate setting, and the sight rendered him breathless and weak in the knees.

Her face was flushed, eyes bright and merry and completely full of love. The gown itself was thin but not totally transparent, offering tantalizing glimpses of her flawless form underneath. The satin flowed over her hips in gentle folds and over barely visible legs until just touching the tops of delicate feet, leaving tiny toes exposed. The entire vision was delectable and so moving to Darcy's soul. Everything about her was perfection and beauty. He knew his aroused state was obvious to her searching eyes, but under the circumstances, there was nothing he could do to stop it.

Elizabeth, not completely unaware of the effect she was having on her husband, was nonetheless experiencing her own breathlessness as she carefully examined the presence before her hungry eyes. On only three occasions had she seen William in anything other than his full attire: while staying with Jane at Netherfield when she had spied him from her window after his ride, soaking wet from sweat and the water pump; once while he was riding; and many months later when he strode through the early morning mist on the day he proposed for the second time.

On all occasions her mind had been clouded with sleep or lack of it, daydreams, and overwrought emotions. The image of him as she had seen him on those three occasions had burned into her memory to return in her dreams, but it always seemed vague and hazy. This, however, was real. This time she was fully in charge of her senses and faculties, and she fully intended to take note of every detail possible.

He looked so young with his face relaxed; all the tension and careful regulation that usually strained his noble features were gone. His eyes blazed a vivid indigo in the half light of the room, shining and intense with bridled passion and deep love. His robe enclosed his broad shoulders and strong arms completely, yet somehow accented the shape underneath to great advantage. His neck was bare and she could see his pulse beating rapidly in the hollow of his throat. The robe was pulled tight across his muscular chest and belted securely at his lower abdomen. She could only see a triangle of his chest to roughly mid-sternum, dark hairs visible, and her fingers literally itched to touch his skin. His robe covered the rest of his body, hugging his slender waist, falling to his ankles, leaving his feet bare.

Elizabeth finished her inspection, letting out an involuntary sigh and sound of surprise. Darcy broke from his reverie and looked quickly to her face.

"Elizabeth, are you well?"

"Pardon?"

"You seem startled. Are you displeased in some way?" he asked nervously.

She blushed furiously and looked away, stammering, "Oh, no, I am fine. It is just that…" she trailed off lamely.

"It is just, what?"

She could not meet his eyes and her face was red. He did not know whether to be alarmed or to laugh at her sudden discomfiture. He lifted her chin gently until she reluctantly met his eyes. "We promised to be completely honest with each other, remember? Please tell me what you are thinking."

"I… well, I was just noticing… that… well," she swallowed and looked at him boldly, "you have nice feet!"

He could not speak for a moment, then burst out laughing. He gathered her into his arms and held her tightly. Still laughing, he said, "My darling Lizzy! You are so very delightful." He pulled back slightly so he could see her face. Grinning broadly, he said, "Thank you, my love. I can safely assert that no one, with the possible exception of my dear mother, has ever commented on my feet!"

"You are making fun of me," she accused, with a playful slap to his chest.

"Of course I am! How could I not? Only you, beloved, can make me laugh so." He kissed her lips quickly, then proceeded to plant tiny kisses along her jaw until he reached her ear. He breathed deeply of her scent and whispered softly, nervously, "Do only my feet delight you, or did you manage to discover other equally pleasing attributes during your inspection?"

During his kisses she had felt the familiar flutters and tingles that she always experienced when he kissed her and had closed her eyes. Speaking, in fact coherent thought of any kind, seemed next to impossible. Even so,

Lizzy being Lizzy, she answered, "Perfectly adequate, Mr. Darcy, I daresay. Unfortunately, so much remains covered that I cannot in truth render a full accounting. Perhaps we can remedy this oversight on your part posthaste so I can answer your query with total knowledge."

Darcy had ceased his ministrations to her neck and was watching her as she spoke, a happy smile on his lips. *Oh how he loved her! How he wanted her!* But he had promised himself that he would control his desires and take this night slowly. He wanted to enjoy every moment with her, every word, every touch, every sound, and every smell. He was determined that she find pleasure and complete joy in being with him, in becoming his wife in every sense of the word.

"All in due time, Mrs. Darcy. First, I have a wedding present for you." He took her by the hand and seated her on the sofa. He went to the armoire and pulled out a square box wrapped with blue paper and tied with a thick blue ribbon. He returned to her and placed it into her lap, kneeling before her. "For you, my wife, always to remember this day, the happiest day of my life."

Elizabeth was slowly shaking her head and tears filled her eyes. "William, you should not have. You have given me so many wonderful gifts already! All I need to remember and mark this day is you... only you."

Darcy smiled, "Thank you, dearest. You shall always have me. Now you shall also have this meager token as well. Open it."

Elizabeth untied the bow and pulled the wrapping away. Inside the box, lying on a bed of dark blue velvet, was a vanity set—brush, comb, and mirror—made of mother-of-pearl with *Mrs. Elizabeth Darcy* engraved on each handle. The craftsmanship was exquisite. She was overwhelmed.

"William, I do not know what to say. They are beautiful! I have never owned anything equal. Thank you so very much!" She leaned over and kissed him soundly.

Darcy beamed at her obvious pleasure. "You would have enjoyed the spectacle, my dear. I have come to realize how lacking my education is in the area of feminine requirements. I have, in fact, studiously avoided the subject in the past. Recently, I have discovered myself extremely fascinated by all the mysteries related to the fairer sex, or more specifically related to you. I scoured my extensive library and found not a single book that could answer the questions I had. I surmised that the only sure avenue open to me was to enter the shops in London that cater to the needs of women."

Elizabeth could picture it clearly and the vision did make her smile. He went on, "I was most relieved to find that I was not the only gentlemen present in the establishments, but I certainly was the most ignorant! Fortunately, the proprietors were remarkably sympathetic and willing to further my education. So, I learned numerous incidentals, which I am certain will aid me in being an understanding husband. As for this particular gift, considering how ardently I admire your beauty and especially your lovely hair, it seemed fitting."

"William, you are too good to me. I truly do not deserve you."

"Nonsense," he replied gruffly, "I love you and enjoy giving you gifts." As he spoke, he absentmindedly reached up under her gown and began running his hand along her right calf. Time stood still for both of them. Instantaneously their mutual desires were awakened and their thoughts became riveted to their need for each other.

Gazing into her eyes with a deep intensity, Darcy took the box off Elizabeth's lap, laid it on the floor, and then rose onto his knees, bringing himself level with her. He slowly ran his hands along the tops of her thighs and around her bottom, pulling her to the edge of the sofa. Her knees parted and he moved closer to her body as his hands leisurely caressed their way up her back, eventually entwining in her hair as he brought her lips to his and kissed her passionately.

She had watched him as if mesmerized as he stroked her body and repositioned himself closer to her. She could not breathe! He was so incredibly handsome and desirable. Her need for him was overpowering. She wanted to see all of him, touch him intimately, and feel him on her and in her. She wanted to become his wife fully with an ache that was nearly painful in its intensity.

She ran her hands up his chest and then under his robe, placing her fingers gently on his shoulders. With slow deliberation she peeled the robe off his shoulders, exposing his upper body as she lovingly ran her palms down his back. He let go of her long enough to remove his sleeves, baring his arms to her tender caress, and then encircled her again, never once leaving her sweet lips.

It was euphoric! The feelings, the taste, their senses overwhelmed. Elizabeth boldly reached down and untied his sash, feeling the robe fall to the ground. Darcy moaned and in one swift, graceful motion rose from his kneeling position, gathering Elizabeth into powerful arms and carrying her to their bed.

Darcy stretched next to his wife's lovely body, careful to keep his hips away from her flesh for the time being. He experienced a momentary stab of fear that he would not be able to keep his self-promise to proceed slowly, bringing Lizzy to pleasure first. His need for her was all consuming and powerful. He may never have been with a woman himself, but he knew that obtaining his own release was an easy task. The finer art of bringing her enjoyment was another matter. That was where his inexperience, coupled with a raging hunger for personal fulfillment and a need to make her his own, could lead to failure. Such was his love for her and his prideful wish to succeed as a giving lover, that he clutched onto his fear and used it to restore his faculties and level his ardor.

Elizabeth's hands were around his neck, fingers massaging his scalp through his thick hair. She was watching him, eyes full of love and trust and desire with only a hint of nervousness. She seemed quite unafraid; however, Darcy knew this could change if he moved too fast. He stroked her cheek and jaw line and neck, all areas he had touched before, successfully bringing her enjoyment. She quivered and sighed, closing her eyes.

"I love you so very much, Elizabeth," he whispered against her lips. "Do not be afraid. I promise to be gentle." He lightly kissed every delicate feature of her face, ending at the sensitive area behind her ear. "You must show me what you like. Tell me in words or, if this embarrasses you, simply relax your body and I will know by your reactions. We shall learn from each other, my precious. Do you understand, my love?"

She nodded and whispered, "I love you, William. I am not afraid." She proved her words by rubbing her hands down his back and turning slightly to her side, loosely draping one leg over his and pulling him toward her. They both gasped simultaneously. She, from the feel of his incredible heat and hardness. He, from her unexpectedly bold action, which threatened to undo him.

He swallowed and inhaled vigorously. He opened his eyes to see her gazing at him, an expression of wonder and a small smile on her lips. He kissed her then, a kiss unlike any they had yet shared. The joy of being able to abandon all restraint and to explore each other's mouths was exhilarating. They surrendered themselves fully to the excitement to be gained from indulgent kisses. For a time all the focus was on the transcendent joy of shared breath and moisture.

Hands began moving of their own volition. Darcy untied her gown and exposed her shoulders and breasts without coherent forethought. Lizzy delighted in the muscles of his back and shoulders and arms. He was soft and rough at the same time, and it inflamed her further. Darcy trailed his fingers down her collar to her shoulder and then to her soft bosom. Fire trailed feathering fingertips; shivers of heat and ice coursed through their flesh.

His mouth left her lips and traveled over her neck. Soft kisses interspersed with tiny nibbles and feather touches of his warm mouth passed across her shoulders and fragile collarbones. Lizzy sighed and trembled in pleasure. Darcy was jolted with almost excruciating waves of satisfaction. Her taste was bliss, her warmth exquisite, her soft vocalizations heavenly. Lizzy arched involuntarily, exposing her neck to his moist lips and tongue, all the while caressing solid shoulders. One would be hard pressed to say who was more deeply affected.

"Beautiful love," he murmured against her throat, "so unbelievably beautiful. How deeply I love you my Elizabeth, my wife." Gradually, so very tenderly, he traveled wet kisses to her breasts. Never had he imagined anything as beautiful as the feel of her flesh under his lips and tongue. It was rapturous! She moaned, pulling his head harder onto her breasts with sharp clenches in his hair.

"William, sweet love. Please do not stop."

He spent endless stunning minutes of ecstasy teasing and tasting the perfection of her bosom, with one hand caressing lightly over her satin-clad waist. He rose, urgently needing to gaze upon her precious face. Her eyes opened, glazed and inundated with a passion never revealed before, as she looked upon him.

Darcy rolled his upper body over hers, heat seeping into her very bones, and leaned up on his elbows to caress her breasts, purposefully arousing her. "Are you well, beloved? Does this please you?"

She swallowed, nodding faintly. "William, I… I cannot describe… your touch moves me so. Oh, please, love, please kiss me!" she moaned, offering lush parted lips with obvious yearning, hands tight on his shoulders.

He reclaimed her mouth, groaning deep in his throat, delving into the depths of her mouth possessively and completely. Lizzy held his neck in a savage grip, meeting his kiss with equal passion and enthusiasm, her other hand exploring brazenly. She involuntarily curved her hips toward him, unwittingly increasing pressure to his leg and other sensitive parts.

"Elizabeth!" he gasped and released her slightly, raggedly gulping for air. He dropped his head to her chest and forced himself to stop moving, frantically seizing the frayed edges of his control.

"William, my love! I am sorry. Did I hurt you somehow?" Her voice was full of anxiety.

Darcy could not explain why it struck him as humorous, but it did. He laughed faintly, breath tickling her sensitive bosom, and shook his head. He kissed each perfect breast and then lifted up to look upon her amazing face. "No, my precious, you did not hurt me. Quite the opposite, in fact. I am frankly becoming undone by the bliss I am feeling being in your arms… touching you… kissing you. I must slow down. Ah, my beautiful wife, you have absolutely no idea how I yearn for you!"

She smiled happily and rose up to his lips. "Yes, Fitzwilliam," she purred, "I do know. I yearn for you as well and do not wish to slow down." She kissed him playfully as she had so longed to do, teasing his lips, tasting the skin of his jaw, exploring the cleft in his chin. Her fingers moved freely over his face and neck, toying with his ear folds as fire ignited anew over his flesh.

He passively allowed her investigation but was tremendously affected. He had managed to regain a semblance of control but he realized with certainty that he could not persevere for much longer. His arousal and ardor had reached a point bordering on pain. God, he needed to make her his! It was an uncontainable force burning through his very soul. He still refused to rush to the degree that he might hurt her or fail to bring her to total fulfillment; however, he needed to step up the pace. He felt her tremors, heard her sighs of longing, and knew what to do.

"Elizabeth," he asked huskily, "may I please see all of you?"

Her answer was to gently push him away as she sat up in the bed. He propped himself up with his arm and avidly watched her. She flushed in embarrassment at his intense stare but daringly did as he wished, gaze averted. She wiggled her arms and the top part of her gown fell to her waist. Darcy's eyes drank in the vision of her newly exposed skin. She was lovelier than he had imagined, absolutely stunning. She gripped the fabric at her waist and, with a quick lift of her bottom, pulled her gown past her hips.

A guttural groan escaped Darcy's throat, startling Lizzy yet sending a massive surge of heat lancing through her body. Darcy snapped out of his entrancement, reaching over and running the back of his hand along her inner thigh as he peeled the gown off her legs, tossing it absently away. Lizzy quivered at his touch, sighed deeply, and closed her eyes.

"My God, Elizabeth! You are perfect and so stunningly beautiful." He swallowed, eyes leaving her body with difficulty to meet her glittering gaze. With agonizing patience he reached to brush trembling fingertips over her skin, collarbone to nipples to ripe breasts to navel and then along her shapely legs. Lizzy was panting in short gasps, examining his intense expression, and discovering the rising ardency gained from his clear adoration of her form and the indescribable titillation of his touch.

Gradually her gaze left his face to move over his body, truly seeing him for the first time. Blushes crept over her cheeks, but she could not pull her eyes from the beauty of his shape. That he was powerfully built she had ascertained even through his clothing, but she had not known the raw manliness evident in the defined muscles of his torso. Black hairs, profuse over his chest but compacting into a heavy patch between his pectorals, trailed in a thick line down a hard, flat abdomen to join a much denser patch at his groin. Her eyes widened and she hastily glanced away, cheeks flushing further at the instant ache felt deep inside her belly. Never had she envisioned such virility or the raging response she felt to all she saw and all he was doing to her. With a shuddering moan, she closed her eyes.

"Lie back, my love," he commanded tensely. She did so as he repositioned himself. Lizzy thought this was it, and she was mildly frightened but mostly elated. She was mistaken. He gently began raining warm wet kisses over her abdomen, firm hands caressing everywhere. The sensations that he educed transcended anything she had yet experienced. He was unrelenting but always tender in his stimulation, arousing her to places unimaginable, the previous fervency insignificant compared to what she now felt. Forever, so it seemed, he caressed and kissed. Not an inch of her skin was left unfazed by his devotion.

Dizziness consumed her. Time lost all meaning. Soft whispers of love flowed from his lips as he traveled about her flesh. Her body writhed and shivered uncontrollably and strange vocalizations emitted from parted lips until eventually the sensations coalesced into a nearly terrifying intensity. All she knew for certain was that she required fulfillment from him immediately or she was likely to perish from the aching need.

"William!" she shouted, "I need you! Please!"

At her cry he moved until fully on top of her. His fiery body pressed into hers as he twined one hand into her hair and around her neck, passionately claiming her mouth with a throaty groan. Simultaneously his other hand grasped the back of one knee, pulling her leg up and around his waist as he joined with her, lovingly consummating their marriage and bond.

Darcy groaned, the joy of feeling his wife surrounding him and at one with him nearly more than he could handle. It was Lizzy's gasp of pain and instant stiffening that restored his clarity.

"Relax, my love," he murmured, "it only hurts for a moment." To prove the truth of his words, he stilled, caressing softly and kissing deeply until she eased. Gazing into her trusting eyes, his own glittering indigo and brimming with adoration, he waited.

"We are one, my beloved. Joined together. Hearts and bodies bound now and forever. Oh, Lord, Elizabeth! How I love you! You are mine and I am yours for all eternity. Release your tension, precious love. I will be gentle." He spoke softly, caressing and kissing.

Lizzy smiled, gently tightening the legs wrapped over his waist and gliding her fingertips over his cheeks. "Love me, William. Complete making me your wife," she whispered, eyes slipping shut in rapture as she lifted her mouth to his.

He closed his eyes and moaned, moving unhurriedly, suppressing his flaming yearning until fervor replaced her discomfort. Afterwards, Darcy would be amazed at himself for finding the control to set a leisurely pace. His restraint was short lived, however, due to her reawakened passion. His pace quickened with a feverish hunger, Lizzy spurring him on. It was nirvana! Pleasure and gratification as never before experienced. They surrendered themselves to the spiraling sensations of pure pleasure and cried each other's names while clinging to each other in a desperate attempt to meld further.

Darcy collapsed onto her, too exhausted and satiated to move. Lizzy wrapped her limbs even tighter about him while tears of joy leaked from her eyes. Neither of them could have verbalized then, or ever, the riot of emotions swirling inside. Suffice to say, nothing had prepared either of them for the satisfaction, contentment, and unadulterated ecstasy of the reality.

How long they lay entwined, their wits rattled, hearts racing, and breathing erratic, they never knew. Lizzy moved first by planting kisses along Darcy's sweat-glistened shoulder and neck, repeating *I love you* as a litany. With a final shuddering exhale, Darcy rose slightly so that he could see his wife. They simply looked upon each other for long moments. Darcy caressed her face and kissed gently. He started to move off her, but she tenaciously clutched him.

"Do not leave!"

"Am I not crushing you?"

"No," she assured him, grasping him even tighter with arms and legs. "I love the feel of you." She blushed slightly, ridiculous under the circumstances, and he chuckled.

"As you command, my wife." He kissed her, lingering over her soft warm lips. "My wife," he whispered, "mine, all mine, and only mine. My Lizzy. Forever. I love you so. We are wholly and utterly one now, my love. I am yours, my heart, forever."

He caressed her body lazily, delighting in her silky skin and firm muscles. His thumb brushed along the edge of one breast where it swelled from under his chest. His kisses traveled over her neck to her ear.

Lizzy tantalized him with hands and legs. She discovered the enticing spectacle of round, tight buttocks. His taut muscular legs, hairs rough against her smoothness, sent shivers up her spine. The musky smell of his familiar cologne now mixed with perspiration and their love intoxicated her. Neither dreamed of breaking the contact, their bodies fused on every plane. Satiation and bliss attained so few minutes ago only whetted their appetite for each other, heightening their senses.

They were both agreeably surprised to find themselves becoming stimulated so soon. Lizzy, having no previous experience to draw from, took it in stride, assuming it was normal. Darcy was frankly stupefied to recognize excitement resurging so soon, his desire for her so intense as to become profoundly aroused mere minutes after such an incredible, soul-unifying crescendo.

He may have been surprised, but he certainly was not disappointed! This time their coupling was altogether different. Following so quickly upon their previous gratification, Darcy was in much better control. His stamina was amplified tremendously, with mutual approval. They kissed and caressed wherever they could reach, both experimenting with altering pressures and rhythms. Gradually they attuned themselves to their partner's sighs and moans as a gauge for what was especially pleasurable. Occasionally they spoke, but they soon found that sensations, actions, and sounds were preferable.

It seemed to continue forever. As one would near the point of bursting, the other would slow their actions, increasing the aching and craving. Time and again they came near the pinnacle only to pull back for further enjoyment. Eventually it was more than they could bear, and both were taken by acute spasms that shook them head to toe in rapture beyond the words to convey.

Quite some time later, they lay blissfully depleted and satiated, limbs entangled. Elizabeth's head lay partly on Darcy's shoulder and partly on a pillow so she could admire his face. They were awake but drowsy, talking softly, enjoying simply being together in such sweet harmony. Darcy played with her hair where it cascaded over his arm, while Elizabeth traced lazy circles over his chest and stomach. They spoke of silly things, small talk, more to hear each other's voices than for any purpose.

The final acts of love had been far superior to any imaginings either of them had entertained. Darcy, never a great admirer of romantic poetry, finally understood. Each day, each moment with Elizabeth had transcended the one before. Tonight they had reached dizzying heights, and it honestly seemed impossible to love her more.

Darcy would have had to confess that he believed his heart would burst if he experienced anything beyond what he felt at this moment. He had told her, when he proposed the second time, that she had bewitched him body and soul, and it was true. Now he knew that she owned him, lived inside of him, kept his heart beating, and gave him purpose. If it had not felt so very right, it might have terrified him.

Real life intruded when Darcy's stomach growled loudly and abruptly as if in response to Lizzy's fingers, which had been playfully examining his navel. They both laughed at the absurdity of it.

"Hungry, darling?" Elizabeth asked. "Have your recent exertions increased your appetite?"

"I have eaten sparsely today, my love. Nerves, I suppose." He rolled onto his side and began kissing her bare shoulder. "I was much more interested in satisfying other hungers so that I ignored my more basic needs. What is food compared to your love?"

"Very pretty. However, I am beginning to experience pangs of my own. The Hamiltons have supplied us with an abundance of food and it would be rude to ignore it," Elizabeth said, but then grinned mischievously as she ran her hand along his inner thigh. "Besides, we must take care to restore our energies, do you not agree, beloved?"

He quickly snared her hand and brought it to his lips, kissing each of her fingers lingeringly. "You minx! I do believe a tigress has been unleashed tonight!" He pulled her to him and indulged in several kisses before again being interrupted by a loud growl from his empty stomach.

"Poor Mr. Darcy!" she laughed.

"Stay warm, Elizabeth. I shall fetch your robe and stoke the fire." With a last kiss, Darcy left the bed and retrieved his robe from where it had been unceremoniously discarded by the sofa.

Elizabeth propped herself up on one elbow, the better to watch her handsome husband. Contentment flowed through her entire being as she lay so relaxed in the large bed. It had been an arduous day full of countless anxieties and abounding wonders. She was tired yet exhilarated at the same time. Happiness was a palpable entity that surrounded her and permeated her very soul. Just observing him performing the mundane task of adding logs to the fire was a pleasure beyond imagining. *How is it possible to love someone this much?* She asked herself. *Is it normal?* Probably not, but it certainly was magnificent and she would not wish it any other way.

Darcy returned from her dressing room with a thick robe and helped her into it. Or more precisely he delayed the process with numerous kisses and caresses, but Elizabeth did not mind. Finally they sat on the rug before the now raging fire with the platter of food on the floor. Darcy popped the well-chilled champagne and poured them each a glass. "To us," he toasted, "the happiest couple on the face of the earth!"

Darcy attacked the superb provisions with relish and Elizabeth was not too far behind. They had fun with the process: feeding each other morsels, licking and sucking each other's fingers, and kissing honey-smeared lips. Eventually even Darcy's appetite was quenched and, with a satisfied sigh, he reclined on an enormous pillow. Elizabeth leaned against his bent knee and gazed dreamily into the fire. Neither spoke. Words were unnecessary. A warm blanket of peace and bliss covered them.

Darcy began to drift into sleep, warm and relaxed by the fire. Lizzy was lazily caressing the leg and knee she leaned against and the sensation was calming. As far as Darcy was concerned, life could not possibly get any better than this. He closed his eyes and sighed.

Elizabeth turned to gaze at her husband. He had a soft smile on his lips, hair in disarray, and one arm raised above his head and the other lying across his stomach. The robe was loosely tied so most of his chest was exposed. She recognized that, despite the intimacies of the last hours, she actually had not had the opportunity to examine her husband's form closely, as she had teasingly told him she needed to do.

He was so beautiful and perfect to her eyes. She had spent the past weeks memorizing his face and intimately knew every inch of it. The small scar on his right cheek was the result of a tree branch while riding when he was fifteen, he had told her. She knew how long it took from the time he shaved until whiskers began to reappear, and that they sprouted first along his upper lip.

She had discovered that his eye color altered depending on his mood or what he wore. When he was thinking passionate thoughts of her, his lips would part slightly and eyelids would flutter. When he was annoyed or concentrating, his jaw would tighten and several small creases would appear between his brows. When he was very angry, his eyes would darken almost to black and his lips would press tightly together into a thin line. She had found that a singular expression crossed his features with thoughts of each person he loved. He had his "Georgiana face" and "Richard face" and "Mrs. Reynolds face" and "Elizabeth face."

At times her hurtful words came back to haunt her. *Your arrogance, conceit… selfish disdain for the feelings of others.* Oh, how could she have thought such things! He would be angry with her if he knew she was remembering those words because they had spent hours discussing the past, their mutual errors, and had promised to learn from them and then put it all behind them. Perhaps in time it would no longer wrack her with guilt, but she continued to loathe herself for the pain she had caused him. Knowing now the depth of his emotions toward those he loves, his loyalty, the profound grief he carries for those he has lost, and his goodness, made it all the harder to forgive herself. Not for the first time she vowed to herself that she would never cause him pain again.

Impulsively she kissed his knee, causing his sleepy smile to deepen, and then gently pushed his leg down while she resituated herself between his legs. He opened his eyes, still smiling, and considered her movements with interest. She carefully opened his robe to initiate her inspection.

"Elizabeth?" he whispered.

She smiled. "I made a promise, sir, to give you a full accounting of all your attributes that are pleasing to my eyes. Never let it be uttered that I do not keep my promises. Now, relax."

"That may be a challenging order to follow, my beloved, if you continue in this manner."

Elizabeth did not reply. Her fingers traveled slowly over him, noting his muscles, counting each rib, graphing the pattern of his chest hair. She reveled in the contrast of smoothness and roughness, felt each of his breaths and the beating of his heart. She grazed rigid nipples and he inhaled sharply. She detected for the first time a bump atop one of his ribs. "What caused this?" she asked quietly.

"I fell out of a tree when I was twelve," he answered. "Broke my rib and lacerated my arm here," and he rolled up his sleeve showing her a long scar along his inner left arm. "Ten stitches. My mother was furious but Father just laughed. 'Boys must be allowed to be boys,' he said." Darcy chuckled at the memory. "My mother kept me abed for a week, and Mrs. Reynolds forced all manner of hideous-tasting concoctions down my throat. I am convinced they punished me due to their own fright, rather than any actual need of my own."

Elizabeth loved how his eyes glowed when he spoke of his family. He did it rarely, the memories being very painful to him. His childhood was much a mystery to her. She could not wait until she was at Pemberley, the place where he grew up, the place he loved more than any other. She remembered how at ease he had been there when they had spent their glorious day together, how he laughed and smiled. Somehow she knew that their relationship and understanding would reach even greater heights once in his home.

"I cannot quite picture you climbing trees," she said, her head tilting to the side. "You seem more the library-dwelling boy to me."

He laughed. "Well, I did rather spend inordinate amounts of time in the library, but I do love the outdoors. I generally prefer riding my horse to long walks, although I am coming to appreciate what can be accomplished on long, solitary walks." He grinned slyly and she blushed, knowing full well to what he was referring. "I was not normally stupidly reckless though. It was usually George…," he stopped abruptly as a dark cloud crossed his face, "… Wickham that baited me into something foolish. He dared me to climb the tree, in fact. Of course, the fault was mine in allowing him to drive me to such follies." He took a deep breath and, with a visible shrug, he shoved the unpleasant memory aside. He looked at her face, shining above him with pure love and devotion. It was impossible, he thought, to stay morose with such beauty to behold.

He tenderly captured one of her tresses in his hand and twined it around his fingers. For long moments they gazed at each other, enraptured by the love they felt. Thoughts of sleep vanished. Darcy started to rise up, intent on taking her into his arms, but she stayed him with her hands. "I am not finished, sir," she murmured and lowered her face to his neck as she stretched fully onto him.

It was her turn to bestow feather kisses to all his sensitive places and to discover the secrets of how to please him. This she did with an intensity and directness that left him beyond breathless… and completely satisfied.

Their wedding night was not yet over.

CHAPTER FOUR

A New Day Dawns

FITZWILLIAM DARCY WAS HAVING the most extraordinary dream of his entire life. Elizabeth was there, although that fact was not unusual since she had graced the vast majority of his dreams for months now. This dream, however, was exceedingly more erotic than any of the previous ones, and, yes, there had been several! Darcy was enjoying this dream enormously and did not want it to stop, so it was with tremendous dismay that he felt the beginning tendrils of consciousness return. He valiantly fought against them, but the tingles in his right arm persisted no matter how many times his subconscious self tried to move the offending appendage.

The cold blast of wakefulness was like a knife to his heart. He had really liked that dream! So acute was his disappointment that one can imagine the soaring heights instantaneously reached when he realized that the object of his dream was in his arms. In fact, it was her head, which at some point during her sleep had crept from his chest to the inner aspect of his elbow, that was causing his arm to burn. The irony of it did not escape him, and he chuckled softly.

Memories of the fine dream, coupled with the vision of her beauty before him, were temporarily enough to drive away the ever-increasing discomfort to his poor extremity. For some moments he manfully bore the pain and watched her sleep. It was an enchanting sight to behold. Her lush lips were slightly parted, her thick lashes resting peacefully on her rosy cheeks, her mane of hair scattered haphazardly about, and her creamy neck and shoulders visible. Darcy could quite contentedly have stared at her all day, but now his fingers had lost all feeling.

Resolving this issue was suddenly one of the most problematical calamities of his life! He did not want to wake her, nor did he want to remove his arm completely. He thought maybe he could roll her gently back towards his body, a pleasurable prospect, but his arm now had not only lost all sensation but refused to comply with his brain's request. He saw no choice but to use his left arm, which would probably mean waking her up.

There seemed to be no other option, so he began to reach for her. Just at that moment, she stretched her body, sighed deeply, nestled closer to his side, and moved her head back to his chest. Darcy sent silent thanks to whichever guardian angel takes care of these sticky situations.

His relief was short-lived, sadly, due to the sudden rush of blood that ignited a blaze of fresh pain in his unfortunate arm. He gritted his teeth, and his whole body tensed and shuddered in his effort not to cry out and wake his peacefully sleeping wife. Eventually the torture subsided and he was able to move his arm again. Naturally he made good use of it by hugging his wife against his side, resting his hand on her silky hip.

Well, that was interesting, he thought. *Certainly a drawback to sleeping with someone that has never occurred to me, but most assuredly worth the experience.* He lifted his head slightly to view the clock. A quarter to nine! Darcy could not remember the last time he had slept so late. Of course, neither could he remember the last time he had slept so deeply and contentedly, nor woken up feeling so amazingly refreshed and blissful. He sighed and closed his eyes again, a joyous smile on his face.

As pleasant as his dream had been, the reality of his wedding night was vastly superior. They had ended their first night of marriage by loving each other before the fire on the bearskin rug. Elizabeth's initiative, coupled with the location of their union, had added another dimension to what they had already discovered to be a most delicious activity. Darcy never claimed to be a particularly creative man, but how he could not have imagined being with Elizabeth in a site other than his bed surprised him. He was a trifle embarrassed, but he now found his mind drifted to all sorts of promising possibilities. Pemberley had any number of secluded areas, both inside and out, that would work nicely. *Good God, man! Listen to yourself!* But the self-chastisement was ignored and the erotic ruminations manifested themselves physically.

His decadent musings were interrupted by movement from his wife. She murmured something unintelligible, stretched, and then rose up from his chest so she could see his face. "You are awake," she said with a happy smile and reached up to brush his hair.

He caught her hand and kissed it. "Good morning, my love. Did you sleep well?"

"Extraordinarily well. I had the most charming dreams. Quite invigorating, actually," she said with an impish grin.

"Really? How so?"

She smiled roguishly. "There was a man there. Could not quite determine who he was, but he made me feel so nice." She purposefully assumed a dreamy expression. "Black hair he had, dark green eyes, rather short…"

Darcy stopped her words with an ardent kiss, lasting just long enough to leave her breathless, and then he released her abruptly. "Does that drive thoughts of this other scoundrel from your mind, or must I search him out and challenge him to a duel?" There was an edge to his voice, but Lizzy did not detect it.

"Hmmm… A hazy memory remains. I fear I may need more persuading."

Darcy brusquely flipped her onto her back, trapping her wrists above her head with one hand. His other clutched her bottom, securing her against his hips with her legs parting naturally to accommodate him. He kissed her deeply, covetously assailing her mouth as far as he could manage.

"Listen to me, Elizabeth *Darcy*," he growled huskily, "You are *mine*! I forbid you to dream of any other but me." He punctuated his intense words with firm presses of his arousal into her pelvis. She moaned and writhed with the pleasurable sensations arising and struggled to free her captive arms, but he held her fast. He moved his lips along her neck and shoulders, tenderly nibbling and sucking.

Her squirming became frantic with the urgent need to hold him, and she arched into his flaming body, moaning and whimpering. "Please, William!" she cried in desperation.

"What do you want, my wife?"

"I need you!"

"Tell me what you need," he commanded.

"I must have you. Hurry!"

His voice was guttural and hoarse with desire and jealousy and a hint of vulnerability. "Say you want *me*, Elizabeth, only me!"

Somehow through the haze of her passion-induced stupor, Lizzy heard and sensed the frailty in his tone. A pang of guilt ran through her and she forced her eyes open. He was watching her with a dreadful intensity. As calmly and softly as possible, she said, "Always and forever it is you, Fitzwilliam. Only you I want and need… " Her words were cut off by a massive gasp of sensual delight as he claimed her mouth, her body, her heart, and her soul.

When they were blissfully spent, he rolled to the side, bringing her with him in a tight embrace. It was a while before either of them had sufficient lung capacity to speak. It was Darcy who broke the silence, "I am sorry, Elizabeth, if I was too rough, if I frightened you." He sounded so miserable and regretful. "I should not have allowed my petty jealousy to govern me. My passion for you overruled my senses."

Elizabeth rose up to see his face and was pained by the sadness she saw where only happiness should reign. "William, look at me," she demanded, and he did. "If there is fault, it is mine for making such a poor jest. My tongue often rules over my reason, as you know." She moved closer, grasping his face in her hands firmly. "I love you beyond the words to express it. It frightens me how much I love you because my very existence is now inexorably bound to yours. I am not easy with these feelings of vulnerability. It is my nature to make light of serious matters or to tease when I am afraid. Forgive me for my thoughtlessness."

He opened his mouth to reply but she stopped him with her fingers to his lips. "Know this," she continued, "You are everything to me. I have never loved another and I never will. I dream only of you and I desire only you. You have bewitched *me*, body and soul, Fitzwilliam Darcy. You are *mine!*" she finished fiercely and kissed him ravenously.

When she eventually released him, he was breathless and flushed, lips ruddy and swollen. She smiled then, a smile of pure naughtiness, as she ran a finger along his jaw. "Besides," she said, "I rather liked what you did to me, if you could not tell. Rough is acceptable now and then."

Darcy was at a momentary loss for words. Her declaration of love using the spontaneously uttered phrase from his successful proposal, followed by the intensity of her kiss, was a thrilling surprise and soothing balm to his fragile heart. He did not doubt the sincerity of her expressed love for him but was uncertain if its depth matched the all-consuming passion he held for her. Equally titillating was her obvious reciprocating ardor. He knew that Lizzy was passionate by nature; nonetheless, he had not allowed himself to automatically assume this would transfer to bedroom activities.

While his mind was still whirling, Lizzy further proved her love and desire for her new husband by snuggling nearer and bestowing kisses to his chest, thus beginning a long interlude of mutual exploration and pleasure.

Quite some time later, blissfully content in their sweet communion and satisfaction, Lizzy broke the silence first.

"William, may I ask you a personal question?" she inquired faintly and with hesitation, not meeting his eyes.

"Of course, beloved, you can ask anything of me. Have we not established this?"

She did not reply hastily; instead, she toyed with the hairs on his chest and kept her face turned away. Darcy frowned, sensing her discomfiture and beginning to feel a rising concern. Just as he was about to force her to look at him, she spoke.

"Before our wedding, when I told you about my fears and nightmares and you shared your past with me, you assured me you were… chaste as I was. I do not doubt your assertions. I know you would never deceive me, yet you…" She paused, not sure of the proper words to say or how to overcome her embarrassment to proceed.

Darcy was flummoxed as to where she was leading. He had been truthful with her regarding his innocence and could not understand her thoughts, especially in light of how amazing the consummation of their union has been. Was she disappointed? Had he failed her in some way? He paled and the fears of inadequacy shoved aside before their marriage came crashing over him. He struggled to formulate a thought but then she resumed her inquiry.

"Perhaps I am merely displaying my own innocence and… ignorance, William, but you seem to be… well, knowledgeable and confident, and… frankly, I did not anticipate… our… joining being so wonderful!"

In a rush of emotions, Lizzy conquered her shyness and embarrassment. She lifted up and actually glared at her husband, as if challenging him to give an explanation.

Darcy experienced a profound wave of relief and, truth be told, no minute amount of egotistical satisfaction at her confession, so he laughed.

Her eyes opened wide and then narrowed dangerously. "Fitzwilliam Darcy! Do not laugh at me. This is serious."

He hugged her tight to his chest and kissed her cheek and, still chuckling, captured her face in his hands and held her eyes intently with his shining blue ones. "Elizabeth, you delight me so. I honestly divulged my virginity to you, and I am abundantly thankful the situation arose for me to do so. I entered our marriage inexperienced, beloved, with no practical knowledge. However, I never claimed to be uneducated. I told you how precocious I was and how adamantly my father assured my education. There are many ways to learn, and Pemberley has a *very* extensive library."

Lizzy's eyes widened and then she laughed. She kissed him lightly. "Will you show *me* these books, Fitzwilliam?" she asked, smiling wickedly.

～❦～

It was nearing ten o'clock before they finally arose from their tousled bed. Darcy was quite famished again and needed coffee. He rang for breakfast while Elizabeth retired to her dressing room to freshen up. Darcy also took the time to clean himself up, pulling on a shirt and breeches at random.

The breakfast tray arrived just as Elizabeth reentered the room. She had clad herself in a lovely burgundy gown that Darcy had never seen before. Her face was pink from washing, and she had hastily pulled her hair back with a white ribbon, so it hung as a tail down her back. Darcy was struck anew by how beautiful she was and how marvelous it was to be married so he could view her in such casual attire. Elizabeth was thinking the very same thought. She adored how handsome her husband looked with his shirt loosely tucked and open at his neck, feet bare. He was handsome in his complete dress, but here was a picture of him that only she would be privy to.

After a quick kiss, they sat down. Elizabeth curled up in the chair, tucking her feet under her. She poured coffee for Darcy and tea for herself. The simple task of serving her husband sent a surge of happiness through her heart. For his part, Darcy could not cease staring at her. After all that had transpired yesterday and last night and this morning, it still seemed dreamlike that they had finally arrived at this place when, for so long, he had despaired of ever being with her.

"You are staring, Mr. Darcy. Do I have a distracting blemish on my face?" she teased.

He laughed, "Sorry, my dear. No, you do not have any blemishes. I am entranced by your beauty, that is all."

"Quite the flatterer you have become, sir. So charming. Who would believe it of you?"

"Well, as I intend to save my best flattery for when we are alone, no one would believe you even if you were to inform them."

"So, am I to infer that you will be devising and practicing said flattery beforehand? If so, you must remember to give as unstudied an air as possible."

Darcy grinned at her reference. "Perhaps I shall occasionally plan my flattery; however, as you are well aware of how uncreative I am, my dear, I would imagine that the pleasing compliments will usually proceed from the impulse of the moment."

They both laughed and she threw a grape at him. "Ridiculous man! Read your newspaper and let me eat in peace!"

He did his best to comply with her request, discovering that it was quite challenging to focus on world events with her across the table. As the meal proceeded, they both relaxed. Neither of them knew it at the time, but they were innocently setting the stage for what was to become a morning ritual for the rest of their lives. Except for those occasions when guests were present or business separated them, they would breakfast together quietly each day in their joint sitting room. Darcy would read the newspaper and Elizabeth would read a book. They would discuss their daily plans or estate business or items from the news. The staff would be instructed not to interrupt the Master and Mistress until they were called for. Even their children would breakfast apart. This time would become a favorite and necessary part of their day.

"What are we to do with ourselves today?" she asked at one point. "Have you made any specific plans?"

Darcy put the newspaper down and gave his full attention to his wife. "Nothing specific," he replied. "We could always stay here all day." He gave his wife a naughty leer. "I am sure we could dream up *something* to occupy our time. Or if you would rather, the village is quite close so we could ramble through it and see if there is anything that you wish to purchase. The Hamiltons have a gig available, if you wish to take a drive in the country or around the lake. The weather appears to be fine enough for a drive. Too bad it is winter, as a picnic would be an agreeable pastime."

She raised one eyebrow. "Oh? Did a law pass of which I am unaware that we can only enjoy our meals outdoors in the spring or summer?"

He was surprised. "I did not mean to imply that such activities are unlawful in the winter, Mrs. Darcy, as you well know! I am solicitous regarding your comfort, however. It is late November and quite cold outside."

Lizzy laughed. "Honestly, William, I thought you knew me better than that! When has the weather ever hindered me?"

"As you wish, Madame. A picnic it shall be. I beg one concession, however. You must endure my fussing over you and not argue if I deem it is too chilly to remain outdoors. Agreed?" She nodded her assent, smiling placidly.

They each retired to their dressing rooms to finalize dressing for their day out. Darcy finished first and crossed the bedchamber to Elizabeth's door. He knocked tentatively. "Elizabeth?"

"Come in," she called.

He opened the door and was startled to see her alone, sitting at the vanity with her arms up, pinning her hair. "Did the maid not respond to your summons?" he asked, fully prepared to complain to Mr. Hamilton immediately.

"I did not summon her," Lizzy said. She noted his baffled face in the mirror and smiled. "I have been taking care of my own hair for years, my love. I am aware that this will likely change once I am at Pemberley, but for now I wish to do it myself. Does this disturb you?"

"Not in the least. I feared the service was lacking, that is all." He stepped behind her and ran his fingers along her neck and shoulders. "Elizabeth, I do not wish you to alter any of your habits at Pemberley. If it pleases you to attend to your own hair, then it pleases me for you to continue doing so. I fell in love with you as you are. I do not desire for you to be anything other than my Lizzy."

She gifted him with one of her dazzling smiles. Love and desire swept through him in a surging rush and he hastily removed his fingers, sensing a sharp and powerful urge to unfasten the buttons of her gown that threatened to overcome him. He retreated to a couple of paces and cleared his throat.

"I intruded on your privacy only to inform you that I am departing momentarily to speak with Mr. Hamilton about our needs for today. I will return for you when all is prepared. Be sure to dress warmly."

"I will." She pivoted the stool around so she could face him. "And William, you do not need to knock, and I shall never think of you as an intruder."

Darcy beamed, once again amazed at how dissimilar she was to any woman he had ever known and how incredibly blessed he was to have found her. "That may take some adjusting to, my love, but thank you."

◦❦◦

They spent a lovely day together, this first day of the rest of their lives.

Darcy commandeered the gig with easy competence. Mrs. Hamilton had prepared a luncheon hamper for them and loaded the carriage with several thick blankets. Darcy looked Elizabeth over carefully before they set out to ensure she was well bundled. She laughed inwardly at his apprehensiveness but kept silent.

To begin with, they drove into the village. It was not a large town, about the size of Meryton, but there were numerous quaint shops to browse through. It was liberating to be able to stroll along together without being halted every few feet by people wishing to converse with them. No one was acquainted with them here, and no one assigned them a second glance. Lizzy quickly realized that she had to be cautious in exhibiting interest in even the smallest trinket because Darcy would insist on buying it for her. In spite of her guardedness, Darcy's arms were encumbered with packages by the end of two hours, and he was forced to rearrange the blankets and hamper to make room in the gig.

Despite Darcy's worries it was a beautiful day, crisp and cool, but the sun was warming and the sky cloud free. Snow had not yet fallen, nor had it recently rained, so the ground was dry. An intermittent breeze wafted but primarily the air was still, rich with the fragrance of winter blooms.

They leisurely drove along the edge of the river toward the small lake, admiring the countryside. Lizzy sat as close to his side as she could possibly manage, blankets covering them both. She rested one hand on his leg, feeling the warmth of him and delighting in his presence. They would stop periodically to marvel at a particular natural feature and take the opportunity to steal a few kisses. Eventually they discovered a level spot close to the lake's edge that seemed perfect for their luncheon.

Once Darcy was satisfied with the comfort and warmth provided by three blankets laid upon the ground, he assisted Elizabeth from the carriage and nestled her snuggly, insisting on placing another blanket over her. It truly was not that cold, but he refused to take any chances that she might become ill. She was beginning to wonder if he would ever relax and thought that perhaps picnic had not been such a good idea after all. She appreciated his diligence regarding her well-being but could not prevent becoming annoyed.

To cover her waspishness, she busied herself with the lunch. Mrs. Hamilton had packed provisions enough for four grown men, including a bottle of red wine. The day was simply too marvelous and Lizzy far too happy in general to remain cranky for long. She also had learned over the past weeks that Mr. Darcy was especially mellow after dining. Today was no different.

They chatted as they ate. Conversation now came so easily to them that it was impossible to imagine that they had ever struggled so. The topics ranged widely from childhood memories to current events to family matters to literature to future plans and various points in between. By the time they had eaten their fill, Darcy was totally untroubled. He laid his head in her lap and read out loud from a book of Shakespeare's sonnets while Elizabeth played with his hair, deliriously content merely to stare at his face and listen to his resonant voice.

After a bit they decided to stroll. They held hands as they meandered, sometimes talking and sometimes silent. They encountered not a soul. It was as if they were the only two people in the world. When passing a large oak tree, Darcy halted, leaned against the trunk, and gathered Elizabeth into his arms. For some time he merely held her pressed tight to his chest. She experienced a profound sense of peace and protection. His warmth radiated out of him, stalwart arms strong about her body, cheek resting on the top of her head.

In due course his soft lips traveled through her hair to her ear and then her neck, raining gentle kisses and sweet endearments along the way. He caressed her back through her coat, drawing her ever closer to him. Elizabeth gave in to the pleasure that his breath and touch elicited. How wonderful to be married so that they could freely allow their emotions to wash over them! Darcy allowed his hands to open her overcoat and travel deliciously about her curves. Lizzy did the same, pressing her body into his, feeling his arousal. Naturally there was a limit; both of them were cognizant that although they were not exactly in public, they were not in the privacy of their bedchamber. The precipice was reached when Darcy noted his hands, as if of their own accord, grasping and lifting her skirts at the same time that Lizzy untucked his shirt while running one delicate hand up his chest. Darcy groaned and knew he was at the edge of his endurance so they regretfully ceased, mutually deciding that, all things considered, it was time to return to the inn.

They packed up in haste and drove as speedily as safety permitted. Darcy bordered on curtness in instructing the servant that they would be dining at seven o'clock and not to disturb them for the rest of the afternoon. He failed to notice the servant's smile of understanding, nor would he have cared.

The door to their room was barely latched before they were in each other's arms, removing clothing as fast as humanly possible. Darcy's jacket and waistcoat were easy enough for Lizzy to manage; the cravat was another matter. Lizzy's fingers fumbled with what seemed like a dozen knots and twists, the process not aided by the fact that she was kissing his neck at the same time.

Darcy was distracted by her lips and focused on removing the innumerable pins binding her lustrous hair, but he became aware of her struggles when a singularly frantic tug at his neckcloth choked him. They both laughed, and Darcy competently removed the offending cravat, giving her free reign to assault his neck while he returned to her hair. Her tresses finally unencumbered, Darcy was mesmerized momentarily by the sensation of her dense silky curls entwined in his fingers.

He was snapped back to reality with a gasp at the sublime currents racing up his body as her hands moved under the shirt she had untucked. The sudden intense need to feel her skin rocked him, so his hands moved to her back and attacked the tiny buttons of her gown. The ever proficient and assured Mr. Darcy was at a loss with the tightly clasped and seemingly inexhaustible row of buttons. The urge to grab the neckline in his strong hands and rend it open forcefully was overwhelming.

Thankfully, as Lizzy did not own that many dresses, prompt inspiration dawned and he moved behind her to see better what he was doing. This led to the added revelation and intoxication for them both of tracing warm kisses down her spine as each button was released. Lizzy bemoaned his absence and the emptiness of her hands but was quickly overcome with shivers of pleasure at his lips on her back. The rest of her clothing, all totally unique to him and rather fascinating, came off slowly as he endeavored to educate himself and also because he discovered the increased arousal they both experienced by prolonging the stimulation.

Finally she was naked before him, trembling from desire, as he lightly traced long fingers over the sensitive skin of her back, waist, and buttocks. He had not yet seen her from this angle. She was beautiful and perfect. He kissed her bared flesh, familiarizing himself intimately with every inch of her backside.

He turned her about in his arms and kissed her sweet mouth, savoring her taste, and teasing her lips. "I love you so completely, my Elizabeth, my wife," he breathed. He gazed into her shining eyes. "You own me, do you know that, my love? I do not exist without you." He kissed her deeply, letting her feel the extent of the arousal derived solely by his love for her.

He removed his shirt in one swift motion and crushed her to his chest. He abruptly took a step toward the bed, Lizzy in his arms, but their feet tangled on the discarded clothing. They both lost their balance and fell onto the mattress, laughing. Darcy landed on his back, Lizzy sprawled on top of him, one elbow connecting forcefully with his nose. They both laughed hard, Darcy massaging his sore but otherwise undamaged nose.

"William! I am so sorry," Lizzy apologized, kissing his nose and face and everywhere else, and then proceeding to finish undressing him.

It was a novel experience and more than a little enjoyable. They laughed as they fumbled with the strange clasps and buttons, taking another step along the road of discovery and comfortable unity in their relationship. The end result of their playful exertions was as one would expect.

With colossal effort and regret, they left their bed with barely enough time to make themselves presentable for dinner. Maintaining etiquette and decency throughout the meal bordered on painful. Luckily, the room was empty most of the time so, between bites, they shared a few kisses and squeezes.

The food was delicious. They ate heartily, both ravenous from the energy expended over the past hours. Darcy was mesmerized by his wife, every movement generating ripples of delight through his body. His need to touch her overwhelmed him. Breaking pieces of bread and fruit, he fed her, lingering on her lips and losing all awareness in her sparkling eyes.

"William, your food is growing cold," she teased, kissing his finger.

He smiled, leaning to nuzzle behind her ear and briefly kissing. "I care not, beloved. Famished I may be, but touching you is preferable. For once your parents are not present to preclude me fulfilling the fantasy of displaying how even the simple act of eating enhances my desire for you."

Lizzy giggled, fingers covering her mouth. "Oh, William! The vision! I wish you had acted on your impulses then so I could see Mama's face, if nothing else!"

Darcy laughed, resuming his seat and picking up his fork. "As entertaining as that may have been, Elizabeth, your father would likely have strangled me. Curbing my inclinations was not always easy, but wise. Thankfully I no longer need to do so. Well, within reason, of course."

After dinner they took a stroll in the silent garden. Darcy talked about Pemberley. The plan was to depart fairly early in the morning since the journey home would take most of the day. Darcy was in a state of uncontrollable bliss that his *Lizzy* would finally be with him in his home... their home. It was a dream he had harbored in his aching heart for so many months that the reality was incredible. Lizzy was excited and anxious at the same time. With Darcy by her side, his strong arms around her, it was difficult to feel any apprehension. However, she could not completely erase the gnawing doubts of her competence as Mistress of an estate such as Pemberley.

For now though, her emotions were captured by her husband. Her happiness was unlimited and her desire simply to be with him transcended any fears. Before too long they returned to their room, wishing to thoroughly enjoy the last night at this place which would forever be special to them. They made love again, slowly and reverently worshipping each other's bodies before they fell into a deep, peace-filled sleep. Lizzy ached in muscles and places she had hardly known existed, but her love for this man who had so wholly consumed her soul surpassed any discomfort. They slept entwined, cuddling and warm.

CHAPTER FIVE

Homecoming

Mrs. Reynolds, housekeeper of Pemberley in Derbyshire, was in a state of jubilant expectancy that she had not experienced since… well, she could not remember a day she had ever anticipated more! Sometime this afternoon her master, Mr. Fitzwilliam Darcy, would return to Pemberley with his new bride. The entire staff had hoped and waited for the arrival of this day for years, but few of them fully grasped the inexplicable joy in this particular day, this particular union.

Mrs. Reynolds considered herself one of the luckiest servants in all of England. At the age of two-and-thirty she had joined the staff at Pemberley, along with her husband who had been a groom. Pemberley had a reputation throughout the country as an ideal estate. The Darcy family had for generations managed their holdings with honesty and generosity. The former housekeeper had been Mrs. Reynolds's aunt. When she began to feel old age creeping up on her, the Darcys had authorized her to recommend a replacement.

Mrs. Reynolds had been employed as a still-maid at a manor in Gloucestershire and was content in her service; however, the opportunity for advancement, coupled with the sterling name of Pemberley, swayed her to accept the position. Any trepidation she might have felt vanished the moment she met Mr. and Mrs. Darcy. For the past twenty-four years she had served faithfully and with ever-increasing happiness.

Over the years she had grown to love the family she tended to. She had watched Master Fitzwilliam mature into a fine young man and Miss Georgiana into a beautiful young woman. She thoroughly enjoyed her duties and was an excellent housekeeper. There had been tremendous hardships and grief along the way. The death of Lady Anne some eleven years ago and of the elder Mr. Darcy six years ago, not to mention the passing of her own husband three years ago, had begotten sorrow in her heart that she realized would never dissipate. Yet the affection she harbored for Pemberley and, more specifically, for the two young Darcys could not be more genuine or profound if they had been her own flesh and blood.

It was this love that had made the past several years so emotionally tortuous. Master Fitzwilliam had from his youth been far too serious and intense, too reserved, and too apt to seek solitude. The burdens that had been thrust upon him at the tender age of two-and-twenty, along with his acute sorrow, had nearly overwhelmed him. If possible, he had retreated further into himself, laughed and smiled less, and erected a rigid shell about his heart. He only had a handful of true friends, including his sister whom he loved to distraction, yet even they often found his tendency toward surliness and bitterness difficult to comprehend or tolerate. Mrs. Reynolds had fretted and worried, but there was nothing she could do but pray.

As Mr. Darcy settled into his role as Master of Pemberley, she had noted a loosening of his stern demeanor. Colonel Fitzwilliam was a loyal companion who would tease the Master and encourage him to socialize more. Also, his friendship with Mr. Charles Bingley was providential. Mr. Bingley was the polar opposite of Mr. Darcy and, by all outward appearances, the two should have loathed each other. Luckily their relationship had created its own path, and the two young men had formed an abiding bond of mutual affection. Mr. Bingley's sunny, effervescent nature was a soothing balm to the frequently brooding Mr. Darcy. Mrs. Reynolds began to believe that her dear Mr. Darcy would break out of his self-imposed prison. Her sincerest hope was that he would find a young lady to mend and fill his aching heart.

Then abruptly, that past April, Mr. Darcy had plunged into a dark pit of despondency and depression unlike anything Mrs. Reynolds had previously witnessed. It was not unlike the immense grief to which the former Mr. Darcy had succumbed when his wife had expired. There was no basis for young Mr. Darcy's anguish, as far as she could ascertain. Eventually he did partially return to the world of the living, but a lingering pain in his blue eyes refused to lift.

Until one glorious day in early September.

Mrs. Reynolds remembered the day vividly, although it had initially dawned virtually identical to all other days. Mr. Darcy was in Town, not expected to return until the next day. Mrs. Reynolds had welcomed visitors to the manor, not a frequent occurrence, but one that happened often enough not to register as significant this time. The visitors, an older couple and their young niece, were polite and gracious.

The niece seemed vaguely uncomfortable and nervous, but Mrs. Reynolds did not dwell on it overly. She executed her duty as tour guide with pleasure, being quite proud of the house and its furnishings. She recalled being a bit startled to discover that the young lady was acquainted with Mr. Darcy as she did not immediately strike Mrs. Reynolds as being in the same class with her master. However, as his personal affairs were for the most part outside her purview, she did not thoroughly ponder the situation.

Toward the end of the tour, the niece became separated from the group. It could not have been more than fifteen minutes before she came bounding around the side of the house to where her aunt and uncle were standing by their carriage, expressing their thanks to Mrs. Reynolds. The lady, Lizzy her aunt called her, was extremely agitated. She insisted on walking back to Lambton, wringing her hands and shifting her feet the entire time she asked to do this. She kept glancing toward the house as if she feared something or someone was going to barge out of the front doors and attack her! It was most unusual. Mrs. Reynolds stood speechless, wishing she knew the root of the young woman's distress, fearing greatly that something terrible had happened and wondering if she should inquire. In the end, Miss Lizzy left, nigh on running down the road toward the bridge.

Mrs. Reynolds stood in the drive for a few minutes ruminating on the odd behavior of Miss Lizzy. She determined that she would ask the other servants if they had seen the young lady after she had been left behind in the gallery. She needed to guarantee that nothing untoward had occurred. She entered the foyer and ascended the stairs to the main floor, but before she could advance any farther than five feet, she was paralyzed with shock when Mr. Darcy, whom she was unaware was even home, fairly flew out of the parlor door. He was frantic, but his face was radiant and he wore the broadest grin. He skidded to a stop mere seconds before bowling her over.

"Mrs. Reynolds," he shouted breathlessly, "send word to the stables to resaddle Parsifal, immediately!" Without another word he dashed around the corner, heading toward the stairs leading to his chambers.

She stood there with her mouth hanging open, only then aware that Miss Georgiana was standing in the doorway, also displaying a ridiculously bright smile. "Hurry, Mrs. Reynolds! Do as he asks and then come back and I shall tell you what is happening. Oh, it is the most wonderful thing!"

The next month had been fraught with emotions and angst. Miss Georgiana had told her the whole sorry tale. That Mr. Darcy was head over heels in love with Miss Elizabeth Bennet was an indisputable fact. What was not so clear was whether Miss Bennet was in love with him. Mrs. Reynolds adored her master and was initially vexed, assuming that any lady who had refused him once was unworthy of him. However, as the truth was revealed, she did understand and eventually recognized that Miss Bennet was precisely what Mr. Darcy so urgently required to heal his wounded heart.

Two months ago she and Miss Georgiana had at long last received the missives they had been longing for. Mr. Darcy's ecstasy at Miss Elizabeth accepting his hand was uncontainable. Mrs. Reynolds had received hundreds of pieces of correspondence from her master over the years, but none remotely similar to the letters he now wrote. Why, she could remit them to a publisher for a book of romantic musings and poetry! Her heart was overflowing with joy.

Mr. Darcy had been quite specific in his orders regarding the new Mistress. His mother's chambers had been aired out and thoroughly scrubbed. Old furnishings had been removed. His plan was to allow Mrs. Darcy to redecorate the rooms at her leisure, so for now they needed only to be clean and comfortable. He had purchased several items that had been sent ahead, including a new bathing tub and washbasin, a new mattress, a stationery set for her desk, and an enormous painting of a landscape. All he had hinted was that the scene was special in some way and he wished it to be a surprise for his new bride. The painting was to be hung, he instructed, in her dressing room behind the vanity.

He had entrusted Mrs. Reynolds to acquire any feminine objects that were essential and to stock the bathing room with the finest linens. Numerous odd packages had arrived from Mr. Darcy, trinkets, he told her, that he picked up here and there: various hair accoutrements, perfumes, ribbons, small pieces of jewelry, a musical snuffbox, robes with matching slippers, a set of silk handkerchiefs, several books, and other odds and ends. These she had carefully distributed as he instructed. The last touch was numerous vases of flowers randomly placed about the rooms, the largest a bouquet of white roses and lavender to be placed on the vanity.

He also had detailed directives regarding his own bedchamber and private sitting room. They, too, were to be thoroughly cleaned. New bed linens and coverings of a lighter design than the dark colors he usually preferred were sent. Some of the more masculine furnishings were to be removed and exchanged with new pieces he purchased in Town or with specific objects from elsewhere in the manor. The small table was replaced with a larger one with two overstuffed chairs. The old rug, a remnant from when the rooms were his father's, was discarded and replaced with a gorgeous Persian carpet of pale blues and golds. The overall effect was subtle; the rooms were already beautifully decorated, but the changes added an airiness that was altogether inviting.

Mrs. Reynolds was not an innocent. She comprehended that her master was of the conviction that his wife would be sharing his quarters much of the time. The former Mrs. Darcy had done so, except for when she was confined or ill, so Mrs. Reynolds was not shocked by this. In fact, it amplified her happiness to know that her master had fallen in love with such a woman.

Mr. Darcy had written to his aunt, Lady Matlock, soliciting her assistance in hiring a lady's maid for Elizabeth. She had gladly done so, sending three women to Mrs. Reynolds to be interviewed. Mrs. Reynolds had settled on a Frenchwoman of thirty named Marguerite, who was an experienced lady's maid. Her recommendations were impeccable, and she had agreed to a probationary period pending Mrs. Darcy's final approval.

The staff had been quite busy over the past weeks ensuring all was in perfect readiness. Mr. Darcy's last letter had arrived the day of his wedding. He directed Mrs. Reynolds to have a light supper prepared, to ignite the welcome torches on the grounds, to have their chambers warm and well lit, and to assemble the senior household staff for a quick greeting of the new Mistress. The flurry of activity that had descended on the normally placid household was concluded. Mrs. Reynolds strolled, for the umpteenth time, through the house guaranteeing that all was flawless. A sentry was stationed by the main road to alert Mrs. Reynolds the moment the Darcy carriage was spotted.

Nothing for it now but to wait....

The trip to Pemberley was uneventful. Lizzy was anxious and excited at the same time. *I am going home!* She kept repeating this to herself so it would truly penetrate her heart and soul.

She valiantly feigned composure and serenity, but the amused curl of Darcy's mouth told her that he was on to her little charade. For probably the hundredth time, she asked him, "How much further to Pemberley?"

"Maybe two more hours, if the weather holds," he replied, leaning closer to her so he could see around her out the window. "Those clouds do look ready to burst any moment. Luckily the road through here is an excellent one, so even if it does rain, we should not be waylaid."

She continued to stare out the carriage window. "It is so beautiful here. Is this Derbyshire?"

"The southernmost regions, yes. I had the driver bypass Derby to avoid the congestion. We are some twenty miles south of Lambton. However, we will divert and enter from the south, rather than the west as you did before. I will let you know when we enter our estate lands. The southerly route passes through approximately five miles of our farms."

Lizzy lifted her brows in surprise. "I had no idea it was so vast!" His use of the word "our" was not lost on her, but she did not comment.

Darcy smiled at her and stroked her cheek. "Yes, it is quite large. It requires several hours to circle the perimeter. Of course, a generous percentage of the land is wild and inaccessible but for horseback. A significant amount is woods, lakes, and rivers, as well as pastures. Game runs free and birds make their homes with little to disturb them except for the occasional hunt. The farmlands are closer to the manor, thus the tenants are within an easy distance." He leaned back in the seat and lovingly caressed her back.

Elizabeth continued to stare out the window. She did not speak and Darcy could sense her tension, but he kept silent, waiting patiently until she was prepared to open her mind to him. In time she did, but her voice was so low he had to strain to hear her. "What if they do not like me?"

"It does not matter if they do not like you. You are my wife and the Mistress of Pemberley. They are your servants and tenants." She jerked her head toward him at his blunt words, a ready retort on her lips. He smiled and stopped the flip rejoinder he knew she was about to make by pressing his fingers to her lips. *That is what I want to see from you, my brave, feisty Lizzy,* he thought. "However, I do not believe, even for one second, that they will not adore you. Nor do I have the slightest qualm or apprehension that you will be the most excellent Mistress that Pemberley has seen in decades, no offence intended toward my dear mother or grandmother."

She peered intently into his eyes, as if searching for any untruth or doubt in his assertions, but there was none. The deep love he felt for her was unmistakably visible, as it always was. Yet, as she examined his eyes, she was again struck forcibly by the unparalleled esteem he held for her. His love for her, although all consuming, unwavering, and unconditional, was not blind or foolish. He knew her faults, her flaws, her weaknesses. He also knew her quality, her personality, her strengths, and her character. His trust in her was in spite of and due to these incontrovertible facts, not out of besotted passion or bedazzlement.

She sighed and relaxed against his chest, burying her face into his shoulder. "You must think me a silly child!"

He smiled into her hair. "You are not silly and, as proven several times over the past two days, you are unquestionably not a child!" They both laughed. "I do think you are worrying too much about all this, Elizabeth. No demands will be placed on you until you wish to assume them. Good heavens, it took me a year to feel secure as Master of Pemberley, and I grew up there! You will have all the time you need. Mrs. Reynolds already likes you and she will assist you in any way you require."

"I do not apprehend how she could have such a fair opinion of me since I acted so outlandishly peculiar. Getting separated, spying on Georgiana, stammering like an imbecile, rushing off across the fields. I would imagine she is horrified that you would deign to be in the same room with me, let alone marry me!" She smiled up at him and he could not resist kissing her.

"Well, therein lies the answer to your question, my heart. Mrs. Reynolds has known me since I was four. Few people understand me as well as she does. For all that she is technically a servant, she has in many ways been a second mother to me. She has observed me through all my years of pain and grief. She knows my character and judgment. She trusts my choices and wishes nothing more than to see me happy. So, if you bring me that happiness, and you emphatically do, and if *I* trust you, then she does as well. It is that simple." He kissed her again, deeply.

Huskily he continued, "You must learn to have the same faith in my assertions regarding your qualifications as she does." He paused to kiss her some more. "Of course," he teased, "it is all a moot point as I intend to keep you locked in my bedchamber for several weeks, at least so I may have unfettered and undisturbed access to you!"

Lizzy grinned. "If you mean to frighten me by that threat, Mr. Darcy, you have failed miserably. Frankly, I can think of no place on earth I would rather be than in your bedchamber, provided you are there as well, naturally." She accompanied her words with sensitively placed caresses and kisses, causing Darcy to groan and close his eyes in mute surrender.

It was some time before he sought to find his voice or even that he was able to. Finally, breathlessly, he begged, "Desist, woman! You win! I shall exact my revenge for this torture, however, so be warned." He moved away from her to compose himself, refusing to acknowledge the expression of amusement and triumph on her face.

Time passed in comfortable companionship. Lizzy was riveted to the passing scenery, all of it lushly green moorland and rolling hills. The River Derwent was a constant companion as the main road wove alongside it, crossing frequently over stone bridges. They traveled through Matlock, but Rivallain, the estate of Lord and Lady Matlock, was not visible. Darcy pointed out the places of interest as they glided by, but they did not halt. Both were too anxious to be home.

As they veered onto a secondary avenue and crossed over a stone bridge spanning the river, Darcy proclaimed, "We are well into Pemberley lands, Elizabeth. Look."

The view was magnificent. The sun was low in the western sky, blanketing the spectacular landscape with soft shadows. To the west and east flowed seemingly endless fields of orchards and perfectly manicured farmland. Small, sturdy stone cottages were scattered randomly. Large numbers of sheep were noted as well as the horses that Pemberley was famous for. They saw a sizeable lake that was fed by numerous small streams from the hills and bordered on its eastern shore by a forest of cedar and pine that appeared to stretch to the horizon.

On her tour with the Gardiners, Lizzy had approached Derbyshire and Pemberley from the northwest, having taken a circuitous route. These were areas she had not seen with any clarity, her return to Hertfordshire being filled with too much dismay to inspect the passing landscape.

She scooted closer to him, resting a hand on his thigh, and he suspiciously watched her. "Do not fear, sir," she giggled. "I promise to behave...for now. How soon to the house?"

"Only a couple of miles now. We will be arriving at twilight. I ordered the torches to be lit." He placed his arm around her shoulders and snuggled her near to his side. He kissed her forehead and then nestled his face into her hair. "My Lizzy!" he breathed, "I cannot express my joy, my elation, to be bringing you home with me. Do you have any idea how deeply I love you?"

Her only reply was a bone-crunching hug. They held each other thus as the carriage proceeded down the tree-lined drive to the gravelly expanse before the entrance portico, not separating until the carriage slowed to a halt.

"How do I look?" she asked him.

"Stunning," he answered truthfully. He kissed her lips tenderly and touched her cheek with his fingertips. "We are home."

Lamps were lit in abundance, giving the house a bright and cheery glow of welcome. Scattered around the grounds were tall torches, lending increased illumination in the gathering darkness of evening. Mrs. Reynolds and Mr. Keith, the steward, waited atop the entryway steps under the wide canopy, both smiling warmly. Darcy led Elizabeth forward.

"Mrs. Reynolds, you remember Miss Elizabeth Bennet? Now it is my boundless honor and joy to introduce you to her again as my wife, Mrs. Darcy."

Mrs. Reynolds curtseyed. Her face was beaming and, in an act of spontaneous pleasure, she took Elizabeth's hands in hers. "Welcome to Pemberley, Mrs. Darcy. On behalf of the entire staff, I wish to express our delight in meeting you. Please rest assured that we will all endeavor to make you comfortable in every possible way. We are at your disposal."

Elizabeth smiled. "Thank you, Mrs. Reynolds. Your kind words ease my heart."

Darcy introduced Mr. Keith. "Mrs. Darcy, welcome. I echo Mrs. Reynolds's greeting and assurances," Mr. Keith said. "It is a tremendous honor to welcome you to the Pemberley household and family."

Mrs. Reynolds turned to her master and curtseyed. "Mr. Darcy, welcome home. All has been prepared as you instructed. The senior staff is waiting inside, and dinner will be served whenever you wish."

SHARON LATHAN

They entered the enormous foyer. The room, with its marble flooring and painted ceilings, brought back fond memories for Elizabeth. Her visit here had brought William back into her life. The beauty and elegance of these rooms had finally coalesced her tumultuous thoughts of him into recognition of the amazing man he was. She stole a glance at him as he walked so proudly by her side, a dazzling smile on his lips. Suddenly it felt so very right to be here, to be with him, that all her doubts and fears vanished as a vapor on the wind.

Elizabeth's eyes fell on the people standing in a row before her. She experienced a moment of embarrassment to have so many stares directed her way, but the looks were universally ones of welcome and friendliness. Darcy took the lead in introducing her to each member of the staff present. The head cook, Mrs. Langton, was a commanding woman, tall and stout. One glance at her features and manner, and Elizabeth could well imagine the formidable competence of her kitchen management. The butler, Mr. Taylor, a man of some sixty years, was bent slightly but robust nonetheless. Mr. Darcy's valet, Samuel, was a handsome man of approximately forty. Mrs. Reynolds explained that the remainder of the staff, both inside and outside, would be introduced to her on the morrow.

Lastly, she was introduced to Marguerite. Elizabeth almost gasped in surprise. Marguerite was an exquisite creature, quite small in stature and build, with blonde hair pulled severely back into a knot and the face of an angel. Her voice was rich and deep for a woman, accented with a trace of her native French. She greeted Elizabeth properly but with warmth. "Mrs. Darcy, welcome. It is a tremendous honor to be chosen to serve you. I understand that my position here is dependent on my ability to please you and serve you competently. To that end, I beg you to express your needs and wishes to me and to hastily inform me of any errors I may make."

"Thank you, Marguerite." Elizabeth was quite moved by the greetings she had received. She addressed the group all together: "Thank you to all of you for your sincere welcome. I have been somewhat nervous regarding my reception, as Mr. Darcy could confirm, but your graciousness and concern for my well-being has comforted me. Thank you, again, from the bottom of my heart."

Mr. Darcy took over, dismissing the staff to their duties. He directed Mrs. Reynolds to have dinner prepared for two hours hence. "I will be giving Mrs. Darcy a tour of our apartments, Mrs. Reynolds. Please see that we are not disturbed. Marguerite, Mrs. Darcy will ring for you when she is ready to dress for dinner. Samuel, I will call for you as well." Curtseys and bows all around, and then Darcy offered his arm to Elizabeth.

They ascended the grand marble staircase, taking a turn to the left and then to the right, heading to a part of the house Elizabeth had not seen during her tour in September. She could not absorb it all! Every wall held a picture, tapestry, or wall covering of incredible beauty. Exquisite furnishings lined the corridors and plush carpet runners of detailed woven designs softly cushioned their feet. Statues large and small occupied wall niches or sat on ornately carved tables. Most of the doors they passed were closed, and hallways branched off to unknown destinations with additional latched doors and staircases. Perfectly spaced oil lamps provided illumination.

"This wing of the second floor is primarily private apartments," Darcy explained. He stopped and pointed down the passageway. "Georgiana's chambers are down there and to the left are guests' quarters. Colonel Fitzwilliam and Bingley have rooms set aside for their use. I suppose we shall need to reassign Bingley's chambers as the current ones are inappropriate for Jane as well. You have seen some of the public rooms on the southern wing, but we will tour them thoroughly tomorrow. Our chambers are up this staircase, on the third floor."

"William, I am lost already! I sincerely hope you plan on staying close by my side or I may wander off some forgotten corridor and never be seen again. I could well become the ghost bride who haunts Pemberley for all eternity." She laughed.

"Never fear, my dear. I intend to keep you quite near, not only so you will not get lost but for other purely selfish motives," he said cheekily. "In truth, Pemberley is not as difficult to navigate as some manors I have been in. Rosings, for instance, is far older, and I have always imagined the original architects taking perverse delight in designing a maze of halls and rooms with the singular intention of confusing the inhabitants. Also, Pemberley is well lit, day and night. I refuse to bump into walls, so I insist on lit lamps in the main rooms and passages. All the rooms and hallways have windows that admit sunlight during the day."

They had reached the third-floor landing and Darcy paused. He gestured to the right-hand passages. "Those rooms are unoccupied and have been since I moved into my father's chambers years ago. Occasionally we have needed to open them for guests, but I prefer guests to stay on the second floor. Someday our children will reside in those rooms." He said the last sentence softly and looked at Elizabeth with tenderness.

She smiled back but could not resist teasing just a bit. "And how many rooms are we to generate occupants for, sir? A girl likes to grasp what she is in for in life!"

"Well, let me think," Darcy thoughtfully mused, "there are at least a dozen empty chambers down that wing and I believe three on this wing, not to mention the others on the western side of the manor, so…" he paused and in mock seriousness began counting on his fingers, pretending to be unable to add it all before he gave up. "It is quite a few, my dear, so I suppose we ought to get busy with the unpleasant task of creating said occupants." He sighed deeply and theatrically, an expression of mournful sadness on his face, "A gentleman must be diligent in his duties."

Elizabeth laughed and took his hand, propelling him forward. "You are incorrigible! Lead the way before I attempt it and get us hopelessly waylaid."

Darcy complied, leading her to a set of double doors to the left. He stopped before opening them and took her face in his hands. "Elizabeth, I have dreamed of showing you these rooms, of having you here as my wife for so long now. I am overwhelmed! Pinch me or something so I know I am not dreaming."

"I shall do better," she said. She wound her arms behind his neck, twining fingers into his hair, and brought his face to hers. She kissed him with wild abandon, pouring her love into the task. He encircled her waist with his arms, drawing her to him so that she was pressed against every plane of his body. She could feel his ardor, his desire and arousal, and she experienced it, too. He buried his face in her neck and inhaled deeply of her lavender fragrance.

She held him tightly, allowing him the time he needed to regain control and steady his breathing. Softly she whispered, "I love you, Fitzwilliam Darcy. Now, beloved, are you convinced of my reality?" He nodded, kissed her lips briefly, and regretfully released her.

Turning back to the doors, he said, "Remember, my love, these rooms were my mother's and she decorated them when she came to Pemberley as a new bride. Therefore, the fashion is more than thirty years old and totally outdated. You will be able to refurbish the chambers however you desire." He opened the door to his wife's modest sitting room and held her hand as they entered.

The room was generous but cozy. His mother had had an observable predilection for green and peach. Lizzy did not dislike the motif, his mother obviously having had exceptional taste, but she knew instantly it was not her preference. However, this was a vague thought as her eyes were drawn to the large windows, the general dimensions of the room, and the fine fireplace. She could easily imagine being very comfortable relaxing here.

Darcy was studying her closely. "I have arranged for a decorator to come from London next week, dearest. He will assist you with finding a style more pleasing to you."

"Truly, William, you worry too much. The room is beautiful. I will grant that some modification would be welcome. I tend to prefer darker colors, earthy tones, you could say. Nonetheless, I would not want to embark on a spending frenzy simply because the colors are not to my liking!"

Darcy laughed, "Now it is you who are worrying too much. The expense is not an issue. I assure you the estate can afford renovating a couple of rooms." Lizzy furrowed her brow. She wondered, briefly, if she would ever become accustomed to money not being a concern.

He led her to her bedchamber. It was arrayed in the same colors and fashion as the sitting room. The bed was ample but not overly huge, and several chairs sat on a beautiful Oriental rug that carpeted the floor. Three other doors were visible. Darcy pointed to one. "That leads to my private sitting room, through which is my bedchamber."

"Where does that door lead?" she asked, pointing to a door recessed in a curtained alcove.

"The nursery," Darcy responded. "It has been unused since Georgiana was born and is empty. Beyond it is another chamber for a nurse." He had come behind her and slipped his arms around her waist, kissing her below her ear.

"Are you planning on practicing the filling of those uninhabited chambers this moment, Mr. Darcy?" she said archly.

"It *is* a bedchamber, my dear, although not the bedchamber I have fantasized seeing you in." He playfully nibbled on her earlobe.

She turned in his arms, smiling wickedly. "Fantasies, is it? Why, Mr. Darcy, how decadent of you! I am shocked to the core!"

He held tighter, "You minx! You have revealed your dreams to me, so do not play innocent." He kissed her heartily but she wiggled out of his arms, giggling.

"We may never complete this tour, sir, if you constantly interrupt." With an impish smile she flounced to the third unexplored door. He followed, smiling foolishly.

This door led to her dressing area. This room, with adjacent bathing area, was larger than the bedchamber. Rows upon rows of drawers, numerous racks to hang gowns, and shelves for shoes lined one entire wall length. Her meager belongings took up no space at all. An enormous floor-length mirror stood at one end. The vanity was magnificent with a dark-blue velvet cushioned bench, dozens of small drawers, and a mirror edged in gold. On the top was a large bouquet of white roses in a crystal vase surrounded by perfume bottles and a musical box. Through the arch, an enormous bathing tub and an elegant stand with a porcelain washbasin and pitcher were visible.

However, Elizabeth noticed none of this initially, because her eyes were immediately captured by the painting on the wall above the vanity. She gasped and her trembling hand touched her mouth as tears filled her eyes. She was speechless.

"William... how... where... I do not understand..."

He was beside her, one arm around her waist, an expression of incomparable exhilaration on his face. "Do you like it, my darling? I discovered it in a gallery in London, quite by accident. It instantly reminded me of Hertfordshire and the meadow near Longbourn where we met on the day you accepted me." His voice throbbed with emotion.

It was a landscape that uncannily resembled her childhood home. The field of knee-high green grasses almost appeared to wave in the sun-kissed air. A small stream cut crookedly through the middle, a narrow stone bridge spanning one edge. In the distance stood a house of beige bricks obscured by the faint wisps of English mist hugging the ground. The work was exquisite, but even if it had been of poor quality, she would have been tremendously moved.

Lizzy could instantly understand why the painting had struck her husband. It was not the moor near Longbourn where they encountered each other that fateful day in late September, drawn to each other as if by magic, but stunningly similar. She could almost see their figures in the haze, finally speaking openly of the love they shared.

Elizabeth's thoughts and emotions were in riot. She wanted to cry, to laugh, to hold her husband tenderly, to passionately make love to him right there. He surprised her continually in his ability to show his adoration for her, his devotion. For an agonizing second she experienced an acute stab of unworthiness. What had she done in life to deserve such an extraordinary man?

The answer was nothing... his love was a gift and she would spend her life dedicated to the task of loving him in return with equal fervor.

With tears coursing down her cheeks, she turned to him and wrapped her arms around his waist, holding him as close as possible, her face pressed against his chest. She could not think of the proper words to express herself, so she merely held him. For a very long while they stood thus, embracing in love without thoughts of passion, content to hear the other breathing, the warmth of their bodies seeping into each other. Unaware of who moved first, Darcy kissed her tears away with the utmost tenderness while they were still locked together in sweet harmony. Softly murmured endearments proceeded from both their mouths in a welter of need to articulate the consuming love they both felt.

Eventually their eyes met, hers shimmering with tears and his the pure blue of a cloudless summer sky. He smiled a smile that lit his face and caused Elizabeth's knees to weaken. "So, you approve of the painting?" he whispered in his melodious voice.

Elizabeth laughed and bent her head to his chest momentarily before looking back at him, mirth dancing in her eyes. "Yes, my love, I 'approve' of the painting." She giggled and hugged him again. "Thank you! It is.... unbelievable. I am at a loss for words. You will never cease to amaze me, William. With each passing day I realize how blessed I am to have you as mine and how I shall enjoy being your wife."

"Well, that is a relief! I was beginning to wonder," he teased, kissing her nose. He snatched her hand and led her toward a door she had not noted previously. He stopped and assumed a melodramatic tone, "The tour commences, Mrs. Darcy! Now to my favorite room in all of Pemberley, or at least hereafter it shall be. The chamber which shall be subjected to the greatest of joys, pleasures untold, passion of the highest order, ecstasy unparalleled!" and with a flourish he opened the door to his bedchamber.

Elizabeth continued to laugh at her husband's silliness as she crossed the threshold. Immediately she was enveloped by a profound sensation of peace and contentment. In one swift glance she knew this room was perfect; it was home. The walls were covered with rich mahogany paneling and cream wallpaper printed with a twining design of autumn leaves. The ceiling was also cream colored with intricately scrolled beams of polished mahogany.

The massive four-poster bed was carved mahogany with curtains of burgundy and gold velvet and a coverlet of cream with burgundy edging.

A gigantic fireplace with a roaring fire gave the room a comforting glow. The Turkish rug was an incredible design in blues and gold. Two large windows, each with gauzy curtains lining thick ones of damask, flanked a set of French-style doors that opened onto a balcony facing south with an incredible view of the fountain-accented lake and extensive lawn. Across the room, beyond the bed, three more large windows faced east. The chamber itself was generous in size but sparingly furnished, creating a sublime atmosphere of openness.

Elizabeth walked about the room touching and admiring. Many of her husband's personal touches were evident: a forgotten book on the bed stand, a miniature of Georgiana, a decanter of brandy and several glasses with *F.D.* engraved on them, a pair of slippers next to the bed, and a small pillow with Parsifal's likeness embroidered on it. She had not previously contemplated what William's tastes might be. Having not seen any of the private rooms on her previous visits, nor when visiting Darcy House in London, she had had no way to make a judgment. Yet, looking about this room, she knew it was absolutely him. More amazing, it was absolutely her! The rich colors, the lack of pretension, and the hominess were precisely as she would desire.

Darcy was watching her intently and nervously. "I had some furnishings removed and purchased the rug and coverlet to replace what I had before, they being quite old. These have been my rooms for many years, my love, so I am afraid they have been indelibly stamped with my personality. However, it is important to me that you find this suite to your liking. Any suggestions you have are welcome."

He moved to where she was standing and took her hands, staring intently into her eyes. "Elizabeth, I am aware that we have not discussed this and I do not wish to embarrass you." He swallowed and then continued with a slight blush on his cheeks. "Convention would dictate that these remain my chambers and you have your own. I would never presume to force my wishes upon you nor request you submit to any action that is unfavorable to you. However, I have been alone for far too long and have no appetite for solitude. My fervent hope has been that you would choose to share my chambers with me at all times. However, I will understand if this is not... Elizabeth, why are you laughing? This is serious!"

"I am sorry, my dear, but... Fitzwilliam Darcy, for all your wisdom, maturity, and authority, you can be such a baby sometimes!" She could not stop laughing. "Any time we allowed convention to dictate our relationship, we ended up miserable. It was not proper for me ever to tour Pemberley, all things considered, or you to rush after me as you did. Rules of society would not have had you dash to Lambton to invite total strangers to dine at your house. And it most assuredly was neither proper nor conventional for us to become betrothed while unescorted and without a prior courtship! I would say that flouting convention has served us quite well, and I do not intend to deviate in this matter!"

She placed her hands around his face and pulled him toward her until their foreheads were touching. "After all we have suffered to be together, after the love we have shared these past two days, did you honestly suppose for one second that, day or night, I would want to be anywhere but right next to you?" she inquired tenderly.

His only reply was to kiss her, deeply and ardently. He pulled back slightly. "I love you, Elizabeth."

"And I love you, William." Kiss.

"You can make any changes you wish." Kiss.

"Thank you, but I love everything exactly as it is." Kiss.

"You will stay with me each night?" Kiss.

"Forever, and all day, too, until you are sick of me." Kiss.

"That will never happen!" Kiss.

"I *can* be annoying at times." Kiss.

"Do you truly think me a baby?" Kiss.

"Only occasionally, beloved, and in the most endearing way. Now hush and kiss me!"

Darcy complied with abundant enthusiasm. Elizabeth unbuttoned Darcy's waistcoat, ran her hands up his chest, and then moved her fingers to his cravat and began working the knots. With immeasurable strength of will, he stayed her hands. With a heavy sigh and a groan, he took a step back and in a trembling voice whispered, "I must be insane!" He ran a hand over his face. "It is time to prepare for dinner, beloved. God knows it is the *last* thing I wish to do right now, but we should." He stated sarcastically, "I am attempting to employ some of that maturity and wisdom you alluded to."

She chuckled shakily and fought against an excruciating urge to overpower his "wisdom and maturity," positive he would capitulate. She managed to behave, though, and they parted reluctantly to their respective dressing rooms.

It took a bit of time for her to figure out how to ring for Marguerite. While she waited, she further inspected the room, opening the many drawers on the vanity and discovering numerous items that had not previously belonged to her. Among the treasures were tiny notes written in Darcy's hand with phrases such as: "Because I love you" or "They sparkled like your eyes" or "It matches your green gown" or "I adore you in red."

A box next to the vase of flowers had a card with "To my wife, my matchless pearl" written on it. She hesitated, but curiosity overcame her so she opened it. Inside rested a spectacular strand of pearls. Elizabeth collapsed onto the bench, too overcome with all that had happened since she arrived at Pemberley to think clearly. Marguerite entered moments later to encounter her mistress motionless and staring off into space.

"Madame, are you well?"

"What? Oh, yes. Forgive me, Marguerite; I am simply feeling a bit overwhelmed."

"I understand, Mistress. If I may suggest a bath? I know that always brightens my spirits."

A half hour later, Elizabeth was dressed and feeling her old self again. She was well aware of why her husband had a penchant for her and pearls, so she decided to wear the gown she had worn at the Netherfield Ball and she requested Marguerite adorn her hair with a pearl-encrusted comb she found in the vanity and, naturally, she wore the necklace. As a final touch she nestled a sprig of lavender and a single white rose between her breasts.

Darcy was awaiting her in his sitting room, which she had not yet viewed. Her eyes were only for her husband, however. Why was it that she still found herself dazzled by how handsome he was? She supposed it was because of her initial reaction to him, that his attractiveness had been marred by a ridiculing, forbidding countenance and a disagreeable nature. *What a fool I was!* she thought, not for the first time.

The fiery expression crossing his visage left no doubt of his opinion of her ensemble. His provocative eyes ranged leisurely down her body and her heart instantly began beating erratically. He walked to her slowly, a sensual smile on his lips. He stopped before her and delicately touched her skin just below the necklace.

"These were my mother's," he said, eyes on the pearls and the neck they graced. "I knew they would be beautiful on you." His fingers moved lightly across her collar and along her shoulder, and then grazed the edge of her gown until reaching the flowers. He met her eyes with one brief, smoldering gaze, and then lowered his face to the flowers. He inhaled their scent, warm breath tickling her skin, and then placed two soft kisses onto the tender flesh on either side of the corsage.

If his sturdy arm had not encircled her waist, Elizabeth was certain she would have fallen. "William," she whispered, almost pleading, arms already around his neck, fingers in his hair.

He was studying her face with its half-opened eyes and parted lips. "You are so beautiful, my Lizzy. I love you so!" The following kiss was encompassing and demanding.

They were lost and they both knew it. Passion had overtaken them and dinner was completely forgotten. Luckily, or unluckily, Darcy's valet chose that precise moment to knock on the door announcing that dinner was served. Even so, it seemed forever before they came to their senses. Darcy cleared his throat huskily before calling out that they would be right down.

He closed his eyes and rested his forehead on hers, moving his hands to her waist regretfully and with a struggle. "I require a moment," he stated flatly.

Lizzy glanced to the front of his breeches and smiled. Her arousal was indisputably intense but without the visible physical ramifications.

Dinner was served in the smaller of the two dining rooms that Pemberley had. (Elizabeth would discover this fact later.) It was the same room she had dined in with her aunt and uncle. They were both quite hungry, luncheon having been a basket shared in the carriage hours ago.

They were mounting the stairs to return to their room when Mr. Keith appeared. "Mr. Darcy," he bowed. "My apologies, Sir and Madame. Mr. Darcy, there is a matter of some urgency. Forgive me for interrupting but I fear it cannot wait."

"Of course, Mr. Keith. Allow me to escort Mrs. Darcy to her rooms, and I shall meet you in my study momentarily."

They proceeded up the stairs. "Do you think it serious, William?" Elizabeth asked.

"I hope not. However, Mr. Keith is not an alarmist and would not disturb me today of all days if it was not important. Do not fret, my love; I will return as soon as possible. If this matter demands my attention for any length of time, I will send word." He kissed her at her door. "Wait for me," he whispered, and then he was gone.

He was gone for more than an hour. He had sent word that he was needed at the stables and was unsure how long it would be. Elizabeth freshened up, donned another nightgown, and used her time to wander around the suite. She meandered about his dressing room, stunned at the quantity of clothing he possessed. His familiar scent permeated the air. The personal items on his dresser were arranged in perfect order, all of them dear to her because they were his. She impulsively grabbed one of his robes and put it on, wrapping herself in his scent and oddly comforted knowing that the soft fabric had touched his body.

She sat before the fire, reading for some time, but began to feel sleepy, so she went outside onto the balcony. The view was stupendous, even at night. The torches were still blazing, casting reflections over the water. She wished William were with her, yet her joy was such that she could not feel too depressed. It was a cold night, but Lizzy was warm in his robe. She sat down on the padded bench and contented herself with waiting.

Darcy returned in such a state of haste that he only paused long enough to allow Samuel to remove his boots, stockings, jacket, and waistcoat. He washed his face and hands quickly, splashed on a drop of cologne, and then rushed into their bedchamber, untucking his shirt as he went. Elizabeth was not there, but he saw the open balcony door.

"You are back!" she said happily. "Is everything all right?"

He bent down and kissed her lips. "Yes, it is now," he replied. "One of my best broodmares was having a difficult birth. The foal survived, one of Parsifal's many offspring, as a matter of fact. The mare, however, had to be put down. I hate having to do it, but on occasion it cannot be avoided." He sighed sadly.

"I am sorry, William. I know how much your horses mean to you."

"Thank you, my love. It is disturbing, but one of the unfortunate occurrences when one breeds horses, or any animal for that matter." He shook his head. "Anyway, it's done now. Why are you out here, Elizabeth? It's quite cold."

"Enjoying the view while I waited for you." For a time they remained silent, both enjoying the breathtaking scenery. Elizabeth unconsciously began caressing his leg.

He looked down at her. "You are still wearing the pearls," he noticed.

She smiled winsomely. "I like them. I thought you might enjoy seeing me wear them… and only them."

He smiled one of his devastating smiles, glanced away briefly, and then sat beside her with long legs stretched on the opposite side from hers. He clasped her cool hands within his warm palms, and said, with his voice low and husky, "How are you faring this evening, my dearest?"

"Excellent, especially now that you are back with me." She smiled, fingers interlacing with his and caressing tenderly. "It is so beautiful here, William. I feel at home already."

"You are home, Mrs. Darcy. Forever Pemberley shall be where you belong."

"I love hearing you call me 'Mrs. Darcy.' You say it with such tenderness and happiness."

He laughed softly, his eyes sparkling. Reaching to feather strokes over one soft cheek, he whispered, "I am happy. Happier than I have ever been, and it is all due to your presence in my life, Mrs. Darcy." He shook his head slightly. "I shall never tire of calling you such." He leaned forward, kissing her nose lightly. "Always, eternally, my Mrs. Darcy."

Lizzy exhaled a gentle laugh, closing her eyes and basking in the feel of his breath and warmth so near her face. Every sense was assaulted, tingling and alive as he bestowed tiny kisses on every feature, interspersing them with breathy endearments.

He paused and their eyes met. Her lips were parted and her breathing uneven, awaiting the pressure of his mouth upon hers. Surely she would die if he did not kiss her soon! He stroked her chin with his thumb, adoring the perfection of her face.

"Mrs. Darcy," he whispered, so soft as to be almost inaudible, as with deliberate patience he slowly approached her mouth, kissing her with a nearly imperceptible touch. He lingered, lips feathering hers, taunting her with languid restraint. She pressed into him but he retreated slightly, maintaining a gentle pressure and movement on her mouth. She moaned and he smiled against her lips, delighting in the ability to inflame her. She wrapped her hands around his neck, pulling him to her while at the same time arching toward his chest.

Darcy committed all his energy to the pleasurable task of kissing his wife. He could feel the cold of the winter air seeping into him, but his lips were on fire. Her taste and moisture and warmth spread from his mouth to his heart and his soul. He teased her, evading her insistence, as he played with her sweet lips. He captured her upper lip and then her lower, tenderly sucking with his lips and then nipping slightly with his teeth. After a time he ever so lightly ran the tip of his tongue over her lower lip.

Lizzy's hands had stilled in his hair, all her focus on the racing torrents of delight his mouth inspired. She had always adored his kisses and the sensations they stimulated, but this was altogether different. She moaned and sighed, heart beating erratically, yet she was paralyzed with the need to consign total attention to what he was doing to her. She was dizzy.

For what seemed like hours, he toyed with her, vacillating between faint maneuvers and enthusiastic provocations. His right hand continually stroked her jaw and cheek while his left tangled in her glistening hair, firmly clasping her head and neck to him. He probed every plane of her mouth—teeth, palate, inner lips, and cheeks—exploring leisurely and thoroughly. In a sudden burst of possessive passion, he groaned boomingly from deep in his chest and crushed her body to his chest, intensifying the kiss beyond description.

Eventually he pulled away, meeting her eyes with a burning stare. "Mrs. Darcy," he croaked hoarsely, "my love, my wife. I so adore you!" He stood, bringing her with him, and then swept her into his arms. She buried her face into his neck, kissing softly.

Instead of laying her onto the bed as she expected, he stood her on her feet next to it. "Stay here," he commanded. He crossed back to the door, latching it securely and pulling the curtains. Then he stoked the fire, adding another log to dispel the cold. Turning back to her, he walked slowly, stripping his shirt and tossing it randomly aside. "If Samuel knew how often my clothes have fallen to the floor in the past days, he would likely resign his post," Darcy joked as he reached her.

Lizzy barely registered his words, so caught was she by the sight of him. She required no prior comparison to know with certainty that her husband's figure was beyond gorgeous. His chest was broad with straight shoulders and defined muscles. Dark, thick hair lightly blanketed his upper torso, gathering densely over his sternum before trailing in a finger-width path down the solid planes of his abdomen to his groin. The bulging muscles of his arms and legs further aroused her. He was so brawny, so virile, and so utterly male. It intoxicated her. Like a magnet her hands moved to caress his milky skin, eyes windows to her devotion and craving.

Darcy was still, observing her with escalating ardency and satisfaction. He was not an egotistical man by nature. His frame was what it was, and he never gave significance to it. As long as his clothing fit well and he was lean and healthy, he was content. He certainly had been told he was handsome on many occasions, yet had assumed it was more a response to his wealth and station. No woman had ever seen his unclothed flesh, so he truly had not known what to anticipate. In these past two days of loving his wife and monitoring her reactions, he had recognized that her entrancement with his body was as profound as his was with hers. The surge of pride he felt was as much for his own ego as for his wish to please her.

Lizzy looked into his intense blue eyes and smiled shyly, a faint blush spreading over her cheeks as she continued her tactile investigation of his chest. "You endlessly chronicle how beautiful you find me," she said quietly. "I have been too bashful to verbalize the same." She paused as she stepped closer, holding his eyes with hers. "You are... stunning, Fitzwilliam. Hard and yet tender. Graceful and powerful. So invigorating, breathtakingly handsome and desirable to me. I love your heart and your soul, and will for all eternity, no matter what your appearance. However, I cannot deny the awesome effect your physical being has on my senses." She finished her earnest speech by wrapping her arms about his waist, hands pressing into his back as she squeezed herself against him, hungrily seeking his mouth.

"My Lizzy," he breathed as he kissed her. He held her tightly to him, caressing her back through her gown. His hands roamed all over her, removing his robe from her shoulders first, then slowly peeling the gauzy gown up and over her head as he stroked her satiny flesh. She shivered with delight, fire and ice piercing each nerve ending he touched.

He picked her up then, carrying her to their bed. "Elizabeth, my darling wife," he whispered as he kissed the sensitive flesh behind her ear, "You are utterly miraculous, enthralling, bewitching, and so incredibly sensuous. You drive me wild with desire!"

His magic hands were everywhere at once, propelling her to a frenzied state of aching hunger. She pivoted to face him, flinging one leg over his hip and locking her foot behind his knee. He understood what she needed and was more than willing to comply. Leisurely, then with increasing ardor, they loved, attaining sweet glory in the embrace of the other.

"I love you; I love you," his voice rasped as he inhaled roughly. "My sweet Lord, how I love you, Elizabeth!" He kissed her face, smoothing tangled hair from her eyes, before he moved to the side. Arms embracing, he nestled her to his heaving chest. "I do not know how I survived all these years without you," he whispered.

"Nor I," she answered sleepily, exhaustion and satiation overtaking her.

Darcy smiled, releasing her only to cover them both and draw the bed curtains. Cuddling her closely, listening to her regular breathing, Darcy quickly fell into an undisturbed and revitalizing slumber.

LIZABETH AWOKE GROGGILY WITH the bizarre impression of having lost something. For several minutes she experienced total disorientation. She was in an enormous, strange bed with dark curtains drawn about. She was alone, and the sensation of emptiness and heartache persisted even though she could not immediately identify the cause. She rubbed her heavy eyes and forced them to remain open. Part of her wanted to retreat back into sleep but the other part, the part that felt uneasy, urged her to wake up. She made herself sit up and, as she did so, her gaze fell on the slight depression in the pillow and mattress next to her. Immediately reality crashed over her consciousness. She knew exactly where she was and the fact that she was alone hit her as an almost physical blow.

"William?" she called, her voice louder than she intended and, to her mild shame, bordering on hysteria. How could she feel so bereft after only two days of waking with his body beside her? Why this sense of panic?

She jumped out of the bed, grabbing her nightgown from the floor where, in their haste, it had been tossed. She pulled it on quickly and had her hand on the doorknob before rationality returned to her clouded mind. It certainly would not do for the Mistress of Pemberley to go dashing through the house in her nightgown!

Calm yourself, Elizabeth! Think! Her first thought was that she was quite cold. William's robe, the one she had worn last night, was lying over the chair so she put it on. Instantly she felt coherency and calmness wash over her.

The combination of warmth and her husband's scent restored her clarity. She realized suddenly and with acute embarrassment that she was being utterly ridiculous. William would not have left her without good reason. All she need do was to ring, and a servant would appear and tell her what was happening.

She inhaled deeply. Looking at the mantel clock, she noted that it was only a little after seven. William must have arisen early. She walked back to the bed and touched the spot where his head had lain. It was cold. She actually felt tears start in her eyes. *Really, Lizzy!* she chided herself, *what would he think to see you acting the lovesick fool!*

Then she noticed the note on the bed stand with her name written in his hand. She collapsed onto the end of the bed and picked it up. *I truly am a fool. Of course he would leave me a note!*

> *Beloved,*
>
> *I woke early, as is my usual wont, not that you would necessarily have ascertained this fact based on these past two days! You were sleeping peacefully and absolutely beautifully. I knew I would be unable to resist waking you if I tarried any longer. I wished to check on the new colt. I will not be long. As much as I love my horses, they in no way compare to you, my precious wife. So strong is my desire to kiss you—even as I write this note I am overwhelmed by the need to do so—that my visit to the stables will be brief. I love you so, my darling.*
>
> *William*

She had no sooner finished reading when she heard the faint squeak of the door opening. She bolted up and rushed across the room without pausing to determine if it was he, not that anyone else would be entering their bedchamber. It *was* Darcy and he had only opened the door enough to peek his head in. His face lit up at seeing her, but she so surprised him that he literally fell against the jamb when she flew into him. He caught her with one arm, the other desperately grabbing at the wall to keep from falling over. He involuntarily grunted and winced when his back made contact with the hard wood.

"Oh, William! I am so sorry. Did I hurt you?" She stepped back a pace so he could right himself, her hands on his face.

"No more than a bruise, my love," he laughed. He shut the door and took her into his arms, kissing her soundly. He reluctantly let go but took her hand

and walked over to the chair by the fire. He sat down and began pulling off his boots.

"Let me," she said, and knelt down in front of him, pushing his hands away and removed his boots.

He leaned back and watched her, a happy smile on his face. She stole a glance up at him, really examining him for the first time, and paused in her task, mouth dropping open.

"What is it?" he asked.

"What in the world are you wearing?" she questioned him in astonishment. Elizabeth would never in a million years have imagined the impeccable Mr. Darcy in such attire. His shirt was of coarse linen discolored from old sweat, open at the neck and without cravat; his breeches were stained with mud and had actual tears in the knees; and his thick coat was threadbare with two buttons missing! Even more incredible to her was how alluring he appeared. The rough clothing, his face unshaven with cheeks flushed from the cold, mussed hair clinging damply to his neck, and the musky smell of horse and earth combined to elicit an odd response from her senses.

He looked down at himself, having totally forgotten what he was wearing in his yearning to see his wife, and blushed scarlet. He stood up quickly. "Forgive me, Elizabeth! I intended to clean up and change," he spluttered. "I only meant to make sure you were still asleep. Give me a moment…" He turned toward his dressing room, but Elizabeth snatched his hand.

She stood up and placed her hands on his chest. He watched her with a mingled expression of bafflement and mortification. "I did not say I disapproved," she said softly, "In fact, you are rather fetching. So… rugged and… wild!"

He stared at her, a tiny frown crossing his features. "Are you making fun of me?"

She stepped closer and ran her fingers along his jawbone. "Do I look as though I am teasing you?"

"No," he swallowed. "However, I do not comprehend how my work clothes would captivate you. I wear these when I train the horses. I am dirty and… unorganized!" She had moved even nearer and was kissing his neck. "Elizabeth, you cannot be serious!" He was aghast.

She spoke softly against his ear, "Did you not tell me that you first knew you loved me when I walked to Netherfield to see Jane? Was I not wild and disheveled? You confessed you found me attractive, sir. How desirable did you find me then?" she inquired with a gentle nibble to his lobe.

"Exceedingly so," he breathed. He grasped her elbows and pulled back so he could see her face. "So, you are telling me that all this time I only needed to don these garments and I would have driven you mad with longing?" He grinned and arched one brow.

"Perhaps," she answered pertly, "I guess we shall never know. It is, however, currently having a tremendously positive affect on me." The ministrations of her hands proved her sincerity. She had untucked his shirt while she spoke and was running her palms up and down his back with ever increasing urgency.

He laughed and shook his head. "I cannot help but visualize all the money I could have saved on clothing if I had only known this fact." Then he kissed her and willingly surrendered to her wishes. "I am beginning to wonder about you, Mrs. Darcy. First you confess that you enjoyed the forceful lovemaking of two days ago, and now you are driven to heights of passion by the mere appearance of me in my rough attire."

"You married a country girl, sir. I am enchanted by raw nature and unpretentious adornments. You, my love, are astonishingly alluring and arousing. It is nearly too much incitement for a simple girl like me to withstand." The truth of her teasing words was quickly proved.

They loved quickly, furiously, and rapturously, not bothering to remove clothing. Darcy collapsed, rolling to the side with Lizzy still held in a snug embrace. She nestled close, burying her face into his shoulder. Darcy was exhausted and, despite lying sideways on the bed half clothed, felt sleep creeping over him. Lizzy rose up on an elbow and smiled as she brushed mussed hair off his sweaty forehead. He smiled back, caressing her cheek gently.

"You can take these off now," she whispered, tugging on the fabric of his shirt.

He laughed, "Thank you for your permission to do so; however, I now find I do not have the energy to expend on the task."

"Allow me then," and she sat up, first addressing the breeches that were bunched absurdly at his knees. She studied him as she worked, not with desire for the moment but with simple delight regarding his figure. "It is amazing, is it not?"

"What is?"

"How our bodies are designed so perfectly for each other. The pleasure we derive from the other's touch and appearance." She blushed and would not meet his eyes. "Does it surprise you, William, or… disturb you in any way at how forward I am and… how wanton you make me?"

"Elizabeth, I am so far removed from being disturbed by your desire for me that there is not an adequate word for the emotion. As to being surprised, well, yes I am; however, not in the way you intimate." She looked at him quizzically, and he smiled. "I am not surprised by your passion, my love. It was your passion that attracted me to you and captivated me. Passion for your family, for your opinions, and for life in total. I always knew you would be a passionate lover. My surprise is that I am the man whom you have gifted with your passion and that I am capable of inciting you so. I am not worthy of it and do not deserve you."

"You are too harsh in your self-assessment, my love. I may be passionate in the ways you have listed, yet you seem to be alluding to the fact that my ardor could be inspired by anyone, and I can assure you that is not the case."

He paled at her words. "No, Elizabeth, I did not mean…"

She shushed him and tugged on his hands until he sat up next to her. She undressed him and then removed her own rumpled nightgown. She kissed him thoroughly before pulling back slightly and gazing into his clear eyes. "Now, my heart, I insist you give me what was so cruelly taken from me this morning."

"What is that?"

"You. In bed naked next to me and holding me so close that we are as one."

Darcy smiled brightly. "Ah, if only all the demands made of me were so straightforward and gratifying to fulfill."

⁂

Mrs. Darcy's first complete day as Mistress of Pemberley certainly began wonderfully enough. Darcy seemed in no hurry to leave their bed once he was back in it with his wife now awake. They cuddled and talked for some time until they were both ready for some breakfast. This they took in his sitting room.

Lizzy had only given this room a cursory glance the previous evening, so she took the time to examine it now. Like Darcy's bedchamber, his sitting room had been decorated in rich colors of forest green and burgundy. Large windows facing to the east offered illumination and a spectacular view of the sunrise. The furnishings were of a lighter wood than in the bedroom. The chairs and sofas were universally soft and comfortable. It was an inviting room; however, she was left with the impression that it was not much used.

"Do you spend much time in this room, William?"

He looked up from his newspaper. "Actually, no." he answered, gazing around as if puzzled by the fact. He frowned. "I am not really sure why. I have tended to spend most of my time in my study working. When I relax in the evenings, it is either with Georgiana in the music room or parlor, or alone in my bed reading." He smiled then and caressed his wife's hand. "Of course now I shall not be alone, and for that I am eternally grateful."

She smiled back. "Well, I like this room very much." She turned a serious face to her husband and he put down his paper. "I have been giving this some thought. In regard to our conversation yesterday, I honestly do not see myself using my chambers all that much. I cannot imagine not wanting to be with you awake or asleep." She flushed slightly and dropped her eyes demurely. Darcy glowed with satisfaction.

"In truth, the only time I can see myself needing to be apart from you is when our babies are born and I will need to be close to the nursery." The mention of *babies* caused Darcy's heart to leap with a jolt of bliss. "As for having my own sitting room, I cannot remotely imagine the need. You told me once that your mother had a private parlor for when she entertained her lady friends. Were you referring to her sitting room way up here?"

"No. Her parlor is on the second floor, across from my study. It is mostly unused now and I had intended on showing it to you today. It is yours to do with as you wish."

Lizzy nodded. "This is what I propose. The parlor is appreciated and I can envision myself needing it from time to time. When Jane visits or Georgiana and I wish to engage in private talk." She smiled mischievously. "The bedchamber, I would like to redecorate, although there is no need to rush into it nor will I alter much since it will be used so rarely. As for the sitting room, we can ignore it. No point in expending time and money on a room that will sit there unoccupied."

"Elizabeth, you know that the expense is not an issue."

"William, please. I appreciate that it is not as far as you are concerned. However, I cannot simply change the way I am, nor do I wish to. Perhaps in time I will accustom myself to my new station in life, but be patient with me."

Darcy leaned over and kissed her cheek. "Forgive me, dearest. Naturally I want you to be comfortable here and to make choices that will ease your transition. I'll tell you what, when the decorator arrives next week, you and he can sit down and plan together. Whatever you wish to do is fine with me."

Lizzy laughed. "Really William, you are far too trusting! What if I decide to choose Scottish plaids or Oriental motifs?"

He cringed, "Point taken. Very well then, *we* shall meet with the decorator. Do you have any opinions on these rooms?" He swept his hand around the sitting room and toward the bedchamber.

"As I told you last night, the bedchamber is perfect. Truly. You and I appear to have similar tastes. I do not wish to change anything, although I would like to see about purchasing an overly large bearskin rug and big fluffy pillows," she said with a suggestive smirk and risqué giggle. He grinned.

She continued, "The sitting room is lovely. What do you think about us using it more often? We can be casual here whereas we cannot if we are down-stairs. We could each have a small desk here, perhaps a couple of bookcases for easy access to our favorite books. Oh, and how about a sideboard for our breakfasts? I so enjoy this time in the morning with you."

"Those are excellent suggestions, my love. Consider it done."

"One other request. I wish to have the landscape hung in here. We must share the joy in the reminder of the day we finally declared our love."

He grasped her hands and pulled her onto his lap, holding her tightly. "Agreed." He commenced lavishing her neck and shoulders with kisses and Lizzy sighed with satisfaction.

***

It was midmorning before they left their chambers. Lizzy had expressed concern that the servants would think ill of her for languishing in their rooms half the day, but Darcy just laughed. "The servants are doubtless consumed with their daily tasks and are giving no thought to our whereabouts. If they are, well, it *is* our honeymoon so they will understand." Lizzy blushed profusely, which made Darcy laugh even harder.

First he sought out Mrs. Reynolds, asking her to arrange for Mrs. Darcy to meet the rest of the staff whenever it was convenient. In the meantime, he told her, they would be touring the rooms on the second floor.

Between Lizzy's brief visit in September and Darcy's continual sharing with her over the past two months, she had a fair grasp of how the manor was designed. Architecturally the house was English baroque, built in the early 1600s over twenty years as an extensive addition to the original house erected a hundred years earlier. That earlier home of the Darcys was now the northern annex, renovated to include the conservatory, grand ballroom, game rooms, and formal dining room on the lower level, and guest quarters above.

The newer mansion was a perfect square with an inner courtyard of cobbled stone in the precise center. Facing in every direction of the compass, each wing offered astounding views of the breathtaking scenery. The entire structure sat on a gentle slope, giving a slightly uneven appearance from a distance. The main entrance, with four ionic columns supporting a generous porch, faced west with the River Derwent yards away past a walled garden and grassy sheep-dotted expanse.

Due to the slope, this side of the house appeared taller with the ground or basement level completely visible. The columned portico with massive double doors opening into the grand foyer with elaborately painted ceiling, ornate carvings, and marble flooring was actually on the ground level, the foyer vaulting a full two stories. The wide stairway led to the main level where the family rooms are located; the ground floor beyond the foyer was exclusively servants' quarters, kitchen and storage, wine cellar, and the like.

On the main level, or first storey, were the library, Darcy's study, several parlors, the music room, sculpture gallery, and guest quarters, among numerous other rooms. Lizzy and her aunt and uncle toured parts of this level during their visit. It would be weeks before Lizzy fully realized how few of the rooms she had actually seen, because the manor was so massive.

The entire third floor was bedchambers. The Master and Mistress's suite covered the whole south-facing wing, Darcy's bedchamber in the southeast corner. This location was ideal, providing a stunning view from numerous windows and a large southern balcony of the vast lawns, gardens, ponds, fountains, and the forest to the hilly east, as well as bathing the chamber with the sunrise and capturing woodland-scented breezes.

For the day's tour, they started in the library. Lizzy had seen it before, in September, and had been quite impressed. The room was enormous with ceiling-to-floor bookcases, almost all filled. Tall ladders on rollers allowed one to reach the highest shelves. Darcy explained how the volumes were organized, each case having a letter designation. He showed her the system of cards in a cabinet that cataloged the books and directed where to find each one. She had never heard of such a technique and found it fascinating. Several chairs and sofas with tables and lamps graced the room. The windows were tall and wide, as all the windows were at Pemberley, allowing incredible views in all directions and blazes of sunlight. She could not help but picture her father in this room and said as much to Darcy.

"Yes," he said. "I deem your father will set one foot in here, and we shall not see him for the length of his visit! It was probably the lure of Pemberley's library which principally swayed him to accept my proposal for your hand."

Lizzy laughed. "Well, that and the fact that I would undoubtedly have run off with you anyway if he had not consented."

She spoke teasingly and absently, but her words struck Darcy and he lightly grasped her chin turning her toward him. "Would you have, Lizzy?" he asked huskily. "Run away with me, I mean."

"Oh! I… Well, it never came to that did it, William? Yet now that I think about it, I remember how worried I was when you took so long in his study. I knew it was silly, that my father would never purposely refuse you, knowing how much I loved you… But then he did not know I loved you yet." She shook her head. "It is all such a jumble, really. I do know that I had to be with you, would die if I could not be. So, yes, I would have run away with you if he had refused. I would have had no choice." She smiled up at her husband and he kissed her, saying nothing.

She cocked her head to the side and began playing with the buttons on his jacket. "So, tell me, Mr. Darcy, which category do I look under for the *special* books in Pemberley's library?"

He flushed and swallowed audibly. "*Those* books are kept in my private collection in the study, under lock and key."

"Shall I be entrusted with a key to this cabinet?" She fluttered her lashes coquettishly.

"I shall contemplate the request, Mrs. Darcy. You are dangerous enough as it is without adding further fuel to the fire!"

Next he led her to the music room. An older pianoforte sat here alongside an enormous gilded harp. A glass case housed a collection of unusual instruments. Darcy explained that many of them were ethnic musical apparatus picked up from other countries over the centuries. Propped in one corner were a beautiful cello and a violin. Lizzy asked who played them.

"Richard plays the cello and is quite talented actually. He and Georgiana have several pieces they play together beautifully. I play the violin, but not very well. Never one to practice," he said in a perfect imitation of his aunt. "My mother insisted I study music but I could never control my clumsy fingers to even pound out my scales on the piano, so she gave up. I had limited success with the violin."

"I would love to hear you play."

Darcy laughed, "No, my love, you truly would not, trust me! Perhaps some evening when I have indulged in far too many brandies." He took her hand and led her to the northern wing. They visited the conservatory and game rooms, and then he led her into the formal dining room.

Elizabeth had never imagined a single room could be so huge. A massive, sheet-draped table in the shape of a "U" filled the space. Darcy told her it could comfortably seat one hundred-fifty people. Lizzy was stunned. The room was beautiful and elegant, as all the rooms were, but there was an emptiness to it, an atmosphere of long disuse with dust thick in some areas.

"We have not opened this room since my mother died," he remarked softly. "She loved to entertain. Here at Pemberley, that is. She did not care for Town. Twice a year, at Christmas and on the first day of summer, we hosted a feast for the tenants and community. Additional tables would be placed in the ballroom. It was a tradition for generations and quite the party, let me tell you! Christmas carols in the winter and music and dancing on the terrace in the summer." He smiled and his eyes were far away with the memory.

"Traditions must be adhered to," Lizzy declared briskly. "This Christmas is too soon for me to prepare a party, but by summer I will have figured my way around. We can arrange for it then, do you agree, my love?"

Darcy was smiling broadly. "Mistress of Pemberley indeed." He placed his arm across her shoulders, drew her close to his side, kissed the top of her head, and then steered toward the next room. Lizzy quickly became lost in the long hallways and vast rooms, all of which had several doorways tucked into draped alcoves leading to more rooms. Eventually she would learn that Darcy spoke the truth: Pemberley was patterned in a clear square and hallways that seemed initially to dissect randomly did, in fact, follow a predictable scheme. However, this would take time and she was abundantly thankful he intended to stay close to her. He diverted from the sculpture gallery and portrait hall for now, stating that it would take too much time to fully appreciate.

They encountered Mrs. Reynolds as they entered the main parlor. She curtseyed and addressed them both formally, "Mr. and Mrs. Darcy, the staff will be assembled in the ballroom in one half hour. After which, luncheon will be served. Does this meet with your approval?"

"Thank you, Mrs. Reynolds. That will be fine."

Lizzy strolled around the room, fondly remembering the miraculous days in early September when she surprised Mr. Darcy and his sister and then enjoyed luncheon and a glorious afternoon in their company. Observing him in his home had released her heart wholly. She vividly recalled sitting here transfixed by his peaceful face and demeanor and realizing that she loved him. Georgiana had played several tunes on her new pianoforte, Lizzy lifting her voice a time or two, while Darcy gazed at her with a tender expression. Naturally it had all worked out, but Lizzy could not help wondering how differently things might have transpired if only they had known the truth of the emotions behind their barely regulated features.

Now he was pointing out features and furnishings, sharing with her the memories attached. His parents had enjoyed having their children with them in the evenings, he told her, and they had generally relaxed here. He and Georgiana naturally gravitated to this parlor as well. The mixture of his childhood memories, the yearlong unrelenting daydreams of Elizabeth here with their children running about their feet, and now the reality that she was his wife bathed him in contentment.

"My father would read a book or newspaper in that chair," he pointed. "My mother would sit in the one alongside it, sewing or reading or singing to Georgiana in her lap. I was usually reading as well. Still do, actually, or I listen to Georgiana read to me. She has a sweet voice."

"Do you sit in his chair?" Lizzy inquired, studying his luminous face.

"No, I prefer the sofa. More comfortable and I can stretch further. I am taller than my father was, so my legs get cramped by the table in front. Suppose I could simply rearrange the furniture; however, I am a creature of habit so things have remained unchanged." He smiled brightly. "Probably could use some shaking up around here, Elizabeth, so indulge yourself."

"I was reflecting on the prospect of how stimulating it will be sitting by your side, touching you on the sofa, so I believe I shall keep the table as it is," she responded with a little laugh. She had moved to the far window as he had been talking and created an angelic vision with the sun shining on her. She was leaning against the wall, so still and calm, watching him. She was enchanting and Darcy was fascinated anew by the mere presence of her. He dazedly observed her for a spell and then found his feet drawn toward her as a moth to the flame.

She looked up at him, caressed his cheek, and smiled. "I love you, Fitzwilliam," she purred, her features awash with love. She rarely used his full name, treasuring it for the most intimate of moments, and her tone was intensely seductive and vibrant when she did. Hearing her call him so here, now, nearly brought him to his knees. He embraced her, nestling his face in her neck, moaning her name with desire and need. In a fluid motion he sat on the window seat, drawing her onto his lap.

He wondered if she grasped how vital she was to him, and whether she recognized that after all of the trials of the last year, the separations, the misunderstandings, the long waiting, and the gnawing urgency he had felt for her, these moments in her arms were like oxygen to a drowning man. He whispered her name over and over as he gently kissed her neck and shoulders. His torrid hunger for her was as powerful as ever, yet his desire to simply hold her was stronger.

Elizabeth ran her fingers through his hair and along the edge of his collar. She knew they probably should not be in this position outside their bedchamber, but she did not care. Being back in this room had evoked clear memories of her wonderful day here with him but also of the horrible separation afterwards. Those awful weeks of not knowing if he still loved her or if she would ever see him again, musings that seemed pointless in the face of Lydia's scandal. She shuddered anew at the pain and despair she had experienced.

Darcy felt her trembling and pulled back. "What is it, my heart?"

She kissed him. "Awful memories of how close I came to losing you. I do not think I could have lived if you had not come back to me, William," she said with a small sob.

"Shhhh…" he soothed, kissing her teary cheeks. "Let it go, Elizabeth. It is history. We are one now and will be forever. I refuse to allow this time to be clouded by the foolishness of the past." His wits restored somewhat, he bestowed a soft but lingering kiss before rising from the seat. He hugged her tight and then released her. He smiled gaily and reminded her they had an appointment to keep.

He offered an arm, "Shall we, Mrs. Darcy?"

She smiled bravely and placed her hand into the crook of his elbow. "Lead the way, Mr. Darcy."

As they walked down another long hallway she had yet not discovered, she inquired, "How many people does it take to keep Pemberley operating?"

He seemed puzzled by the question. "I am not sure the exact number. As many as is needed to get the jobs done."

Lizzy smiled inwardly. To him, who grew up surrounded by innumerable servants, the question would seem ludicrous.

The ballroom near the formal dining room was so mammoth that it dwarfed the latter chamber. Lizzy speculated that all of Longbourn could fit into this one room, and she would not have been far off. Details of the elegant room were ignored for now, however, as her eyes were drawn to the array of people in front of her. They were separated, accidentally or on purpose she did not know, into small clusters, rigidly at attention and wearing pristine uniforms. Mrs. Reynolds and Mr. Taylor, the butler, stood formally in front. In unison, everyone in the room bowed or curtseyed. The perfection of it stunned Lizzy.

Mrs. Reynolds stepped forward. "The staff awaits your inspection, Mr. Darcy."

"Thank you, Mrs. Reynolds."

Lizzy felt the urge to laugh. It was all so stiff and slightly ridiculous to her. One glance at her husband's visage, though, and she reconsidered. This was his world. Here he was the Master. In the weeks of their engagement, she had seen only her "William." He talked about his home and his duties frequently, to the point where she understood much of what life at Pemberley must be like. During that time, the stern, commanding presence of "Mr. Fitzwilliam Darcy, Master of Pemberley" had faded, and she had forgotten that side of him. In all honesty, she had never actually seen that side of him.

She saw it now and experienced a surge of pride. What she had originally deemed haughty arrogance was in reality nobility, authority, power, and superior confidence. Here was a man utterly assured of his place in life and his responsibilities. He gave orders and expected them to be carried out without question.

With sudden insight she put all the pieces together. How a man of enormous capabilities, absolute command, and control over such vast properties and lives could be laid low by consuming love for a woman he thought he could not have. How this vulnerability and helplessness would engulf and stagger him. Perhaps to a degree he had needed to be humbled, yet all Lizzy could feel now was fresh pain and thankfulness that he would suffer no more.

She decided immediately that there was no possible way she would remember all their names, so she did not try. There was the kitchen staff, commanded by the iron fist of Mrs. Langton. The footmen, under the authority of Mr. Taylor. The household staff consisted of a dozen maids and numerous helpers and answered to Mrs. Reynolds. The outside staff, gardeners and maintenance men, led by the head groundskeeper, a Mr. Clark. Marguerite, Samuel, and Mr. Keith stood off to the side as they were under the direct and only command of Mr. and Mrs. Darcy. Darcy explained to Elizabeth that the grooms and stable boys would be introduced later at the stables. She maintained her composure, but was inwardly overawed and suddenly understood how her husband could not possibly know the precise number of staff.

Afterwards they retired to the smaller dining room, the "breakfast room" as Darcy called it. Lizzy was feeling more than a little overwhelmed, so she was thankful for the reprieve. As soon as they were served, the servants exited and shut the doors firmly behind them. They had done the same at dinner last night and it mystified her.

"Do the servants always leave?" she inquired. "At Longbourn they remain in case we need something."

Darcy reached over and took her hand, bringing it to his lips for an intoxicating kiss to each of her knuckles before tenderly sucking the tip of each finger. "If they remained, I would not be able to do this," he declared with a mischievous grin and a smoldering gaze. Lizzy was instantly breathless and weak. How was it that his eyes on her and one touch of his lips could arouse her so?

Before she lost all restraint, not that she was necessarily averse to the idea, she flippantly retorted, "Am I to understand that the Master's commands include keeping me sequestered behind closed doors to be at his disposal?"

He continued to ravage her hand, now having progressed to the sensitive flesh of her palm and inner wrist. "I warned you, Madame, did I not? I desire unfettered access. You should be grateful I permitted you out of our chambers at all today." His exploring mouth was sending shivers of excitement coursing through her body.

"Does the Master's absolute control extend to me?" she stammered, finding it extremely difficult to speak.

"Your vows included the promise to obey, my love." He wormed one finger under her sleeve, pushing it up to her elbow with his lips following. "Do my requirements perturb you, beloved? I would never wish to force unpleasantness upon you," he said with a playful nibble to her inner elbow.

"William!" she pleaded, her voice a husky whisper.

He smiled with satisfaction. "Are you begging me to stop, dearest wife, or to carry on?"

"I…" The truth was she wanted desperately for him to have his way with her right then, but she could not bring herself to say it. She felt his smile on her skin, and then with one last kiss, he released her arm, gently returning the hand to her lap. Their eyes met, his full of passion and a hint of amusement, hers glazed with forlorn yearning.

"Eat your food, Elizabeth. You will need your strength as I intend to carry you to our bed the second we are finished." And he did exactly that.

CHAPTER SEVEN

A Stroll in the Garden

THAT EVENING, AS ELIZABETH prepared for dinner, she could not stop
smiling. Her happiness was boundless.

Marguerite fussed with her hair, creating a masterpiece arrangement Lizzy would not have thought possible. The only disruption to her joy
came when she contemplated her limited wardrobe. Her father had scraped
together as much money as he possibly could for her and Jane; however, most
of it had gone toward their wedding gowns and trousseau. She and Jane had
managed to purchase cloth for two dresses each, which they sewed themselves.
At the time Lizzy, in her innocence, had deemed this more than adequate. She
had never been the type of woman to trouble herself with fashion or style. Her
gowns were functional and comfortable. She owned only two fancy gowns,
her wedding dress and her white ball gown; however, even they now appeared
dowdy and plain amidst the splendor of Pemberley.

The question was how to broach the subject with Darcy. She persisted in
harboring feelings of embarrassment regarding the topic of his wealth. Should
she blatantly solicit money for gowns? She shuddered at the thought.

She decided to wear her burgundy gown. She reached for the pearls,
but Marguerite interrupted politely suggesting that the rubies would be a
preferred accessory.

"Marguerite, I do not own rubies."

"Begging your pardon, Mrs. Darcy, but you do. I was instructed to relinquish this into your keeping," and she pulled a small key from her pocket, "It opens the closet with the Darcy jewels. I regret that there has not been the appropriate time. Please forgive me."

"Of course," Lizzy murmured, amazed anew. "Which cabinet is it?"

The cabinet was floor to ceiling and about one foot wide. Inside, lying on cushions of velvet was a staggering assortment of jewelry. Necklaces, bracelets, earrings, rings, hair clips, brooches, and more in every gem she had ever heard of and some she did not recognize. Many of the pieces were quite old and of a style that Elizabeth could never imagine herself wearing, yet they were all exquisite. Her hands trembled as she touched the spectacular ruby necklace that Marguerite indicated. "Could you please assist me, Marguerite? I do not think I can manage."

She stood before the mirror for one last inspection and was started by a deep, sonorous voice. "You are exceptionally captivating tonight, Mrs. Darcy."

She whirled around to see her husband leaning against the doorway, arms crossed and eyes lazily exploring her body while an inviting smile danced on his lips. He was wearing a blue coat, naturally, with matching blue breeches and a waistcoat of green with gold stripes. She decided to match his bold inventory of her appearance by doing the same. To her pleasure she noted the increased flame in his eyes. She smiled wickedly. "You surprised me, Mr. Darcy."

"You assured me I was welcome in your dressing room anytime and that I am not required to knock. Is the offer valid, Madame?"

"Yes, it is, although you might take caution not to sneak so. You are liable to frighten poor Marguerite into a heart seizure," she said with a laugh and a wink to her maid, who had placidly busied herself straightening the vanity.

Marguerite calmly turned toward her mistress, her face a study in serene indifference, intoning unemotionally, "I warrant my heart is able to withstand the shock, Madame. Will you be requiring my services further, Mrs. Darcy?"

"No, Marguerite, thank you."

"Very well. Sir... Madame," and with perfect curtseys, she left.

Lizzy peered at her husband, who remained insolently lounging in the doorway, "You scared her," she teased, and turned back to the mirror.

"It appears to be a failing of mine," he remarked dryly. He came behind her and stroked the curve of her hips before clasping his hands about her waist and pulling her against him, nibbling along her neck at the same time.

"You are so beautiful, Elizabeth. I love you immensely." She could feel his heat; desire and craving evident in how he embraced her.

She melted against his body. "Have you not yet gotten enough of me, Mr. Darcy?" she sassed. "Have I not satisfied you sufficiently?"

"You have satisfied me, my heart, lavishly and in ways previously undreamed of. But, enough? No, there is no risk of me ever reaching a state of over-saturation. Your love, your existence in my life, is as crucial as food and air." He ceaselessly kissed and caressed as he spoke. "I see you found the jewelry cabinet. The rubies are lovely on you, or rather your beauty augments their loveliness."

"Perhaps it is merely an odd coincidence; however, it seems that you are forever attempting to delay our meals with your amorous attentions."

"The fault is entirely yours, my wife, for being such a temptress. I am only a man and cannot be expected to control myself when confronted with such succulent delights before me."

"Why, sir, I was under the mistaken impression you were a gentleman!"

He laughed and turned her around, taking her face into his hands, "I see I have accomplished my goal of deceiving you. Would a gentleman do this?" he asked, and claimed her mouth in a kiss of incredible depth and implication. When he at last pulled away it was to see his wife's face suffused with passion, eyes half open and breath shallow. He gazed upon her, mightily thrilled at his ability to inflame her.

Eventually she calmed enough to meet his eyes. "No, my husband, I do not believe you are a gentleman, and I cannot express how happy that makes me!"

Darcy smiled and kissed the tip of her pert nose. "Come, Mrs. Darcy, let us not delay our meal any longer. I can survive in the knowledge that I may not be a perfect gentleman, but perish the thought that I am a brute who starves his wife!" He offered her his arm and led her out the door.

They passed the door to his dressing room and Lizzy started giggling. "What have I done now to amuse you, my love?"

Still laughing, Lizzy replied, "I had a sudden vision of barging into your dressing room, which is only fair I might add, and catching you in a state of undress. How would your valet respond to that?"

Darcy smiled, "Samuel is exceedingly prim and proper, *and* unmarried. I believe I have upset him enough these past two days by not adhering to my strict schedule and usual decorum. He probably *would* suffer a heart seizure!"

He glanced at his grinning wife. "Are you giving me fair warning, my love? If so I should prepare Samuel for the eventual improprieties of my wife. He is an excellent valet and I would hate to lose him."

Lizzy lifted her chin impudently. "Prepare him as you see fit, Mr. Darcy, but do not expect any fair warnings from me. Sneaking and surprising are the rules of this game."

Dinner, naturally, was delicious. The servants left the room, returning with the next courses only when Darcy rang for them, but he kept his seat and did not torture his poor wife. They were both quite happy so the atmosphere was lively.

"Dare I inquire, dear husband, what the itinerary is for the rest of the evening? Or had you planned a recap of our after-lunch activity?" she asked with a playful flutter of her lashes.

Darcy lifted one eyebrow. "Said activity is never far from my mind, dearest; however, I am willing to ponder alternative pursuits, provided you are involved."

"William, I would like to take a walk. We have been cooped up all day, marvelous as it has been." She gazed at him warmly and caressed his knee. "Nevertheless, I am feeling the need for some fresh air."

He rose and bowed gallantly, saying, "I am yours to command, beloved. A walk it shall be."

They exited the dining room and discovered the butler standing at attention. He bowed. "Mr. Darcy, Mrs. Darcy. Sir, I have an envelope that Mr. Keith gave me to convey to you when you finished dining." He handed Darcy a large envelope, which Darcy glanced at quickly, seeming instantly to glean the contents.

"Thank you, Mr. Taylor. Would you please place this on my desk for now? Could you then please ensure the terrace lamps are lit and retrieve our gloves, my coat, and Mrs. Darcy's pelisse? We will be in the gallery."

"At once, sir," and with another bow to each, he left.

Darcy took her hand and led her to the gallery. Lizzy had not been in this room since her visit in September and had almost forgotten how astounding the works of art were. There was so much beauty in this one room that she imagined one could never fully absorb it all. Darcy strolled alongside her, offering insights into and the history of several of the pieces. He told her that his grandfather had first begun collecting the marble statues after he and Darcy's grandmother had taken a trip to Italy. His father had acquired a few pieces, but it was Darcy who was especially stirred by sculpture. He had added more than half the pieces. He was so enamored with the art form that he had insisted on a bust of Georgiana. She had agreed but finagled him to also have a bust made of himself, hence the image before which Lizzy now stood.

Lizzy was as enraptured by the image now as she had been three months ago. It fascinated her how cold stone could appear so alive. How was it possible to capture his beauty, strength, and gentleness in a rock? Darcy had been distracted by a footman bringing their coats, so he was surprised to see his wife staring so intently at his likeness.

Lizzy was mesmerized. She sensed his presence near her and said dreamily, "Your face was the cause of my separation from Mrs. Reynolds and my aunt and uncle. I could not look away. I know now that I was already falling in love with you, but I had not admitted it to myself. Being here at Pemberley, surrounded by the beauty of your home, focused my tumultuous emotions. However, it was as I beheld this," she reached up and brushed the shimmering cheeks and lips of the bust, "your face so gentle and loving even in stone, taunting me it seemed with a fond gaze, that I desperately wished to be favored with... I knew then that I hopelessly loved you."

She turned to him, his flesh-and-blood face so close to her own, with those impossible blue eyes piercing her soul and his countenance resplendent with emotion. He cupped her face in his hands, caressing soft thumbs over her cheeks. He opened his mouth as if to speak but words failed. He swallowed, tears threatening to spill. Lizzy linked her hands behind his neck, drawing him to her. "I love you, my darling, with all my soul," she whispered. They kissed then, a slow, tender kiss not of passion but of deep faithfulness and belonging. He enfolded her in his arms, embracing securely.

Eventually Darcy spoke, "Shall we stroll in the moonlight, my heart? It is cold out tonight so I shall have ready excuses to hold you and kiss you to keep you warm."

She laughed. "As if you need valid excuses."

It was a cold night but clear with the moon at three-quarters and bright. Billions of stars were visible. They walked leisurely, hand in hand, along the wide terrace that ran the length of the southern side of the manor. Several stone benches and secluded alcoves with arbors of trailing vines were spaced along the railing. Darcy unerringly led her to the eastern edge of the terrace and down the steps to the moonlit lawn beyond. He crossed the grass to a looming wall of brick and climbing vines that sheltered an array of pathways weaving through a secluded garden.

"This garden," he informed her as they strolled, "is considerably smaller than the ones located to the southeast. It is a private garden for the family only. I come here most nights to breathe the fresh air and gaze at the sky before retiring. Mr. Clark knows it is a habit of mine, so he typically will wheel the protected flowers out from the conservatory until after I complete my stroll. You will find, my love, that he is an incredible gardener who has trained his staff well. No seasons pass without at least a few blooms and greenery."

He chose a trail lined by a row of rosebushes, currently without blooms, of course. The gravel passageway twisted and turned until finally terminating at a clearing with a large gurgling fountain of four sea nymphs pouring water from pitchers. The fountain and pebbled expanse were completely shaded by an enormous, ancient oak tree and bordered with a profusion of vines and shrubs. Most were dormant, but the fragrance and color of the protected winter blooms of jasmine, camellia, hyacinth, paper-white narcissus, and hellebore filled the air. The only illumination was the moon and starlight shimmering and reflecting off the water.

Darcy sat on the edge of the fountain and pulled Elizabeth onto his lap. He wrapped his large overcoat about her and she nestled into his chest. "I love gazing at the stars," Darcy remarked softly. "The immensity of the universe with the vastness of space and uncountable heavenly bodies is so outside our control and power. What is man compared to such awesome magnificence? It is a humbling experience to note one's insignificance."

"'Miserable mortals who, like leaves, at one moment flame with life and at another moment weakly perish,'" Lizzy quoted.*

Darcy smiled, "'There is nothing nobler or more admirable than when two people who see eye to eye keep house as man and wife, confounding their enemies and delighting their friends.'"**

They continued to play the quote game, but Darcy proved the victor. Lizzy laughed, conceding defeat, and then arose to walk among the flowers. Darcy sat in complete contentment watching his lovely wife in the moonlight.

"When Jane and I were younger, we would sometimes steal out at night

*Homer, *The Iliad*
**Homer, *The Odyssey*

when all were asleep. We would lie on a blanket under the stars and talk about our dreams."

"What do young girls dream of?"

She giggled. "Handsome princes on gallant white steeds charging in to whisk us off to crystal castles with spires reaching to the heavens."

"Alas, my steed is black and Pemberley has no spires. Pity that your dreams have been dashed."

"Well, at least the handsome part is true so I shall endeavor to overcome my acute disappointment." She had picked several fragrant buds, tucking them in her hair and at her bosom. Lastly she snipped a strand of jasmine, weaving it into a garland. She approached her husband, still sitting on the fountain's edge, and crowned his head with the aromatic adornment. "Now you are a prince," she teased. "Two out of four is tolerable."

Darcy clasped her legs to pull her onto his lap again, but she danced lightly away, tinkling laugh ringing. "If you desire to whisk me away, my prince, you must catch me first!" She gave a merry chase but his longer legs proved his asset, and he caught her at last.

The devious gleam in her eyes should have warned him. He leaned down to kiss her but she moved in quickly and securely caught his lower lip with her teeth. She nibbled tenderly, running the tip of her tongue along his lip, sucking slightly. Her hands were not idle, firmly stroking up his inner thighs and over his hips, fingers barely brushing his most sensitive regions.

Darcy had never experienced anything like it. How did she know to do this? *From you*, came the answer. She was intoxicating and he was instantly aroused. His befuddled mind relaxed his grip and she scurried away, dashing down the path toward the house, effervescent voice floating back to him, "Revenge is sweet, beloved!"

He groaned in misery then laughed, remembering his satisfied gloating at lunch and in her dressing room. He followed slowly, needing the distance to restore his irregular heartbeat. When he reached the terrace, he could see her moving about in his study. He entered and she was standing placidly by his desk, an expression of contrition on her face, although with Lizzy, penitence was as equally suspect as naughtiness. She came to him, softly placing tiny hands on his chest, and in a little-girl voice asked, "Still love me?"

SHARON LATHAN

"More than ever," he answered, bestowing a kiss to her forehead, cheek, nose, chin, and finally her lips.

She smiled brightly. "This is your study, is it not?" He nodded. "I wondered if it was, when I was here in September." She flushed in embarrassment. "I did not read anything, but I saw papers with your handwriting and your seal. I could picture you sitting at that desk, working. It's a beautiful room, William."

"Have a seat, Elizabeth. Since we are here, I have something to discuss with you." She did as he asked as he retrieved the envelope given to him earlier by Mr. Taylor, and then he sat beside her, taking her hands. "I recognize that discussions of my wealth are uncomfortable to you, my love, and I appreciate that as it is further proof of your true reasons for marrying me." He smiled at her.

"Nonetheless, we cannot ignore the facts nor can I discount my responsibilities to you as my wife. When I was in London last, I had my solicitor draw up legal documents regarding my will and settlement for you. That is what is in this envelope. The exact details can be deliberated later. The gist is this: When I die, a settlement of thirty-thousand pounds will be yours, along with a yearly income of three-thousand pounds. Pemberley will forever be open to you as your home, as will Darcy House in London. Ownership of Pemberley will pass to our eldest son with further details regarding future children to be decided when the time comes."

Lizzy was stunned. Darcy smoothed her cheek and kissed her softly. "For the present, since I selfishly intend to live a very long time to love you, I have set aside a monthly allowance for your personal use. The intention is not to prohibit what you spend but to render easy access to funds as you need them without requiring you to solicit me or Mr. Keith. The bills will be kept in a locked box in that cabinet over there. If at any time you need or want something beyond what monies you have available, you must only ask. Do you understand so far?" She nodded, speechless.

He continued, "Household funds are in a separate account. In time Mrs. Reynolds and I will teach you how it all operates. As I have assured you, dearest, I am making no demands. Pemberley is a very complicated estate and it will take you time to learn it all, if you even chose to do so. All you must understand now is that any decorating you wish to do or furniture you wish to purchase, that sort of thing, is *not* a personal but a household expense. The monies are limited; I am not the King after all!" he laughed. "However, you would have to be excessively extravagant to seriously jeopardize the estate."

"Lastly, you are aware that I have a decorator arriving next week, which should be Wednesday. On Monday I have arranged an appointment for you with a dressmaker in Lambton. Her name is Madame du Loire, and she has fashioned many of Georgiana's gowns. Mrs. Reynolds suggested this course. I hope it meets with your approval, dearest?"

"William, I truly do not know what to say. You are so conscientious and far too generous! You continually stagger me with your ability to contemplate my needs. Thank you!"

"Elizabeth, you flatter me with your kind words. Business I comprehend easily. Women's necessities are still much a mystery to me. We must educate each other. As always, Mrs. Reynolds and Georgiana, when she returns later this month, will be your principal resources. They know what is available in the region and what should be obtained from Town. Now, enough of that!" He stood up briskly and locked the envelope safely in his desk. "I am overcome with the urgent yearning to unwind with my wife in our sitting room. To hold her in my arms reminding her of my fervent love, devotion, ardor, and happiness. Shall we, Mrs. Darcy?"

When Lizzy entered their sitting room, comfortable and resplendent in her nightgown and robe, Darcy was already reclining on the chaise lounge before the fire. He had an open book in his hand and momentarily did not hear her, so engrossed was he. She smiled. He had finally given up reading the book he had labored over during their engagement and had succumbed to the reality that reading was out of the question for the time being. It was refreshing and heartwarming to see him content and able to relax.

She settled herself between his legs, back tight against his chest. He entwined his legs with hers and hugged her close, one arm over her shoulders with a hand resting between her breasts. He kissed the top of her head and told her he loved her. Lizzy could honestly say she had never been happier in her entire life. He began reading aloud and his melodic voice soothed her.

Darcy became aware that his wife had fallen asleep when he asked her a question and she remained silent. "Elizabeth?" he whispered, but there was no response. It was not precisely the ending to the evening he had envisioned, yet oddly the fulfillment of having his wife's warm body in his arms was intensely gratifying in its own way. He held her for a long time, until the fire had died to embers, listening to her breathe and feeling her vitality. Carefully as not to wake her, he carried her to their bed. He stretched out beside her, marveling how even in her sleep she came to him, nestling close.

THE NEXT SEVERAL DAYS passed in much the same manner. Lizzy and Darcy were together almost twenty-four hours a day, and they were incredibly blissful.

While they lounged in bed on their second morning at Pemberley, their fourth day of marriage, Lizzy confessed with some embarrassment her actions the previous morning when she had awoken without him by her side. He laughed out loud, which she considered blatantly unfair.

"Forgive me, beloved; however, I had this vision of you running through the halls in your nightgown. I venture to speculate that any fright I might have given poor Marguerite yesterday would pale in comparison to the panic amongst the house staff at that sight!"

"You beast!" and she hit him with a pillow, which led to him grasping her wrists to stop her, which lead to them kissing several times. When she came up for air, she continued the topic. "I was going to apologize for accidentally pushing you into the doorway yesterday, but now that I think of it, it was your entire fault anyway, so I shall not."

"How do you reason it was my fault?"

"You should never have left me in the first place!" she declared with a pout. "You have set the standard, Mr. Darcy, by being entirely too wonderful, so your desertion was an overwhelming shock. My feeble wits could not handle it and

I acted precipitously. Your bruises are therefore the penalty for your cruelty. Nonetheless, I shall be magnanimous and will even kiss your aches away. Turn over," she commanded.

She actually was surprised and remorseful to note a small bruise over his mid-spine, which she dutifully kissed. However, she was more taken at the pleasing sight of her husband's backside. Using all the strength she could muster, she massaged his shoulders, back, and derriere. Darcy moaned with pleasure, his eyes closed. Elizabeth, for being so delicate, had incredibly strong hands.

As expected, her innocent conduct eventually took on a decidedly sensual flavor. She straddled him at his waist, sitting on his bottom, directing her attentions first to his shoulders, massaging as hard as she could. He tried to caress her knees but she slapped him and told him to behave, earning a chuckle. For thirty or so minutes, she diligently applied herself to kneading and manipulating every muscle. Darcy slipped into a daze of relaxing euphoria, unaware, for a time, of Elizabeth's presence. That was until she scooted off his bottom to his legs and began squeezing his rump and thighs. Her strokes gradually turned from firm and deep to soft and caressing. She traveled over and under his hips, down outer and up inner thighs. His breathing changed from deep and relaxed to sharp and fitful.

He rumbled her name deep in his throat, begging, and she ceased, lying fully onto his back and kissing the nape of his neck as she ran her fingers through his hair, before meeting seeking lips as she rolled off. Darcy gathered her into his arms, passionately kissing her with a ravenous hunger. He pulled away and met her eyes, those beautiful eyes that had intrigued and captivated him almost from the first moment he saw her in Meryton.

"What you do to me, love. So beautiful... exciting... precious. My wife, my only love, my soul." His endearments and declarations were incessant as he kissed her eyes, lips, nose, cheeks, chin, and neck. They made love slowly initially, quickening as their mutual passion grew.

Darcy whispered words and phrases of love in a pattern that would become very familiar. Like a dam overflowing, words poured from his lips, verbalizing his emotions and burning need. "God, love... I never dreamed loving you would be so... spectacular, exhilarating! Your skin... like silk... your hands, Oh Lord, your hands, Lizzy!... touching my skin... it is electric, flames... burning my flesh... shivers through me..." He moaned hoarsely, voice low and grating. "Your scent... I am delirious... your moans and sighs of pleasure... for me... my love... mine always... only!"

The pace accelerated, Darcy stridently moaning as he loved her. "Elizabeth, I love you... God how I need you! You squeeze me so tight... your legs, your arms, your body... made for me... love me, my darling! Now!"

Coherent language was lost as passion overcame them both with uttered cries and whimpers, shudders through every nerve and pore. Total abandon and uninhibited release. Two individuals joining as one. Souls combined in the purest expression of love. For timeless minutes they merged and were no longer separate.

If the journeys varied, the destination was the same. It was a beautiful period of discovery for them both. As they explored each other's bodies and grew daily more aware of their own sensibilities, their intimate relationship blossomed into a fullness and union of souls unreservedly profound. As the initial days turned into the first week, the last vestiges of any embarrassment or awkwardness totally disappeared. At times they were playful. Other times they were serious and tender. Sometimes they were swept away with their passionate hunger. Yet always they were moved by the melding of their spirits, the harmony, and the love that defied logic by growing deeper with each passing day.

Once they emerged from their chambers, it was rarely with any particular destination in mind. They simply wanted to be together. Their keenest desire was to learn more about how the other thought and felt. The intimate nature of their communication evolved as they each had suspected it would once they were married.

Darcy no longer suffered the pain of his loneliness and grief. Wounded areas of his heart were unearthed and healed, some of which he was ignorant even existed. The past no longer haunted him, and he was able to remember and share the happy memories without the instantaneous ache of sadness overwhelming him.

As for Lizzy, she gave herself to him wholly. Her rigid independence, self-reliance, and need to prove herself all shattered before the force of his love. To be essential to another human being, to be vulnerable, to have another assign themselves generously and selflessly is the ultimate expression of true love, and they understood how lucky they were.

Most days they moseyed around Pemberley. Slowly Lizzy began to acquaint herself with the manor's layout. Darcy was correct in stating that it really was not that confusing. The hallways were set up in a linear fashion and the rooms universally square or rectangular. Perhaps not overly imaginative, but it was easy to navigate. By the end of her first week as Mistress, she was confident enough to wander on her own around the main floor, which she did on those few occasions when Darcy was occupied with a business matter. Nonetheless, she was constantly amazed and, frankly, significantly intimidated by the vastness of the house and by the plethora of art, furnishings, history, wealth, and beauty that Pemberley housed. The more she saw, the more she was awed by the responsibilities her husband carried on his broad shoulders.

The staff was mysteriously everywhere and yet unobtrusive at the same time. Lizzy never once actually witnessed a maid cleaning, yet the manor was spotless. A footman materialized magically when Darcy needed one, then vanished as speedily. Darcy greatly impressed Lizzy by knowing the names of each of them, always making eye contact, and unfailingly inserting "please" and "thank you" into each command. The staff's devotion to their master and to Pemberley was apparent in their manner and in the pristine condition of the house.

Lizzy had learned much about the estate's interests during her engagement. Darcy's pride and pleasure regarding Pemberley were unmistakable. Unwittingly, conversations about his home, both then and now, had given Lizzy tremendous insight into the business affairs that her husband managed. She knew that his income stemmed not only from Pemberley itself but also from investments, trade, and industrial and commercial enterprises in England and abroad.

Nonetheless, the bulk of the estate's income came from agriculture, livestock, cotton milling, and horse breeding. The farmlands were extensive and offered varying produce, including fruit orchards and grains. Two mills used the power of the River Derwent and modern technology to process the grains and shorn wool. Livestock consisted primarily of sheep with a few goats and wandering fowl. The wild game was generally left unmolested except for the occasional hunting parties Darcy allowed and, of course, for their own table.

Her husband handled all of these aspects of Pemberley's business efficiently and dutifully. However, Lizzy had rapidly established that his heart lay with his horses. Darcy was a horseman through and through. He confessed to her that, if it were possible, he would happily consign all his responsibilities to someone else and immerse his energies into breeding and training the fine horses of Pemberley.

Thus it was on Lizzy's second day that Darcy enthusiastically escorted her to the stables. The complex that accommodated the horses, carriages, and equipment, and the massive staff necessary was only slightly smaller than the main house. It too was a marvel of exquisite architecture and craftsmanship. At two stories high, the building could easily house all the staff, store the equipment and numerous carriages, and shelter the horses. A high arch facing south opened onto an enormous courtyard amid the complex where the animals were groomed and cared for. The thoroughbreds were separated from the working horses, each with their own handlers and grooms.

The weather had taken an abrupt turn for the worse. Ominous clouds hovered on the horizon, and Darcy assured Lizzy that it would snow by that evening. Despite the cold, the grooms went about their duties. They acknowledged Darcy's presence and, as always, Darcy addressed each of them by name.

Lizzy did not ride and was actually quite frightened of horses in general. That was not to say she did not value the beauty and majesty of the species, and it was immediately apparent even to her uneducated eyes that the thoroughbreds of Pemberley were magnificent. Darcy seemed intimately acquainted with each one of them. Parsifal, naturally, had the best stall and was visited by his master first. Treats were given and he was again introduced to Lizzy, who overcame her fear enough to stroke his soft nose.

Darcy knew of Lizzy's apprehension, so he thought it best to take her to the new colt first. Who could not fall in love with a baby? They arrived just as one of the grooms was about to feed the young animal. Darcy assumed the task and encouraged Lizzy to assist him. One look into the playful, sweet face of the foal and she was captured. Before long she was kneeling in the straw, Darcy beside her, holding onto the makeshift milk bladder and nipple while the colt suckled. It was a fantastic experience. Despite all expectations to the contrary, Lizzy bonded with the foal and would become a frequent visitor. She named him Wolfram, after Wolfram von Eschenbach, the poet who wrote *Parzival* from which Darcy had taken Parsifal's name. This brought a huge grin to Darcy's lips and filled his heart with joy.

Next he took her outside to the training pen where a staggeringly feisty stallion was actively being broken. Heedless of what anyone might think, Darcy pulled Elizabeth against his chest, wrapping her with his thick greatcoat. Holding her tight to keep her warm in the gathering gloom, he explained the process unfolding in the corral. Elizabeth was both fascinated and horrified.

"It looks to be rather dangerous," she said.

"Yes, it can be. The stallions are incredibly strong and unpredictable. One must attain the perfect balance between harboring that strength and controlling it. The mares tend to be slightly more docile, but not by far."

"And you do this, William? You get in there with these perilous animals?"

"When I can. Unfortunately, my duties do not allow me the freedom I would wish to be consistently hands on."

"Well, I am glad for that! It terrifies me to think of you in there. Have you ever been hurt?"

"No more than an occasional bruise or the wind knocked out of me. Once I had a mild concussion after being thrown, and there was the time I injured my thigh." He outlined his wounds with the same concern as if mentioning a paper cut.

Lizzy shuddered. She wished she could forbid him doing something she considered so reckless, but she had no right. One look at the intense emotion on his face as he watched the trainer at work, and she knew she would never wish him deprived of an occupation he so enthusiastically enjoyed. For his sake, she would exhibit interest in the stables and the world contained therein, but it would never be easy for her.

As Darcy predicted, the rain and then snow hit that evening. The intermittently inclement weather made exploring the extensive grounds beyond the immediate surroundings impossible for most of the winter. Instead, Darcy took her to random chambers on the top floor and pointed to features visible from the windows. When seen between storms, the panoramic vista was breathtaking.

Pemberley Manor rested on a gentle hill so, from the third story elevation, the countryside appeared to stretch for endless miles to the hazy horizon. She saw the pastures, orchards, and forest laid out like a patchwork quilt. She had a bird's eye view of the incredible and varied gardens, the Maze, the ponds and streams, the trout lake with fountains, and the Cascade waterfall with the Greek Temple barely discernible above. In September she had strolled through a couple of the gardens closest to the house, but her emotions had been so taut and her sensibilities so acutely affected by the man next to her that she scarcely recollected any of it.

Now they stood before the tall window, Lizzy enfolded in Darcy's strong arms, watching the snow gently blanket the earth and vegetation far below. Darcy's lips were near her ear, intermittently planting soft kisses as he spoke.

"Up above the Greek Temple is a secluded grotto," he told her. "There is a tiny pool sheltered by tall pines, elder, and willows. The pool is fed from underground so it is perpetually tranquil, acting as a mirror. The trees and bushes are so thick that when you enter, it is as if you have been transported to another world. When I was a child I would escape there with a book or my journal or nothing, just wanting to be alone. I would pretend I had magically left Earth for Mars or Jupiter. I even attempted to write a story once, relaying my adventures as the conqueror of this other planet." He laughed and Lizzy smiled at the vision of Darcy as a young boy. "I do not know what ever happened to that story, although I would surely be mortified if it was unearthed!"

He tightened his grip around his wife and continued, "I had not visited the grotto for years until this past June. After Rosings and then attempting to drown my sorrow in London and too much brandy, I returned to Pemberley. The first place I thought of was the grotto, which surprised me after so many years, but I went again and again as if compelled. I did my best self-examination there.

"As you know, beloved, I did not expect ever to have you in my life, to be given this chance to prove my love to you. I only wished to become a better man, to learn from my mistakes. The peace that pervades the place soothed me beyond words. I remember musing once, fleetingly so as not to hope where no hope seemed forthcoming, that if ever I was so blessed as to earn your love, I would take you there. It would become our special place. I only wish the weather allowed me to do so now, but I must content myself with fantasies until the spring."

He smiled down at her. She brought her hand up to caress his face, meeting his loving and intense gaze. She grasped his neck and pulled his head to her, meeting his lips with a hungry kiss. She turned in his arms and encircled his waist, pressing her body to his, and whispered, "So, describe these grotto fantasies. Or better yet, employ this gift for pretending you appear to possess and show me, right here and right now."

Darcy did not hesitate. In quick long strides he crossed the room, locked the door, and returned to her arms. Between kisses and increasingly indulgent and fervent caresses, he painted a picture of hanging branches with dappled sunlight leaking through, gentle breezes, soft grass carpet, and the heady aroma of earth and pine and wild honeysuckle. If the room was cold, neither of them felt it; the heat they generated abundantly adequate.

These pleasant diversions during the long cold afternoons were not an unusual occurrence. Pemberley was a very large house and, aside for the servants, who were under strict orders to discreetly vacate any room the Master and Mistress entered, Darcy and Lizzy were alone. Darcy was discovering the sublime exhilaration of making love to his wife outside their bedchamber. Nothing quite compared to the comfort of their bed or the rapture of cuddling afterwards and falling asleep in each other's embrace. However, there was an element of naughtiness and danger attached when they were elsewhere that was intoxicating and tremendously arousing to them both. They understood that these dalliances would become a rare event once Georgiana returned, so they recklessly luxuriated in the activity in her absence.

On the fourth day of Lizzy's residence at Pemberley, she was alone in her parlor waiting impatiently for Darcy, who was discussing a business proposal with Mr. Keith. She was standing by the window watching the snow falling when Mrs. Reynolds knocked at the open door.

"Pardon me, Mrs. Darcy, am I disturbing you?"

"Of course not, Mrs. Reynolds. Please come in."

"Mr. Darcy asked me to discuss the Christmas arrangements with you."

"Oh! Very well. Please sit down. How can I help you?"

"Christmas for the past several years has been a quiet affair. Mr. Darcy prefers this, as does Miss Darcy. Usually a few guests are invited, Mr. Bingley and his sisters on occasion, Colonel Fitzwilliam, and twice Lord and Lady Matlock have graced us. Now that you have joined the family, Mr. Darcy requested that you have the final authority on who was invited as well as the arrangements and festivities."

"I see." Lizzy hesitated. "The truth is, Mrs. Reynolds, I have given minimal thought to Christmas, my mind being focused on my wedding and not getting lost in the corridors! I rather imagined the holiday would proceed as Mr. Darcy and Miss Georgiana have traditionally done so. I will confer with Mr. Darcy regarding the guest list and proffer the invitations. Perhaps you could enlighten me as to the usual festivities?"

"Certainly," and Mrs. Reynolds launched into a detailed report of a typical Pemberley Christmas. After a half hour, Lizzy had a great deal to ponder. She told Mrs. Reynolds that she would talk to Mr. Darcy and meet with her again tomorrow. While Mrs. Reynolds was there, Lizzy enlisted her assistance in another matter she had been brooding on. It was the first time she and the housekeeper had said more than a few words to each other, and although the conversation did not result in much decision making,

Lizzy still felt as if she had taken a small step toward assuming her role as Mistress of Pemberley.

❦

Two days later Lizzy was awoken by the sensation of something velvety with a lovely aroma brushing across her face. She opened her eyes to see her husband's handsome face hovering over her. His jubilantly dimpled smile, sparkling blue eyes, and disheveled hair were enough to instantly set her heart racing. It took her a moment to realize that he held a pink rose in his hands and it was this with which he was gently tickling her face.

"Happy anniversary, my precious wife," he declared in his rich, musical voice. "Elizabeth my love… my light… my heart… my pearl… my lover… my Lizzy." He unceasingly grazed her face, neck, and shoulders with the rose, sprinkling kisses between his endearments. "One week ago today, you made me the happiest of men, Mrs. Darcy, my beloved." He kissed her deeply then, pulling her body onto his, caressing her back with his hand and the flower.

"My husband, I note you are wearing your trousers. Under the present circumstances, is this not a ludicrous encumbrance?" she tantalized, planting nibbles to his neck.

"Nothing that cannot be easily rectified, my love." He laughed. "I did not think it wise of me to traipse to the conservatory unclothed. The staff has been shocked enough lately at my lack of modesty and propriety."

"You went to the conservatory this morning?" she asked with slight alarm.

"I needed to pick this for you," he touched her adorable nose with the rose, "and those as well." He waved his hand about the room and the five vases of varied flowers scattered about the chamber.

Lizzy sat up in bed, unconscious of the heavenly sight she presented to her husband, and smiled radiantly at the array of blooms. She turned her smile onto Darcy, devastating him further with love and desire, and teased, "You are doing it again, Mr. Darcy. Being entirely too fabulous, spoiling me beyond endurance, and setting the standard so high that you may exhaust yourself in an effort to reach higher than the previous pinnacle!"

He rose and kissed her quickly on the cheek. "Let me worry about that," he responded, and then left the bed before her beguiling charms drove further thought away. He returned from his dressing room swiftly with an enormous box, which he placed on the bed in front of her.

"William, you must cease buying me gifts! I do not require such gestures."

"Whether you require them or not is irrelevant, Mrs. Darcy. I will shower you with presents because I am entirely egocentric and I extract pleasure from admiring your happy face! Humor me, if nothing else."

She pretended a scowl, but could not maintain it for long. She opened the box and gasped in shock. She pulled out an ankle-length pelisse of russet wool, lined and edged with sable. It was by far the most exquisite garment she had ever owned. With a squeal of glee, she robustly hugged her husband and then stood up on the bed, wrapping herself in the lush softness of the coat. The luxuriant contact of the fur on her bare skin was positively vivifying. She pranced seductively about the bed, making Darcy smile and laugh aloud.

"You see," he gushed, "the pleasure is wholly mine. I am selfishly overcome with joy." He clutched her legs and drew her onto his lap. "Now let me see what other self-serving indulgences I can secure."

Just prior to noon, Lizzy sat in Darcy's study while he worked at his desk. She pretended to read a book, but was more fascinated with inspecting her husband. A small crease sat between his brows as he concentrated. He rolled the quill in his fingers and rubbed his chin when ruminating. Occasionally his lips would silently mouth the words on the document before him. Frequently he would sigh or harrumph or aah or curse or grumble, without being aware he did so. Lizzy adored simply observing him, learning more about him in these unconscious mannerisms.

A knock at the door led to the entrance of Mr. Keith, who requested a moment of Mr. Darcy's time. With alacrity, and a thankful nod to Mr. Keith, Lizzy rose and left the two gentlemen alone. Mrs. Reynolds stood outside the door. "Is everything ready?" Lizzy asked.

"As you requested, Mrs. Darcy."

"Thank you!" and with a brief squeeze to Mrs. Reynolds' hands, Lizzy flew up to her dressing room where Marguerite was waiting.

About forty-five minutes later, Mr. Darcy emerged from his study, asked a footman where Mrs. Darcy could be found, and was told that she was in the conservatory. Darcy walked speedily, already lamenting the absence of his wife. He called to her when he entered, and her voice came from the far side of the room. He made his way around the profusion of potted plants and trees. The tableau before him stopped him dead in his tracks.

A clearing had been made and a luncheon was arranged as if outdoors, hamper and all. Elizabeth stood, wearing her lightest muslin summer gown with only a thin chemise underneath and satin lawn slippers. Her hair was down, with the side strands twisted into an elaborate braid in back. The warmth of the conservatory, the aroma of the blooms, the sunlight shining through the ceiling and walls of glass, along with the blanket on the floor, created the perfect summer scenario.

"Happy anniversary, Fitzwilliam!" Lizzy approached her stunned husband and without preamble began unbuttoning his coat. "I know it is a poor substitute for your grotto, so we must pretend." She laid his coat aside and then kissed him. "I could not forget the day you made me the happiest woman in the world, my love. One whole week you have tolerated me! You have earned a medal, but instead you will get only lunch. Now sit. I shall serve our food."

Lizzy also had a gift for her husband. "It is rather silly," she blushingly remarked when she handed him the small box. "I did not have the foresight to buy a real gift for you. Instead I recalled an inane French novel I read when I was a girl, a poorly written romantic piece of tripe. There was this one thing I thought sweet, in my girlish idea of romance."

Darcy opened the box and saw a small satin pouch with a drawstring closure. "Look inside," Lizzy said, biting her lip in nervousness. He pulled out a long slender tress of her silky hair that had been braided and tied on each end with fine thread. "You see," she explained, "now you will permanently have a small part of me with you even if I am not there."

He stared at her in unbelief. "You thought this was silly? This is... astounding! Elizabeth, I do not have the words!" He kissed her tenderly and held her chin with his fingers. "My love, I resort to buying gifts because it is what I am accustomed to. You look inward to your heart and give far more generously than I. I will cherish this and bear it with me for all my life. I so love you, Elizabeth."

It was a lovely afternoon. There is something mysterious about picnics—even indoor ones—that immediately causes one to feel mellow and whimsical. One week of wedded bliss, and they both already had scores of memories to record into their journals, not that either of them would ever forget the passion and joy of these first days.

Chapter Nine

Shopping!

M ONDAY ARRIVED AND LIZZY was slightly ashamed, but she could not deny her excitement. Never in her entire life had she been able to shop without worry for the cost. She still was not sure she could manage it, but she intended to try. Darcy seemed as eager as she was. She had learned early in their engagement that he adored buying gifts for those he loved—for her, of course, but also for Georgiana and even his cousin Richard or Bingley. He was almost absentminded about it, simply seeing something that he knew they would enjoy and purchasing it on the spot. It was endearing.

Although she felt somewhat like a child let loose in a candy store, she understood that her excursion today was necessary. Each day, as she wandered about Pemberley, the awareness of her new station in life became increasingly apparent. If for no other reason than to make her husband proud that he had married a simple country girl, she would present herself as exactly what society demanded from the Mistress of Pemberley.

She wore her new pelisse over her gown, feeling more regal than she ever had. She tucked a wad of her pin money into her reticule, just in case, and met her smiling husband in the foyer.

First they had luncheon at the Carriage Inn, one of Lambton's oldest and most prominent establishments. Lizzy blushed initially at the number of stares her appearance on the arm of Mr. Darcy engendered, but his air of indifference and obvious pride at her gracing his side calmed her. She was introduced to several people, all of whom had heard of Mr. Darcy's marriage. "Word travels quickly in these small communities, as you well know, Elizabeth," he whispered.

After luncheon Darcy and Lizzy walked to Madame du Loire's salon. Along the way they encountered a distinguished older gentleman who approached the Darcys with a broad grin.

"Why, Mr. Darcy! How fortunate I am to meet you so unexpectedly. This must be the Mrs. Darcy we are all hearing about." He bowed deeply to Lizzy. He had a very open face and Lizzy found herself liking him immediately.

"Mr. Vernor," Darcy replied with a happy smile, "you are correct. This is my wife, Mrs. Darcy. Mrs. Darcy, may I introduce you to our closest neighbor, Mr. Henry Vernor of Sanburl Hall."

Lizzy curtseyed. "Mr. Vernor, it is a pleasure to make your acquaintance."

"Thank you, Mrs. Darcy, however, I must insist that the pleasure is entirely mine. I am certain that Mr. Darcy has warned you that the rumors of your grace and beauty have preceded your entry into our little community. Now I shall be able to brag to all that I beheld you first and can glowingly proclaim that the rumors pale in comparison to the reality that was before me."

Lizzy was a bit shocked at Mr. Vernor's ebullient charm and assumed Darcy would be miffed, so she was further surprised to hear him laugh boomingly. "It sunders my heart to disappoint you, my old friend, but we have just come from the Carriage Inn and I was honored to introduce my lovely wife to a number of the denizens of Lambton. Tell me, Vernor, how much have you scoundrels wagered on who would espy my wife first?"

Mr. Vernor feigned indignation, "Darcy, you wound me, sir! A true gentleman would never wager on such a thing." His words, however, were denied by the wink he gave to Lizzy and by Darcy's continued laughter.

Darcy turned to his wife, who was beginning to find the entire encounter extremely amusing. "You see, my love, Lambton offers little in the ways of diversion so the *gentlemen* frequently resort to petty indulgences to offset the boredom. I know for a fact that there has been a long standing wager as to when I would enter the esteemed state of matrimony and to which society lady it would be. How did those bets turn out, Vernor? Any luck, my friend?"

Vernor assumed a visage of tremendous mourning. "Mr. Creswell won on the age. There was some debate since you were eight and twenty when you became betrothed, but the wager was for age at marriage, so Creswell edged out

Sir Cole. Sadly for us all, although undoubtedly happily and wisely for you and Mrs. Darcy," he bowed again to Lizzy, "you ventured outside London society, a move none of us anticipated."

Lizzy laughed, "I do not believe my husband anticipated it either, Mr. Vernor. His chagrin was tremendous, let me assure you." With a twinkle she glanced at her husband. "He fought valiantly against it, but in the end we ladies usually achieve what we want, is that not true, Mr. Vernor?"

"Most definitely, Mrs. Darcy. When it comes to matters of the heart, the fairer sex has the distinct advantage."

"My wife is far too generous, Vernor. She led me on a merry chase in which I was all too delighted to engage." He briefly kissed Elizabeth's hand, saying, "The prize was well worth the effort." Darcy was beaming and Vernor could not mistake the looks shared with his wife as anything other than the deepest love. Vernor had been a great friend to Darcy's father, and his son, Gerald, had been a childhood playmate of Darcy's and was one of his dearest friends still. The families were close so it warmed Vernor's heart to see the young man finally so happy.

Darcy turned his attention back to Vernor and clapped him on the shoulder. "It brings joy to my heart to know I have disrupted the gaming. By the way, where are you heading? Will you take a glass of wine with me?"

"Gerald is meeting me and would undoubtedly delight in visiting with you, too."

Darcy nodded. "I am escorting Mrs. Darcy to Madame du Loire's. Let's plan soon for a game of billiards at Pemberley?"

Mr. Vernor winced. "I do not think I have quite recovered my pride from your last thrashing at billiards, Darcy." He addressed Lizzy, "Your husband is the champion billiard player in all of Derbyshire, Mrs. Darcy. Last summer was the first time anyone had beaten him in a decade, and then it took Mr. Hughes, our next best player, to accomplish the feat."

Darcy scowled and glanced at his wife. "I was distracted most of last summer with personal matters and Hughes caught me on an off day."

Vernor smiled, completely misapprehending Darcy's reference. "Yes, I imagine you were distracted, and we now all comprehend the reason. Mrs. Darcy, my wife and the other ladies of Derbyshire are anxious to meet you. As soon as Mr. Darcy is willing to share, you must dine with us."

"Thank you, Mr. Vernor. I shall look forward to it."

Lizzy spent an exhausting afternoon admiring fabrics and accessories finer than any she had ever owned. Darcy had made it abundantly clear that she was to be outfitted fully, top to bottom, with expense not an issue. With Phillips as chaperone and lending two strong arms as baggage carrier, she shuffled from one shop to another purchasing new slippers and boots, nightgowns and robes, undergarments, stockings, bonnets and hats, outerwear, gloves, and more. The focus was winter wear, naturally, so the fabrics were heavy wools and velvet with fur for warmth. By the end of the day, she had three new gowns quickly altered to her dimensions by the seamstresses in attendance and another two dozen gowns to be made with fabrics acquired from the drapers.

Madame du Loire was a genius. Lizzy had often lamented her, shall we say, less than curvy figure. She was not generally the type to follow fashion, nor was she particularly vain. Nonetheless, with four sisters shaped full and lush, Lizzy could not help but notice the obvious difference in her own form. Her mother had frequently and mournfully commented on Lizzy's overly svelte physique, loudly bemoaning it as a probable deterrent to any man finding her attractive. All her young adult life, Lizzy had scoffed at her mother's words, but deep inside she had harbored feelings of inadequacy.

Darcy's wanton approbation of her body and his frank and blatant intoxication with her feminine shape had erased most of her uncertainties. Even so, she was amazed and delighted at the skill Madame du Loire employed to enhance her limited assets and accentuate her attributes. She taught Lizzy how to manipulate stays and gathers and lace and numerous other things to present a more pleasing and alluring vision. Considering her husband's already over-whelming amorousness for her, Lizzy was not totally sure this was a wise plan! Thoughts of how he would be affected by her new attire brought a blush to her face as well as shivers of desire, most inappropriate in the current setting.

Late in the afternoon, exhausted but exhilarated, Lizzy said her final farewells to shopping. The purchases were packed up and secured into the carriage, but Lizzy opted to stroll along the streets of Lambton. With Phillips as escort she headed to meet her husband, passing numerous shops of interest. The desire to buy needless items for Darcy burned in her chest; however, the hour was growing late so she made mental notes and bypassed them for the time being.

Later that evening, after dinner, Lizzy and Darcy relaxed in their sitting room. Darcy had carried out Lizzy's requests and the room had been rearranged. The painting was now hanging over the fireplace mantel directly across from the doorway so one's eye was drawn to it immediately upon entering the room. A mammoth new carpet, which Darcy had discovered on his last trip to London, had arrived the day before. It was a Serapi Persian rug, plush and thick, patterned exotically with soft golds and greens. It lay in front of the fireplace and dominated the room. The chaise and two chairs with ottomans sat before the flames. A breakfast sideboard stood against one wall with their small dining table nearby. Lizzy had unpacked her favorite books, placing them into the bookcase with Darcy's. Lizzy had fallen in love with a petite desk she had discovered in one of the guest's chambers, so it had been relocated to their sitting room and placed close to Darcy's desk in one corner before the window. The room was cozy, serene, and inviting. In truth, they had spent scant time relaxing in any of the downstairs rooms, much preferring to be here, together and informal.

So it was tonight. Lizzy sat at her desk and Darcy was at his. They were not quite close enough to physically touch, but the desks were arranged in a rough "V" so they could converse easily if necessary and could view each other unobstructed across the negligible space. Darcy had removed his coats and cravat. The household account ledger was in front of him, and a minute crease twisted between his brows as he concentrated. Lizzy was in her nightgown and robe and alternated between watching her husband and the task she worked on. As always, he distracted her by his very presence, but pleasantly so.

She was amused at how he fidgeted while he worked. He held his body straight and erect, but his fingers were incessantly moving, either twirling his quill or stroking his chin or, as now, playing with a palm-sized glass ball. She was further fascinated at how dexterous he was in his unconscious toying. He absently tossed and rolled the little ball, balanced it on his fingertips and even reeled it across his knuckles, not once taking his eyes or focus off the ledger. She shook her head in amazement, smiled, and returned her deliberations to her letter.

She had completed a long, detail-filled correspondence to Jane, which she had been composing in bits and pieces for several days. She missed Jane, even as content as she was at Pemberley. At odd moments throughout her day, she would find herself thinking of her sister, wondering what she was doing and how she would react to something Lizzy was saying or doing. Mostly, Lizzy was curious about whether her sister was as happy in her marriage as she was. Lizzy adored Mr. Bingley and was certain he loved her sister, so she was not particularly worried about Jane's happiness. No, she simply missed sharing in that happiness and being able to talk about her own felicity.

Also, Christmas was fast approaching and although Lizzy was delighted at the prospect of spending the holidays with her husband and new family, it would be the first holiday season in her life without her parents and sisters. It was a bittersweet reality, which led to the task before her. She and Darcy had discussed the Christmas plans, and he had embraced the idea of a major celebration. For more than ten years, since his mother had died, Christmas at Pemberley had been a quiet affair. He felt it was time they put past grief behind them and commemorated the season as it deserved to be.

To that end, Lizzy had penned formal invitations. Darcy had insisted on inviting the Gardiners, so one invitation had been written to them. Another had been written to Col. Fitzwilliam and yet another to Lord and Lady Matlock. Georgiana would be returning to Pemberley in a little over a week. Col. Fitzwilliam and his parents, who had been gracious enough to keep Georgiana in Town during these first weeks of the Darcy's marriage, would be bringing her home when they returned to their estate in Matlock for the winter.

Lizzy had won the affection of the Matlocks while in London during her engagement. It had been a tortuous battle, what with Lady Catherine's vocal disapproval and attempts to thwart Darcy's marriage to "the country upstart." However, eventually Lizzy's natural charm and wit, along with the obvious love Darcy held for her, had swayed the Matlocks. Lizzy was far from comfortable with them, imposing characters though they were, but she respected them. Mostly, she knew how valuable they were to Darcy, so she had declared they should be invited for Christmas Day as well.

Lastly, Darcy requested the presence of a friend of his from Leicester, a Mr. Stephen Lathrop, and his young wife Amelia. Darcy had met Mr. Lathrop years ago at Cambridge, and the two had become friendly, being of similar temperaments. Mr. Lathrop owned a small estate in Leicestershire and his father had died this past year, leaving Mr. Lathrop without any family except for his wife of one year. She was Scottish so her family lived quite far away, and Darcy thought it would be a nice gesture to have them join the Pemberley festivities, understanding thoroughly how grief stricken his friend would be this holiday. Lizzy had not met them, but was very pleased to include them.

Inviting Lady Catherine and Miss Anne was positively out of the question. Lizzy had gently broached the issue, but Darcy, in a rare display of anger toward his wife, had flatly refused even to consider it or to discuss the subject. Lizzy feared the breach between the two was irreparable and it saddened her. She was quite content never to set eyes on Lady Catherine again, thinking her in all ways a horrible woman. Nonetheless, she was Darcy's aunt, sister to his mother, and as the schism was a direct result of her existence, it pained her.

Logically she knew that it probably had been an inevitable event since Anne and Darcy would never have married, neither of them desiring it. Lady Catherine would undoubtedly have been furious at whomever Darcy had chosen to wed over her daughter. Still, logic aside, Lizzy could not stop feeling a bit guilty and wished she could facilitate reconciliation. If it ever happened, it would not be now, so Lizzy pushed the matter from her mind.

Darcy closed his ledger with a snap and stretched his neck, sighing deeply. Lizzy had finished the last invitation, to the Lathrops, so she rose and handed it to her husband.

"The last one," she declared. "How does it sound?"

He took it from her, claiming her hand in the process for a brief kiss. He smiled up at her. "I am certain it is as well written as all the others, my love." As he read, Lizzy stood behind him and began massaging his temples with her fingers. She then ran her fingers through his hair, massaging his scalp to relieve the tension she knew he felt after concluding long columns of mathematics. She traveled to his neck and shoulders, kneading firmly with her surprisingly strong hands. Darcy groaned and dropped his chin to his chest. "That feels so wonderful," he sighed.

"Your muscles are too tight," she stated. "How did you ever manage without me to do this?"

"Samuel is actually a fine masseur," he mumbled, "although, the end result of his attentions was never as pleasant as yours!" He clasped one hand and pulled her around and onto his lap. She laughed and then kissed him soundly as her hands resumed their devotion to his shoulders. Darcy untied her nightgown, slipping one hand inside for his own form of massaging.

Lizzy faltered and gasped against his lips. "Sir!" she teased, playfully slapping at his probing hand, "I cannot complete my wifely duty of easing my husband's pain if you distract me so!"

Darcy chuckled and resumed his provocative activities with stubborn persuasion. "There are countless ways to ease my pain, my heart. We simply have differing ideas at the moment. However, I am supremely confident that I can modify your direction with alacrity."

To further prove his point, he fluidly arose with her secured in his arms and carried her into their bedchamber. In the end, he was correct and Lizzy did not balk in the slightest.

L IZZY LAY DRIFTING OFF to sleep, bare back pressed firmly against her husband's chest, his heat seeping into her and his strong arms holding her tightly. As always, she was overwhelmed by the incredible peace and joy she felt in the presence of this man she loved so totally. His breath tickled her shoulder as he slept with his head next to hers, the power and strength of him apparent in every muscle of his body as he held her securely. He could not be any closer unless he crawled under her skin! She loved his need to cuddle and, oddly enough, had no trouble sleeping with him so near. In fact, her need to feel him beside her had become a necessity.

Her sleepy musings turned to Christmas. Lizzy zealously anticipated the holiday, even though it meant disruption to their idyllic solitude. She was anxious to renew and deepen her friendship with Georgiana, and she knew William missed his sister. Col. Fitzwilliam was a kind and humorous man, sure to add laughter to the festivities. The elder Fitzwilliams were much more stoic than their youngest son, but they were polite and they were now her family. Memories of her introduction to them in London returned to her, and with those remembrances freshly recalled, Lizzy fell asleep.

London, some five weeks previous

It had been agreed upon by all that the trousseau and wedding gowns for the two Bennet sisters must be acquired in Town. At the behest of Lizzy, Mr. Bennet rather than Mrs. Bennet, had escorted his daughters to the home of his wife's brother, the Gardiners, in Cheapside. Mr. Darcy and Mr. Bingley had accompanied them on their journey in their own carriage, both wishing that they could ride with their fiancées, but such arrangements were frowned upon without proper chaperones.

The first few days were spent in a whirlwind of shopping. Aunt Gardiner accompanied the girls while Mr. Darcy and Mr. Bingley entertained Mr. Bennet and Mr. Gardiner. Mr. Darcy enthusiastically shepherded his soon-to-be family to his club and other favorite haunts. Mr. Bennet was delighted to pass hours in the Darcy House library, a fraction the size or quantity of Pemberley's but impressive nonetheless. Col. Fitzwilliam joined the men whenever his duties allowed him to do so, and Lizzy was certain her father had not had so much fun in years. One night her uncle and father did not even return from Darcy House, and the next day all the gentlemen suffered from headaches they tried unsuccessfully to hide!

Most evenings they all dined at the Darcy townhouse on Grosvenor Square. Darcy proudly introduced Lizzy to the staff there, much smaller than the staff at Pemberley. Mrs. Smyth, the housekeeper, was terribly formal and distant, unlike Mrs. Reynolds, but quite efficient. Darcy House was modest and soberly decorated with few of the flamboyant embellishments found at Pemberley and far fewer rooms. The garden was graceful and beautiful with several secluded areas, although not huge. Darcy showed Lizzy the chambers that would be hers and, as at Pemberley, she saw no reason to alter them; however, these intimate details could not be openly discussed during their engagement, so she evaded the issue of redecorating for the present.

All in all, she was delighted with the house and overjoyed at the chance to observe Darcy in the comfort of his home. The stolen moments alone that they contrived were significantly more intense and amorous, dangerously skirting the edges of propriety. It was not until after they were married that he would confess how tortuous it was for him to have her in his home without being her husband. His desire for her had overwhelmed him and, he admitted, the nearness of his bedchamber, where so many dreams of her had transpired, exponentially added to his distress. It was during this time that Lizzy became fully cognizant of the hidden passion of her betrothed and the tremendous effect his passion had on her!

Darcy and Bingley managed to keep their presence in London quiet, not wishing to attend any of the usual social obligations that came with their station. Caroline, much to Lizzy and Jane's relief, had accompanied the Hursts to Bath for a short vacation. With Georgiana still at Pemberley until the week before the wedding, the only extended family to deal with were the Earl and his wife. This could be problematic.

It had started, not shockingly, with Lady Catherine. In the first days after their engagement, Darcy had written his sister Georgiana, Mrs. Reynolds, and Cousin Richard glowing letters of his bliss at Miss Bennet accepting his hand. His letter to his uncle had been more formal but filled with personal revelations of his joy. Darcy was fairly close to his Aunt and Uncle Fitzwilliam but knew they would be shocked and dismayed at his choice of wife. Ultimately none of this mattered to him; however, his regard for their opinion and wish for their sanction was desired. His letter to his Aunt Catherine had been extremely formal and terse; he had not forgiven her for her inappropriate actions at Longbourn.

Despite his irritation, Darcy had not expected the rabid vitriol of his aunt's attack against his fiancée. The letter she sent in answer to his news was lengthy and malicious. First she had responded to his announcement with a scathing denouncement of his character. According to her, he had *betrayed his dear mother's memory by callously abandoning Anne to spinsterhood*. She said he was *selfish, irresponsible, and a black mark on the ancient house of Darcy*. There was much more and it did hurt; however, he was a self-confident man who knew the truth about his own character, so he could mainly ignore his aunt's horrid words. It was when she viciously condemned Elizabeth personally that he responded with outrage and steely resolve. Lady Catherine had assaulted his honor as a gentleman and accountability as husband and protector of his wife, and he was beyond offended.

Lizzy never knew the full content of Lady Catherine's letter. She probably would not have known the letter existed if she had not been at Netherfield the day it arrived. Darcy and Bingley were playing chess while the ladies sat nearby when the footman brought the gentlemen the day's post. Darcy's stack was large, as always, due to the numerous business interests he managed. He flipped through it quickly stopping with a frown upon spying his aunt's hand. It had been a week since his engagement and his letter had only posted four days ago, so he was surprised at the haste of her reply and even that she had replied at all.

Later he would condemn himself for not having the foresight to open the letter in private or for not controlling his temper. As he read his face darkened visibly, eyes as black agates and lips pressed into the thin line signifying tremendous anger. Forgetting where he was in his wrath, he jerked from his chair uttering a vile curse and stormed from the room. Needless to say, the three other occupants of the room were stunned speechless.

Bingley had more experience with his friend's temper, so he recovered quickly, stammering to assure the ladies that all would be well. After a moment of paralysis, Lizzy rose to follow Darcy. He had disappeared from sight, but the blanched face of a maid down the hall was indication enough of the direction he had taken.

She found him in the library, staring out a window. At first glance he seemed calm, but in the short time of their acquaintance, Lizzy had learned to recognize the signs of tension in his body—and never had he been as tense as he was at this moment. Fury emanated from him in nearly visible waves. Lizzy approached him silently and gently laid her hand on his arm.

He jolted in surprise and looked at her with such ferocity on his face that she flinched. "Leave me be, Elizabeth," he commanded flatly in a voice that brooked no argument.

Nonetheless, she refused. "No," she said firmly, "Talk to me, William."

He stared at her in shocked ire at her refusal and then turned his gaze to the window. He fluttered the letter in the air. "My aunt is not pleased about our engagement," he said with massive understatement.

Lizzy surprised him further by actually laughing, and his scowl increased. "I find no humor in this, Elizabeth."

"Really, William! Did you imagine she would embrace me with open arms and host a party? Lady Catherine made her opinion of me quite clear at Longbourn, an event that we should essentially be thankful for since, left to your own devices, you may not have gotten up the nerve to propose again." She said the last bit teasingly and rose onto her toes to kiss one cheek while caressing the other. He continued to stare at her, clearly torn between crushing her into his arms or further ranting about the letter. In the end he did neither. He sighed and walked several paces away before turning back to look at her. He was in turmoil and had no idea what to say.

Lizzy moved a bit closer to him but kept a space, sensing he needed some distance. "William, I am indifferent to what your aunt has to say about me or us. I love you with all my heart and you love me. She cannot alter that, can she?"

"Of course not!" he said in a strangled tone.

"She is angry at her dashed hopes for you and Anne. I am not a mother yet, however, I can partly sympathize. It does in no way justify her actions or words, but you must try to understand a little."

Darcy shook his head. "Elizabeth, it is more than that. She has slandered you personally, your character and virtue and qualifications as my intended. This I cannot forgive."

She drew closer before replying softly, "Did you not initially doubt my qualifications and connections, beloved?" His countenance paled and his mouth fell open at her words, and she rapidly closed the gap, taking his beloved face into her hands so he would not turn away. "The difference is that you now know my character and virtue and you love me. The only truth that matters is us and our love. The rest will resolve itself or it will not, but it is inconsequential as long as we are unified in our commitment."

Darcy sighed again and rested his forehead against hers, arms enfolding her. "How are you so wise, my love, for one so young?"

She smiled impishly and kissed him lightly. "It is a secret, Mr. Darcy. You cannot expect a girl to reveal all too soon can you? Then where would the mystery be?"

He laughed. "Very well. I shall let Lady Catherine stew and rage if she must; however, I refuse to listen."

Darcy waited a couple of weeks before he addressed his aunt. His letter was blunt and formal. In language that permitted no error, he informed her that he would forever revere her as his mother's sister but that his loyalty was to Elizabeth. Until she accepted this incontrovertible fact and rendered his betrothed the esteem due her as Mistress of Pemberley and Mrs. Darcy, she would not be welcome in his life.

Unbeknownst to him at the time, Lady Catherine had been busy spreading her disgust to Lord and Lady Matlock, and anyone else who was willing to listen. The news of Mr. Darcy's engagement had disseminated expeditiously through the ton, rumors galore based on little in the way of truth. Darcy's supreme happiness conjoined with his general disdain for London society was such that he gave no consideration to what gossip may be circulating. The opinion of his uncle and aunt was another matter. In both instances, he confidently believed that Elizabeth's charms would eventually prevail. The fortuitous trip to Town presented the opportunity for him to introduce his fiancée to the rest of his mother's family.

Upon arriving with the Bennets, Richard informed Darcy of the letters from Lady Catherine to his parents and the confusion they harbored over Darcy's choice of bride. Col. Fitzwilliam had sung the praises of Elizabeth and made no secret of the love Darcy felt for his bride-to-be. The Fitzwilliams cared very much for their nephew and they trusted the opinion of their son, so they were willing to forestall jumping to any conclusions. All the same, Lord Matlock was prepared to forcefully remind Darcy of his duties to Pemberley if his choice of wife was as poor as Lady Catherine intimated. The Earl was a realist and the patriarch of a noble family. Love and romance have their place, but not at the expense of tradition, duty, and honor to one's name, country, and ancestry.

On their fifth evening in Town, Lizzy and her father accompanied Mr. Darcy to the Matlock townhouse for dinner. Strangely, Lizzy was not at all nervous. Perhaps it was her naïveté, but truly it was simply her nature and character to not be intimidated. Darcy observed her sunny face and gay personality as she chatted with him and Mr. Bennet in the carriage and his pride and love swelled. She was amazing. So fearless and brave, so vibrant and luminous. If his uncle and aunt disapproved... well, they would be fools and he knew they were not fools.

Per Darcy's behest, the dinner party was to be an informal one—just the immediate Fitzwilliam family to meet Lizzy and Mr. Bennet. Aside from the necessity of being introduced to Lord and Lady Matlock, Darcy wished for his betrothed to become reacquainted with his cousin Richard. The Darcy and Fitzwilliam families were generational friends, their affection and accord preceding by decades the marriage of Lady Anne Fitzwilliam to James Darcy.

Richard, three years Darcy's senior, was his oldest playmate and confidant, the two nigh on inseparable when younger. More so even than with his aunt or uncle, it was desirous that Richard and Lizzy grow comfortable with each other. Darcy was not too concerned, the two having already established a rapport in Kent. In fact, at the time the native charm and ebullience of Col. Fitzwilliam, in sharp contrast to his own reticence, had been mildly irritating. Observing the easy familiarity that arose between the woman he loved and his cousin would have birthed a raging jealousy if he did not know Richard's strong abhorrence to the very idea of marriage!

Joining them would be the eldest Fitzwilliam brother and heir to the Matlock earldom, Jonathan, and his wife Priscilla. Darcy had never been close to his older cousin, but there was a fondness nonetheless and he was pleased to have Jonathan as part of the party. Darcy's youngest cousin, Annabella, was not able to attend, her Society duties as Lady Montgomery preferable to meeting her cousin's country fiancée. Not that she voiced this opinion in such blunt language, but Darcy well knew Annabella's superior attitude to be everything once accused of him.

Introductions were made in the imposing foyer of the Matlock town-house near St. James's Square, the party then gathering in the parlor for a short spell before dinner. Lord Matlock was dazzled immediately by Miss Bennet's charm and liveliness. Lady Matlock was equally captivated, but her gaze rested most often on the face of her dearly loved nephew, marveling at the animation and peace that infused his countenance even as he maintained his typical reserve. It was no mystery why Darcy had succumbed to her, Miss Bennet being as gregarious as he was taciturn. They say opposites attract, and here was a clear example of the old adage, as well as a visible illustration of how love opens one's soul.

Mr. Bennet was the archetypical country gentleman. Proper to be sure, but somewhat irreverent, intelligent, and with a piquant wit and wry humor. Lord Matlock, for all his elevated rank, was the master of a country estate and appreciated men such as Mr. Bennet for their unpretentious mannerisms. In no time at all, the two men were engaged in a friendly discourse of modern literature versus the classics.

Dinner was a lively affair with conversation flowing from all sides. Lord Matlock and Mr. Bennet conversed easily on numerous topics, with Lizzy joining in frequently. Col. Fitzwilliam, always full of stories and anecdotes, kept them entertained and even managed to elicit a laugh or two from his sober brother and pompous sister-in-law. Darcy was content to placidly observe his fiancée enchant his relatives, contributing now and then to the general conversation.

Retiring again to the parlor after dinner, the atmosphere relaxed further. Some light entertainment was engaged in, Mrs. Fitzwilliam being quite accomplished on the pianoforte, but primarily it was an amiable setting for deeper communication as they sipped tea and brandy. Lady Matlock spoke adoringly of Derbyshire and Pemberley, reminiscing to Lizzy of her own days as a new bride relocating to an unfamiliar land.

"You have seen Pemberley, I am taken to understand?" Lizzy affirmed Lady Matlock's inquiry. "It may seem imposing, Miss Bennet, but the Darcys have made it a home. And never fear, Fitzwilliam is the soul of patience and kindness. You will be most happy there, I am sure."

Lizzy blushed faintly. "Thank you, Your Ladyship. I am anticipation itself. I have no doubts that Mr. Darcy will lead me gently."

She smiled up at her betrothed, who stood nearby with Richard at his side. He smiled faintly in return, eyes sparkling.

Richard nodded, his eyes mischievous as he gazed to his cousin's face. "Indeed, Mr. Darcy is patience personified. All can attest to the fact. Even his horses declare it so!" They collectively laughed, Darcy blushing slightly but meeting Richard's teasing gaze.

"Sadly a lesson I could never impart to you, cousin. Your horses habitually choose to throw you rather than listen to instruction."

"That happened one time, and I was fifteen and the horse refused to jump that creek!" He turned to Lizzy with a chuckle and sly glance toward Darcy. "He, braggart, was twelve with a horse larger than mine and cleared the creek without hesitation! Very well, I concede. You are the superior horseman. I, on the other hand, excel at dancing and witty conversation."

"You are now witness, Miss Bennet, to what shall henceforth pervade your existence whenever these two are in the same room together." Lady Matlock interjected with a laugh. "They delight in baiting the other, have since they were children, and likely will be doing so in their senility."

"Miss Bennet knows it to be true, having confessed to me the dreadfulness of William's dancing and conversation in Hertfordshire."

Lizzy laughed gaily. "Colonel! You tease as well as color the truth. I said that Mr. Darcy refused to dance, not that he danced poorly. He quite proved his skill at the Netherfield Ball, dancing with the grace of a gazelle."

"Grace of a gazelle? High praise, indeed. Is this true, Fitzwilliam?" Lord Matlock grinned at his nephew's discomfiture.

Darcy coughed, color high but face alit with humor as he gazed upon his impish fiancée, "Miss Bennet is being generous, as always. I managed to avoid stepping on her feet or making a total fool of myself, but in my particular case it remains fortunate that dancing skills and engaging repartee are not the only inducements to affection."

They all smiled and chuckled, even Jonathan. "Quite so," he offered. "I abhor dancing and socializing more so than you, William, and that is saying something, yet my wife tolerates me. One's beguilements and personality can be well hidden secrets for only select individuals to divine."

"I concur, Mr. Fitzwilliam," Lizzy nodded. "Rather like a fine bottle of aged red wine. The cork must be removed; the wine poured out and allowed to breathe. One must wait patiently for the aroma to rise in the air to captivate those who wish to partake of its delights. The wine warms in the glass as the flavor softens and mellows, exposing its true essence." She paused, her gaze locked on Darcy's startled but tender eyes as he focused on her to the exclusion of all others in the room. "Some people are structured so and are abundantly worth the wait," she finished in a soft whisper.

"Well spoken, Miss Bennet," Lady Matlock glanced between the two lovers and then shared a pointed look with her husband.

As they were preparing to leave, Lord Matlock took Darcy aside for a private exchange. "I like her, my boy, enormously. There is absolutely no doubt she loves you. Her father is a gentleman and their manners are impeccable."

"Thank you, sir. Your opinion means a great deal to me." Darcy smiled slightly, privately thanking Lizzy's maneuvering to ensure that her father and not her mother had accompanied her.

Lord Matlock peered at his nephew intently. "Nonetheless, what if I do not approve? She is not quite in your class, manners notwithstanding. What if I agree with your Aunt Catherine?"

Darcy returned his gaze with the same intensity. "Sir, I would be grieved, as I am with Lady Catherine's attitude. However, my choices are just that… mine. Elizabeth is my life. I am nothing without her."

Lord Matlock nodded, still watching his nephew's face. "And Pemberley?"

Darcy was silent, thinking how to respond. "I understand what you are asking, sir. All my adult life I have placed Pemberley's needs before my own." He paused. "I believe I have been a worthy Master of Pemberley, that I have carried the Darcy name proudly. I searched long and hard for a woman of quality, someone strong and brave, intelligent and wise, empathetic and giving. All the characteristics the Mistress of Pemberley must have. I am not a fool, Uncle. Elizabeth has all this and so much more. I have fallen in love with a woman my equal, if not superior. Yet all of this is inconsequential compared to the fact that she loves me and I her. Her paramount value is in this truth."

Lord Matlock smiled then, a bright smile. "Your father would be very proud of you, Fitzwilliam, as would your mother. They loved each other, as you know. It is an emotion uncommon in our society. Both of them were better human beings because of it. I do approve of your Miss Bennet. You have my blessing, for what it is worth," he ended wryly.

Lord and Lady Matlock attended the wedding, as did their two sons. Lady Catherine was not invited, having ignored Darcy's second attempt at reconciliation. He would make no further gestures. Miss de Bourgh was invited and sent a gift along with her heartfelt blessings. Unfortunately she could not attend without her mother. Darcy's happiness was so profound that he spared little energy in grief over his aunt. As Lizzy had said, it would eventually resolve itself or it would not. They were one now, and that was all that truly mattered to either of them.

CHAPTER ELEVEN

A Surprise for Poor Samuel

Elizabeth? Wake up, my love." Darcy sat next to his sleeping wife, gently smoothing her hair as he whispered softly into her ear. "I cannot leave without a farewell." He kissed behind her ear tenderly. "Lizzy? Open your eyes."

"William?" she mumbled sleepily.

"Indeed," he laughed softly, "who else would it be?"

She yawned and stretched, opening her eyes briefly before nestling deeper into the mattress. "Come back to bed," she murmured. "I am cold."

Darcy smiled and tucked the thick covers about her. "I must go, love. Mr. Keith is waiting for me. You can return to your slumber, but I had to tell you I love you before I left." He kissed her forehead and cheek and then her lips. It was a mistake… her arms somehow freed themselves from the snugly placed covers and twined about his neck as she drowsily pulled him into her embrace, deepening the tiny kiss he meant to bestow.

He sighed and happily gave in to her demands for a moment. With regret he untangled her hands from his hair, kissing each palm. She was dazedly looking at him, still more asleep than awake. "Why are you dressed? What time is it?" She started to rise, but he restrained her.

"Remember, dearest? I need to inspect the fisheries today. I shall return for dinner, I promise." Her hands were clasped in his and he kissed her fingers. "I shall pine for you terribly and will be thinking of you incessantly." He chuckled mildly. "So much so that I am not sure how effectual I will actually be! It shall be a test of my fortitude."

She was fully awake now. Aware that it was absolutely ludicrous but unable to curb her emotions, she felt tears burn her eyes and her chin beginning to quiver. In a small voice she said, "I shall be desolate without you, Fitzwilliam. Please be careful and return quickly!"

Oh, the power she had over his faculties! Why was it that every time she spoke his full name he melted? With a groan he kissed her energetically, wrapping his arms about her as best he could with blankets and a comforter in the way. He stroked her back and readjusted his body so he was lying next to her, some tiny part of his foolish brain conjecturing that as he was clothed and she under the covers, his control could be maintained. *Only a few kisses*, he told himself, *to placate me during my separation from her.*

It was some twenty minutes later before he arose from the bed. The few kisses had evolved into far greater diversions. Lizzy was akin to a slippery eel in her ability to extricate herself from swaddled covers. Darcy could not relate how it occurred, but in no time at all, she was on top of the comforter, limbs entwined with his. Thoughts of timetables, schedules, and prior commitments fled under the forces rushing through his body. Even after two weeks of marriage and the passion that had inundated his existence, he was still amazed at how rapidly he responded to her touch; nay, even her presence was enough! His arousal was immediate and marked, his need for her vehement.

Somehow his coat was discarded haphazardly, but the remainder of his clothing stayed, neither of them wishing for the delay. One would assume they had not made love in months instead of just the previous night, their hunger raging and consuming them as it did. Their lovemaking was frenzied but no less rhapsodic.

As he buttoned his breeches and straightened his waistcoat, smiling at his divine wife, his love was too profound to experience any regret. He was behind schedule now, but the memory of her and the tingling sensations coursing through his veins vastly outweighed any time concerns.

He finished adjusting his rumpled clothing as she arose from the bed, standing before him in all her glory. She buttoned his jacket and tamed his mussed hair with her fingers. "There," she said, "you are presentable. And tremendously handsome, I daresay." She smiled and kissed him lingeringly.

"I love you, Mrs. Darcy, and shall miss you." His hands traveled over her body and he nuzzled her neck, planting one last kiss on her earlobe before he pulled away. As if fearful of losing his restraint yet again, he turned abruptly and strode rapidly to the door, pausing for one last look and a devastating smile as he closed the door behind him.

Lizzy sighed, eyeing the bed but knew she would not be able to return to sleep. Besides, she did have plans for herself today. She retrieved her nightgown from the floor wondering, not for the first time, why she even bothered donning one each night. Her husband did delight in removing it, she mused with a becoming blush, which was an incentive to maintain the habit.

Their sitting room felt emptier without Darcy, and Lizzy did not like dining alone, so she ate quickly. This was the first day in over two weeks that they would be apart for more than an hour or two. Even when Darcy had needed to attend to business, he had been brief or had worked while she sat nearby. The realities of life at Pemberley were gradually invading their idyllic solitude. Darcy had postponed today's outing for several days, but he could no longer ignore his responsibilities. It was sad; however, Lizzy was determined not to mope about but instead to benefit from the time alone.

First, she met with Mrs. Reynolds in her parlor. Over the past week, they had conversed on a number of occasions, primarily about the Christmas festivities. Lizzy was gradually growing more comfortable with the housekeeper and had began inquiring about other topics relating to the manor's management and tasks that she should eventually assume.

Mrs. Reynolds was all that Darcy had declared she was: benevolent, amicable, patient, supportive, and incredibly elated to have Lizzy as mistress.

Mr. Keith had graciously penned a detailed report of all the Pemberley tenants and their families. Lizzy's initial task with Mrs. Reynolds was to discuss the holiday gift boxes for the tenants. This was an old tradition that had been maintained over the years but without the personal touch of a Mistress. Lizzy decided this was a perfect commencement of her duties and a splendid way to acquaint herself with the folks who devoted their service to Pemberley.

She hoped that Georgiana would wish to accompany her. Darcy had never insisted on Georgiana undertaking the tasks properly expected of the Mistress of Pemberley since this was not her role and she was too young. However, he did believe it imperative that she learn what being the mistress of an estate entailed since she would someday marry. He and Lizzy had conferred and decided that Lizzy joining the family afforded an ideal opportunity for them to be educated together.

Using a map of the estate and her knowledge of the surrounding area, Mrs. Reynolds figured it would take two to three days to deliver the packages, allowing time to socialize. A rough agenda was laid for the days prior to Christmas. The gifts were to be individualized based on each family's needs. That was where Mr. Keith's and Darcy's intimate knowledge proved to be invaluable. Darcy had been proud of Lizzy when she broached the subject of tackling this chore. He had willingly put aside his own business, and they had sat for more than two hours talking about the tenants while Lizzy jotted down the information. Mrs. Reynolds imparted personal tidbits about the children and wives. Armed with this data, Lizzy had dictated meticulous lists of purchases to be made, victuals to be prepared, and game to be dressed for each family.

Next, they finalized the menus for Christmas Eve and Day. Mrs. Langton managed the kitchens with an iron fist and required little in the way of instruction. Lizzy had requested the inclusion of some of her personal favorite dishes and asked to be shown the daily menu for her approval, yet other than that, no changes needed to be made. As far as the holiday preparations were concerned, Mrs. Langton was abundantly capable, having served the Darcy family for more than twenty years. Although Lizzy had heard rumors of Mrs. Langton's grousing about the extra work, Mrs. Reynolds assured her that the cook was never happier than when overtaxed and that her belligerence was a well-honed personality trait used to perfection in her superior management of the kitchen staff.

"I am confident that Mrs. Langton will provide adequately for all our guests," Lizzy said, marking a check on her list, "and that she will command the huntsmen aptly. Now, I see that the groundsmen have been trekking into the woods for holly, ivy, and mistletoe. I want to drape the entire manor if possible!"

"I have instructed them, Mistress. I have purchased ribbon to tie the boughs and lace through the vines. I inventoried the stock of candles and ordered several dozen additional. Mr. Taylor will be directing the footmen to unpack the decorations in storage, and the maids will oversee any cleaning or repairs. This will be finished by the end of the week. With your permission, Mrs. Darcy, I would request that we refrain from the final trimming until Miss Georgiana arrives."

"Absolutely, Mrs. Reynolds." Lizzy smiled. "It shall be wonderful to have

Miss Darcy home. Our acquaintance was unfortunately fleeting before the wedding, therefore not conducive to forming a sisterly relationship, as I desire ours to be. Also, Mr. Darcy misses her terribly."

Mrs. Reynolds continued, crossing items off her own list as she went, "The guest chambers are being prepared. Col. Fitzwilliam will most likely stay here rather than at the Matlock Estate. I have chosen the largest of our couple's suites in the north wing for the Lathrops, if this meets with your approval, Mrs. Darcy."

"I will trust your judgment in this matter, Mrs. Reynolds, since the guest rooms are unfamiliar to me yet."

"Thank you, Mistress. I doubt if Lord and Lady Matlock will tarry over night; however, I have taken the liberty of preparing a suite for them as well. The weather can be unpredictable this time of year."

"Excellent." Lizzy examined her paper with a small frown. "Well, all appears to be in order. The Yule log has been cut and dressed, the pianoforte tuned, and menus arranged. The house is impeccably clean as always, and games and activities have been concocted and equipped for..." She sighed and shyly met Mrs. Reynolds kind eyes. "Mrs. Reynolds, I must confess to you how tremendously I appreciate your collaboration with me. You have been patient and thoughtful and exceedingly supportive. I am well aware that you did not need my input on any of the planning; nonetheless, you have embraced my interference and have taught me so much. I cannot thank you enough."

Mrs. Reynolds blushed faintly. "Mrs. Darcy, may I speak freely?" Lizzy nodded. "The Darcys are dear to me, as is Pemberley. I flatter myself that I know Mr. Darcy well, or at least as well as a servant can ever know one's master. His joy since his marriage to you, Mrs. Darcy, is beyond anything I have ever witnessed from him. That fact alone would induce me to welcome you and, frankly, endure any hardship on my part in the process.

"However, this has not been the case. If I may be so bold, I sincerely like you. You are intelligent, lively, honorable, and most importantly, you love Mr. Darcy and Pemberley. I am discovering that these discussions and educational opportunities with you are a source of pleasure to me. Therefore, the thanks are entirely mine, Mistress."

Lizzy was overcome and speechless, eyes glazed with tears. Mrs. Reynolds lightly patted her hands then rose, resuming her brisk, efficient manner. "Is there anything else, Mrs. Darcy?"

"No, I believe we have covered the list for now."

"Very well. Luncheon shall be served early, as you requested, and Phillips will be awaiting you in the foyer when you are ready."

"Thank you, Mrs. Reynolds." With a curtsey, she left. Lizzy remained seated for a while, thinking. Her mind turned to William, wondering where he was at that moment, what he was doing. She shook her head. *Do not start down that path!* A knock at the door interrupted her reverie. "Enter."

A maid approached and handed her a letter. "This just arrived, Mrs. Darcy."

"Thank you. Your name is Hannah, is it not? I am slowly learning."

"There are many of us, Mrs. Darcy. I still cannot remember the names of all the footmen." She giggled and then flushed, realizing belatedly that she was being too forward.

Lizzy, however, laughed the tinkling laugh they had all grown accustomed to hearing in the usually quiet house. "Thank you, Hannah. That comforts me."

The letter was in actuality an invitation addressed to Mr. and Mrs. Darcy of Pemberley from Sir John Cole of Melcourt Hall. There was to be a Twelfth Night Masquerade Ball. Lizzy's heart fluttered in excitement mixed with no slight amount of trepidation at the news. She had never attended anything so formal in her life, and it would be the first social outing with her husband. She shrugged. Sooner or later she had to meet the families of Derbyshire and afterwards the *ton* of London. A ball was as fine a place as any to begin!

For the afternoon, Lizzy had decided to drive to Matlock for some shopping. Phillips and another footman named Georges attended her. The town of Matlock was larger than Lambton and a mere ten miles further south. Marguerite, who had resided there for the past eight years, had supplied her mistress with a list of the finest shops the town had to offer.

She spent several lovely hours acquiring gifts for her parents, sisters, Charlotte, Georgiana and, of course, William. The funds that Darcy had allotted her were more than adequate for all she wished to purchase. So much so, in fact, that she could never envision spending them all. She even picked up a few odds and ends for the tenants and the servants, and still had a surplus.

Once she was home, dressing for dinner, her aching heart conquered her. Darcy had not yet returned and the loneliness of the long day without his smiles, kisses, tender touch, and lush, masculine voice caught up to her. She wore a new gown, fashionable and of a highly daring style. She chose the sapphires and Marguerite dressed her hair strikingly, permitting several curls to fall over one shoulder.

The sun was setting, casting the gardens into deeper gloom, before Lizzy heard her husband's unmistakable resonant baritone and firm tread in the hall. Her heart skipped a beat and every ounce of willpower was called forth to forestall her rushing from the room and into his arms. Instead, she sedately strolled out of the parlor where she was lurking to see him hand his coat to a footman and speak with Mr. Keith. He was dusty and windblown with a dark shadow of beard. She smiled brightly, content merely to gaze at him until he finally noticed her in his peripheral vision.

He halted mid-sentence and broke into a beaming grin as his eyes roved over her entire form. The footman disappeared, as they always seemed capable of doing, and Mr. Keith murmured something about discussing these matters on the morrow as he quit the area. Darcy was unaware of it all, paralyzed by the heavenly vision of his wife.

"Mr. Darcy, welcome home."

"Thank you, Mrs. Darcy, I am happy to be home." He kissed the hand she offered, slowly and with a decidedly improper caress. He took a step closer to her, peering intently into her eyes. "Elizabeth," he whispered, "I have missed you and could easily, without the slightest thought to propriety, ravish you this very second."

Lizzy laughed and tossed her head saucily. "Well then, Mr. Darcy, it is fortunate that I have been far too busy to miss you at all, so my emotions are in check!"

"Not even the tiniest bit, my love?" He teased the tip of his tongue over one palm.

"Perhaps a time or two, husband. So many duties the Mistress of Pemberley must attend to, you see." Her eyes twinkled but her voice was more than a little shaky.

He smiled and again raked his eyes seductively over her body. "You were not thinking of me when you selected this specific gown, my dearest wife?"

"Do you like it? It is new!" she asked, suddenly sounding more like a giggly teenager as she posed and twirled around, dropping a flirtatious curtsey.

Darcy laughed gaily. "I like it enormously, Mrs. Darcy. I especially admire that there are only these three buttons and one sash keeping it on your body."

"Shocking, Mr. Darcy! I pray Samuel has drawn a cool bath for you as your temperature appears to be elevated. Shall I accompany you to your dressing room, husband?"

"I am considering the vast number of empty chambers between here and my dressing room, so it would undoubtedly be prudent for you to wait for me in the parlor." His kiss brushed her cheek briefly but nonetheless sent a thrill through Lizzy's veins. "I shall not be long, my love."

Lizzy watched him until he climbed the distant stairs, a naughty gleam that he did not detect sparkling in her fine eyes.

Darcy had finished washing and shaving, a damp towel draped about his shoulders. Samuel was inside the closet retrieving the garments Mr. Darcy had indicated he wished to wear, while Darcy pulled on his trousers.

"Enchanting view, Mr. Darcy. Quite rejuvenating!"

Darcy spun about, his expression of laughable fright and shock rapidly replaced with an expansive smirk. Lizzy had quietly opened the well-oiled door and was only a couple of feet behind her husband, leaning audaciously against the wall. Before either of them could utter a word, poor Samuel exited the closet and, upon spying Elizabeth, he yelped, dropped the clothes onto the floor, blanched, and then blushed scarlet.

Lizzy averted her face, biting her lip to avoid bursting into gales of mirth. Darcy barely glanced at his valet, eyes fixed on his wife. "You may retire, Samuel. Thank you, I no longer require your services."

Samuel stammered something inaudible and dashed out of the room. Lizzy could contain herself no longer and laughed helplessly. Darcy pinned her to the wall with his arms locked on either side of her waist. "You deserve to be disciplined severely for such behavior, wife. What shall your punishment be?"

"I do not figure that my behavior warrants a reprimand, Mr. Darcy! You started this little game, remember, and I did give you fair warning. If you failed to alert your valet, the fault is entirely yours." She affected a pout and primly downcast her gaze. "However, if you truly feel that punishment is necessary, I shall be an obedient wife. Your earlier threat of ravishment sounded particularly distasteful. I am sure my lesson would be learned by such chastisement."

She coyly fluttered her lashes and ran one hand the length of his torso, shoulder to hip. Darcy leaned slowly and enticingly toward her as if to plant a kiss, but then paused mere inches from her upturned lips. "I rather imagine withholding ravishment would be a greater torture, my love. Yes, now that I reflect on the issue, this shall be your penalty." And with this pronouncement, Darcy withdrew a pace, smiling at his wife's expression of surprise and thwarted desire.

Darcy's satisfaction at beating his wife at her own game was short lived, however. When it came to teasing, Darcy might have been learning quickly, but

Lizzy was the master. She shrugged her shoulders and studied her fingernails with deep intensity, declaring unconcernedly, "As you wish, husband. I accept my sentence and will now leave you so I may ruminate on my faults and failings. I shall meet you in the dining room properly demure and sober."

As she concluded her contrived and transparently spurious little speech, she kissed Darcy primly on the cheek yet managed to *accidentally* brush her breasts against his bare chest and her hand over his nether regions as she turned toward the door.

She had not taken a single step before her wrist was captured in a vise-like grip and she was spun around and again pinned to the wall, this time by her husband's entire body. Although Lizzy had begun this little game, she was nonetheless taken aback by the lustful response of her husband. Before she could utter one sound, he had claimed her mouth in an ardent kiss, lifted her skirts to her waist, and begun to attack her undergarments with confidence.

Thus far they had always made love lying down in some manner. The positions had varied somewhat, leaving Lizzy constantly amazed at the diverse ways the human body could be manipulated. So naturally she assumed Darcy would take her into the bedchamber or at least fall to the floor here in his dressing room, which frankly is what she had fantasized. Never would she have entertained the concept of him pinning her to the wall and loving her beautifully and intensely right there.

Darcy sank to his knees with Lizzy entwined, time necessary to regain use of weakened muscles. Lizzy slowly planted kisses on his shoulder and neck, moving to his face. He cupped her in trembling hands, tenderly stroking her cheeks with his thumbs. "Precious love," he whispered, "amazing, beautiful, giving."

She pulled back and smiled at him, his eyes tear filled. She kissed each of his crystal blue eyes and then his lips, murmuring, "Was this another recommendation from those books you forbid me to view?" as she playfully nibbled his lower lip.

He chuckled softly, flushing lightly. "Yes, I confess it is. Your surprise entrance afforded the perfect opportunity. Nonetheless, I am sorry if I startled you. Elizabeth, my heart, you drive me mad and all reason escapes me!"

Lizzy laughed. "Do you hear me complaining, beloved?"

Needless to say, Darcy did not finish dressing in a timely manner and dinner was kept waiting. Luckily, the kitchen staff was becoming accustomed to these delays so the fine cuisine was served without noticeable deficiency when the Darcys, blushing and smiling and giddy, did arrive.

Later, as every night thus far since coming home to Pemberley, they relaxed in their sitting room. Darcy sat at his desk attending to business correspondence, and Lizzy had the piles of purchased gifts from her excursion to town scattered over the floor as she wrapped them for delivery.

"William," she said suddenly, "I forgot to tell you of the invitation we received from Sir Cole. He is hosting a Twelfth Night Ball, a masquerade ball."

Darcy nodded, not looking up from the document he was examining. "Yes, they hold one every year. It has become a standard Derbyshire event. My parents considered it the highlight of the season."

"Do you always attend?"

"I have a few times, maybe three or four. You know I do not much care for dances."

"Oh. Well, if you do not wish to attend, I understand." Lizzy could not control the tone of disappointment creeping into her voice.

"Elizabeth, look at me. My reasons for disdaining these sorts of events in the past are no longer relevant. I will assuredly never be one who shines above others at an assembly, nor will I ever pretend to adore conversation with persons unknown to me. On the other hand, I am now married, most happily I must add, so I am no longer the prime bull presented for inspection. I will be the proudest man in all of England to escort you, dearest wife, to any and all social engagements to which we are invited. Who knows, I might even surprise you and be witty and charming and a veritable dancing aficionado."

Lizzy glowed and leapt into her husband's arms, kissing enthusiastically all over his face. "Thank you, William! I promise I will make you proud and we will have a marvelous time!"

"I have no doubt whatsoever, my heart. Of course, you realize you will need to acquire a ball gown," he remarked with a small grin. "I daresay this is not an onerous task?"

"I have several lovely gowns, William, thanks to your generosity."

"No, beloved, for a ball such as this you will require something special. Madame du Loire will be able to attire you properly, and I shall reap the benefit by arriving with the most stunningly beautiful woman in the entire known universe on my arm. She, in turn, will save all the best dances for me and I shall be the envy of all the men at the ball. You see how selfish I am?"

"No more than I, dearest, for I shall be attended by the prime bull of Derbyshire! How fortunate am I?"

T HE DARCYS APPROACHED THE day of Georgiana's return home with
mixed emotions.

Darcy adored his sister and had missed her enormously. Far
too often in the course of his adult life, business and social requirements had
separated him from her. One of the fortunate consequences of settling into
marriage had been the prospect of dwelling exclusively at Pemberley, with only
occasional forays to Town necessary. All too soon Georgiana would be a woman
and leaving him for another man. He lamented the very thought and did not
wish to squander the time he had remaining as her guardian.

Lizzy was fond of Georgiana even though they had spent little time
together. She pined for her own sisters, surprising herself, in truth, at how
oppressive the quiet and solitude of Pemberley often felt when she had passed
many an hour wishing for such quiet and solitude at Longbourn. The relationship she and Georgiana had forged thus far promised to be a sisterly one, and
Lizzy recognized that this was a crucial necessity for both of them.

Nonetheless, neither Elizabeth nor Darcy relished having their tranquil
honeymoon shattered. The three weeks since their wedding had been
magnificent. The freedom to express their love in any way they desired,
anywhere they desired, was liberating. Darcy, especially, felt as if a locked and
guarded chamber had been opened in his soul. His entire life he had regulated

his emotions, rigidly controlled his actions, suppressed his own desires, and dwelt in a world where honor and dignity and appearances were prized over compassion and happiness and passion. In three short weeks, that man had all but perished and Darcy's spirit had danced at the wake.

His joy was not exclusively a product of his love for Elizabeth and the marvelous expression of that love, but also from the result of the peace that came from loosened strictures to his character. Where he once feared impropriety or performing in any way considered imprudent or sensational, he now dreaded reestablishing those traits. When he fully dwelt on his life thus far, he admitted honestly that careful adherence to society's rules had brought him mostly grief. Amazingly, breaking from that mold, laughing and smiling openly, and bending the rules on occasion had not caused Pemberley or the world to come crashing down!

Now they would be surrounded by guests, mostly family to be sure, and the test would be whether Darcy reverted to his somber, serious self, or allowed joyfulness to bubble forth. One look at his lovely wife's face and he did not doubt the answer.

They made love leisurely, cuddling afterwards as they conversed and tenderly caressed until passion ignited yet again. Rising late, they tarried in their sitting room until after noon, cognizant that, for the next two weeks, they would be expected to arise earlier than they had so far done and to break fast with their guests. Darcy caught up on correspondence and several business transactions while Lizzy wrote letters. Her gifts had already been sent, and the tenants' gift boxes were prepared and waiting for distribution over the next several days. After lunch Darcy rode off on Parsifal to visit a couple of the farms.

The final Christmas details and needs were completed. Holly and ivy vines trailed along the terrace railings and a sizeable pile of each remained to decorate the inside banisters. The maids had gleefully pounced on the occasion to design elaborate mistletoe ornaments to dangle throughout the manor. The Yule log was dressed, Mrs. Langton had the mealtime essentials well in hand, and the guest chambers were cleaned and stocked. Pemberley and its new Mistress were ready!

It was late afternoon when a footman announced that the Matlock carriage was approaching, and Darcy and Lizzy prepared to greet their guests before the main entrance.

Col. Fitzwilliam alighted first, reaching in for Georgiana, who jumped out with all the enthusiasm of youth and launched into her brother's waiting arms.

Darcy had never been able to contain his joy where it involved his dear sister. He twirled her about, laughing gleefully, before setting her on her feet and kissing her cheek. "I missed you, Georgie! Welcome home."

"William! It is good to be home," Georgiana replied breathlessly and then turned rapidly from her grinning brother to her new sister, standing cheerily at his side. "Elizabeth! It is wonderful to see you again!"

The two young women embraced each other. "Welcome home, Georgiana."

Georgiana gestured at the bright flambeaux along the front drive and entrance that illuminated the trailing boughs of holly and ivy. "Pemberley is so beautiful! I do not remember it ever lovelier. What a sensational Christmas it will be!"

Darcy greeted his cousin heartily. "Darcy, old man, you are positively beaming! Married life surely agrees with you," Col. Fitzwilliam decreed.

"More than I could possibly verbalize, cousin. Someday you must give up your reckless bachelor ways and discover the joys of matrimony."

Richard shuddered. "Not too hasty, Darcy, not too hasty. Mrs. Darcy, if I may be so bold, you are radiant. Shocked I am, to tell the truth," he said, with a sly glance at Darcy. "Personally, I thought you would be weary of this old codger by now!"

Lizzy laughed as the Colonel bowed and kissed her hand. "Not yet, Colonel. Perhaps in a week or two."

Lord and Lady Matlock had approached the small group on the veranda and were smiling pleasantly. Darcy welcomed them formally to Pemberley, and they both greeted Lizzy with warmth.

"Please," Darcy said with a step toward the house and the offer of his arm to his aunt, "let us hasten to the parlor where it is warm and tea awaits."

Georgiana linked her arm through Lizzy's, smiling shyly. "My brother is glowing, Elizabeth, and so are you." She blushed. "I cannot convey in words how delighted I am for you both."

"Thank you, Georgiana. We are blest, especially now that our family is with us. I trust your trip here was not overly arduous?"

"Not in the least, aside from being anxious to arrive. Cousin Richard is thoroughly entertaining. His stories nearly induce me to wish I were male so I could join the military."

Lady Matlock laughed her throaty laugh, "Richard exaggerates, my dear Georgiana. I am certain you would discover that the realities are contrary to his stories. Nonetheless, his wit does pass the time."

Col. Fitzwilliam raised one brow and feigned shock, "Exaggerate? I?" while Lord Matlock chuckled.

Tea was served in the main parlor, to the particular relief of the fatigued travelers. The ladies sat on settees by the table while the gentlemen conversed in a knot by the fire.

"Lady Matlock, William and I have readied your suite if you and Lord Matlock desire to abide for the night."

"Thank you, my dear; however, I believe we will recommence our journey after dinner, if you do not object. It is not much further, and I am afraid our older bones prefer the comforts of home." She smiled and lightly touched Lizzy's hand, "I would be honored if you would address me as Madeline. We are family now, Elizabeth."

Lizzy blushed, "I am touched, Madeline. Thank you. William and I are pleased you and Lord Matlock will be sharing Christmas with us. I admit I am rather fond of Christmases with copious masses of friends and family underfoot."

"Georgiana informs me that your uncle and aunt will be celebrating here as well?"

"That is correct. They will arrive three days hence. Also, a gentleman friend of William's from Leicester, a Mr. Lathrop and his wife, are expected the same day. The poor man lost his father this past year, and my husband extended an invitation as a way of cheering him. Plus, I do not think they have visited together for well over a year."

"I do believe I met Mr. Lathrop a time or two, several years ago. He was at Cambridge with William, correct?"

"Yes. They met there."

"Ah, yes, I do recall. He sojourned at Darcy House one summer while the two men were off term. Agreeable young man, I seem to remember, serious and reserved yet generous and polite." Lady Matlock laughed softly. "Quite like William, in point of fact! I contemplated at the time whether the two of them ever actually conversed with each other, both being so taciturn." She glanced pointedly toward the man in question, who was smiling, effulgent, and laughed loudly at some anecdote of his cousin's. "How changed he is now. Perhaps Mr. Lathrop has found the same fount of joy in his marriage as my nephew has."

Lizzy blushed prettily. Darcy sensed the scrutiny upon him and turned his radiant face, eyes immediately alighting on Elizabeth. For a moment only their gazes locked, yet that moment spoke volumes of the love and devotion the two shared and it was nakedly visible to all in the room.

Lady Matlock smiled and Georgiana positively glowed.

Dinner was a lively affair. Even the generally shy Georgiana was gregarious. Darcy said little, preferring to observe his family and to bask in the joy of the occasion. It had been more years than he cared to recollect since Pemberley had hosted such a gay party, and it would be even more festive with the arrivals of the Gardiners and the Lathrops.

Richard and his parents resumed their journey to Rivallain shortly after dinner. The Colonel planned to return in two days and would stay at Pemberley for a week during the holiday before he was expected to return to his regiment in London. This left Georgiana alone with Lizzy and Darcy, a pleasing prospect as they all desired to enjoy this brief episode of intimate family time.

For the first evening since Elizabeth had arrived at Pemberley, they lounged in the parlor. Georgiana eagerly seated herself at her new pianoforte and graced her brother and his wife with her marvelous playing. Lizzy accompanied Georgiana by raising her voice in song for three tunes while turning the pages. She had a lovely voice, a sweet lilting alto. Darcy sipped his brandy and contentedly smiled at his wife and sister, feeling a profound sensation of fulfillment wash through him.

Georgiana's yawns signified time for retiring. Together they walked along the lengthy corridor to her second-floor chambers where Darcy kissed his sister tenderly. "Sleep well, Georgie."

Lizzy accompanied Georgiana into her room, telling Darcy she would be up shortly. However, *shortly* ended up being nearly two hours as the two young women gratified a mutual craving for the type of conversation that only females appreciate. Lizzy entered their bedchamber with a big smile on her face, missing her husband yet oddly serene in the happiness and completeness that had permeated her life and soul. Darcy had fallen asleep propped up on several pillows, hand with book atop lax where it had fallen by his leg.

He is so beautiful, she thought, standing beside him and tenderly caressing his hair. She put the forgotten book on the bed stand and crawled cautiously under the covers. He was covered to his waist but unclothed and, with a start and pang of guilt, she felt the cool skin of his shoulders. She gently touched his cheek and said his name. He sighed but did not waken initially, so she was forced to speak louder and tug on the pillows and his body to facilitate repositioning him supine and under the blankets. Darcy was a tall man; broad shouldered with not an ounce of unnecessary fat and heavily muscled. Additionally, she had discovered that her husband slept deeply, practically comatose in his slumber. Luckily for Lizzy, he stirred groggily but enough for her to communicate his need to lie down, which he did, naturally gathering her into his arms and nestling close. For the first time it was Lizzy's warmth seeping into her husband's body and in short order they were soundly asleep.

❧

The next two days passed in a whirlwind of activity, affording the lovers scant time together, and they were both exhausted by nighttime. Darcy was on horseback from sunrise to after sunset, traveling from north to south over Pemberley lands and attending to numerous affairs that had been neglected. For this separation Lizzy could honestly declare she was too busy to miss her husband… not greatly anyway.

The entire first morning after Georgiana's return was spent abetting and directing the final garnishing of the house. There was such a profusion of greenery scattered about the manor that it resembled a forest that had sprouted over night. Small candles were tactically nestled amongst the branches to be lit at night, representing the twinkling stars of the heavens. The dozens of mistletoe ornaments that the maids had so delightfully created were strategically suspended over doorways and alcoves. The Darcy kissing bough, a century old heirloom constructed of silver and finely polished china painted with Christmas scenes, had been meticulously cleaned and restored to pristine condition with fresh, aromatic greenery and ribbons hanging from the bottom. It was hung reverently in its traditional place over the fork of the grand staircase.

Another heirloom of the Darcy family had taken Elizabeth's breath away. It was a nearly life-sized crèche carved from wood and intricately detailed. The set was complete, including the traditional stable animals and the Wise Men. As per custom, the crèche was situated in one corner of the dining room. The entire chamber had been elaborately decorated with a fine gold tablecloth, ivy, autumn leaves, Christmas candles, and more. Tableware of fine Chinese porcelain was brought forth, five different patterns with a holiday motif. These, along with freshly polished utensils and sparkling crystal glasses, were a crowning touch to the already dazzling room.

That afternoon and all the next day, Elizabeth and Georgiana visited the tenants and delivered the holiday gift boxes. Georgiana agreed to go, reluctantly. Her shyness was acute and Lizzy felt guilty for coercing her into it, but Darcy had insisted and Georgiana would not dream of disobeying her brother. Thankfully, by the end of the first day Georgiana was relaxed, touched by the gratitude from the families they met and amazed by the realities of the world around her, the world that made her life possible. She took a huge leap forward in maturity by viewing the lives of these simple folk closely for the first time.

For Lizzy it was as if she had returned to Hertfordshire. These unpretentious, pragmatic, and earthy people were not far removed from the society she had grown up in. She had studied the information on each family and greeted them as old friends. It would not be the slightest understatement to declare that, by the end of her visits, Elizabeth Darcy was almost universally adored throughout Pemberley, and the news of her kindness, generosity, humor, and genuine solicitude had spread like wildfire throughout all of Derbyshire.

December the twenty-third saw the arrival of the Gardiners, the Lathrops, and Col. Fitzwilliam, all within a few hours of each other.

Richard arrived early in the morning and he and Darcy promptly disappeared for a ride and some shooting, a favorite pastime that Darcy had not indulged in since his marriage. By luncheon they were home, the kitchen newly supplied with several pheasants, a turkey, and two grouse that were not needed but accepted graciously. After lunch Darcy arose purposefully and, implacably grasping his wife's hand and placing it in the crook of his arm, announced bluntly that he had "private estate business to discuss with his wife."

Darcy strode unwaveringly toward the staircase leading to their apartments. Lizzy smiled and teasingly proclaimed, "Estate business, Mr. Darcy? Should we not be en route to your study?"

Darcy paused and studied his wife seriously. "I was envisioning our discussion transpiring in our bedchamber, Mrs. Darcy; however, if you prefer my study for the resolution of our estate affairs, I am amenable to oblige your desires." He grinned.

Lizzy considered, for several minutes actually, and then tossed her head flippantly and propelled her husband toward the stairs. "I shall concede to your inclination at this time. The study shall remain undisturbed, for the present."

"Is that a promise or an allusion that there shall be an occasion where my study *may* be disturbed, my love?"

"You do spend large quantities of time there working so diligently, slavishly attending to odious tasks, and are thus in need of relief and diversion. As your wife, Mr. Darcy, it is my solemn duty to ease your suffering in any manner feasible, even if said remedy is impetuous or unsought."

They had reached the second-floor staircase, when Darcy halted abruptly and pulled his wife into his arms, kissing her ardently. "Elizabeth!" he growled, "no further teasing. I am desperate for you. Two days without loving you, without giving you pleasure, without your warmth surrounding me. Oh God, I must have you now, my love! Please… come with me."

He grabbed her hand and stumbled through the first available door, thankfully an empty guest chamber. Darcy scarcely had the presence of mind to lock the door before he was gathering her into his arms. Lizzy, only marginally less aroused than he, withdrew a pace to peer about the unfamiliar room. She clutched his hand and hurriedly crossed to the sofa, commanding him to sit, which he speedily did.

They loved each other fully until spent utterly, bodies melting together and breathing heavily. They stared, imprisoned in the other's gaze for long moments as they embraced and caressed.

"Fitzwilliam Darcy, would that I could convey how miraculously exquisite you are when aroused and when we…" she closed her eyes and kissed him tenderly. "I do not have the words," she whispered. "My heart is bursting with love for you my husband… my darling… my lover and my soul."

He smiled, fingers caressing her lovely face. "My wife… my precious wife. Shall I chronicle how resplendent your face is in your rapture? You are luminous: your eyes shining with devotion and excitement, your lips swollen and ruddy from my kisses, a light sheen of perspiration gracing your perfect brow, your cheeks sanguine with desire. Always you are beautiful, my Lizzy, but never more so than when you give yourself to me intimately."

They kissed, tenderly and languidly, not wishing to part until finally Lizzy spoke softly, "William, my legs are numb."

He chuckled, taking his kisses to her throat and ear. "Then I shall carry you to our bed, dearest, where I intend to undress you gradually as you undress me, after which I intend to kiss and caress and nibble," accenting his proclamations with demonstrations, "every inch of you until you are aroused anew and begging me for the satisfaction only I can offer." He lifted her easily with his strong hands, readjusted his clothing and hers, checked the corridor, and then swept her into his powerful arms.

For over an hour they loved, Darcy fulfilling his promise and wholly gratifying his wife, and himself.

~❦~

The Gardiners arrived around three in the afternoon. Lizzy and Darcy, refreshed and glowing, welcomed them to Pemberley. Despite the difference in their ages, Darcy got on famously with Lizzy's uncle and was genuinely glad to see him. The Gardiners had become acquainted with the Colonel in London and at the wedding, and Richard's sunny disposition was such that Lizzy could not imagine anyone disliking him. After a brief respite in the main parlor, the gentlemen retired to the billiard room, Darcy with a lingering caress and kiss to Lizzy's hand.

Lizzy accompanied her aunt to the suite set aside for them; Georgiana left to practice carols on her pianoforte. Her aunt wasted no time in commenting on Lizzy's obvious felicity.

"Oh, Aunt Violet, I cannot express in mere words how happy I am! Marriage is vastly superior to anything I could have envisioned."

"Well, my dear, at least marriage to the right man is!" They both laughed. "How are you finding Pemberley? Overwhelming?"

"Yes, a little. William has been patient and attentive, escorting me everywhere, hardly leaving my side. Mrs. Reynolds, in truth all the staff, have been enormously supportive and kind. I do have so very much to learn, though."

"Is Mr. Darcy pressuring you in any way?"

"Oh no! Quite the opposite. He is immeasurably patient and actually seems nonchalant regarding the subject. He dotes on me profoundly. I fear I shall quickly become horribly spoilt if he does not desist."

Her aunt laughed. "I doubt this, Lizzy. It is not in your nature to be unappreciative or influenced by luxury. Embrace his love and allow him to express it. I believe it is good for both of you. Mr. Darcy is altogether more buoyant and amiable, and you have a steadiness and peace hovering about you. It is refreshing to see you both so well matched. I reckon I need not ask how the physical aspect of your relationship fares," she continued in that forthright manner of hers, "as it is clearly written upon both your countenances and obvious in your demeanor."

Lizzy unwittingly assumed a dreamy expression. "Aunt, it is everything you told me and more. William is... amazing, wonderful, gentle, and passionate. I am so very blessed and satisfied." She blushed then but her aunt chuckled.

The Lathrops arrived around six. Mr. Lathrop was much shorter than Darcy, about the same height as Lizzy, stocky with a ruddy complexion, blond hair, and hazel eyes. His wife Amelia was the same height as her husband, full figured, plump, with green eyes, fiery red hair, and a profusion of freckles. Darcy greeted his friend with delight, ushering them inside the manor rapidly as snow was beginning to fall. Introductions were made in haste as all parties, especially the Lathrops who were fatigued from their extended journey, needed time to freshen up before dinner.

Lizzy counted this meal the first official feast of the season and had planned accordingly. There were ham, turkey, and pheasant, an abundant variety of vegetables and breads, pastries and pies and puddings. The large table was laden to capacity, the guests animated, and the atmosphere celebratory.

Lizzy sat Mrs. Lathrop to her right. It was apparent that the young woman was weary, yet still she was talkative and pleasant. Her lovely Scottish lilt was musical and husky. Conversation flowed and Lizzy was drawn to her outgoing, candid nature. She was quick witted, spirited, and occasionally verged on crudeness, but Lizzy liked her.

Per protocol, the ladies and gentlemen separated after dinner for a spell, Lizzy hosting her guests in her newly redecorated parlor. Between the irrepressible Amelia Lathrop, the unpretentious Violet Gardiner, and the clever Elizabeth Darcy, the naïve and shy Georgiana received a lesson in humor and scintillating repartee!

The party gathered together again in the music room where Col. Fitzwilliam was induced to accompany Georgiana with the cello. Darcy stood behind the seated Lizzy with his fingers lightly resting on her neck, unaware that Mr. Lathrop stood behind his wife in the identical inadvertent pose.

"Col. Fitzwilliam," Lizzy declared, "you play beautifully! I am tremendously impressed."

The Colonel bowed. "Thank you, Mrs. Darcy; you are very kind. I fear I am rather out of practice. The only opportunity I have to indulge my meager musical talent is here at Pemberley."

"My husband claims to be as poor a proficient on the violin, yet now I begin to speculate he may not have been totally forthright. How would you evaluate his skills, Colonel, as one artist assessing the other?"

Richard smugly appraised his faintly frowning cousin. "Ah, Mrs. Darcy, you place before me an interesting dilemma. If I judge his talents paltry, then we shall all take pity and not wish to embarrass him by prevailing upon him to play, thus depriving us entertainment, but he shall thank me and be in my debt. If, however, I laud his gift, extolling the unsurpassed skill he wields, then all shall beseech him to grace us with a tune to our delight but I shall likely be soundly pummeled once alone."

They all laughed. Mr. Lathrop chimed in with his soft voice, "I shall save you, Colonel. Darcy has not seen me for many months so would not likely horsewhip me."

"Do not be too confident, Lathrop," Darcy interrupted with a growl.

Undeterred, Mr. Lathrop continued with a grin, "Darcy often played at Cambridge and is quite good, although he abhors performing for crowds. Except for that one time, remember, Darcy?"

All eyes were on Darcy, brows raised in question. Richard stifled a chuckle and Mr. Lathrop was grinning broadly. "This is blackmail, old *friend*." Darcy said, trying not to smile.

Mr. Lathrop spread his hands innocently, "Simply a reminder of what is possible with the appropriate... influences."

"What manner of *influences*, Mr. Darcy, pray tell?" asked Mrs. Lathrop with a dimpled smile. All were staring at Darcy with varying degrees of humor with the exception of Georgiana who was frankly baffled.

Darcy cleared his throat. "Very well. Georgiana, play 'Largo' by Handel and then 'Minuet in G' by Bach." Darcy took a moment to tune his instrument, refusing to make eye contact with anyone, and then indicated to his sister that he was prepared.

Lizzy waited with bated breath, anxious to hear her husband, yet feeling tremendous remorse that her thoughtless teasing may have led him to humiliate himself. She acutely recalled her own chagrin at having been coerced by Lady Catherine to display her weak pianoforte abilities. Darcy, however, was reticent by nature and therefore more apt to embarrass.

Upon the first strains, she knew her fears were groundless. Darcy was no virtuoso but he was talented, far surpassing what she had imagined based on his assertions. He and his sister played beautifully together and the entire room was spellbound.

The applause was sincere and lengthy. Darcy bowed and then turned to his cousin. "Richard, one more with your assistance." Colonel Fitzwilliam took his place at the cello and smiled at the sheets placed before him by Darcy. Georgiana indicated she was ready and they launched into a sterling rendition of "Ode to Joy" by Beethoven, eminently apropos for the season.

Georgiana's skill and stamina were put to the test this night. The impromptu concert led to a swell of hidden talents brought to light as the guests' boldness and merriment increased. Lizzy and Mrs. Lathrop lifted their voices, as did Mr. Gardiner, who revealed a pleasing tenor. Mr. Lathrop chimed in on occasion with an unexpectedly deep bass belied by his soft speaking voice. The crown of the evening was Mrs. Lathrop raising her beautiful Scottish alto a cappella for three folk ballads: "I Once Loved a Lass," "Mary Queen of Scots' Lament," and "Blow the Candle Out."

❧

Lizzy sat at her vanity, Marguerite having been dismissed, absently brushing her hair as she smilingly recalled the evening's events. There seemed no doubt all had enjoyed themselves, and therefore the night could only be credited as a resounding success.

Lost in her reverie, Elizabeth did not notice her spouse's entrance until he gently took the brush from her hand and assumed the task. She smiled brightly at his reflection in the mirror. He loved to brush her hair, so his usurping was rapidly becoming a sort of ritual. Lizzy closed her eyes and sighed with contentment.

"It was a successful evening, wouldn't you agree, William?"

"Unquestionably. Our guests were well fed and marvelously entertained. I harbored no doubts whatsoever that the Mistress of Pemberley would triumph admirably."

"Thank you, love, however, I deem that a greater portion of the acclamation should go to Mrs. Reynolds and the rest of Pemberley's outstanding staff. And no small amount of praise to you, dear husband."

"I? Elizabeth, I did nothing but attend and partake."

"Nonsense. You were a gracious host and stunned us all by your performance on the violin." She looked at him then via the mirror with a playful lift of her lips. "You misrepresented the truth, dear husband. With only one brandy consumed you dazzled us with your skill. I was amazed and delighted, despite your previous assertions to the contrary!"

Darcy blushed and remained silent. Lizzy's smile broadened. "So tell me about the *one time* at Cambridge and what *influences* were necessary."

Darcy winced and then briskly put down the brush, patted his wife's shoulder, and seriously pronounced it was time for bed, becoming all 'Master of Pemberley' as Lizzy called it, as he strode solemnly from the room. Lizzy laughed gaily and chased him, cornering him by the fire. He valiantly attempted to dissuade her, but between tickling and pretend pouting, she finally forced him to capitulate and sink onto the edge of the bed.

Passing a hand over his face, he mumbled, "Perhaps when I am in my dotage, I will live this down." He glared at his grinning wife, "You really want to hear this?" She nodded and he groaned.

"During my years at University, there were only three times I… overly indulged, shall we say. The last was one month prior to the end of my stay. Some thirty of the lads threw a farewell party of sorts for me, Lathrop, and a few other gents who were finishing as well. Sometime toward the wee hours of the morning, when we were all far into our cups, someone, I do not know whom, which is just as well as I probably later would have murdered him, brilliantly decided that music was in order. Instruments of all sorts materialized from Lord knows where. I think I was the only one present at the time who had some musical talent, although it aided me naught in the state I was in."

He paused and groaned again, putting his face in his hands. "We thought we were marvelous and played for hours, so the story goes. Frankly, few of us remember any of it." He started laughing into his hands. "So stellar we credited our abilities that serenading the entire compound seemed a good plan, so we took our genius to the streets. The Dean dubbed us the 'Squealing Pig Orchestra' and immortalized us by creating a plaque with all our names on it. To this day it hangs in the Hall of Records and probably will long after I am dead."

Lizzy was laughing so hard she was breathless. Darcy grabbed her and tossed her onto the bed. "You owe me now, Mrs. Darcy, and you shall pay."

He tickled her mercilessly, head to toe, revealing sensitive zones she hadn't known existed. Arousal was guaranteed and abundantly welcomed. Darcy's arousal, in fact, and Lizzy's assistance in heightening his state were the incentives necessary to cease his tickling torture. The playful mood reigned as they nibbled with titillating bites, stimulated with romantic pinches and squeezes, and beguiled with amorous kisses.

Each day their lovemaking changed, evolving to new heights of delight as they learned more about their own bodies' responses and how to control their passions. Darcy, as the leader in most instances, had discovered a stamina and mastery he would not have thought achievable a month ago. On occasion their ardor overwhelmed them and they willingly and gleefully relented to their consuming need. However, usually they desired to prolong the act, reveling in the intoxication of a protracted interlude as their urges amplified leisurely. The resulting release was not necessarily superior, but their unions always intense and gratifying, and the steady nature of an unhurried pace led to a fulfillment as prolonged and languid as the journey itself.

Such it was tonight. Their afternoon assignation had so tremendously satisfied them that now there was none of the previous urgency. Their passion built gradually, their desire tender and nurturing, and their devotion, reverence, and faithfulness overruling their lust. Caressing ceaselessly and kissing temperately, they reached a release that was extended and joyous, flowing over them in soft, soothing waves, and leaving them trembling and awash in profound emotions of serenity and belonging and security.

They nestled close, gripped by their love and happiness. Lizzy kissed Darcy's chest just as she drifted into sleep and he tightened his arms about her, kissing her head and smiling with contentment. "I love you, Elizabeth," he murmured as sleep claimed him.

A S THE LONG YEARS unfolded, the Darcys would experience a multitude
of Christmases at Pemberley. Some would be intimate family affairs,
and on other occasions the manor would be overflowing. In time, their
children and the children of relatives would exponentially boost the festivities.
The traditional Darcy feast for the tenants would resume and occur annually
for decades. The Darcy heirlooms would proudly regain their historic locales,
along with the candles and greenery and ribbons eventually further augmented
by the Christmas tree. The vast majority of the holidays would be joyous gatherings with delightful memories, such as the year Lizzy's birth sac burst while
kissing her husband under the kissing bough on Christmas Eve and the year
their eldest daughter became betrothed during the Cole's Masque. Thankfully
the somber years were infrequent, the saddest being the first season after Mr.
Bennet passed, although it would also mark the only time all the Bennet sisters
managed to gather at the same time.

In truth, this particular Christmas would not necessarily be counted
preeminent, yet through the blissful years of their life together, Lizzy and Darcy
would agree that it held a very special place in their hearts. The reason was
simple: it was their first.

Christmas Eve dawned cold with ominous dark clouds threatening despite
having dropped fresh snow in the night. All the guests were slow to rise,

preferring to stay snuggled under warm blankets. As there were no particular plans for the morning hours, it mattered not. The Darcys, as host and hostess, strove to attend to their duties and so departed their chambers far earlier than they wished or had grown accustomed to. Darcy held Lizzy's hand in the crook of his arm as they walked.

Abruptly Darcy stopped, causing Lizzy to collide with him, but prior to her uttering a sound, he propelled her backwards into an empty side corridor.

"What…" she began but he shushed her with a hiss and a finger to her lips.

"The Lathrops," he whispered, pointing and cautiously sticking his head around the corner. Lizzy peered around his shoulder and stifled a laugh at the sight before her. At the bottom of the stairs, Mr. and Mrs. Lathrop had discovered one of the strategically positioned mistletoe balls and were dutifully obliging the custom.

"What shall we do now?" Lizzy asked her husband with a grin. At roughly the same moment, they looked upward and noted that they too were precisely under another mistletoe ornament.

"How many of these baubles did the maids fabricate, anyway?"

"I believe they were considering all the places the footmen frequent," Lizzy said with a chuckle.

"Whatever the motivation, it is a ritual with historic dictates that we would be severely remiss to not observe." Darcy stated firmly, capturing his wife's mouth equally as firmly in an ardent kiss.

It must have been the day for espying lovers beneath mistletoe, for Col. Fitzwilliam's chambers were down this very hallway and, with a chuckle, he ducked back into his room and busied himself until he deemed the corridor was clear.

The Pemberley occupants drifted into the breakfast room in spaced interludes throughout the morning, all with smiles on their faces and some with flushed cheeks and downcast eyes. Mrs. Langton and her fine staff had outdone themselves. The morning repast was stupendous with every imaginable type of breakfast cuisine. Mr. Gardiner had readily ascertained, as only a rabid angler can, that Mr. Lathrop shared his penchant for the avocation. Darcy assured them that the trout and other fish well stocked in the lake would happily acquiesce despite the half-frozen water. With obvious zeal, the two men quit the table, not to be seen until late in the afternoon.

The ladies decided a walk was in order. Darcy frowned, noting the persistent gloom and foreboding clouds as well as the slick pathways. He attempted to dissuade them, but Lizzy was insistent.

"We shall take care, Mr. Darcy, I promise. You need not vex yourself," Lizzy assured him.

"Georgiana," he turned to his sister, "I will trust you to keep to the safest paths closest to the house." He glanced at his wife's faintly scowling visage, pointedly ignoring her and declaring to the group in general in a tone which booked no argument, "Miss Darcy is most familiar with the walkways and knows which are best maintained and level. Please follow her lead."

Assuring that Georgiana and his wife were properly attired, Darcy pulled Lizzy aside. He buttoned her coat for her as he whispered, "Be careful, love, and return if it begins to snow or rain. Promise me."

"William, you are being silly," she began but he cut her off with a piercing look, eyes darkening somewhat, and that small crease of annoyance flashing between his brows.

"Elizabeth Darcy, do not argue with me. Stay with Georgiana."

"Yes, dear."

Once outside, Aunt Gardiner turned to her niece with a smile. "Mr. Darcy certainly is protective."

"Too much so at times, yet it is endearing; irritating but endearing!" They all laughed. Lizzy related their honeymoon luncheon experience and they laughed even harder.

Georgiana spoke then, in her quiet voice, "My brother has always hovered in this manner. I do believe nothing frightens him other than the thought of someone he loves being hurt. He still refuses to allow me to take my horse out without a groom shadowing me even though I have been riding since I was five!"

"I am afraid you are a more tolerant lass than I," said Mrs. Lathrop, "I confess to being a bit of a rebel. My parents turned gray over my antics. Do you ever defy him, Miss Darcy?"

Georgiana was genuinely shocked. "Never!"

Despite Darcy's concerns, the ladies had a lovely walk through the snow-dusted gardens. Georgiana proved to be an excellent tour guide, pointing out with amazing knowledge the plant and tree varieties. They lingered for a short rest at the water nymph fountain and then Georgiana unerringly ushered them through the hedge maze.

While they rambled, they babbled together serenely. Mrs. Gardiner and Georgiana happily conversed about Lambton and its environs as Violet remembered them from her youth, including her memories of Georgiana's parents. Lizzy and Mrs. Lathrop established a friendship that would persevere throughout their lives.

"How did you and Mr. Lathrop meet?"

Amelia smiled sweetly. "His family has interest in a sheep farm near Motherwell. My father is a baron of the region, and we were introduced when my father invited Mr. Lathrop to dine with us. It was love at first sight; however, my father required a bit of persuading! He was not too content with the idea of his daughter marrying a Sassenach." They laughed. "He eventually consented, yet I do not believe he shall be entirely resigned until I have presented him with a grandchild or two."

"How do you find Leicestershire, compared to Scotland?"

"Have you ever been to Scotland, Mrs. Darcy?"

"No, I have not been so fortunate."

"It is far colder there. Rainier and very green with heathers and mosses in abundance. I mourn the absence of certain trees and flowers that only grow there. Mostly, though I miss my family. I have two older brothers and three younger sisters. Our house was perpetually loud and raucous. I never imagined I would miss it, but I do."

"I understand how you feel. I have four sisters and spent much of my time escaping to the solitude and silence of the woods and meadows. Pemberley is beautiful and I love it here, yet it is imposing compared to Longbourn where I grew up, and very quiet. It is pleasant to have people in the house."

"Even if we are disrupting your honeymoon?" Mrs. Lathrop said with a gentle laugh.

Lizzy blushed prettily. "Merely a brief hiatus, I think. The honeymoon shall continue unabated for a long while, I trust."

"It is a delight to have made a 'love match,' is it not, Mrs. Darcy? I have learned that love often does not enter into the arrangements among the upper classes of England. This was a shock to me as these social considerations are not as important to the Scottish. Mr. Lathrop broke more than a few rules in marrying me, and his father did not approve."

"I am sorry, Mrs. Lathrop. Was it uncomfortable for you?"

"Initially. My husband, contrary to his gentle demeanor, has a strength and stubbornness of astounding proportions. He tenaciously stayed the course in his devotion to me, and his father eventually capitulated. We established a tenuous peace between us prior to his death."

"Mr. Lathrop sounds very like Mr. Darcy. Both are tenacious and stubborn. No small wonder they are such good friends."

They laughed. "They also appear to have similar taste in women, Mrs. Darcy, if I may be so bold as to declare that I think we are quite similar in our temperaments. Outspoken, independent, and with no lack of stubbornness myself, I sense this in you as well."

Lizzy smiled. "Along with a heavy dose of pride and misjudgment. Flaws that were almost our undoing, yet oddly aided us in coming together." Lizzy noted Mrs. Lathrop's quizzical expression and laughed. "It is a long and horrid tale. Perhaps later I shall tell you of it."

Speaking of her husband and touching on the subject of their convoluted and painful journey toward matrimony brought an ache to Lizzy's heart that could only be assuaged in his arms. As soon as she returned to the house, she sought him out. She had a vague idea where he would be, and a footman confirmed her suspicion. Upon entering the library her eyes immediately spied him alone and in his favorite chair by the far window, his back to her, and wholly lost in the pages before him. Her heart surged and skipped a beat as she rushed toward him silently on the thick carpet. She wrapped her arms around his shoulders from behind, burying her cold face into his neck. He gasped in surprise and shock from her chilled nose.

"Who is this?" he demanded in mock severity.

"Are there a plethora of women who attack you in the library, Mr. Darcy?" Lizzy began loosening the knots of his cravat, planting cool kisses along his neck.

"No. I must confess this is the first occasion ever." He closed his eyes and tilted his head to allow her freer access.

"How remiss of me," she mumbled, "I vowed to kiss you in every room of the manor. I am slipping hideously in my promises. What are you to think of me?"

He chuckled and grasped her hands, pulling her onto his lap. "I will happily aid you in fulfilling your vows, Mrs. Darcy. Lord knows there is probably a mistletoe ball in each room to lend credence to the venture if we are discovered." He rubbed her rosy cheeks and bussed her icy nose before seizing her mouth in a deep kiss.

He broke away reluctantly, snuggling her close to his body with her head resting on his shoulder. "You all returned safely, I presume?"

"Yes, my dear worrywart of a husband. No one fell or caught their death of cold." She laughed but he frowned and held her tighter.

"Nothing wrong with being cautious, Elizabeth."

"Of course not, love, but you must admit you fret excessively on occasion."

He was silent for a while and then spoke very softly, "I suppose I do worry overly. It is just that… I could not bear to have anything happen to you, Elizabeth, or Georgiana either. It is my responsibility to assure your safety and protection. I fear… failing in some way and losing you."

She gazed into his eyes and kissed him tenderly. "Forgive me, William. I shall aspire not to try your patience nor cause you anxiety. Nevertheless, you surely realize that you cannot control everything, my dearest. Accidents do happen."

He shuddered. "Please, love, let us not discuss this now. Hold me tight and kiss me instead."

She smiled. "With pleasure, Fitzwilliam, with pleasure."

"I love you so completely, Elizabeth," Darcy groaned, crushing her against him and kissing her ardently for a good long while.

"Ice skating, Elizabeth? You cannot be serious. Did you not satisfy your itch for outdoor activities earlier today? It is snowing outside!"

"Lightly snowing, William; the small pond is frozen solid, and I never tire of outdoor activities. Besides, I am not an accomplished ice skater, as I am informed you are, so the opportunities are ripe for you to clutch me tightly or perhaps even fall on top of me into a soft snowbank." She said the last with a mischievous twinkle and he could not stop himself from laughing.

"You are incorrigible, Mrs. Darcy." They stood in the hallway outside the parlor where their guests were lounging after lunch, except for Mr. Gardiner and Mr. Lathrop. The anglers had apparently lost all sense of time in their pursuit of the elusive fish, so a basket of food had been delivered to them.

She stepped closer to him, fingering the buttons of his coat. "You will arrange this for us, my love, will you not? And join us in our frivolous pastime as my savior if nothing else." She looked up at him through her lashes.

He smiled, tenderly fingering her chin and cheeks. "My love, I shall likely chastise myself later for confessing this; however, I would doubtless grant you anything within my capacity to give, such is your power over me."

In short order they were bundled snugly and laced into their skates. Mrs. Gardiner had opted to rest in her chambers, and Mr. Gardiner and Mr. Lathrop were still captivated by the trout pond, leaving Darcy and Col. Fitzwilliam to escort the ladies. Once Darcy relinquished his initial pique, the idea of ice skating actually sounded pleasant. He had not skated in several years and had almost forgotten how enjoyable the experience was. Georgiana had truthfully enlightened Lizzy on her brother's abilities, which he displayed in a rare example of exhibitionism by effortless gliding onto the ice and rendering a dazzling figure eight with a spin on one foot before grinningly approaching his stunned wife.

"Braggart!" she declared, to which he bowed grandly before taking her hand. He tucked her in close to his side and set a measured pace. Lizzy was not truly as inept as she hinted but had decided to enjoy the deception for now, to the point of already eyeing the snowdrifts along the edge, thus saving the joy of seeing her husband's surprise later when she smugly revealed her competence.

The small pond, as it was called, was indeed smaller than the other water bodies of Pemberley; it was roughly forty feet in diameter and shallow, allowing it to freeze quickly and easily. The purpose of the pond, Lizzy had been told by Darcy from the upper windows of the manor when he gave her the "tour" of the grounds, was primarily for winter skating and as a summer home for minnows, frogs, toads, and several species of ducks.

They passed a lovely two hours, twirling and floating, as the snow steadily fell in gentle flakes. Lizzy *accidentally* fell only once, picking a particularly cushy heap; however, her ploy failed. Darcy merely laughed and offered his hand. Once she was safely on her feet, he bussed her rosy pouting lips and slithered away, leaving her standing there with her mouth open.

"Mr. Darcy!"

"Come along, Mrs. Darcy; catch me up! I am wise to your charade."

Col. Fitzwilliam had surreptitiously observed this little interplay, cataloguing it with all the other amazing actions, words, and expressions he had noted from his cousin, and marveling at the phenomenon. It was as if the Fitzwilliam Darcy he had known all his life no longer existed. No, he reconsidered, that was not accurate. Darcy had always had the propensity to laugh and joke, and was renowned in fact for his clever wit, but always with reserve and caution attached. Very few people, a mere handful in truth, could say they knew the relaxed side of his personality. Richard doubted whether Georgiana could claim to have witnessed her brother in a completely undone state and, with one glance at her shocked yet radiant face as she, too, observed Darcy's antics, he knew he was correct. A Darcy who laughed boisterously, kissed and touched in public, smiled foolishly, blatantly ignored rules of propriety by whisking his wife off to their bedroom, and who teased and conversed affably was a new creature entirely. Richard could not be happier.

The final crescendo to the afternoon was a snowball fight started by Lizzy with a well-aimed lob at the back of her husband's head. The game was on with all of them breathless, cold, wet, and smiling brightly by the time the snow began falling in earnest with a rising wind, prompting them to quit the pond. They met up with Mr. Lathrop and Mr. Gardiner, blue lipped and shivering, but also grinning broadly and proudly sharing their day's results with the group, who displayed the appropriate amount of enthusiasm.

The staff scrambled to draw hot baths for all. Lizzy sank into her bathing tub with a grateful sigh, reclining and closing her eyes as the warm water seeped into her frozen, aching muscles. As she began to drift off into a doze, she was jolted awake by a soft whisper and the sensation of hands grazing over her shoulders and then down her arms. She yelped and thrashed wildly, sending a spray of water flying through the air, soaking her husband whom it was, naturally, standing behind her.

Her panic and anger was rapidly replaced by amusement at the sight of Darcy in his robe, droplets hanging from his nose and chin and an expression of incredulity and mortification flowing over his handsome face.

"Fitzwilliam Darcy!" she declared crisply, "How dare you frighten me this way?" Any attempt on her part to be stern was nullified in part by her nakedness and location, but mostly by the comical and heavenly vision of her spouse.

Lizzy had long marveled at the varying miens of the man before her. Darcy's aspect could be haughty, domineering, blasé, grave, and forbidding; in all ways a face not to be trifled with. Then there was his tender, passionate, joyful, and smiling countenance, approachable and youthfully innocent. His most adorable face was the one he now wore: his "puppy face," as Lizzy dubbed it. With his blue eyes slightly drooping, brows knitted, pallor marked, and full lips parted in confusion, he looked more an errant little boy than the Master of Pemberley.

"Elizabeth, forgive me! I did not intend to frighten you. I should have spoken louder. How thoughtless of me! I shall leave you."

"William, wait!" she yelled with a laugh halting him at the door, although he kept his eyes averted. "You did startle me, which would have been avoided if you had only announced your presence in a less shocking manner. Nevertheless, I am not averse to your being here, depending on what your intentions are," she finished playfully.

He glanced at her, pallor replaced by a blush, and her smile deepened. *How can a man of nine-and-twenty suddenly look about twelve and be absolutely delectable!*

"Your bathing tub is quite large… "

"You purchased it, my love," she interrupted.

"Yes, well…" he cleared his throat, "I thought at the time that you would appreciate it and that it could easily accommodate two, if such a situation arose," he concluded lamely, waving his hand vaguely.

"You imagine now to be one of those *situations?*"

He flashed a grin, meeting her eyes hesitantly. "The maids have to carry dozens of pails, so I merely thought to spare them filling another tub."

"How considerate of you."

"Yes. I also recognized how cold you were and thought perhaps the added body heat would be welcome. I would not wish you to fall ill."

"Mr. Darcy, you are the epitome of English chivalry."

He was smiling brightly now, "puppy face" replaced by the more familiar one of passionate promise.

Lizzy laughed. "William, you are shivering and the water is growing cold. Hurry up, but lock the door first."

He needed no further encouragement, and his robe was discarded hastily. He positioned his body behind Lizzy, wincing at the hot water on cool skin. She reclined gratefully against his chest, sighing and closing her eyes.

"Hmmm… This is better. Why have we not previously considered this?"

"*We* may not have; however, *I* unquestionably have."

She was befuddled. "Yet you have not acted on the inclination. Why?"

He was silent and she could sense a hesitancy and slight tension in his body, even as his fingers lightly stroked her arms. She tilted her head to peer up at him and noted a faint blush on his cheeks. She frowned. "William? Whatever is the matter?"

He met her eyes with a level gaze. "Elizabeth, I love you to distraction. You know this, I am certain." She smiled and nodded. "On occasion, in truth fairly continuously, I am… inundated by my need for you. I do not merely refer to our intimate relationship, for that is only a fragment of my desire for you. When we are parted, even for miniscule periods, I yearn for your presence. The ache is tangible and only assuaged by your voice or touch or simply seeing your face." He traced her jawline with one finger.

She pondered his serious expression with heightened misery. "Does this yearning and need for me disturb you? You wish it otherwise?"

His eyes widened at the catch in her voice and note of pain, and his hand firmly cupped her cheek. "No, Elizabeth, God no! You misapprehend my words or I chose them poorly. Please, allow me to rephrase. You lend purpose to my life and I am an empty husk without you. My fear is that my… demands could in any way intrude upon you or become burdensome. I frightened you by coming in here, selfishly considering only my desire for you without contemplating if you needed solitude or preferred your privacy. You have had precious little of either since we have wed, and I would not want to be the cause of your dissatisfaction."

She maneuvered around to face him, water sloshing. "My darling, you are being a baby again." She smiled and kissed him, happy to feel her dismay evaporating and his eyes softening. "You are forgetting several facts. First, I am terribly forthright, a character trait you are painfully familiar with. If I need solitude, I *will* tell you. Second, I am as insanely in love with you as you are with me. If we were keeping score, I would venture to guess I have invaded your private sanctuaries and isolation far more often. You need never worry being welcomed by me. Just do not sneak." She concluded with a precise assault to his ticklish zones, water flying.

The only sure method of halting her antics was to clutch her with strong arms and distract with a deep kiss. "Elizabeth, have I told you lately how utterly amazing you are?" He nibbled along her neck while delicately caressing her shoulders. Oddly enough, at least for the moment, his original intention of fulfilling yet another fantasy by making love in the water was not foremost in his mind. He had spoken honestly regarding his desire for her presence. Merely holding her, knowing he was welcomed and wanted to the same degree, was a balm to his heart. How could he doubt her love? He was ashamed of himself for entertaining the notion.

Thoughts of lovemaking may have momentarily fled his consciousness, but they had dawned with alacrity on Lizzy. Her hands were not content to remain in one area. She ran her palms over his torso, hairs silky and buoyant from the water. Oh, how she adored touching him! Darcy naked and wet was an ambrosial vision. She was ceaselessly energized by his solid, defined muscles, replete with raw power emanating from every pore. His skin was flawless and creamy, as soft as satin, and radiating heat and supreme masculinity. In each line and plane of his perfect body, she sensed strength, protection, fortitude, virility, and intoxicating sexuality. He was the embodiment of all things male and subsequently accentuated her femininity as nothing in her experience ever had. Lizzy knew her love for Darcy was profoundly deeper than merely physical, but, oh, how he aroused her!

She pressed against his chest, moaning softly. "William," she whispered, "I love you so."

"My Lizzy," he sighed, grasping her shoulders lightly and pulling her back a space. He smiled, ran the tips of his fingers over her face, and then reached for the soap. "On your knees," he commanded quietly as he rose to his. He lathered his hands and proceeded to fastidiously cleanse her body, lingering over each area. Lizzy followed his lead, quickly light-headed from the combined awareness of his hands gliding over her and hers sliding over him. It did not take long for the caresses to become stronger and more intimately focused, sensations raging uncontainable until the urgent necessity to unite as one overwhelmed them.

Darcy frantically clasped her body against his, forcing her to stillness, and kissed her roughly before gulping for air and control as they sank entwined into the slick water. "I do not want to rush this, beloved! I have dreamed of making love to you here for a very long time."

"How long have you dreamed of this, my heart? And are your dreams being fulfilled?" She leaned down and sharply bit his earlobe, nibbling bites trailing along his wet neck.

"Far longer than it would be proper for me to divulge if I wish to maintain my reputation as a gentleman. As for the content of my dreams… as vivid as they were, none has remotely resembled the reality of your love, Elizabeth. Despite the stories amongst my peers, I had no true notion of the physical pleasure and absolutely not a clue as to the spiritual and emotional gratification I have attained in you, my wife."

They kissed deeply and playfully. Hands touching everywhere: backs, breasts, arms, necks, faces… slipping nimbly in the filmy water. Oh, the ecstasy! Darcy was a man possessed. Some part of his mind was amazed anew at the love and desire he felt for this woman, his wife. Even throughout the long, hideous months of wanting her, he had not fully appreciated how utterly she would consume his existence or how vital she would be to his happiness.

Further, as he felt desire growing beyond what seemed physically possible, as the torrents of throbbing heat surged through his body, as breathing and heartbeat erratically pounded in his chest, and as rapture dominated and crashed over him, he acknowledged the ignorance and innocence of his former self. In all ways that mattered, he had been born and became a man on the day she married him.

～❧～

Lord and Lady Matlock arrived late in the afternoon, blowing in with the wind and snow. Now all the Christmas guests were present and accounted for, and introductions were executed. Once again the outstanding Pemberley staff exceeded all expectations and served a lavish feast. The after-dinner activities were fairly subdued, all being fatigued from their daytime pursuits. The gentlemen renounced their usual private entertainments in favor of joining the ladies in the parlor. Hot cocoa and spiced cider was served as an accompaniment to a platter of sweets, fruits, nuts, and other finger treats. Conversation was sporadic and tempered.

Georgiana sat quietly and embroidered. Lady Matlock and Mrs. Lathrop had formed an easy acquaintance, based primarily on the fact that Lady Matlock had distant Scottish ancestry and adored the Highlands. She had visited there often in her youth, as her family owned a manor near Inverness, so they now conversed amiably. Darcy, contentedly sipping his cup of cocoa, sat near Mr. Lathrop in a far corner, the two old friends softly speaking as they renewed their association by reliving memories of bygone days and filling in the recent gaps. Lord Matlock read by the roaring fire, lulled in short order into a doze. Lizzy, Richard, Mrs. Gardiner, and Mr. Gardiner sat at the card table and played whist, the Gardiners teaming up against Lizzy and the Colonel. The card table was by far the liveliest spot in the room, yet even there a halcyon atmosphere prevailed.

Lady Matlock retired first, rescuing the Earl from embarrassing himself by snoring while he drowsed. Georgiana followed soon thereafter. The game ended, the Gardiners the ultimate victors with two sets won to Lizzy and Richard's one. Darcy and Mr. Lathrop's conversation had evolved naturally to the topic of their mutual bliss regarding their wedded states, prompting both gentlemen's thoughts to deviate toward their lovely wives. As the party began to break up, it was clear to the remaining guests where the newlyweds' musings lay. With gentle smiles of understanding, the Gardiners and Richard extended their good nights. Mr. Lathrop and Darcy claimed their spouses and wasted no time with excessive adieus.

Darcy and Lizzy parted to their respective dressing rooms with a slow kiss, Darcy commanding her to wait for him to retrieve her before entering their bedchamber—a request that puzzled her, but she agreed. In no time at all he entered wearing nothing but a robe, as Lizzy preferred, and assumed the task of brushing her hair. No words passed for some fifteen minutes, each content simply to enjoy the moment. Darcy reveled in the sensation of her sumptuous hair crackling with life in his hands, while Lizzy succumbed to the pleasure of his radiant warmth behind her and the soft kisses and caresses he interspersed while he brushed.

When he spoke, his voice was husky, sending thrills down her spine. "I have an early Christmas present for you, my dearest wife. Do you wish to see it?"

"How coincidental! I have an early present for you as well, and somehow I gather we shall both greatly benefit from our respective gifts," she replied with a saucy smile. She rose from her seat, turning to face him as she leaned against her vanity, blushing faintly. Focusing on his expectant but puzzled gaze, she continued in an enticing whisper, "Today, my love, you fulfilled a fantasy of yours, to my tremendous pleasure, I hasten to add. Perhaps you would welcome sharing a fantasy of mine?"

He raised a brow and grinned. "As you wish, dearest. I am at your disposal."

Her blush increased and she swallowed nervously but met his gaze boldly. "Nearly every evening, you enter my dressing room and brush my hair as I sit on my bench. You kiss my neck softly and caress my neck and shoulders with your beautiful fingers." As she spoke she demonstrated his movements with her own fingers lightly brushing her skin. Darcy gulped, groin clenching. "Time and again I have visualized you proceeding further to my back and then down my arms as you seductively peel my robe away," and she slowly removed her robe, letting in fall in a puddle of satin at her feet.

Darcy gasped and blinked in disbelief. She was wearing the sheerest, clingiest, and shortest chemise he had ever beheld, thigh-high silk stockings secured with lacy garters, and nothing else. Intelligible speech was literally impossible. She stood patiently, observing with a thrill of satisfaction his obvious excitement. Serenely she glided toward him until there was only the bench between them. Bending slowly until her lips were touching his right ear, she murmured, "Do you wish to hear what I then imagine, my heart?" She sucked his earlobe and he could only groan a raspy yes. "I dream of you loving me here, in my dressing room, too overwhelmed with your need to walk even to our bed."

He froze in shock, staring at her in incredulity. What she was suggesting was in point of fact a fantasy he had harbored and vividly enacted in his dreams. Like all his more exotic fantasies, he had intended to work toward implementing them gradually as he deemed her receptive. Despite her openness in their intimate relationship and her astounding passion, he nonetheless was flabbergasted that she would fabricate such a fantasy and then beseech and obviously lust after him in this manner! Aghast he might be, but assuredly he was not unwilling to capitulate wholeheartedly to her supplication. A slow, sensuous grin diffused his face.

Happily, so very happily, he granted her wish. As they were learning with each passing day, their love knew no bounds. The joy they derived from each other was intense and infinite, acceptable and expressible in a multitude of ways and places.

Bliss was attained as easily as always, Darcy dazedly lurching to the bench and sinking gratefully as his legs trembled. Elizabeth sat on his lap with her head thrown onto his shoulder. Both were panting in ragged gasps, needing a number of minutes to regulate heartbeats before speech was possible. She turned her lips to his neck, kissing tenderly. "Thank you, Fitzwilliam. I do not have the words. I love you."

He smiled. "And I love you, precious wife. Feel free to share any other fantasies you entertain. I live to please you."

She kissed his mouth, chuckling softly. "Yes, you assuredly do please me, husband." She rose then and exited to her water closet, returning shortly having freshened up and straightened her skimpy attire. Darcy was robed, leaning against the doorjamb, and still breathing heavily.

She approached him and lightly placed her fingers on his shoulders. "You have a gift for me, Fitzwilliam?" Her lovely, radiant face tilted toward his; expectant aspiration already reawakening, to her fortunate spouse's delight.

He nodded, cleared his throat, and licked dry lips before he could speak.

"Yes. Elizabeth, you are breathtaking and I am overwhelmed." He kissed her tenderly, exploring every part of her mouth before releasing her, clasping her hand and ushering her into their bedchamber. "Close your eyes, beloved."

He halted and moved behind her, encircling her waist with sturdy arms and pulling her firmly against his body, and then whispered into her ear, "As you wished for, my lover. Open your eyes."

Lizzy grinned and laughed sensuously. Darcy had fulfilled her request by procuring an enormous bearskin rug and five generous, plush pillows situated precisely in front of the blazing fire. The room was lit solely by the fire and a smattering of candles randomly placed. A bottle of wine and two glasses sat by the rug. She turned in his arms, snaking her hands about his neck and fingering his hair, drawing his lips to hers.

"Happy Christmas, husband," she murmured as he ambushed her mouth zealously, releasing her eventually as his knees were still weak from the desire stirred by her *gift*.

"Sit, Mrs. Darcy, and I shall pour us some wine. I, frankly, need it as you have effectively unhinged me."

She laughed as she sat. "Poor Mr. Darcy."

He grinned as he handed her a glass. "On the contrary, dearest, I am the luckiest man alive and emphatically not complaining. To us, on our first of a century of Christmases." They clicked glasses and sipped.

"A century?"

I selfishly intend to live a very long time to love you. After ng, I believe I shall require a hundred years, if not more, to ous ways to please you." He sat with her between his legs, is knee. He sipped his wine, watched her fire-burnished face, ed with the ribbons tying her chemise together.

d stroked his other leg where it draped over her lap. Time passed a ank their wine and each placidly enjoyed the presence of the other, speaking occasionally but mainly silent.

"William, I love you." She spoke softly and smiled with her eyes as well as her lips.

He bent near, gazing intently into her eyes, and then kissed her gently but thoroughly, tasting the wine on her tongue. His lips traveled to her cheek and along her jaw to her ear, nibbling the lobe and then tickling her with the moist tip of his tongue. "I adore you, Elizabeth. I worship you, I respect you, I lust for you, I admire you, I cherish you, I love you ardently.

My wife, lover, companion, mother of my children, my soul, my heart..."
His endearments fell fainter until they ceased as he devoted himself to the
task at hand.

Lizzy sighed, excitement rising at his intoxicating touch. He pulled away,
leaving her panting, and reached under a pillow. He handed her a small box
tied with a red ribbon.

"A gift, dearest, although after your innovation and precociousness, as
displayed most recently and on various other occasions this past month, I
remain hesitant at the wisdom in presenting it to you. I must trust that you
will take pity on your older husband and not strive to incapacitate him." He
was smiling as he spoke and Lizzy blushed, even though she had no idea what
he meant.

She opened the box and removed a tiny brass key. She looked at him in
bafflement. "It opens a cabinet in my study," he answered her questioning
expression. "Only I have the other key. The cabinet secures my most private and
personal effects: my journals, letters from you, mementos... and a set of books."
He paused, staring at her as her brows rose and a naughty grin appeared.

"Books? How sweet of you, William. Always desiring to improve my
mind. I promise I shall apply myself diligently to the cause and will practice
as often as feasible."

"You minx!" He tackled her and tossed her onto the pillows, lying fully on
her and kissing hungrily.

⚜

Lizzy did not rouse at the knock to their door but did at the hoarse rumble
of Darcy's voice, felt as well as heard through his chest where her head lay. She
stretched and nestled closer to his side, his arms immediately tightening their grip.

"Is it morning already?" she asked sleepily and yawned expansively.

"I fear so." He nudged her gently, rolling to his side with her in his embrace
until he could see her face. "Happy Christmas, Mrs. Darcy," he murmured with
a tender kiss as he stroked her hair.

"Hmmm... Happy Christmas, beloved. Must we rise straight away? Or do
we have time to cuddle for a spell?"

"I believe an obligatory episode of Christmas cuddling is in order," he said
with a smile.

With a mixture of joy for the holiday and regret at departing their warm bed, the Darcys embarked upon their day. Lizzy joined her husband in their sitting room, having bathed and dressed, stunning Darcy as she approached in a resplendent gown of cream and emerald green taffeta. Marguerite had once again dressed Elizabeth's hair elaborately, clips with emeralds and diamonds sparkling nearly as brightly as her fine eyes.

Darcy caught his breath and then smiled expansively. He took her hands, kissing each palm. "Lovely, Mrs. Darcy."

"Thank you, Mr. Darcy," She curtseyed. "You are quite dashing as well, husband. I believe Samuel and Marguerite are consorting again." She laughed, fingering the emerald green waistcoat he wore.

"Heaven forbid we clashed. Come, my love, our guests await and I am famished."

Traversing corridors and staircases abounding with greenery, ribbons, and candles, along with the surfeit of mistletoe balls, the Lathrops joined the Darcys and the Matlocks, all attired in their holiday finery. Christmas greetings flowed. Georgiana, Col. Fitzwilliam, and the Gardiners were already in the dining room partaking of the fabulous Christmas morning spread. Mrs. Langton had cooked three versions of the traditional Christmas pudding frumenty as well as a vast array of sweet rolls and pastries. Further greetings ensued as Darcy went directly to the coffee and then piled his plate with food, pausing for a tender kiss to Georgiana's cheek.

"Happy Christmas, brother."

"Happy Christmas, my dear. All is well, Georgie?"

"Very well. Shall be better still once I open my presents from you," she teased shyly, earning a raised eyebrow.

"Was I required to supply a present today? Must have slipped my mind."

She giggled. "Nothing ever slips your mind, brother. I have no fears."

"Or is it that you have been peeking in the parlor again?" he asked with a stern expression, causing Georgiana to blush and stare intently at her plate. Darcy laughed. "Father was not able to break you of the habit, so I shall not try. Nonetheless, you must bear the anticipation along with the rest of us until after church."

The modest chapel of Pemberley was an old yet beautiful structure located an easy distance from the manor in a small, unnamed village exclusively for the needs of Pemberley's workers. In fair weather the family would walk to church. Today, however, although the sky was mostly cloud free, the wind was brisk and snow had covered the ground some two inches deep, so the carriages were employed. Lizzy had previously attended services twice with Darcy since their marriage.

The Bennets were fairly regular church attendees, although it was Mary who embraced the tenets of religion most strongly. Lizzy, frankly, had taken church and the Bible greatly for granted. That is not to say she was a nonbeliever, simply that her day-to-day life had proceeded with scant thought to Biblical principles. Darcy, on the other hand, had been raised in a family of staunch Anglicans and was deeply devout. His grandfather, James Darcy, Sr., had met the famous John Wesley and had embraced many of the Methodist's views.

James Darcy had not gone so far as to publicly break with the Church of England, but he had striven to incorporate certain doctrines into the teachings at the Pemberley Chapel. He had secured their current minister, Mr. Lyndon Bertram, who was then a young man and a pupil of Mr. Wesley's. The decision created a stir and minor scandal at the time, but James Darcy had that healthy dose of pride and stubbornness that seemed inherent in the Darcy men. Now, some forty years later, Mr. Bertram was an old man, yet hale and with no plans to retire any time soon.

The Pemberley party arrived at the church and was greeted by Mr. Bertram and his wife Sarah. Lizzy liked the elderly couple, Pastor Bertram being a serious quiet man of few words and his wife the quintessential grandmotherly type. Milling about the courtyard were the inhabitants of Pemberley and the nearby communities who attended services here. Naturally Christmas brought forth a substantially larger crowd than normally seen. Lizzy was amused to note Darcy assuming his Master of Pemberley pose, reserved, somewhat aloof, and serious, as he greeted people with a curt nod and isolated comments.

Georgiana, on the arm of her cousin, shyly greeted a number of the wives and children she and Lizzy had met during their visits. Darcy cocked one brow in pleased surprise and smiled faintly.

The church was decorated with holly branches and festive candles. The service itself centered around the birth of Christ, unsurprisingly, with carols and readings from the Holy scriptures as well as a short missive from the *Book of Common Prayer* and one of John Wesley's sermons on the Epiphany. To the delight of all, the service ended with a short play recounting the story of Mary and Joseph searching for the elusive inn in Nazareth, live donkey and all, as performed by the children of the parish. It was thoroughly adorable, despite the uncooperative ass and the Christ babe who refused to cease wailing. The entire congregation exited with laughter and smiles of joy.

After church, visiting was brief due to the wind's resurgence and the threat of fresh snow. Once returned to Pemberley, all retired to the warm parlor, Georgiana hastening to the pile of wrapped gifts in the corner. Darcy smiled indulgently at his sister, secretly pleased at her childish behavior as he was not yet prepared to relinquish his grip on her life.

A light repast of mince pies, scones, plum cakes, tea, cocoa, and coffee were furnished to stem the tide of hunger until the Christmas feast was served in mid-afternoon. Gradually the gifts were passed out, everyone wishing to take their time to prolong the enjoyment. Georgiana was not disappointed, her brother having procured several pieces of sheet music, a stunning brooch of aquamarine, three gowns, and new leather-bound journal with her name embossed in gold.

With extreme effort, Darcy had forced himself not to inundate Lizzy with gifts. He knew she retained a residual discomfort regarding his wealth, their wealth in fact, although she was hesitant to regard it so, and he sensitively acknowledged her delicacy. Therefore, he avoided jewelry or furs or anything else overly expensive, opting for personal items. He bought her books he knew she wanted, a stationery set with her new name printed on the letterhead, two gowns, a shawl of exquisite Chinese silk, and a letter seal with 'E.D.' entwined amid the Darcy crest. This latter gift brought tears to her eyes. The combination of her initials boldly and permanently displayed with the ancient family symbol touched her, lending a magnified reality to her station and the history involved. Unfortunately the setting was inappropriate for her to thank him as she wished, so she settled for a dazzling smile and fleeting caress to his hand.

For Darcy, Lizzy felt that luck had been on her side. Marguerite had directed her to a bookstore in Matlock and, after she introduced herself to the owner, he had diligently applied himself to obtaining whatever she wished. Then, while strolling randomly down the sidewalk, she had spied the perfect gift in a shop window. The remaining two purchases had been purposefully sought. Thus, Darcy was jubilant to unwrap three books he coveted: Admiral Horatio Nelson's *Letters and Dispatches*, Walter Scott's *Tales of My Landlord*, and a volume of poems by Thomas Gray.

"Elizabeth, how did you acquire *Tales of My Landlord*? It was published not a month ago!"

"I charmed Mr. Stevens. Promised him Mr. Darcy of Pemberley would inform all his friends how accommodating he was. Then I fluttered my lashes."

Darcy laughed. "Well, however you managed it, I do thank you. This is wonderful."

Lizzy handed him the smaller gifts: a new dressage horse whip and saddle blanket, and a waistcoat of pale blue to match his eyes, strangely enough the one color he did not already own. Her final gift rendered Darcy speechless. It was an eighteen-inch-tall, intricately carved ebony statue of a rearing stallion with a man mounted. The workmanship was unparalleled.

Darcy sat with mouth fallen open. Lord Matlock and Col. Fitzwilliam leapt from their chairs, converging on Darcy and the statue with combined enthusiasm and expressions of awe.

"Unbelievable!" exclaimed the Earl. "Wherever did you find this, Elizabeth?"

Richard was equally amazed and blurted before Lizzy could respond to Lord Matlock's inquiry, "It is a Ferrier! You found a piece by Lambert Ferrier in Lambton?"

All eyes were on Lizzy, her husband's breathtaking in the delight and love they showed. She blushed. "Matlock, actually, at that little shop on Second Street…"

"Landry's establishment?" Richard interrupted in astonishment and Lizzy nodded. "I have never seen anything of this quality in there." He whistled sharply. "Fortunate day for you, Darcy. Your wife possesses the luck of the Irish to stumble across a Ferrier in Matlock! Now I am truly jealous of you." He smiled and winked at Lizzy. Lord Matlock was caressing the statue as if were made of gold, and Darcy continued to stare at her, his eyes teary.

Lizzy was flabbergasted by the response. All Landry had said was that it was a collector's piece. Lizzy knew little of art, so even if he had told her it was a Ferrier, it would have meant nothing. She only recognized fine craftsmanship in a general way and had been struck mostly by the faint resemblance to Parsifal and her husband in the statue.

She smiled at Darcy. "It surely was blind luck, William, I confess. I merely thought you would appreciate the figure as it mirrors Parsifal and you. I may not particularly care for your horse, but he is an elegant and noble creature… as are you," she finished in a whisper. Darcy was overwhelmed as the entire room faded from his consciousness. He leaned over, taking his wife's chin in his fingers, and kissed her lightly. He met her eyes and was further lost. Only the abrupt sound of his uncle clearing his throat broke his concentration, and he blushed scarlet as he pulled away from Lizzy's lips with effort.

"Yes, well, job well done, Elizabeth, well done," declared the Earl as he resumed his seat, grinning broadly.

The opening of presents absorbed the bulk of the early afternoon. There was rampant laughter, expressions of awe and delight, and pleasurable conversation. The gentlemen accompanied Darcy to his study, reverently, to select the perfect location to display his statue, after which they repaired to the game room where Darcy skillfully defeated each of them in billiards. The ladies visited contentedly.

Christmas dinner was served promptly at four. The feast lavishing the table eclipsed the last evening's repast. There was enough food to satisfy twice as many diners: venison, goose, turkey, an assortment of vegetables, gravies, rare fruits such as oranges and pomegranates imported for the occasion, breads, souse, trifle, fruit and plum cakes, and a variety of pies. The remains of their banquet, as well as from the servants' feast, which would occur later in the evening, were to be distributed to the two orphanages in the vicinity and the neediest tenants on Boxing Day. The courses were proffered in spaced intervals, allowing time for digestion and conversation.

The weather had deteriorated substantially, with snow swirling and drifting as the wind howled. An after-dinner stroll in the garden was unfeasible and therefore deferred in favor of a ramble through the Sculpture Gallery, Portrait Hall, and conservatory.

Mr. Lathrop was impressed. "Darcy, you have acquired some spectacular pieces since I was last here."

"Miss Darcy, your bust is an amazing likeness," Mrs. Lathrop exclaimed. "As is yours, Mr. Darcy. Superb artisanship. Mrs. Darcy, will you have a bust sculpted as well?"

Lizzy was genuinely taken aback. She had not considered the notion. She turned to her husband and saw an identical expression of mystification.

"In truth, Mrs. Lathrop, I had not given the prospect any deliberation," Darcy said. "Thank you for the idea. Mrs. Darcy's beautiful face should be here next to mine." Darcy smiled at his wife's blush.

"Mr. Darcy, I do not believe my husband and I ever expressed how awestruck we were by the art collection of Pemberley," Mrs. Gardiner declared. "I allege no expertise in the artistic realm myself; however, I adore museums and viewing the works of the masters. Your collection rivals any I have observed in London."

Darcy bowed graciously. "Thank you, Mrs. Gardiner. My family has amassed the pieces gradually over the centuries. I can personally accept few accolades."

Paintings and sculptures were scattered throughout the entire manor. Those that graced the gallery were the rarest and dominated by marbles. The Portrait Hall, in truth the long hallway leading to the ballroom and formal dining hall, exclusively housed paintings of the Darcy family. The oldest, from 1438, was a group portrait of Alexander and Clara Darcy with their three children. When Lizzy had initially beheld this painting a week after her arrival at Pemberley, she had been stunned by the resemblance of the eldest son, also named Alexander, to her husband. The boy in the painting was approximately eleven and had the clear blue eyes of his mother, chestnut brown hair, and a serious set to his mouth, all of which were the image of the current Master. Lizzy smiled each time she viewed this painting, visualizing their future son.

The entire hall was a revelation of Darcy features. Blue eyes cropped up frequently. Brown hair dominated, although there was a smattering of redheads and numerous blonds. The men were usually tall and lanky with broad shoulders. Darcy's chin cleft was a newer attribute, first noted on Emily Darcy, his grandmother, in 1760. Almost universally the men appeared serious and aloof, rarely showing the slightest smile, whereas the women displayed more good humor. Pemberley Manor and horses served predominately as backdrops.

Darcy's parents had been painted shortly after their marriage, the love evident on their faces, even eliciting a small smile from James Darcy. A later portrait of Anne Darcy and her two children, commissioned two years after Georgiana's birth, clearly captured a beautiful yet pale and tired Anne. Georgiana was a chubby, adorably bright toddler. Darcy at thirteen was incredibly tall, nearly six feet and grave, with a keen intelligence manifest in his eyes but also a lingering grief. This grief would consume his eyes further as the years progressed, until Elizabeth.

No one commented, but the thought was on all of their minds. Darcy, however, was gazing at his parents and marveling at the absence of pain in his soul. He missed them naturally, and always would, yet the melancholy was no more. He looked down at Elizabeth, squeezed her arm firmly to his side, and smiled charmingly.

Entering the conservatory at the very end of the northern annex was akin to stepping into summer. The snow continued to fall, blanketing the ground and the glass roof, yet the flowers and bushes inside bloomed. The room was perpetually warm and humid, fragrant and colorful. The group impulsively broke up as they strolled among the greenery. Darcy purposefully steered Lizzy to a far corner well concealed by an enormous weeping maple and pulled her into his arms. He held her against his chest and she closed her eyes in happiness, devouring his heat and strength.

"Are you enjoying your first Christmas at Pemberley, my love?" He inquired, resonant voice vibrating in her ear.

"I am enjoying my first Christmas with you, beloved. We could be on the moon and I would be delirious with joy. William, I have not had the opportunity to thank you properly for your gifts." She tilted her face up to meet his eyes. "The gowns are lovely; the shawl is stunning; you know how I love books; and the stationery set is perfect and useful. Mostly I must tell you how touched I am by the seal. I am a Darcy! I know it is ridiculous, yet I still forget at times. I suppose I have been a Bennet for too long." She laughed and he smiled.

"Have no fear, Mrs. Darcy, I shall remind you a hundred times a day if need be. I will never allow you to forget you are mine." He tenderly caressed her cheek, then cupped her face with his hands and lavished light pecks all over her features.

Col. Fitzwilliam's voice from around the tree successfully quashed any further romantic enticements, sadly. Darcy frowned and scowled at his cousin in annoyance, Richard merely raising one eyebrow and pointedly ignoring him. Lizzy took Georgiana's arm and, with Lizzy giving her husband an amused glance, the sisters resumed their walk.

"Fine day, Darcy, wouldn't you agree?" Richard asked with a grin.

"Tremendous," Darcy replied with dripping sarcasm and Richard laughed.

The remainder of the evening passed in varied pursuits. Georgiana delighted them all on the pianoforte. Carols were sung, Richard adding his talents several times, as did Darcy twice. Refreshments were furnished, although no one was particularly hungry. A rousing game of charades was highly successful, as was a lively round of musical chairs, with Georgiana the ultimate victor. Richard challenged Darcy to a bout of darts. Darcy was fully aware he would lose miserably, to which Richard proclaimed it was healthy to be humbled periodically. Upon this decision, the gentlemen repaired to the game room for port, brandy, and manly activities.

The ladies retired to the parlor, ending what was universally agreed to be a first-rate Christmas with quiet conversation, cards, and a mind-boggling game of dictionary that they were all far too weary to take seriously.

Lizzy retired hours earlier than Darcy, the gentlemen capping their evening off rowdily. She was deeply asleep when he staggered into bed and only marginally aware of him gathering her into his arms. The urge to tease him the next day for his raging headache was potent, but she resisted. After all, she rationalized, fun was had by all and he deserved to celebrate as he deemed appropriate. Instead, the ladies allowed their smug smiles to speak volumes as to their lack of sympathy. Suffice to say, this Christmas would be remembered by all for a multitude of reasons!

CHAPTER FOURTEEN

The Days In-between

SOMEWHERE IN THE WEE hours of the morning, Lizzy's sleep was invaded by a loud rumbling. She attempted to ignore the annoying sound but eventually her consciousness fully returned, along with the recognition of what the sound was. Her husband was snoring! In a month of marriage, this was a first. There had been a couple of instances where she had been mildly roused by his deep respirations and warm breath tickling her neck, but never had he snored. Of course, this was also the only night he had fallen asleep after having overly imbibed, which most likely was the catalyst. Lizzy rolled over, surprised to find Darcy's back to her, another first. She nudged him but his reverberations did not cease, so she grasped his shoulder and tugged. He rolled over heavily, snorted, and resumed his singing. Lizzy was vaguely irritated yet could not resist smiling and kissing his cheek. Even snoring and inebriated he was handsome, and he was hers. She pushed the hair away from his eyes, mesmerized by the thickness of his lashes and the play of shadows on his face in the dimly moonlit chamber. *Oh, how I love him!*

Suddenly she remembered the key. The locked cabinet with private books had been a running joke between them since their honeymoon. She had been surprised, pleasantly so, yet rather confused by how competently her purportedly virtuous new husband had performed. That is when he had spoken of the specifically topical books used to enhance his education and how they were kept in a safe place. She had teased him several times about sharing the books with her, in truth not very interested as she was amply content and satisfied to allow him to dominate and teach in the intimate portion of their relationship.

Even thinking of the books now did not pique her curiosity as much as the fact that he had entrusted her with a key to his personal and private items. His vulnerability, honesty, and faith in her and their bond caused her heart to swell. Lizzy paused for a moment in her tender caresses. *Have I given myself as wholly to him as he has to me? Would I trust him with my journals? Yes, I would, without hesitation, for I have given him all of me.* She recollected his confession on Christmas Eve of how he yearned for her and was inundated by his need. Those phrases had registered as encapsulating precisely her emotions for him. The little brass key was symbolic. His soul was hers utterly, and likewise he owned her. The only reason he had not given it to her immediately is that Mr. Darcy was learning to tease!

Nonetheless, she was inquisitive and wide awake. She kissed his full, puffing lips and left the bed. Snaring one of his thickest robes and a lamp, she quietly tiptoed through the empty, diffusely lit corridors to his study. Passing by the parlor, she glimpsed the glow from the Yule log shimmering on the slumbering boy in the chair beside the fireplace. She paused and smiled. The older offspring of the servants were awarded the honor of tending the Log to ensure it remained perpetually alight through Twelfth Night, per tradition. Tonight, Phillips's son Caleb had been assigned the duty. The blanket had slipped to the floor and Lizzy hankered to cover the boy, but she knew he would be mortified if he awoke realizing the Mistress had caught him dozing, so she left him undisturbed.

The cabinet in question was a grand, antique armoire of ornately carved oak. There was an identical armoire against the opposite wall, also locked securely, in which were kept the estate documents, ledgers, funds, and such. Lizzy had previously been given a key to this cabinet, the only other keepers being Mr. Keith, Mrs. Reynolds, and Darcy, naturally. Lizzy lit an additional lamp and then unlocked the door to Darcy's personal storage area. Her eyes were immediately drawn to the array of correlative leather-bound books filling the top shelf and roughly half of the second. She retrieved the first book, his journal with *Fitzwilliam Darcy* etched on the cover, and opening it to the first page, she began to read.

The first paragraph elicited a smile. It was dated November 10 of 1801, his thirteenth birthday, and he had written in his firm, precise hand a dry narrative of who he was, where he lived, his family, what he was studying with his tutor, and other pertinent particulars. It was detailed but wholly devoid of any emotion or insight. Then he wrote:

"My father gifted this unfilled book to me for the express intent that I initiate inscribing my daily musings, undertakings, and activities of import. I extended my gratefulness, however, deemed it essential in the interest of maintaining frank communication and honesty to inform him that the concept of elucidating personal minutiae betwixt the pages of a book was ludicrous and demeaning. He assured me that it was a worthy endeavor, one that he has partaken in since he was a young man, and further guaranteed my future appreciation in possessing a catalog of my memories. I persist in judging the exercise inane; nonetheless, I shall trust my father and obey his dictates."

Lizzy laughed out loud. So like him to overanalyze even the simple matter of keeping a journal! She returned the slim volume to its designated space. It would consume months if she ever wished to read all the books, so instead she proceeded to the third shelf. Here were stacked several cigar boxes of varying sizes and brands. The oldest by appearance contained an odd assortment of what she could only assume were his "mementos." There was a glass jar filled with a disgusting collection of dead bugs and spiders, oddly shaped knots of wood, ten rocks of diverse colors and textures, a small case with pinned moths, the well-preserved flattened corpse of a toad, and a book with meticulously fine labeled drawings of leaves.

Clearly the treasures of a young boy, although Lizzy could well remember her own fascination with the oddities and marvels of nature. Each subsequent box revealed the maturing Darcy as his possessions grew more sophisticated: a lock of his mother's hair; numerous other sketch books of flowers, trees, animals, insects, and more, all detailed and labeled; programmes from an astounding number of operas and plays; letters from his father, mother, sister, and other loved ones; the reports of his marks from Cambridge (all excellent, Lizzy noted); stamped passage and boarding tags from excursions abroad; and a vast amount of other odds and ends, many of which indubitably held meaning only fathomable to Darcy.

The last box was entirely devoted to Lizzy. A parchment note lying on top of the items was addressed to her:

"*My dearest, most precious wife,*

Conscious as I am of your formidable and boundless curiosity, my beloved Elizabeth, it is doubtless that you have hastened with alacrity to my armoire and books contained therein, have dutifully scrutinized each page of text and illustrations, and are already formulating diverse methods of employing your newfound enlightenment to shock me! I render this allegation yet wish to assure you, my lover, that I harbor no anguish or repulsion at the idea. I am yours to do with as you will. My only chagrin is that I am too much the gentleman to wager with Vernor and the gang as to how long it takes you from the key's presentation to when you utilize it. I envision you tiptoeing through the corridors early Christmas morning; however, I may be amiss by a day or two.

Eventually you shall make your way to these boxes. I trust that, after a month of wedded bliss, you will be sufficiently enamored with me so as to not be appalled nor amused by my cloying sentimentality. I jest, for in truth we both know that our mutual love has afforded me the latitude to relinquish the rigid walls of reticence I had erected. I can now relax my guard without shame or fear of rejection, and it is all due to you, my darling wife. I have not the words to convey how you have touched my life. All that hides in this cabinet is yours to explore, my love. You already possess the key to my heart and soul, and the greater value lies therein.

Yours for all eternity,

William"

Lizzy was laughing and weeping simultaneously. Would he believe that she had *not* first examined the special books? Yes, because despite the rapture savored in the physical aspect of their marriage, the joy of their two lonely souls redeemed and melded into one was unparalleled. She was moved by his declarations of love and faith yet also tickled by his humor and accurate assessment of her actions. With a smile she turned her attention to the box.

Among the anticipated letters she had written during their separations while betrothed were some surprises: one of her handkerchiefs, confiscated she knew not when; a green ribbon loosened from her bonnet that she had completely forgotten to retrieve from him; the hairpin he had intentionally and scandalously removed so he could play with a lock of her hair; the crown of jasmine she had placed on his head at the fountain; the stub of the life candle from his birthday party; one of the gold ribbons worn in her hair at their wedding; a pressed and dried gardenia that she had tucked behind his ear one day while walking; the cork from the champagne drunk on their wedding night; the programme from the symphony performance attended while in London; and so many other little tokens.

Lizzy was amazed. She knew that her William was a romantic, but she had not comprehended the depth of his sentimentality. The astounding plethora of memorabilia collected over his lifetime belied his thirteen-year-old assertions of the inanity of cataloguing his memories and displayed how mawkish he had always been despite his cool exterior. What a complex man she had married!

Lastly, she turned her attention to the books. There were six of them of differing sizes. The largest was a medical textbook devoted to human reproduction and sexuality from the clinical viewpoint. She flipped through it quickly, noting numerous comprehensive illustrations and exhaustive chapters covering everything from bodily systems to diseases to pregnancy. She made a mental note to absorb the latter so she would be prepared for what she prayed was a timely blessing.

The remaining books were decidedly more carnal in nature and brought a ready blush to her cheeks. Perhaps Darcy was correct in keeping these books from her, she thought, as an acute rush of embarrassment washed over her. The illustrations and text were blunt, inclusive, and graphic, clarifying the question of her husband's competence in the bedroom!

The clock chimed five, startling Lizzy. She had been here for almost two hours. She grabbed one of the books at random for perusal at her leisure, folded the letter under the front flap, and made her way silently back to her chambers. Darcy was soundly asleep but no longer snoring. She secreted the book in her bed stand, crawled under the covers, and nestled close to her husband's warm body. He sighed deeply, pulled her into his embrace, sleepily murmured her name, and kissed her forehead without waking. Within seconds she was asleep.

Lord and Lady Matlock departed that morning after breakfast. Lady Matlock embraced Lizzy warmly, thanking her for a delightful Christmas. The Earl, looking a wee bit peaked, kissed her hand also thanking her, and smilingly assured her that he would gladly thrash his nephew if he maltreated her in any way. Lizzy laughed and with a nod to her husband pledged to accept the offer if necessary.

The three younger men were all rather pale, wincing in the bright sunlight and trembling. They spent their day in quiet pursuits, primarily in the library with the draperies drawn. The servants, although somewhat bleary eyed from their own night of revelry, had boxed up the feast residuals for the orphanages. Lizzy insisted on delivering them herself, and Amelia agreed to accompany her. The two orphanages nearest to Pemberley were large establishments housed in solid brick buildings, full to capacity, maintained and financed by the combined charity of the prominent families of the Shire and the local parishes. The first was actually on Pemberley lands in the tiny village and was managed by the Church, the second in Baslow and operated by the Catholics.

Lizzy was overwhelmed and fiercely moved by the children's pleasure and charm. Each of them was adorable in their own special way, appreciative, playful, and loving. Her wonder and joy in observing their delight was immense. This simple Boxing Day tradition would translate into another Mistress of Pemberley benevolence, as Lizzy would volunteer most every Friday afternoon at the Pemberley orphanage in the years to come.

For the inhabitants and guests at Pemberley, the eleven days between Christmas and Twelfth Night were memorable and exceedingly pleasurable. The weather was primarily clear, if extremely cold, another three inches of snow dropping only one other night. This fairness allowed for frequent walks, more ice skating, fishing twice again with Col. Fitzwilliam and Darcy partaking once, horseback riding, and the annual winter fox hunt for the gentlemen of the region. The men socialized at the coffeehouse once and The Red Deer pub twice, while the ladies strolled through Lambton shopping. For the most part, they remained inside the manor enjoying its warmth and homey comforts, excellent entertainments by the diversely artistic group, games of all varieties, conversation, and fine dining. Afternoon retreats to the upper chambers for napping and intimate occupations were not uncommon.

The Lathrops and Gardiners were to stay until the ninth of January. Richard, unfortunately, was required to return to his regiment in Town on the third. Madame du Loire delivered Lizzy's ball gown on the second, performing the final fitting personally. The women were all twittery and gushy, casting numerous sly glances Darcy's way, much to his embarrassment but escalating excitement.

Lizzy had precious few private moments to glance through the book she had taken from Darcy's cabinet and no opportunity to discuss his letter, personal memoirs, or the books with him until the morning of the twenty-eighth. Between the whirlwind of activities and host duties and Darcy's indisposition the day after Christmas, they had secured no private time at all. This day she decided, with deliberate planning, to wake her husband early and monopolize the entire morning. Such was her anticipation that she slept poorly, yet undeterred and with bounding heart, she slipped out of bed at the crack of dawn to freshen up and garb herself in Darcy's favorite gauzy nightgown. She returned hastily. Darcy slept supine with one arm across her empty pillow as if reaching for her. He was lulled into partial awareness by the pleasurable sensation of his wife nuzzling and kissing his neck while caressing his chest.

"Hmmm..." He sighed, impulsively hugging her tightly and lacing his fingers through her cascading hair. Far more asleep than awake, he nonetheless sought her lips and kissed her lazily and then with increasing ardor as he roused further in response to her insistence. Once she sensed he was completely awake, she pulled away from his iron grip, not an easy task, and sat up on her knees.

"Elizabeth," he pleaded, voice hoarse from sleep and desire, "please..."

She halted his words with a finger to his lips. It was then that he fully noted her attire and his grin spread. "Happy anniversary, my darling husband," she said in a throaty whisper while lightly running her fingers over his face. "Did you forget, my love, that today marks one month of our wedded bliss?"

"No, beloved. I simply intended to allow you to sleep longer before I gave you your gift," he replied, reaching up and firmly tugging on one of the ties to her gown.

"Would you prefer to resume your slumber then? Or can I interest you in an alternate bedroom activity?"

"I shall assume those are rhetorical questions requiring no answer." Another tie released.

"Very well then." She reached across his body, deliberately, for the book resting on his bed stand. Somehow the third tie came loose.

"Ha!" he laughed harshly when he saw the book. "How long have you had that?"

She primly pursed her lips and lifted her chin, "Let us just say that you would have lost your bet with Mr. Vernor, had you made it." He continued to chuckle as another tie was undone and she slapped his hand. "Focus, sir."

"I am," he mumbled, but she ignored him.

Lizzy opened the book, trying unsuccessfully not to blush. "Page five is promising, as is thirteen. However, twenty intrigues me. Of course we could attempt all three." She said the last in a whisper, cheeks flushed, and eyes downcast.

Darcy watched her with amusement and overwhelming love. "You promised not to incapacitate me, love. I *am* only human."

She smiled and met his twinkling eyes. "I made no such promise. You merely asked me to pity your advanced age and presumed I would acquiesce. Besides, I have the utmost faith in your stamina and capabilities."

"Ah, a challenge!" he declared, briskly snatching the book from her hands. "The gauntlet has been thrown! Let me see, page five... Hmmm, yes it is doable." He slyly glanced at her bright face, turning the book to the left and studying it intently. Lizzy giggled and lay at his side with her head on his shoulder so she could see the pages. He flipped to page thirteen and employed a clinical tone, "Interesting, very interesting. Excellent choice Mrs. Darcy, if you deem yourself adequately flexible. Your taste is impeccable." She hid her rosy face in his upper arm, shaking with mirth. "Now, page twenty. Intriguing indeed! Allow me a moment to peruse the text to comprehend the finer nuances..."

Suddenly the book was jerked from his grip, tossed onto the floor and Lizzy's lips descended onto his forcefully. He rolled her to the side clasping her tightly, one hand cupping her face. "Elizabeth," he breathed, "I love you wholeheartedly. Happy anniversary, beloved." He released the last tie to her gown and, with a happy smile, peeled the silky fabric away from one creamy shoulder, kissing the exposed flesh softly and murmuring *"page five"* before claiming her mouth. He stroked her arm with feather touches, no urgency in his actions as of yet.

They lay facing each other for a long while, kissing and caressing, legs entwined, allowing their passion to rise gradually. Lizzy's suggestions, all intoxicating to Darcy, would require tremendous control on his part and the truth was that he did not think he could manage all three positions in one lovemaking session. He appreciated his wife's confidence in his sexual prowess, but he knew his own limits. He adored her innocent enthusiasm, though, and was determined to please her now and forever.

His kisses traveled over her neck, following the trail blazed by his fingers until reaching their destination at her bosom. Lizzy moaned softly as Darcy rolled her onto her back. "Sweet, delicious wife," he murmured as he kissed her breasts, Lizzy arching into him as her hands moved over his shoulders.

"William?"

"Hmmm?"

"I have a confession about the book."

He lifted so as to see her blushing face. "A confession?" His fingers assumed the task of delighting her breasts as his lips feathered over her neck to the tender spot behind her ear.

Lizzy moaned and shivered. "Yes," she responded breathlessly. "The truth is that I have been too occupied to more than glance at the book. Ooohh… Fitzwilliam, pity please! I am trying to speak!" She grasped his head, pulling his mouth away from her neck so she could meet his eyes.

He grinned. "As you command, my love. You were saying?" He gave his attention but lightly caressed his hand over her hips and buttocks.

"I did note page five, but as for thirteen and twenty… I selected them at random. The first I saw the pictures was when you turned to them."

He was honestly surprised. "How long have you had the book?" She told him the whole tale, how she had snuck down the morning after Christmas and found his note and examined all his mementos.

"I cannot believe you collected so many trinkets, William. You are so romantic and sentimental! I love this about you. Mostly I love that only I know this about you, and that you have shared yourself with me so completely. You amaze me." He was blushing and she pulled his face to her, kissing him ardently.

"I still am stunned about the books," he mumbled.

"Ridiculous man! Do you not yet comprehend how satisfied I am with you? I trust you to please me and teach me and be the leader. On occasion I shall surprise you, beloved, never fear. After all, I am the clever one, remember?"

He laughed and rolled onto his back, taking her along until her body was fully on top, embracing her tightly and wrapping her legs under his, squeezing her thighs. His hands traveled over her back and bottom as he kissed her probingly. "Lesson one, Elizabeth Darcy: Whenever you feel the urge, I am happy to submit to your dominance in our bed. As you did on our one-week anniversary and in your dressing room. I find it… intensely arousing."

"Do you? This is good to know." She rocked her hips into his, adoring the sensation of his firm muscles flexing along her outer thighs where he held her captive. She caressed his sides, gliding fingers along the solid ridges of his chest and abdomen as far as she could reach, squeezing and tickling, while she assaulted his neck. He moaned, one hand entangled in her hair as he inhaled her scent.

"Elizabeth, beautiful Elizabeth, my lover. I need you so." Gently but clearly clutching her hair, he sought her lips. They kissed deeply, starved for each other's breath and taste. Tongues mingled, lips suckling lips as they writhed against each other with passion rising. Darcy, always wondrously graceful in his power and strength, rolled and then rose to his knees with Elizabeth secure in his arms and nestled on his lap. Arms wound over his shoulders and hands flattened on his back, Lizzy nuzzled his neck and bestowed tiny bites.

"Precious love. My Lizzy." He arched his neck, moaning and hugging her tight. "Remember page five, my heart?"

She giggled and focused on his expectant face. Playfully they loved, experimenting with the illustrations from the book, but mostly blissfully caught up with the sensations derived so lusciously from each other. Embracing tightly as they merged and moved in perfect unison.

"Fitzwilliam, my darling husband," she whispered, glazed eyes locked. "I love you… I live for your love and touch… your eyes on me… your voice… your mouth… your skin…" Each phrase spaced as she kissed and caressed his chest and shoulders. "Your words of devotion… I so adore you!… I want you… so utterly you belong to me… and I to you… my soul."

It was powerful; Darcy was amazed at his control and stamina in light of his wife's wanton need. As expected, he was unable to withstand all three pages, but neither cared. Their release was blinding, leaving them both shaken and blissfully satiated.

Later they lay entwined, dozing in their happy exhaustion. Lizzy caressed his chest lazily, running the tips of her fingers through his hair, inhaling deeply of his masculine smell. "William?"

"Yes, beloved?"

"I am a little afraid of the books."

"Afraid? I do not understand."

"Do you ever wonder if our lovemaking will always be like this? Will we, perhaps… run out of new experiences or get bored?"

"No."

"How can you be so sure?"

He was silent for a spell, collecting his thoughts. He understood this was one of those moments where, despite his previous inexperience, his overall maturity and worldliness gave him a certain wisdom she lacked. "Elizabeth, I will eternally love you and desire to make love to you. I know this for certain. Right now the activity is novel and perhaps that lends a dimension to it that will not be there twenty or thirty years from now.

"Yet by then our love will have grown stronger. We will have had children together, been through hardships, created memories, and built a marriage that is deep. We may not be tearing our clothes in passion or making love three times a day, although maybe we will," he laughed and kissed her head, "yet when we do love each other it will, I believe, be stronger and more powerful, as can only occur between two souls who have bonded for so many years. This is how it is meant to be. Do you understand?"

He lightly grasped her chin and turned her face to his, surprised to see tears in her eyes. In alarm he cupped her cheeks and kissed her. "Beloved, please do not fear! I will always desire you, Elizabeth. We can discard the books if you wish." She halted him with a kiss, long and deep.

"Why do you put up with me?" she finally said. "I am so silly and you are so wise!"

"Neither is true, Elizabeth," he interrupted, "and I *put up with you* because I could not survive without you." He kissed her eyes and then her nose before continuing. "Happy anniversary, my precious wife, today and every day for all my life I will love you and thank God He brought you to me. This I can assert with confidence." He laughed softly as he stroked her hair and playfully nibbled her lips. "I have not tired of riding my horses after all these years, so how could I tire of riding you? You, precious Elizabeth, are profoundly superior."

The preparations for the Ball consumed most of Lizzy's thoughts. As the imminent event drew nearer, Lizzy's original excitement and blasé attitude was replaced by a fair amount of nervousness. She was apprised of several facts regarding the Masque, which either calmed her or escalated her anxiety. Firstly, the annual Cole Twelfth Night Masquerade Ball was a Derbyshire extravaganza dating back more than fifty years and was *the* premier social affair.

The fact that the surpassingly eligible bachelor, the *prime bull* as he put it, Mr. Darcy of Pemberley, had only deigned to attend four times since his coming of age was a minor scandal, viewed by some as a hideous breach of propriety. This philosophy signified the momentous weight ascribed to this singular celebration and Lizzy's opportunity to make a positive impression as Mrs. Fitzwilliam Darcy, Mistress of Pemberley. It was in no way vanity for her to rightfully surmise that all eyes would be on her for a variety of reasons.

Knowing this, Lizzy was uncertain whether she was happy or dismayed to discover that, although a "Masque," few masks were worn. The tradition of actually attempting to disguise oneself in the relatively insular community of Derbyshire had long ago been deemed ludicrous. Therefore, the style had faded only to be affected by the more frivolous—usually single—attendees who sought an air of mystery.

Darcy had flatly refused even to consider wearing a mask, ever. Lizzy had initially been relieved, since the idea held no appeal to her either, yet as the import of the Ball registered fully upon her consciousness, the comfort of hiding behind a mask did seem providential!

Then there was the gown itself. Lizzy trusted the genius of Madame du Loire and, having beheld her gown, she could abstractly proclaim it a masterpiece. Yet therein lay her disquiet. Lizzy had never in her life entertained the notion of donning such a fabulous garment. It was so far removed from her character to cover herself with yards upon yards of finery. She recognized that if ever there was a night she needed to be comfortable with who she was, it was this night. How could she possibly be "Lizzy" dressed like this? Of course, she was no longer just "Lizzy"—she was Mrs. Darcy, and desired to present herself as such to please her husband and impress the denizens of Derbyshire. Oh, the dilemma! It gave her a headache.

Lastly, Mr. Vernor had informed Darcy that Sir Cole had agreed to sanction the waltz for two dances this year. The scandalous Viennese dance had gained reserved favor last year when the Prince Regent had introduced it at a royal affair in the palace. The older members of society had suffered a collective case of apoplexy, but the younger elite had secretly applauded the Prince's action. Outwardly they nodded sagacious agreement with their elders, yet the dance persisted in popping up throughout the cotillions and balls of the ton. Lizzy had frankly been shocked speechless to learn that her shy, priggish, and rigid husband had learned the dance years ago when touring Austria and practiced further two years ago while in Paris. Lizzy was ragingly jealous to imagine him dancing so intimately with another woman.

This intelligence had been disclosed to her four days after Christmas. They had all returned from one of their excursions into Lambton where, while the men dallied at the pub, Mr. Vernor had enlightened Darcy about the waltz. Resting in their sitting room for the afternoon, Darcy disclosed this information to Lizzy along with his experience in dancing the waltz and his great willingness to teach her if she wished it. Lizzy was dumbstruck, primarily at the idea of her husband knowing the notorious dance, but also at the concept of performing it herself. Darcy, she could easily tell, was quite enamored by the vision.

He gazed at her expectantly until finally she stammered, "You dance the waltz! But... you do not like to dance... any dance! How did you learn..." She blushed profusely. "With whom did you... I have heard it is so, so... intimate!" She was inexplicably furious and leapt from her chair with the probable intent of storming from the room, but Darcy grabbed her arm.

"Elizabeth, stop. You are being silly," he began, but her angry face halted his words and he released her arm. With a final glare she did storm out of the room and into her dressing room, slamming the door with astonishing vigor. Darcy stood in the middle of the room in a welter of emotion. Anger, dismay, amusement, and bewilderment warred internally. With stunning clarity, he realized they had just had their first married fight and he was absolutely at a loss as to what to do. *Well, a letter is out of the question*, he thought with irony as he fell into his chair.

If Darcy boasted one character trait above all others, it would be his ability to succinctly and reliably rationalize. The problem was that he did not always possess all the necessary evidence to form a perfect conclusion, ergo the disastrous first proposal to Miss Elizabeth Bennet. Mrs. Darcy was another matter. Darcy would never be so presumptuous as to assert that he wholly understood his complex, adorable wife, but in their time together he had amply gleaned the nuances of her thinking, character, and actions.

Most importantly, he loved her ardently and refused to allow her to feel any pain, if it was within his power to relieve. Therefore, he shoved his emotions aside, another trait he possessed, and allotted himself the time necessary to ponder all that had happened, what she had said and not said, and what he knew of her until he reached a conclusion. After a prayer and a deep cleansing breath, he approached her door.

He heard a faintly muffled sound from within that he thought might be crying, piercing his heart. He knocked softly. "Elizabeth?" No answer. "Elizabeth my love, we must talk. May I come in, please?" It was some time before he heard a muted yes.

She stood leaning against the wall by the small window, arms crossed. Her face was averted but he instantly knew, based on his intimacy with her body, that she had been crying but was also still angry. He longed to hold her with a palpable ache but he paused just inside the door.

"Elizabeth, I beg your forgiveness on several counts. First, I have been horribly insensitive to your feelings lately regarding the Ball and what I now begin to comprehend might be anxiety on your part. I am unbelievably obtuse at times, and I believe this is one of those times. I take the society and denizens of Derbyshire for granted. It has forever been a part of my life and I am remiss, outrageously so, for not remembering that you are acquainted with few of our neighbors.

"In addition, I am so much in awe of your ability to converse and socialize with strangers that it frankly never occurred to me that you may be nervous. Perhaps you are not and I am, again, leaping to a false conclusion. I can only surmise your nervousness, based on the few subtle signs I have noted—as you have chosen, if I may risk incurring further wrath, not to share your feelings with me." He noted that she jerked slightly at his last statement and almost turned toward him.

He hesitated momentarily to collect his thoughts. "As for the waltz, I must tell you that I am offended and hurt that you would infer, knowing me as well as you should, that my learning the waltz in any way means that I have been intimate with another woman."

She hung her head and her shoulders shook, making it nigh on impossible for him not to move to her. "Oddly, at the same time, your jealousy and possessiveness is charming and gratifying to my ego. I suppose the logical denouement is that we humans, even those who love each other as profoundly as we do, still need reassurance and reiteration."

He took a few steps closer to her before continuing. "Both times I danced the waltz, it was painful to me and I was under great duress. I can bore you with the details later if you wish. Any proficiency I claim is due to Georgiana." Lizzy was so startled by this that she spun around, her mouth agape.

"Georgiana!" she blurted, her tear streaked face so precious to him.

He smiled and stepped close enough to wipe the tears away with one finger. "When Bingley told her I had danced it in Paris, with the intent of embarrassing me—which he succeeded in doing—Georgiana would not let it rest. You know how weak I am when it comes to granting the wishes of those I love, so I capitulated and taught her." He shrugged. "It is not unusual, actually. Who else do you think teaches her to dance?"

He stroked her cheek as he cocked his head and knitted his brow. "By the way, you have obviously deduced that I do not like to dance. This is not true. I abhor balls with all the protocol and vapid conversation that attend them, and I detest being on display. However, I enjoy dancing and have been told I am accomplished. One could even say I am light of foot!" he chuckled. "I have simply never been properly partnered, except for one time during which I behaved idiotically."

Lizzy was crying again and fell into his arms, burying her face into his chest. "William, I am a fool! Please forgive..." He checked her apology with a deep kiss, and she responded fervently with a rapid transposition of her despair and anger to passion. Darcy swept her into his arms and swiftly carried her to their bed. He held her tightly, locked to her mouth as he gently sat on the bed with her in his embrace.

He pulled back mere inches and met her eyes. "Elizabeth, my love, there is no other but you, never has been, and never will be." His voice was low and husky as he stroked her face, tenderly kissing her eyes and nose and every other feature. His fingers moved to the clasps on her gown, beginning the familiar process of undressing each other, a process they had discovered early on to be tremendously stimulating.

At last they were naked, crazily aroused yet peacefully content enough in their love simply to enjoy the sensation of touching each other. They knelt in the middle of the enormous bed, face to face, the unencumbered access to their bodies allowing for languid exploration. There was not an inch of Darcy's sumptuous six-foot-three-inch physique that Lizzy did not adore.

His many scars were the evidence of a rugged youth and badge of a virile adulthood. A light dusting of freckles across the fair skin of his shoulders created a pattern she enjoyed tracing with her fingertips. The downy hair on his chest, the strong pulse in the hollow of his throat, every muscle defined and firm, and his hands... Oh, how she loved his hands! Not only how they felt on her body and the passion his skillful fingers could incite in her, but the very look of them: strong with calluses on the palms, yet soft with long, refined fingers. Then there was his face with piercing blue eyes, lush lips, strong jaw, cleft chin, and noble English nose all combined masterfully. She touched all of him, arousing him with her devotion.

Darcy equally worshipped his wife. Elizabeth was so alive and vibrant and spirited that he frequently found himself freshly amazed at how petite she was. Her bones were so delicate he wondered she did not break in their wild passion, her body svelte yet firmly muscled, skin velvety smooth and flawless, and breasts that perfectly fit his large hands. He towered over her and around her, but rather than prompting a sense of dominance, his potent manliness activated a profound need to protect and satisfy her.

He loved the small mole located precisely where her right buttock swelled from her back, her narrow waist, the dimple at the base of her spine, her pink nipples, her fragility, the thin wrists that he could encircle with his thumb and index finger, her dainty ears, and her face. He could and often did become enraptured by her face. Elizabeth was beautiful by any standard, but what captivated Darcy was the vital force and character that shone on her countenance and primarily in her fine eyes.

He kissed her and she responded with fervor, as they held and touched and squeezed and teased. He trailed his mouth along her jaw to her ear, whispering, "Best beloved, do you remember the first time we touched?"

She hesitated for only a second. "When you assisted me into the carriage at Netherfield. I remember, yes."

"We have not spoken of that event. What, if anything, did you feel?" He nuzzled her neck, planting feather kisses while his fingers lightly traced up her backbone.

"Initially I was merely surprised that you would extend the courtesy as I thought you disliked me. A bit angry, too, with what I perceived as presumptuousness. The way you looked at me though... it disturbed me. I could not decipher your expression, but I was captured by something in your eyes and the warmth of your hand."

He was studying her eyes, smiling softly as they relived an odd yet now happy memory. "I felt a jolt rush to my heart and my hand tingled all the way home. I did not understand it and was troubled. I still am not sure what happened. I know I did not care for you then, and I do not believe it was a sexual response. Perhaps it was like a signal, if I had been listening, that there was more between us than I imagined. It affected me and I relived the moment in my dreams, yet I cannot explain it. I do know one thing; it was the first time I consciously accounted you handsome." She smiled and ran her fingers through his hair.

Darcy caressed his thumb over her lips and jaw as he cupped her face. "I did not plan to take your hand. It was impulsive. The instant I touched you, I knew I had acted from a desire to feel you, not out of courtesy. I was stunned by the emotions rushing through me. Prior to that moment, you had intrigued me but only as a challenge to my intellect, an enigma I failed to comprehend. I thought you lovely but no more so than many other women I had seen. At least this was my reasoning.

"You had already invaded my dreams," he smiled and blushed mildly, "and I thought of you incessantly. I think I needed to touch you so I could rid myself of this obsession, rationalizing that the dreams were not reality. I was a fool. The instant your skin met mine, I was yours. I knew I loved you. Of course, you know the rest, how great my self-deception and denial."

He took her face into his strong hands and drew closer, raptly staring into her eyes. "Elizabeth, I have touched other women's hands and never, not once, have I felt anything, not a ripple. In addition, I have never dreamt of another. Whatever... sensual... dreams I have had in my life were vague with no discernable partner. You were vivid, much to my shame. I pictured you in stunning detail and that touch, as brief as it was, lived in me and came alive and grew with each dream. I love you, my Lizzy. No one compares to you."

By the afternoon of the fifth, Lizzy was relatively calm and excited at the prospect of the Masque. She owed her renewed peace solely to her husband. His mild chastisement for her not sharing her anxieties had struck a nerve. After making love, they had cuddled and talked for hours, Darcy effortlessly ignoring any misgivings regarding his duties to their guests. His wife was precious to him, and her peace of mind was of paramount importance. His assurance to her of this incontrovertible fact alone was enough to placate the majority of her concerns.

Although Darcy was cautious not to label her silly again, Lizzy realized that she was precisely that. Her place in his life was indelible not because of the license that legally bound them, but because of the invincible love that connected them. Simply stated, Lizzy had nothing to fear from the society of Derbyshire, or anywhere else. They belonged to each other in a love and devotion that exceeded logic. They both ended up laughing at how ridiculous they occasionally were in their vulnerability.

Darcy taught her the relatively basic steps of the waltz while still in their bedchamber, theorizing that if she could learn in this setting, then dancing while in a ball gown would be facile. If his generally well-honed ability to rationalize did not succeed as he had deduced, the unforeseen result of ending back in their bed was delightful and welcomed.

Over the next several days, Lizzy practiced with Darcy in the more appropriate location of the music room with Georgiana at the pianoforte, accompanied by both the Lathrops and the Gardiners, who happily embraced the fun. Once over her initial embarrassment at the close proximity of her partner, she found the waltz immensely enjoyable. In truth, much of her pleasure was *precisely* due to the closeness of Darcy, yet in no small measure was it also due to the graceful, swaying motions of the dance.

January 5, 1817

MARGUERITE FUSSED OVER LIZZY like a mother hen, but the result was stupendous. Lizzy's gown was a multilayered masterpiece. The dress was white satin with slightly puffed sleeves ending midway down the upper arm. The sleeves were edged in cornflower blue chenille tied in a petite bow. The same chenille edged the dress in a crossed fashion over the legs and along the hem and demi-train, exposing a white silk organdy petticoat edged with the finest Parisian lace.

Layered over the dress was a drape of midnight blue crepe edged with a braid of the blue chenille and lace. This darker overdress fastened at the left shoulder and fell across the left side of her bosom and back, pleated tightly under her breasts, and gathered under her right breast to fall in soft waves over her hips and buttocks to her knees. The bodice and back were low-cut in a V shape with an inch double frill of the Parisian lace over the shoulders. Slippers of white kid and satin elbow-high gloves completed the ensemble.

Her hair was pulled loosely to the right cascading over her shoulder in full curls secured by a bandeau of pale blue satin adorned with sprigs of honeysuckle and campanula. She wore the sapphire necklace Darcy had gifted her upon their engagement. Lizzy felt like a fairy princess!

Her husband waited in the grand foyer with bated breath. The only hint Lizzy had yielded was that he should wear blue. Darcy preferred blue anyway and, aware that Samuel and Marguerite had undoubtedly compared notes, he trusted his valet's selection. Therefore, he stood on the marble floor wearing a dark-blue formal jacket and matching long trousers of fine wool, the pale blue waistcoat Lizzy had given him, white linen shirt, and an elaborately knotted silk cravat. Mr. Lathrop stood nearby, suppressing a laugh with difficulty, while the others loitered in the parlor.

When Lizzy materialized on the landing, resembling to Darcy's eyes every iota the princess from a fairy tale, his breathing halted for a full minute and his heart skipped several beats. Lizzy blushed under the stunned scrutiny of her husband, loving him increasingly with each step she moved toward him. His smile was radiant and his eyes glowed. If only he knew how impossibly handsome he was when he smiled and gazed upon her in this manner, yet much of his charm was in his total ignorance of his attractiveness and allure.

He kissed the gloved hand she offered, meeting her eyes. "Mrs. Darcy, you are majestic. I am spellbound by your beauty."

She curtseyed and beamed. "Thank you, Mr. Darcy. May I repay the compliment and say that you are an Adonis? Supremely handsome and dapper."

"Elizabeth is here!" Georgiana exclaimed, dashing to her sister and followed closely by the others, who quickly surrounded Lizzy with gushing praise. Grinning indulgently yet conscious that this could continue for hours, Darcy rapidly called for Elizabeth's coat and ushered her into their waiting carriage. Once settled and on their way, Darcy turned toward his wife, retrieving a small box from his pocket.

"For you, beloved. I ventured a guess, the gown a mystery of mythic proportions. Upon revelation, I warrant this bauble will accent nicely."

The *bauble* was a silver brooch some two-inches in diameter in a vague sunburst design with inlaid diamonds and sapphires. Accounting it anything less than exquisite would be an insult. Lizzy was, again, overcome by Darcy's generosity and impeccable taste. He pinned it to her left shoulder where the overdress gathered. It was perfect.

Darcy, painfully cognizant of the fact that for the next eight or so hours proper decorum would prevent him from overtly touching or kissing his lovely wife, made use of the time the ride afforded. Carefully, of course.

Melcourt Hall, home of the Cole family for close to a hundred years, was an enormous brick structure almost as imposing as Pemberley. Sir John Cole, a frail widower well into his sixties, managed his estate with a vigor and efficiency contrary to his appearance. His three sons had gradually assumed most of the responsibilities; however, Sir Cole unequivocally reigned. The eldest two sons were married and the youngest, Percy, only a few years older than Darcy, had recently become betrothed to Mr. Creswell's eldest daughter, Laura.

This development gave Miss Creswell a certain distinction amongst her peers, several of whom gathered strategically so they could simultaneously gossip and admire her engagement ring while maintaining constant vigil on the entryway. The anticipation was elevated this year. As a high point on the Derbyshire social calendar, the Twelfth Night Ball provided the unattached participants the best chance to make a lasting impression on each other.

For the newly plighted, such as Miss Creswell and Miss Sylvia Bristow and Miss Joy Worthington, it was the final opportunity to carefully flirt, giggle, and tease. Additionally, this year's prime topic of speculation was the revealing of the country nobody who had stolen Mr. Darcy. To state that a dozen hearts had been broken, tears shed, and pillows punched would not be an exaggeration; however, none more so than Miss Bertha Vernor, daughter of Henry and Mary Vernor.

The Vernor family had for generations been the closest to the Darcys, both in physical proximity to their lands and in relationship. Gerald Vernor was only months older than Darcy and the two boys were close all through childhood and well into their adult years, only drifting apart somewhat over the past four years since Vernor's marriage. As often transpires after matrimony, Gerald began passing more time in Derbyshire with his wife and new son while Darcy tended toward Town. Nonetheless, the two often met, hunted, and rode together, and Darcy had hosted Gerald and his wife Harriet at Pemberley numerous times.

Miss Bertha had fallen in love with her brother's friend when she was a young girl of sixteen. It was fairly common knowledge to all except for the object of her affection who, not surprisingly, was unbelievably dense about such things and would not have been interested anyway. Still, Miss Bertha pined and hoped, counting on the intimate association between the two families to assist her. Her mother had been devastated by the news of Darcy's marriage, railing at length to anyone willing to listen, especially her husband and son, both of whom cared too deeply for Darcy to wish for anything but his happiness. If that happiness had been acquired with Bertha, the rejoicing would have been profound, but affairs of the heart could not be controlled.

The Vernors had not yet arrived as the flibbertigibbets surrounding Miss Creswell prattled and cogitated. "I heard she refused to eat for a week!" declared Miss Nanette Stanhope.

"Ridiculous," Miss Rose Creswell snipped. "Dear Bertha may be heartbroken, but she would never behave so foolishly."

"Well, I think anyone who chooses to bemoan Mr. Darcy thusly is idiotic," Miss Bristow primly stated. "Aside from Pemberley, he had nothing to offer. Altogether too dull, in my opinion."

"Oh, pooh, Sylvia! Listen to you!" Miss Suzette Lynam sputtered with a laugh. "I recall how you nattered on and on after he spoke with you at the opera two seasons ago. 'He has the bluest eyes, Suzie. And so tall! My neck ached from looking up at him!'" They all laughed and Miss Sylvia blushed.

"Fortunate it is then, Sylvia, that Mr. Reynolds is mere inches taller than you," Miss Trudy Mills teased.

Miss Bristow tossed her head, "At least I am affianced. Trudy, were you not equally all aflutter when Mr. Darcy danced one set with you at the Masque two years ago?"

More laughter all around, and then Miss Greta Creswell spoke in her quiet voice, "Poor Bertha. We should not tease at her expense. She truly cared for Mr. Darcy, not that any fault can be laid at his feet for not returning her sentiments."

Miss Joy Worthington patted Miss Greta's hand. "Do not fret over Bertha, dear Greta. I understand that Mr. Bates has been calling recently. If she is wise, she will accept his suit."

"Have any of you attained any specifics about the new Mrs. Darcy?" asked Miss Laura Creswell. "All my Mr. Cole knew was that she came from Hertfordshire. Not London Society at all."

They collectively gasped and shook their heads. Miss Nanette replied, "My brother Aaron was relating that he met Mrs. Darcy in Lambton a few weeks ago." Most of them had already heard the tale of how the eldest Mr. Stanhope had been introduce to Elizabeth at the Carriage Inn, but for the sake of a meaty story, they all affected ignorance. "He said she was pretty but rather plain, polite and friendly but seemed shy. Mr. Darcy, he said, was clearly besotted."

Sage nods all around. "She has bewitched him, obviously," declared Miss Suzette. "I would not have considered it possible to ensnare Mr. Darcy so, but plainly she found the way."

Miss Amy Hughes spoke for the first time, stunning them all when she proclaimed, "I have met her."

"Miss Amy! How dare you keep such juicy information from us!" chastised Miss Laura. "Pray tell us."

Miss Hughes blushed. As the youngest of the group, just eighteen and out in society only this past year, she was more reserved. "It was in Madame du Loire's salon a few weeks ago. I was there for my fitting. Mr. Darcy escorted Mrs. Darcy in and then left while she shopped." Her blush deepened and she leaned forward, whispering, "He actually kissed her when he left!" This time their gasps were sincere and, if they had been so bold as to admit it, stemmed primarily from jealousy.

"Did you speak with her?" Miss Stanhope asked, all listening with rapt suspense.

"Yes. We were there for over an hour. She was delightful. Witty, charming, and beautiful."

Miss Mills interrupted with the declaration that the Vernors had arrived. Sir Cole at that moment was greeting Mr. Vernor and his wife, Bertha with her brother and sister-in-law next in line. Lord and Lady Matlock were approaching as well. Out in the drive a long line of carriages slowly edged forward, the Darcy carriage among them. By the time the Darcys alighted, the young women had welcomed Miss Bertha, avoiding any further mention of Mr. Darcy, while maintaining their surveillance.

Lizzy had vanquished her trepidations. Her delight in the atmosphere surrounding the festively decorated home, zeal to dance with her husband, eagerness to become acquainted with the other young married women of Derbyshire, and general encompassing bliss had successfully enthused her. The usually stoic and uncomfortable Mr. Darcy discovered that, for the very first time in his entire life, he actually anticipated a ball. It was therefore with boundless pride and a beaming smile that Mr. Darcy entered the grandly embellished foyer of Melcourt Hall with his radiant bride on his arm.

A mild hush fell over the room as nearly every eye in the place fell on the couple, both of them well aware of the scrutiny. Darcy paused theatrically, delighting in the attention for indubitably the only occasion in memory and probably the last. The caesura spanned mere seconds, but the desired effect was obtained. Within minutes the word raced through the manor that the Darcys had arrived.

Sir Cole welcomed the young couple effusively, Lizzy charming him instantly. Lord and Lady Matlock hovered nearby and greeted Lizzy warmly, further causing a stir. If the redoubtable Matlocks so approved of the new Mrs. Darcy, then the rumors of her inappropriateness that had spread throughout the region surely were ungrounded.

"Elizabeth dear, you are breathtaking," Lady Matlock pronounced with a kiss to Lizzy's cheek. "Nephew, allow me the honor of introducing Mrs. Darcy to the Vernors. Mr. Vernor, Mrs. Vernor, my niece Mrs. Darcy."

"Mrs. Darcy, it is a delight to see you again," Mr. Vernor bowed. "I do trust your first month at Pemberley has been pleasant?"

"Immensely so, Mr. Vernor, thank you for inquiring. Mrs. Vernor, it is a pleasure to make your acquaintance."

Darcy had greeted Gerald with enthusiasm and turned to his wife. "My dear, this is Gerald Vernor, an old friend, although he did tergiversate and attend Oxford. Mr. Vernor, my wife, Elizabeth Darcy."

"Mrs. Darcy, it is a joy to meet the woman who captured my wayward friend's heart." Lizzy laughed and curtseyed, sensing immediately the same open amiability in the son as in the father. He lightly touched his wife's elbow, "My wife Harriet Vernor."

Harriet Vernor was a tall woman, slim but slightly mannish in her build, with an unattractive horsy face but yet startling green eyes. As soon as she spoke, however, her homeliness faded. Her voice was dulcet and rich, and she spoke with an easy humor and pithy wit. Lizzy liked her instantly, and the two fell into an effortless conversation as the group moved into the main hall.

The following forty-five or so minutes were expended in a flurry of introductions, as seemingly the entire population of Derbyshire drifted toward the Darcys. The Matlocks remained near, lending nonverbal support to their niece, while Darcy, although remarkably more extroverted than usual, nonetheless cut an imposing figure. Few were brave enough to cross the formidable Mr. Darcy.

In general, the inhabitants were gracious and welcoming, willing, apparently, to delay a hasty judgment regarding the new Mrs. Darcy. The thinly veiled insults and condescending glances were rare and met with the glare and particular set to the jaw displaying annoyance from Mr. Darcy, which none wanted directed their way. Harriet amused Lizzy with a running acerbic commentary whispered in her ear. By the time the strains from the orchestra commenced, Lizzy's mind was a muddle of names. Therefore, she was ecstatic to have her handsome husband claim her for the first set. She had promised Lord Matlock the second set and Mr. Vernor the third, but the remainder were all for Darcy.

The orchestra chose a moderate minuet to warm up the crowd, followed by a lively cotillion. Lizzy and Darcy had a marvelous time. The opportunity to completely erase the unpleasant aspects attached to the memory of their disastrous encounter at the Netherfield Ball was crucial. Neither of them could now deny the attraction they had felt even then, nor did they wish to. Yet for months afterwards Darcy had tried to blot her from his mind, and Lizzy had refused to even entertain the notion of enchantment with Mr. Darcy.

Tonight they allowed their love and mutual enthrallment to wash over them. Lizzy noted that indeed Darcy *was* an excellent dancer! So tall and elegant and graceful, every touch of his hand piercing through her gloves, the intoxicating whiff of his cologne as he glided near, intense gaze boring into her, the tiny lift to his lips now recognizable as humor and veneration, and the soothing timbre of his voice as he prattled nonsensically each time they passed all combined to far surpass any dancing experience of her life.

"I love this dance," he began.

Lizzy smiled. "Indeed, most invigorating."

"So many couples."

"It is an accommodating room."

"Pemberley's ballroom is larger, however."

"Do you intend to talk all through the dance, Mr. Darcy?"

"I have been advised it is proper etiquette to do so… Do you not agree, Mrs. Darcy?"

"Only if one's partner is worth conversing with."

"I see… am I classified as worthy or unworthy?"

"I believe I need more evidence to judge… pray continue, Mr. Darcy."

On and on it went, Darcy never losing his train of inane babble, even when parted for a turn with the next lady in line. Lizzy watched him from the corner of her eye, frequently making contact with his gaze, as they moved through the set. He spoke little to anyone else, except for one young woman approximately

Lizzy's age whom he greeted with a soft smile. She, oddly, was a deep shade of pink and decidedly uncomfortable, puzzling Darcy.

"Who is the young lady in yellow?" Lizzy asked when again engaged with her husband.

"Miss Bertha Vernor, Gerald's sister," he replied softly with an edge of bafflement in his voice.

"You unnerved her, it appeared."

"I cannot imagine how… I have known her all her life… she is like a sister to me."

Lizzy laughed, "My love, you are impossibly obtuse!"

"I beg your pardon, Madame!"

"I can almost guarantee she does not see you as a brother." Darcy's confusion increased for a full minute before he finally grasped her implication, after which he blushed profusely, covering his discomfiture with the Darcy scowl. The dance ended with Lizzy's tinkling laugh as she took his arm and steered him to the bowl of wassail.

The next sets were the shorter quadrilles. Lizzy danced the initial two parts with Lord Matlock while Darcy squired his aunt. The Earl made few attempts at conversation, the fast pace and intricate steps of the dance demanding all his attention. Lady Matlock apparently was quite diverting, as Lizzy could see her husband struggling to remain reserved and focused. Lizzy danced the middle parts with Mr. Gerald Vernor, Darcy partnering Mrs. Vernor. Lizzy and Darcy finished the set together.

The dining hall was lavishly decorated, the long tables arranged in rows facing toward the door with the main table slightly elevated lengthwise before the far wall. The Darcys were seated at the main table with Sir Cole, the Matlocks, the Vernors, Sir Arthur Levings of Parwich Hall, Lord and Lady Newburgh of Hassop Hall, Sir James and Lady Harpur of Calke Abbey, and numerous others whom Lizzy had not yet met.

Lizzy sat diagonally across from her husband and between Lady Harpur and a man introduced to her as the Marquis of Orman. Lord Orman was a handsome man perhaps a year or two older than Darcy, unmarried and charming. Lady Harpur said little, whether from shyness or lack of interest in her dinner companions Lizzy could not discern. Darcy was flanked by Sir James Harpur and Mrs. Mary Vernor. Within earshot sat Lord and Lady Matlock and the remaining Vernors.

Dinner was spectacular. Conversation and laughter flowed. Lord Orman was engaging, thankfully for Lizzy, as Lady Harpur said barely two words. Darcy spoke primarily with Sir James and Mr. Vernor, joining in with Lizzy and Lord Orman on occasion.

"Mrs. Darcy," Lord Orman said, "I understand you are from Hertfordshire?"

"Yes, My Lord, you have heard correctly. Are you familiar with the region?"

"Not much, I confess. I have traveled through on my way to London; however, I have not tarried in the area. Do you miss your home?"

Lizzy smiled. "I miss my family somewhat, but Pemberley and Derbyshire are my home."

"Of course. Forgive me, Mrs. Darcy, I meant no offense."

"None taken."

"Did you leave a large family behind?"

"Four sisters and my parents, as well as cousins. Fortunately, Meryton is not a great distance, and it is the lot of us women eventually to leave our parents for our new families. I am content." Lizzy glanced at Darcy, who was apparently absorbed in his plate, but she noted the tiny crease between his brows and well knew what it signified.

"Of course." Lord Orman continued. "Still, it must be difficult to leave what you have always known for the unknown."

"You would be mistaken, My Lord. It has not been difficult in the slightest. I am exceedingly comfortable here. The scenery and natural formations are widely diverse and majestic here in Derbyshire. Far more so than Hertfordshire, which is pastoral. Unfortunately the weather has not been kind enough to allow me the opportunity to explore as I would wish; however, this will be remedied in the spring."

"Do you appreciate the out of doors then, Mrs. Darcy?"

"Oh yes, very much."

"You ride, I presume."

"Actually, not at all. I prefer to walk."

He was taken aback, "How odd. A Darcy who does not ride. Who would have believed it? I would rather have imagined horsemanship a prerequisite for matrimony amongst the Darcys." He seemed to be teasing but Lizzy found the comment a trifle rude. Apparently, her husband did as well.

"I fear you are hasty, Orman, in forming assumptions regarding the character of the Darcys." He spoke softly but with an edge that Lizzy recognized as irritation and his eyes were a flinty blue. "A person's caliber is not dependent on a particular accomplishment, nor can a host of accomplishments accurately illustrate one's quality."

It was a true statement voiced in a flat tone, but Lizzy, who knew her husband so well, understood he was casting aspersions. Orman knew it also, and there was a moment of silence before he laughed, "Touché, Darcy."

The conversation turned then to topics more general. The men spoke of politics and the resolving crisis with France. Lizzy struck up a conversation with Mrs. Vernor and Mrs. Samantha Cole, a woman in her late twenties and the wife of the middle Cole son, Joshua. Mrs. Cole reminded Lizzy of her younger sisters, giddy and not terribly bright but humorous and entertaining. Her favorite topics were fashion and society gossip, of little interest to Lizzy; however, she did realize that a fair amount of knowledge on both subjects could be to her advantage so she joined in. She and Mrs. Vernor shared several amused glances, but Mrs. Cole's insipid chatter did pass the time pleasantly and, oddly enough, Lizzy did like her.

As they stood to leave the table, Lord Orman leaned close to Lizzy and said softly, "I hope I did not offend, Mrs. Darcy. You appear an intelligent young woman and I enjoyed our conversation. I would like to be counted a friend."

Lizzy was terribly uncomfortable and momentarily at a loss. Darcy, she noted quickly, was on the other side of the table speaking with his aunt, apparently unaware of Lord Orman's attention. Lizzy took a step backwards, smiled pleasantly, and met his eyes frankly. "Thank you for the compliment, Lord Orman. I can assure you that whomever my husband counts as a friend is also a friend of mine. As I am a new inhabitant of the area, I am leaving these decisions to him. It is far too easy to arrive at swift and errant judgments."

Lord Orman bowed and retreated slightly but continued undeterred, "Would I be too bold to ask if I may secure your hand for a dance set, Mrs. Darcy? Or does Mr. Darcy make those decisions for you as well?"

Lizzy was stunned, a ready retort on her lips, but they were both startled by Darcy's deep voice. "Mrs. Darcy is free to fill her dance card with whomever she chooses." He stood next to her, towering over Orman by at least five inches, calm, and impassively gazing at the Marquis as he offered his arm to Lizzy.

Lizzy smiled brightly at her husband as she placed her hand on his arm, and then turned to Orman. "Thank you, Lord Orman; however, all dances are promised to my husband, by my choice." She curtseyed and he bowed.

"Perhaps another time then, Mrs. Darcy. Mr. Darcy." He bowed again and moved away.

"Interesting man," Lizzy commented sardonically.

"He is a scoundrel, Elizabeth. I cannot fathom what Sir Cole was thinking to seat him at the head table, and close to me. He knows we despise each other."

"As bad as all that?" She said with an arch smile. "You must fill me in, William! I am becoming quite enamored with the local gossip."

He looked at her in shock and then, seeing a feigned vapid expression on her face, he laughed. "Perhaps, darling, you should steer clear of Mrs. Cole and her cronies for the remainder of the evening. They are corrupting your good sense."

To their heightened amusement, Lady Matlock and Harriet Vernor approached at precisely that moment to steal Elizabeth away with the express intent of introducing her to more of the married ladies of the region. Darcy relented only after his aunt promised to be cautious. "Fret not, William, I shall take care of her."

They had re-entered the ballroom. The orchestra played softly in the background as the two enormous and absurdly ornate Twelfth Night cakes were wheeled in. Harriet explained, "One cake is for the women and the other for the men. Pieces are cut, and the man and woman who receive a piece with the bean in it are crowned King and Queen for the night. It is all silly fun."

As the pieces were cut and distributed to those who wished to partake, Darcy not surprisingly refusing as he had every year he attended, Harriet and Lady Matlock escorted Lizzy about the room. There were an abundance of women roughly Lizzy's age or a bit older who welcomed her graciously. Mrs. Samantha Cole fawned over her as if they were old friends, proudly presenting Lizzy to her sister-in-law Mrs. Katherine Cole and soon-to-be sister-in-law Miss Laura Creswell. There was the usual gushing over the dress and brooch and hair, intermingled with cunningly worded inquiries as to how she and Mr. Darcy had met, the wedding details, her family connections, and so on. Lizzy had a marvelous time.

Most of the young women were delightful and, if like Mrs. Samantha Cole they were not overly astute, Lizzy found them genuine and gracious. There were a number who reminded her vividly of Caroline Bingley, but Lizzy had fun with them as well. Three women in particular, Mrs. Alison Fitzherbert, Mrs. Julia Sitwell, and Mrs. Chloe Drury, connected instantly with Lizzy, as had Harriet

Vernor. Before the night was over, the four women had arranged a date for tea the following week at Mrs. Fitzherbert's home, Tillington Hall, near Eyam.

The Queen was Miss Bertha Vernor and the King a Mr. Rufus Sitwell. It seemed clear to Lizzy that the young Mr. Sitwell was delighted to have the opportunity to stand next to Miss Bertha and dance as the Royal Couple for the next set. Lizzy had rejoined her husband for the "crowning" and whispered as much to him.

"He may have competition," he responded. "I have been informed that Mr. Bates has been calling on Miss Bertha."

Lizzy smiled. "My, what an old gossip you are, Mr. Darcy. When we are home, we shall have to compare notes."

"I have plans for when we return home, my lovely wife, and they do not include comparing notes." He stared seriously straight ahead, but feathered one finger over her knuckles where they lay on his arm, sending shivers thrilling up Lizzy's spine.

The orchestra announced the next dance, the sarabande. Darcy and Lizzy took their places, memories again assailing them as the music began. The tune was different than at the Netherfield Ball, but the steps the same. Neither of them attempted conversation. Instead, they focused on each other to the exclusion of the entire room. As pleasant as the experience was, it was also rather dangerous. The two lovers nearly did lose sight of where they were, drawing closer with each turn than the dance strictly intended and becoming mildly aroused. Luckily, the music ended before they foolishly crossed any lines of propriety, faces flushed and panting imperceptibly. The following dances were livelier, a gavotte and then a gigue.

Darcy was willing to continue for the next set, but Lizzy opted for refreshments and fresh air. Darcy secured two cups of wassail and gingersnaps, happily guiding his wife outside to a secluded alcove on the terrace. Lizzy did not have the chance to take a sip before her husband had claimed her mouth in a preferable activity.

"Elizabeth," he sighed, breathing heavily against her parted lips, "you are so beautiful. I am torn asunder. Part of me desires never to leave as I am swollen with pride in proclaiming to all how blessed I am in having procured the hand of such a magnificent woman. Yet I also long to be alone with you." He kissed her lingeringly, caressing her face and neck, and murmuring, "Glorious wife. You take my breath away. I am nonplussed by my mood of felicity!"

"Are you truly enjoying yourself, beloved?"

"Yes, I honestly am." He sounded as surprised to admit it as Lizzy was to hear it. "Dancing with you, introducing you to my friends, simply having you here with me, Elizabeth; I cannot express how happy I am." He laughed boisterously. "Thank you, my love! I now understand how enjoyable these events can actually be and why people attend them. I never comprehended it before."

Lizzy smiled gleefully and kissed his cheek. "William, you are so cute! I love you!"

He lifted one eyebrow, still smiling and stroking her swanlike neck. "Cute? I am not certain how manly it is to be labeled 'cute,' Elizabeth."

"Your manliness is without dispute, my love, but do not worry, your cuteness shall be our secret."

They passed another ten or so minutes in merry seclusion, entering the hall arm and arm in time for the waltz. Some thirty couples were brave enough to dare the infamous dance, all but three of them married. The full assembly gathered in the ballroom, pressed into every available space to observe. The general atmosphere was one of eager anticipation with only a few outright expressions of indignation or wrath.

The Darcys took their place, irrefutably one of the best-looking couples on the floor. The Viennese waltz was a fast-paced dance of unrelenting circular movements with numerous twirlings and rotations. It was fluid, graceful, and vigorous. Despite its reputation, the intimacy was not as scandalous as many envisioned. The partners stood at nearly extended arm's length, the man's right hand lightly on the woman's waist with her left hand resting on his shoulder. His left arm stretched at chest height, acting as a shelf for her right hand. Their bodies never actually touched.

The orchestra played "Una Cosa Rara" from Vincente Martin's opera, one of the original waltz pieces written. The music was beautiful, and it was heavenly to dance with the full symphonic blends swirling about them. Lizzy and Darcy had eyes only for each other. It was amazing, exhilarating, and enormous fun. Only one other intimate activity transcended the rapture of this dance. When the music ended, the room erupted in applause.

For the second turn, some ten new couples boldly joined in. A Mozart waltz was performed this turn as wondrously as Martin had been. The actual steps of the waltz were not complex, rendering the dance easy to learn and execute. Those who possessed a natural grace, such as the Darcys, excelled. Of course, it was a new dance, so few of the participants could claim expertise, which meant that few of the spectators could necessarily find fault. Therefore, the acclamation was thunderous, with even the skeptics rendering grudging approval. Overall, the decision to allow the nefarious dance born in the bordellos and peasant dance halls of Europe was a triumph, and presented another step in the path of preeminence for waltz-type dancing.

For the remaining sets, the orchestra reverted to standard, accepted English country dancing. Darcy led Elizabeth to an isolated seat and, after a kiss to her hand, left in search of refreshments. Lizzy watched him weave his way through the press of people, taller than the majority of them so it was easy to follow his progress. She sighed in happiness and closed her eyes briefly.

"You dance the waltz as if born to do so, Mrs. Darcy."

The voice jolted her out of her reverie and she looked up into the eyes of the Marquis of Orman. "My Lord, forgive me. I did not see you approach."

"It is I who should beg forgiveness, Madame. I believe I interrupted your rest. You must be fatigued after such a vigorous dance." He was smiling strangely and peering at her far too boldly for comfort.

"This would be twice tonight you have been mistaken, sir. I am not fatigued. Merely catching my breath and capturing a moment of solitude until Mr. Darcy returns with our refreshments."

"Ah, so he is to return. Pity. I was rather hoping he had deserted you. May I?" He indicated the empty side of the sofa, but without waiting for an invitation, he sat and leaned toward Lizzy. "Are all the women of Hertfordshire as beautiful as you, Mrs. Darcy? If so, I must travel there immediately. Perhaps I shall be as fortunate as Darcy."

Lizzy recognized with alarm that the Marquis was inebriated. She did not wish to make a scene nor to have Darcy discover him here. She glanced around quickly and did not see her husband's towering form anywhere near. "I appreciate the compliment, Lord Orman. However, I believe it improper for you to offer it and to be sitting so close to me. Please stand a pace away, sir."

"Beautiful and spirited, too. I can understand why Darcy married you. The Monk of Pemberley found his match, and the heart of every young maiden in England was broken."

Elizabeth was furious. "Marquis, I will overlook this hideous breach of manners for the sake of peace at these festivities and because I deem you are not fully in charge of your faculties. I will not, however, sit here and listen to you any further. Please excuse me." She stood to leave but he grasped her wrist tightly.

"Orman! You *will* unhand my wife this instant, or I promise you will not live to see the light of day." One glance at Darcy's enraged face and Orman flinched, releasing Lizzy's hand as if it were on fire. Darcy was livid, visage dark and perilous, flinty eyes boring into Orman with a chilling intensity. Without blinking or removing his glare, he handed the cups to Elizabeth. "My dear, take these and find Lady Matlock. I will join you momentarily." His voice was calm but colder than Lizzy had ever heard it. She took the cups and left without a word.

A backward glance revealed Darcy firmly and ruthlessly propelling the unresisting Marquis out of the hall. Oddly, no one in the near vicinity seemed to have noticed any of it. Lizzy found the Matlocks sitting with the Vernors, elder and younger, and tremblingly told them what had transpired. Lord Matlock and Henry Vernor rose instantly and exited the hall. Harriet and Lady Matlock comforted Lizzy.

"That man has always been trouble," Lady Matlock proclaimed. "I cannot fathom what Sir Cole was thinking, inviting him tonight. You can be sure he will hear about this."

Lizzy was further distraught and felt tears rising to her eyes. "Oh no! I do not wish for this to be made into a scandal. Mr. Darcy abhors talk and would be so angry."

Lady Matlock looked at her sharply. "Elizabeth, do not fret. It will remain discreet and William would never be angry with you for this. You said no one noticed. Harriet, dear, take Elizabeth into the library. I shall tell Mr. Darcy where you are."

Some fifteen minutes later Darcy entered the library. Lizzy was calm, talking softly with Harriet, who rose when Darcy approached. "Thank you, Mrs. Vernor, for attending to my wife."

She curtseyed. "It was my pleasure Mr. Darcy. Elizabeth, I shall see you soon."

"Thank you, Harriet, for everything."

The second the door closed behind her, Darcy dropped his pose of serenity and knelt before Lizzy, taking her face into his hands and studying her raptly. "Beloved, are you well? Please forgive me for allowing this to occur.

What did he say to you? Did he hurt you in any way?" His voice caught and he swallowed.

Lizzy shook her head quickly and put her arms around him. "William, I am fine. He did not hurt me and nothing he said is of any import. He was intoxicated and rambling. There is nothing to forgive." She smiled, "Your timing was excellent, as I was about to kick him. How would that have looked? You are my hero." She kissed him teasingly, but he would have none of that and clutched her to his chest, kissing her possessively.

"I should have had him thrown out earlier when he insulted you," he growled. "He is damned fortunate I did not kill him tonight!"

She peered at his frowning face. "Did you... do anything to him?"

He inhaled deeply and then smiled, "Such as trounce him within an inch of his miserable life? It was tempting, but no. Somehow I did not think you would wish to dance with me covered in blood." He ran his fingers over her cheeks. "Elizabeth, are you positive you are well? You must tell me the truth." He continued to peer at her with the familiar Darcy intensity at full force while gently massaging the wrist Orman had grabbed.

"I am fine. I was angry more than anything. I despise rude people and did not want this wonderful night ruined."

Darcy kissed her wrist and mouth tenderly and then rose. "Nothing is ruined, my love. If I have not lost track of time, there is still one more dance set before the play." He held his arm out. "May I have the honor, Mrs. Darcy?"

They were the last couple to join the line. It was a frolicsome dance to end the evening, and by the completion, Lizzy and Darcy had put the whole episode with Lord Orman behind them. Smiling and breathless, they accompanied the parade of merrymakers into the dining room, which had hastily been converted into a playhouse. The stage spanned the far wall, an enormous curtain concealing the preparations from the audience being ushered to their seats. The Darcys' seats were in the fifth row. As soon as the lights were dimmed, Darcy clasped Lizzy's hand, interlacing his fingers with hers.

It was now after midnight; therefore, Twelfth Night was officially over and it was now Twelfth Day, the traditional day of Christ's Epiphany. The Coles had, for all the years of their Masque, separated the entertainment into two parts: feast and dancing followed by a stage theatrical. This year Sir Cole had hired a troupe of pantomimes from London for the first act. As expected, the comedic company delivered a riotous, irreverent performance. The play chosen was the classic English fairy tale *Jack and the Beanstalk*, executed brilliantly with smashing audience participation. Mugs of wassail had been passed around for the obligatory cheers of "Waes hael," as well as small bags of beans to throw at the giant when instructed. Lizzy had never witnessed anything quite like it nor laughed so hard in her life.

After an intermission, the audience took their seats for the last half of the production. For the dramatic portion of the theatrical, Sir Cole had hired a renowned company from Birmingham to perform the new play by E. T. A. Hoffmann, *Nutcracker and the Mouse King*. This latest piece had been written just that year and not yet translated for the general masses; therefore, it was an amazing treat. Darcy, especially, was fascinated by the Prussian author's stories, so he was delighted and utterly spellbound. Lizzy privately found it too somber but highly imaginative, nonetheless, and magnificently acted.

The end of the theatricals effectively capped a marvelous evening. Visiting, drinking, and nibbling continued for several hours more, although Darcy and Lizzy tarried for some forty-five minutes only. Lizzy renewed her teatime appointment with Harriet, Mrs. Fitzherbert, Mrs. Sitwell, and Mrs. Drury. Darcy thanked his aunt for comforting Elizabeth after the Orman debacle. Invitations were extended by Darcy to several of the young couples of his circle for dinner two days hence, before the Gardiners and Lathrops departed. He spontaneous planned this without consulting Lizzy, to her surprise, not because she minded but because she would have thought him weary of so much entertainment.

Finally in their carriage, nestled close for warmth as well as the yearning to touch each other, Lizzy sighed and contentedly rested her head on Darcy's inner shoulder. He kissed her head and stroked her arm. She arched her neck and peered at her husband's smiling face. "You were the handsomest man there, my love, and I the most fortunate of women because I get to go home with you."

"Flatterer! It is not necessary, beloved; you already have me."

"I can only speak the truth. Now kiss me, Mr. Darcy, and then tell me about the *plans* you have for when we get home."

He did not answer her inquiry but did acquiesce to her request by kissing her searchingly in sheer delight. The short carriage ride home passed swiftly, both of them gasping shallowly with barely enough forethought to cease their activity before the footman opened the door. The cold blast of winter air restored clarity sufficiently to enable them to ascend the staircases in relative calm.

The manor was dimly lit and quiet. A fire was smoldering in their bedchamber, but otherwise the room was dark. Darcy barely managed to keep his hands off his lovely wife during the long walk. He drew her back against his chest the moment they entered their room, latching the door simultaneously. His hands stroked voraciously over her hips and thighs as he delivered sensuous kisses along the silky nakedness of her neck and collarbone.

"Oh, my sweet, delicious wife. How is it possible to love and hunger for you more with each day that passes?" He suckled her earlobe. Lizzy moaned, pressing herself firmly against him. "You render me breathless with desire, my lover. So beautiful. Dancing with you was equally a pleasure and an agony."

"Agony?" she asked in a bare whisper.

He turned her in his arms, cupping her face with his hands, thumbs caressing. "I want you so, my beloved. Do you know what exquisite torture it is to be so close to you, to feel your touch, gaze upon your enchanting beauty, and yearn to make love to you with every muscle in my body, yet not be able to even kiss you?"

She smiled. "Yes, William, I do know. Were you fantasizing again, beloved?"

"Always. Carefully, however, or the entire assembly would have been witness to Darcy of Pemberley's more personal and private attributes."

Lizzy laughed, reaching down while kissing his lips lightly, she said, "I would rather keep those marvelous attributes for mine eyes only."

"You forever shall, Elizabeth. Now, stay here a moment." He added a log to the fire and then lit a couple lamps, returning hastily to where she patiently stood. With a stunning smile and graceful bow, he asked, "Mrs. Darcy, may I have this dance?"

She giggled at his silliness, but curtseyed properly, "You may, Mr. Darcy."

In a flawless waltz position, humming Mozart in perfect pitch, he swept her about the room. Full orchestra music was unnecessary. As regally as at the Masque, their clothing impeccable and movements as one, they floated. The flowing, elegant steps proceeded naturally as they raptly adored each other. As they glided through the sensuous swaying motions, Darcy incrementally lured her closer to his body until they touched. His left hand grasped Lizzy's right, fingers interlaced, and he kissed each finger before placing their enfolded hands against his heart. They danced, twirled, and wove in unity and rhythm as their passion heightened. Both were panting and light-headed with a burning desire.

Darcy steered her to the edge of the bed, laying her down smoothly as he hovered above her, supporting himself so as not to crush her. "I love you, Elizabeth," he murmured and then engulfed her mouth with a hungry urgency. One seeking hand traveled leisurely over her body, tantalizing her through the filmy satin of her gown as she arched to meet him. With a throaty groan, he pulled away from her lips momentarily, studying her rapturous face, and continuing to arouse her with his fingers as she gasped and trembled while skillfully arousing him. They kissed again as if starved, delirious with rising ardor, wanting to be joined together intimately as if life depended on it, yet unable to break from the consummate rapture of shared breath.

Raining moist kisses over her neck, he peeled the delicate fabric off one shoulder, traveling to her exposed bosom for gentle kisses. In time he moved to kneeling on the floor between her legs. Caressing under her skirt and petticoat until the urgent craving to love each other consumed them, they joined forcefully and blissfully.

"William! My heart, oh God, how I love you!" She clutched his shoulders under his jacket, succumbing to the joy of him, the love and passion that consumed her now and always. On they loved, heaven attained eventually as they molded bodily and melded spiritually.

Darcy collapsed onto her. Words were temporarily impossible, all effort expended on breathing. Lizzy's wits resurfaced first. Running her fingers through his hair, her head turning to kiss his cheek, she murmured, "Fitzwilliam, my lover, I adore you more than life."

Darcy lifted on an elbow, fingering along her face with one hand while the other embedded into the curls spilling over her right shoulder. He kissed her tenderly. "You are beautiful, my wife. All night I watched you dazzling and charming the citizens of Derbyshire, and pride consumed me. I cannot believe you are mine, my Lizzy, my treasure. I am the most fortunate of men."

She smiled, "We are both fortunate, husband. Now, I want to feel your glorious naked body surrounding me as we sleep. You have blissfully exhausted me, so I shall need your assistance to undress."

He chuckled, kissed her lightly. "I am not certain I can stand, so we may need to help each other!" They did, the process of unclothing the other eliciting a mild state of reoccurring arousal, but in the end they were blessedly spent and required sleep. At least for the moment.

CHAPTER SIXTEEN

The Long Winter

WINTERS IN DERBYSHIRE TENDED to be harsher and longer than in Hertfordshire. In the days immediately following the ball, the weather turned threatening: ominous clouds gathered and persisted unabated for weeks, occasionally disbursing sheets of rain or snow. Those brief episodes when the sky cleared were grabbed expeditiously. After the Masque, life in the region settled into a protracted period of waiting. For the younger and more society-craving citizens, it was an agony of boring days and nights passed in impatient endurance until the spring thaw permitted the mass exodus to London.

For Lizzy, it was the most blissful period of her life. She had her moments of restlessness when the need to stretch her legs overwhelmed her until she would brave the cold and her husband's frown for an extended turn about the frozen gardens. Otherwise, she found that each day brought new wonders, numerous activities both at Pemberley and with her new friends, family time, duties and lessons to learn as Mistress, and always overshadowing it all, the love for Darcy that grew daily.

Until the ninth of January, Lizzy devoted every possible minute to close communion with her aunt and uncle. Darcy and Mr. Lathrop also sensed the need to strengthen their friendship. Lizzy and Amelia became confidantes, a development that greatly pleased the gentlemen. Amelia revealed to Lizzy and

Violet that she had recently confirmed she was with child. The two women were ecstatic for her, Lizzy plying her with questions and Violet offering words of wisdom. Tentative plans were laid to meet in Town during the coming May, if Amelia's pregnancy allowed.

On the evening of the eighth, the day before their guests were to depart, the Darcys hosted the dinner party that Darcy had impulsively arranged during the Masque. Along with the Lathrops and the Gardiners, there were Gerald and Harriet Vernor, George and Alison Fitzherbert, Rory and Julia Sitwell, Clifton and Chloe Drury, and Albert and Marilyn Hughes.

Gerald Vernor and Albert Hughes were the two closest friends, dating from Darcy's youth. These three, along with Richard Fitzwilliam and George Wickham, had been nearly inseparable when young. Darcy and Hughes were avid billiards players and, by the tender age of seventeen, had so mastered the game that no one in all of Derbyshire could supplant them as the county's champions. Darcy, Vernor, and the future Col. Fitzwilliam had in common a passion for horses. Wickham was younger than the other boys and had shadowed them more than anything, although they had honestly considered him a friend until he went wild as a young man at University.

Rory Sitwell had become acquainted with Darcy at Cambridge. Neither man had met the other before, so it was a pleasant coincidence to establish a mutual friendship with someone from home. Sitwell's personality was similar to Darcy's and Lathrop's: reserved, taciturn, serious, dry witted, and aloof. Vernor, Hughes, and Col. Fitzwilliam inclined toward affability, jocularity, and gaiety. They were an odd group by all outward appearances, but like Darcy and Bingley, their opposite natures blended. Among the many traits the men did have in common were moral uprightness and fierce loyalty to their families and community.

George Fitzherbert and Clifton Drury were well into their late thirties and, although Darcy knew them from town, they were not close friends. Normally Darcy would not have been disposed to invite them to dine at Pemberley; however, Lizzy's positive impression of their wives had pleased Darcy, so he had happily included them.

Aside from the apparently confirmed bachelorhood of Col. Fitzwilliam, Darcy was the last to find happiness as a wedded man, an event that may have caused dismay with the young women of Derbyshire but pleased his friends immensely. The natural gulf that had appeared between them at

Darcy's persistent single status while they were married and beginning their families had spawned a faint distress, not that any of them would have acknowledged it.

All of Darcy's compatriots had chosen their wives based on affection to one degree or another. None of them was as wealthy as Darcy nor had his responsibilities, yet they too had felt the pressure to marry wisely within the strict dictates of society, and all of them had done so. Therefore, the shock at Darcy, of all people, breaking the mores as he had in marrying Elizabeth Bennet had staggered them.

Gentlemen may not tend to gossip to the extent that women purportedly do, although this allegation could well be a misrepresentation; however, these men had shared many a baffled conversation regarding their friend's decision. Now, having been introduced to the new Mrs. Darcy, noting her beauty and grace and decorousness, and observing Darcy's clear infatuation and joy, their relief and comprehension improved.

The dinner was a success. With the assistance of Mrs. Reynolds, Lizzy planned a perfect evening. Georgiana had begged to absent herself from the party, an understandable request, and since Mrs. Annesley had returned from her holiday with her family, Georgiana dined with her companion in her chambers. Lizzy had met Mr. and Mrs. Hughes briefly at the Masque. Marilyn Hughes was currently six months into her first pregnancy and had not felt well at the Ball, prompting an early departure. Fortunately, she felt well enough to attend the Darcy dinner party, and Lizzy found her delightful.

Lizzy entertained the ladies in her parlor after dinner and they all bonded easily. Aunt Gardiner, far older than all the rest and, therefore, with little in common with them, happily sat silently in joy at seeing her niece make new friends. She well remembered how difficult it had been for her to leave her family and intimates as a young bride. Love for one's husband was of the utmost importance, yet female companionship was also essential.

In addition, Violet knew that Lizzy would eventually reach a point where her separation from Jane would overwhelm her. Having other young ladies nearby with whom she felt an affinity to comfort her and fill that void was indispensable. She was correct in her assessment. Over the course of time, these women would form deep alliances, sustain and succor each other, offer advice and wisdom, and raise the next generation of Derbyshire citizens to carry on the tradition of friendship and community.

Lizzy shed several tears over the departure of her aunt and uncle and the Lathrops, but she was comforted first in the knowledge that they would see each other in a few months and then again in Darcy's arms. Lizzy had insisted that, except for the remains of the Yule log, which by tradition had to be packed away on Twelfth Day, all the other decorations stay up until after the guests departed.

Therefore, no sooner had quiet descended on the manor and Georgiana retreated to her pianoforte than Elizabeth purposefully grasped her husband's hand and fulfilled her vow by leading him to each hanging mistletoe globe for a kiss. They managed to keep all proper and chaste until the third floor. By the time they reached the last ball dangling just outside their sitting room door, the twenty-fourth not counting the Darcy kissing bough, the individual kisses had evolved into a ceaseless passionate one that persisted well into the bedchamber and beyond.

They spent the entire day in their chambers together, both desperately needing the time together after the crush of visitors over the past fortnight. Darcy was amply content to embrace settling into the long winter at Pemberley without too many social or business pressures. The occasional dinner party or hunt or dance or afternoon at billiards would be interspersed with the necessary forays to the mills or stables or tenant farms, but winter in Derbyshire effectively cast a stasis over all occupations.

In the past, Darcy had heartily succumbed to the season for the afforded joy of hours spent reading in the library, long rides, catching up on delayed projects, and blessed solitude. This year he would have all that with the added favor of sharing it with his wife, not to mention the pleasure of lazy hours in their bedroom.

Despite his newfound delight in showing off his wife at social events, Darcy was primarily a creature craving privacy. His shyness and natural tendency toward reserve would always be a part of his character, no matter the emancipation of his soul. Lizzy, although not the slightest bit shy or reticent, did cherish peace and quiet and solitary pursuits. The young lovers discovered that they were strikingly akin in more ways than they had imagined.

Darcy truly thought his wife would be fit to rip her hair out after a month of forced imprisonment inside Pemberley's vast, echoing corridors, and Lizzy honestly thought he would tire of her constant presence in his sanctuaries. They were both astoundingly in error. By the time the spring thaw came, necessitating

Darcy's increased excursions to the farms and Lizzy's spurred enthusiasm for outdoor activities, they would be so devoted and enslaved to each other that the separations would be agony. Yet for now, they settled in to the peace and leisure of the winter with relish.

❧

"Fitzwilliam, I have a request."

It was mid-January and the Darcys were breakfasting in their sitting room as they always did, except for Sundays before church when they broke fast with Georgiana. Darcy looked up from the newspaper into the serious face of his wife. He smiled. "Ah, 'Fitzwilliam' is it? I suppose that dictates the necessity for my undivided attention."

Lizzy blushed, lowered her eyes for a moment, and then met his amused stare. "I have been thinking…"

"Very dangerous, that is," he interrupted with a grin.

"Stop that and listen!" she chastised, trying not to laugh. "I would like to learn how to drive a curricle." She was firm and met his surprised face with lifted chin. "Can you teach me, love?"

He opened his mouth to speak but then closed it when he realized he could not think what to say, so startled was he at her request. Lizzy scooted to the edge of her chair and leaned toward him in her enthusiasm. "I have expressed to you my desire to begin volunteering weekly at the orphanage; I have received several invitations to tea with the ladies, and upon occasion I need to shop in the village, so I deduce that being able to freely travel without having to disturb a groom would be advantageous. Additionally, it would give you something to do, beloved. You are becoming entirely too lazy." She smiled at him winsomely.

Darcy lifted one brow. "That accusation I shall not deign to repudiate. Seriously, Elizabeth, your logic is flawed. It is the duty of the grooms and footmen to escort you and ensure your protection. However, that is not my main concern." He took her hands. "My love, handling a curricle is not as easy as it may appear. Yet, even that is not as much an issue to me, as I know you are bright and competent. It is the horses. They are unpredictable and you are inexperienced and afraid of them."

"I have considered all of this. You can ensure that the horses employed are the most placid. I will never be in any rush to get anywhere; therefore,

225

they need not be spirited. I shall travel no further than Lambton or to visit Harriet or Marilyn. You would be teaching me, and I will submit to your timetable. I do not anticipate mastering the curricle swiftly and am not foolish enough to dash pell-mell into an enterprise that has the potential of danger attached."

Darcy stood up and walked to the window, staring out at the murky sky. Lizzy sat silently. She had noted early in their engagement that this was what he did when ruminating on a perplexing matter. Often he would abruptly rise from his desk, usually mumbling unintelligibly under his breath, fingers fidgeting, and stare blankly out a window until the resolution emerged. Usually she found it humorous to observe how his visage would brusquely transform from glowering and plagued to animated and determined as he vigorously strode back to his chair. Today, the overall effect was not as threatening as he rigidly stood there in his robe and nothing else with hair tousled and absently toying with his sash. Nonetheless, Lizzy knew him well enough to understand his turmoil.

"In addition, dearest, I do have some experience driving a carriage. My father taught me the basics when I was young and would on occasion let me take the reins. As for the horses," she rose and approached his back until she was just behind him, "I have been thinking about that, too. One thing that horrible man Orman said did resonate."

Darcy twitched when she mentioned the Marquis's name and turned to peer at his wife. She continued, "I *am* a Darcy, and it is not proper that I should know so little about horses nor be afraid of them. I reason that this endeavor will acquaint me with horses in a general way and then you can teach me to ride."

Darcy was shaking his head slowly. "Elizabeth, I do not care if you ride or despise horses. It matters naught to me. I would never wish for you to attempt an employment that may cause you pain or anxiety."

"William, it matters to me. This is something I need to do, for the reasons I have told you and more." She stood before him now, running her hands along the edge of his robe as she met his eyes. "I want to see all of Pemberley, and you stated much of it is inaccessible except by horseback. I do not suspect I shall ever be an accomplished horsewoman, and I would appreciate it if you avoid assigning me Parsifal's sister or baby brother." She laughed and he smiled. "Yet, this is a challenge I desire to conquer and I can only triumph with your help."

Thus it was that for the subsequent month or so, the Darcys could be found in the courtyard on clear days with the smallest and sturdiest curricle in the carriage house and two of the six horses deemed by Darcy and Mr. Thurber, the head groomsman, as the most steadfast, unflappable, and manageable. Darcy and Mr. Thurber were both impressed at Lizzy's bullheaded stubbornness and inexhaustible application. Within days she could competently navigate up and down the lengthy avenue before Pemberley. Darcy hovered close by on horseback as he trailed her about, prepared to physically launch himself onto the out-of-control vehicle if necessary; however, that never occurred.

The unpredictable weather did not allow for consistent application to Lizzy's lessons, but by the end of January, Darcy deemed her adequate. Once Darcy and Mr. Thurber jointly declared Lizzy competent, Darcy graduated to teaching her how to handle a phaeton. The phaeton, although larger than a curricle, was still rather small. Darcy made it abundantly clear to his wife and to the entire stable staff that Mrs. Darcy was never to be allowed to commandeer a phaeton on her own; however, he reasoned that if she could adequately drive the larger vehicle, then a curricle should offer few challenges.

For the following two weeks, between sporadic storms, Lizzy devoted her energy to conquering the unwieldy carriage as well as her own rising temper. Darcy was the soul of patience; however, he was also exorbitantly comprehensive and privately harbored continued feelings of unease at the whole concept of her driving out, alone, with a curricle.

"No, Elizabeth. You must keep a tighter grip on the reins. The animals will not respond appropriately if you do not command them." His large hands clasped hers and squeezed painfully to exhibit, for the hundredth time, the force necessary. Lizzy gritted her teeth and pressed her lips to halt the sharp retort she wished to make. "Always you must retain focus and use every muscle of your arms and shoulders. You are not naturally as strong, thus the greater the need to concentrate and exert yourself." He frowned as he adjusted the leather straps about her gloved fingers.

"This is nonsense, William!" she snapped. "I will not be taking the phaeton, only the curricle, which I drove perfectly. This is just a waste of time! You are stalling and purposefully finding fault. You do not want me to succeed, do you?" She glared at him and he glared back.

Normally, Darcy loved her spirit, but right now he only experienced a tremendous urge to bend her over his knee and paddle her. Instead, with effort, he took the reins into his hands and coldly intoned, "Very well, Mrs. Darcy, let us go back," and without further conversation he briskly slapped the horses' rumps and hastened down the avenue to the stable yard. He pulled to a skidding stop and vaulted out, striding with contained fury to Mr. Thurber and leaving Lizzy sitting on the seat.

She bit her lip, remorse at her outburst warring with her aggravation. Darcy was intently speaking with Mr. Thurber, who glanced blandly at Lizzy as he nodded his head in agreement with whatever his master was requesting of him. Lizzy climbed down by herself and waited with growing vexation. Mr. Thurber left with a flurry of activity ensuing at his orders while Darcy stood with rigid back to his wife.

Within minutes, several grooms had hitched the curricle and saddled Parsifal. Darcy swung onto his stallion's back in one powerful motion, settled, and only then looked to Lizzy. His countenance was calm but stern, eyes a deep blue and jaw set. Lizzy knew this look, and it was not a pleasant one. She flinched briefly and then collected herself and met his glower full on. His eyes narrowed dangerously, grew even darker, and his jaw muscle contracted with a spasm.

"Go ahead, Elizabeth," he demanded with a gesture at the curricle. "Drive. Down the lane toward the road. Speedily as you can. Go!"

Lizzy was seething. She would show him! She took her time, breathing deeply to calm herself, careful to check the horses and hitch and rigging as taught, sitting attentively with feet planted, and grasping the reins firmly before she flicked them and gave the command. She sedately and adeptly steered the twosome in two circles about the large front courtyard, studiously avoiding Darcy's stare, before she urged the animals to a trot down the boulevard. She cautiously picked up speed. Darcy had previously drilled into her the law, as he saw it, of maintaining a slow pace. However, he had just told her to go faster, so she urged the horses into a moderate canter.

The sensation was exhilarating! Although the curricle was not truly moving very fast, the flow of the chill wind on her face as the scenery sped by was enlivening. She laughed. Suddenly, the sharp staccato blast of a gunshot erupted to her right and Lizzy yelped as several events occurred simultaneously. The horses reared slightly in fright and then leapt forward with a jolt into a run; her own shock caused her to loosen her grip on the reins momentarily; and the jarring from the bolt ahead nearly unseated her as she rapped her head smartly against the metal sidebar.

She saw stars and gasped in a moment of panic, but she rapidly recovered as the instruction drummed into her by Darcy assailed her consciousness. She locked her legs and arms, violently clutched the reins as she leaned slightly into the forward momentum of the animals' panicked direction, and eased back on the reins firmly but gradually. Vocalizing the calming words Darcy had taught her, she increased the pull on the horses as they swerved and lunged ahead.

She began freshly to panic as her efforts seemingly had no effect when two facts invaded her awareness. One was the imperceptible slowing of the horses' pace and the other was her husband racing along beside the curricle. Just as Darcy twisted precariously out of the saddle to grab one of the bridles, the horses precipitously skidded to a stop. Lizzy was thrown abruptly forward, sheer luck and clenched legs keeping her from toppling over. Only Darcy's superior horsemanship kept him from plunging off Parsifal, and even in Lizzy's state of breathless distress, she was awed at how fluidly he handled his mount as he righted his body and spun about. He was at her side and dismounted before she had even taken a breath, heaving her out and into his crushing embrace in one expeditious move.

Lizzy began to tremble hysterically but before she could relax into the sturdy grip of her husband, he pushed her away, grasped her upper arms roughly, and shook her until her teeth rattled. "Do not *ever* make me do something like this again, Elizabeth Darcy! Do you hear me?" His face was black with anger, but tears were in his eyes.

Lizzy's mouth fell open in shock and her mind could not comprehend the whirling emotions as his mouth descended onto hers in a bruising kiss. The kiss was brutal and thorough, albeit short, and then she was enfolded in his arms and pressed tenaciously into his hard chest.

The sound of a horse's hooves barely registered as her sobs and gasps mingled with the wheezes resonating through his shirt. "Is all well, Mr. Darcy?" Mr. Thurber inquired. Darcy nodded and waved a hand, unable to speak, and the wrangler retreated.

"You..." she sobbed, "you... did this... on purpose?"

His intonation was weary when he finally spoke. "I needed to show you how dangerous it can be, Elizabeth. I am sorry." His voice caught and he swallowed. "But you were not taking this seriously enough." He gently fingered her chin and lifted her face to his, raptly examining her eyes. He was emotionally spent and it showed in his gaze. Lizzy nearly collapsed as a torrent of shame rushed through her. She wanted to hide and cry some more and beg forgiveness and then kiss him, but he suddenly released her and she swayed.

"Climb back in, Mrs. Darcy," he demanded curtly in a tremulous rasp. "Take it back to the stable." He remounted Parsifal and looked at her with glazed eyes and a wan smile as she gaped at him. "Like falling off a horse, my love, you must get back on immediately. Hurry up, but be careful. I shall be waiting for you in our chambers. I need to kiss you and hold you for several hours to overcome the fright you have given me." With a last weak smile and a blown kiss, he heeled Parsifal and took off across the meadow in a blinding flash.

For the first time in her marriage, Elizabeth was afraid to approach her husband. Certainly not because she thought for one second he would harm her, but due to her acute shame and fear of seeing disappointment on his face. Therefore, she did not hurry as he asked, but dawdled in the stables, sluggishly climbed the staircases, and entered their bedroom subdued and stealthily. He stood with an elbow propped on the mantle and staring into the fire and twiddling an empty glass in one hand, the other in a fist over his mouth. His torso was bare although, oddly, he still wore his breeches and boots. She observed him silently, detecting no overt tension or anger but rather weariness. She could not see his face until he suddenly sensed her presence and turned.

All she saw was love. He glowed as he did immediately after they made love, the expression in his shining eyes one that she recognized as pure joy and adoration. He placed the glass on the mantle and, without a word, held his arms open. In a flash and with a sob she was there, holding him as he held her, with tenderness and belonging. He sat onto the sofa, cradling her on his lap and soothingly caressing her back and shoulders as he unpinned her already partially loose hair. Neither spoke, Lizzy trembling with unshed tears as he purred placatingly.

Twining fingers through her hair, he tasted her lips, feathering and delicate. With immeasurable patience he began unbuttoning her gown, baring her to his airy touch. He had never undressed her so slowly. It was unfathomably erotic yet tranquilizing at the same time. She relaxed into his body, hands lax as he stirred her senses. For endless minutes he focused on her bared breasts, arousing her gradually with fingers and then mouth.

He clasped her body to his and with balletic grace fell to the bearskin rug. He stretched beside her, examining her face as he resumed the caresses to her chest. Elizabeth never felt as beautiful as she did when William stared at her. His eyes pierced her soul, love and transcendent admiration naked. Words were unnecessary and they uttered none. Passion coursed through her as a torrential wave, every touch rocking her with heat, yet she was mesmerized by his eyes, his face in total so enchanting.

Raptly watching her, he ran his hand down her abdomen and hips, divesting her of the dress completely. With his eyes never leaving her face, even when she closed her eyes in rising euphoria, he allowed his fingers to play over her supple flesh. With nothing but his masterful touch he roused her, lovingly bringing her to utter fulfillment until she cried his name, begging him in desperation to stop before she died.

Immediately, he crushed her shivering body to his. "Oh, my God, William," she spoke shakily, "I truly think at times I shall perish from the power of what you do to me!"

He kissed her forehead, speaking softly, "I will never let you die, Lizzy, not from pleasure or anything else. Without you I cannot survive."

She smiled into his crystal eyes. "Nor I without you, best beloved."

Darcy's "test" did accomplish the goal of proving to him that Lizzy could handle herself in the little carriage. He accompanied her about for the next two weeks as she ventured further afield until he was comfortable with allowing her to wander off alone.

Nonetheless, on the day in late February when she wheeled off to visit Mrs. Harriet Vernor, a mere five miles away, Darcy was beside himself for the entire four hours she was gone. He paced in his study, found endless excuses to wander into the main parlor so he could peer onto the drive, and finished not a stitch of the work piled on his desk.

When she arrived home, flushed and glowing from satisfaction and a delightful afternoon with her friend, Darcy marched her immediately up to their chambers. In general a man of few words, Darcy had recognized that the preferred method of alleviating his tribulation and expressing his devotion was to simply hold, kiss, and tenderly make love to his wife. Since he did this remarkably well, Elizabeth had no complaints.

Aside from such upsets as curricle lessons, one other ball in late February, and the few sudden minor troubles about the farms, life for the Darcys followed a relatively predictable routine every day. Lizzy and Darcy were both historically early risers, Darcy especially so. His normal pattern prior to matrimony was to wake just after dawn and go for a long ride. This activity was replaced by an exceedingly more pleasant one: waking his wife shortly after dawn, generally in a state of partial arousal, and making love. After that, they would contentedly snuggle and doze before rising for a leisurely breakfast in their sitting room. Perhaps twice a week, as weather permitted, Darcy would leave his deliciously satisfied wife in resumed slumber and take Parsifal for a vigorous race across Pemberley's vast pastures, returning for breakfast.

Mid-morning was passed in his study attending to various business matters, while Lizzy either sat reading nearby or met with Mrs. Reynolds while Georgiana was with her tutor. Darcy, to his pleased surprise, preferred to have Lizzy sit with him and discuss the business at hand. Initially it had not occurred to him to share the minute details of the estate management with her, not because he doubted her intelligence, but simply because he had never talked to anyone about his affairs, except Mr. Keith, of course.

Her gentle probing questions and enthusiastic interest had encouraged him to answer her inquiries with increasing clarity and depth. Darcy knew his wife was bright but was astonished at how adroitly her mind grasped certain things. Darcy was a linear thinker, eminently logical and rational, unemotional regarding business, cunning in his problem-solving abilities, meticulous and thorough. Lizzy rationalized in a circular manner, embraced her emotions in her reasoning, was astoundingly adept at comprehending complex issues in mere minutes while simpler tasks often escaped her understanding, and had an earthy and ingenious approach to resolution. It was a combination of acumen that perfectly complemented, assisting Darcy in a way he never would have imagined.

One such incident occurred in early March. Mr. Keith approached Darcy one morning at his desk as Lizzy sat sewing in her chair.

"Mr. Darcy, a difficulty has arisen between Roy Alton and Howard Hayes once again. This time it is over the rights to the well."

Darcy scowled and sighed. "Those two cause me more grief than all the others combined. What about the well?"

"Alton claims that Hayes has not been maintaining the well as he is instructed to do, and the pumps are now malfunctioning. Hayes refutes this, placing the blame, naturally, on Alton whom he states has intentionally sabotaged the pumps in order to slander him. None of it makes sense."

"Are the pumps completely irreparable?"

"No, but certainly not adequately functional, especially with the weather, to sustain the families' requirements."

"Did we not address this same issue three years ago? We set up a schedule of maintenance times and duties..." Darcy trailed off as he rummaged through his files.

"Order each of them to dig a well on their own lands." Lizzy spoke from her chair, still intent on her needlework. Both men paused and stared at her.

Darcy glanced at Mr. Keith, who raised his brows and shrugged. "Elizabeth, that would not solve the immediate problem."

She looked up at the men as if they were impossibly dense and rolled her eyes. "Of course, they would need to fix the current well first. After that, though, they should start working on their individual wells."

They continued to stare at her with mixed expressions of confusion and patronization. Lizzy sighed, "They are acting like children, so treat them as such. Separate them, take the object of their current tantrum away, and distract them with something else. In this case the arduous chore of digging a well in the frozen ground. That ought to distract them from their petty bickering for several months, and they will be too busy grousing at you to pick on each other."

She smiled winsomely at their dawning understanding and astonishment. "In addition, you will have to set a deadline and enforce it by destroying the current well, or they will just ignore you."

Darcy looked at Mr. Keith and they nodded. "Yes, that might just work. Write up a contract, Mr. Keith, and I shall confront them tomorrow. Arrange for the equipment they will need. Is there anything else?"

"No, sir. I will take care of it."

He left and Darcy peered at his smug spouse. "Proud of yourself, Mrs. Darcy?"

"You would eventually have arrived at the same conclusion, my love, in several years or so."

At least twice a week, Lizzy spent the morning hours with Mrs. Reynolds. Like Darcy, Mrs. Reynolds was overwhelmingly patient and delighted at the aptness of the new Mistress. Mathematics failed Lizzy, so Darcy handled the accounts as always, but she readily grasped the inner workings of the household staff and their interpersonal relationships. Like her husband, she learned each of their names and made a point always to address them individually.

Unlike her husband, Lizzy was naturally congenial and not as formal with the servants, thus taking the time to familiarize herself with aspects of their personal lives and characters. This added insight greatly assisted her in dealing with troubles as they arose and with moving freely about the manor, thus intensifying her knowledge of the inner workings of Pemberley. Little by little, she assumed a portion of the duties from Mrs. Reynolds.

"Mrs. Reynolds, tell me about the summer festival for the tenants. I would like to reestablish the tradition."

"Wonderful idea, Mistress! We can easily plan this and the tenants would be delighted. Generally Mrs. Darcy held the event in late June or early July. The planting is primarily done, and it is not terribly hot yet. The festivities were fairly straightforward: a feast and dancing."

Lizzy was nodding, "Yes, this should be perfect. Mr. Darcy, Miss Darcy, and I will be journeying to Town in April for two months, as you are aware. We can set the date for…" she perused the calendar on her desk, "July tenth? Yes, that is good. I will discuss this with Mr. Darcy. We can detail the menu and agenda before we leave. Excellent! As always, Mrs. Reynolds, I count on your forthrightness and assistance. I still have so much to learn."

Mrs. Reynolds patted her hand. "You minimize your progress, Madame. I have never seen anyone learn as fast as you have." Lizzy blushed. "Mr. Darcy is pleased, I can tell." She stood to leave. "By the way, ask Mr. Darcy about the summer festival the year he was fifteen." She smiled and left.

Lizzy wasted no time. She entered Darcy's study to find her husband bent in his chair, mumbling and cursing as he searched for something in the bottom drawer. He did not hear her approach until she was right behind him and spoke.

"May I help?" He jerked up, his mien a mask of consternation until he saw her beloved face and he melted.

"You already have, beloved, by warming my heart before I erupted in a serious temper due to my own disorganization and forgetfulness."

"Pah! You are perhaps the *least* disorganized or forgetful man in the world!" She moved around his chair until she faced him, leaning close with her hands resting on his thighs. "I find that if I take my mind momentarily off the dilemma at hand, the answer will spontaneously emerge. You merely need something to distract you, my love. I believe my arrival is fortuitous." With that proclamation she kissed him, slowly and teasingly playing with his lips.

"Hmmm… You are partially correct, dearest wife, as ideas are materializing in abundance, although none of them solve the prior problem, yet I am no longer concerned." He whispered against her mouth, grasping her waist to pull her onto his lap.

She smiled and gently bit his lower lip before pulling away. She laughed at his sudden expression of childish petulance and clasped his hands. "Such a baby! Come with me, little boy," as she tugged him up and led him to the sofa. She sat close to his side, draping her legs over one of his, one hand entangling in his hair as the other dexterously manipulated the knots of his cravat. "There. Is this not preferable? Now you can have your way with me, Mr. Darcy."

Without hesitation, he did. Kissing thoroughly and caressing where possible while fully clothed, the lovers delighted in a time of rapturous amusement. Darcy's coats were unbuttoned and Lizzy lovingly fondled his chest while nibbling on his exposed neck, finally murmuring into his ear, "So, enlighten me as to the memorable event surrounding the summer festival when you were fifteen."

Darcy had been pleasantly attending to his own diversions along Lizzy's bodice when she spoke. He choked on his startled indrawn breath, coughing and sputtering alarmingly. Lizzy covered her mouth to keep from laughing. "What..." he wheezed, "How did you..." gasp, "Who told you about that?"

"Mrs. Reynolds."

He groaned and leaned his head back against the wall. "I should dismiss her!"

Lizzy snickered as she moved in to assault his now further visible neck and chest. "Nonsense! I am sure it is in your journal for me to read anyway, so confess, Mr. Darcy."

"Oh Lord, have mercy; why did I ever marry such a meddlesome pest?"

"Flattery will not save you." She smiled at him seductively and batted her lashes. "Now, speak!"

"On one condition. If I divulge my secret, then you must do the same. Agreed?" He was grinning.

Lizzy's eyes narrowed and she pursed her lips speculatively. "I could just read your journal."

"I can wrest the key from you by force, if need be, likely enjoying myself in the process."

"Beast! I am sure Mrs. Reynolds will tell me if I ask."

"Not if I order her not to. I *am* Master here." His grin had broadened.

"Oh, alright! Agreed," she declared with a feigned pout and she stuck her hand out to shake on it, earning a laugh from her husband.

"When I was a young, foolish fifteen, I fancied myself madly in love with Mrs. Langton's daughter, Eloise. She was seventeen, buxom, blonde, and a notorious flirt." He was blushing but laughing at the silly memory. "I spied on her whenever I could, which she well knew and used to her advantage to torture me. Wickham figured it out and teased me mercilessly. He was a mere thirteen, but had already cornered a number of the looser girls for kisses and fondles. I found that behavior disgusting, as you know, but I was besotted and reckoned myself pure in my affection.

"He dared me to kiss her and then taunted me with unflattering names. A boy's ego is easily bruised, so I determined that I would make my move at the festival. It was amazingly easy to arrange, Eloise being the flirt she was and more than willing to accommodate the young Master. I was just beginning to truly enjoy myself when Wickham, the demon, arrived with Vernor, Hughes, Richard, and my parents in tow."

He groaned and covered his eyes with one large hand, still grinning though, and continued, "The taunts of the gents I could handle, but my parents were aghast. I was forced to publicly apologize to Eloise and to her parents. Mr. Langton was still alive then and he dwarfed his wife, if that gives you any idea of how intimidating a presence he was. I have never been so humiliated in all my life. My mother did not speak to me for a week, and my father lashed me with a switch so as to render me unable to sit for several days." He peered at his giggling and tremulous wife through his fingers. "The kiss was nice, though."

"Ha!" she barked and attacked his ticklish rib cage with her fingers, dissolving them both in laughter.

"Mercy!" he pleaded breathlessly. "Now it is your turn to confess, Mrs. Darcy. Your first crush and kiss."

"I am afraid you shall be hideously disappointed, my dear. I do not have a good story to tell. My first crush was when I was eighteen and I briefly imagined myself smitten with the butcher's son, who was some five-and-twenty years old and did not even know I existed. My mild case of enchantment with the perfidious Mr. Wickham was next, and then you. Aside from my father and uncles, you are the first and only man ever to kiss me."

Darcy smiled brightly and tenderly caressed her cheek. "You are mistaken, my Lizzy. I am not disappointed in your confession in the slightest." He kissed her lightly. "I do not have to fear suffering by comparison."

"Silly man! If you do not yet know what your kisses do to me, then I shall have to improve my manner of exhibiting my ecstasy and unfettered joy." She roughly seized his mouth and fell back on the couch, taking him with her. Past crushes and kisses were forgotten in the rush of present passion and unparalleled love. She administered a long, drugged kiss, taunting his lips with her tongue and exploring the warm softness of his mouth thoroughly. Breath and moisture mingled as they savored the taste and feel of the other.

His coats were discarded somehow and her skirt lifted to the knees with his seeking hand, before he came to awareness. Pulling away with a struggle he said, "Do not move an inch, dearest." Striding quickly, he drew the drapes and locked the doors, not that anyone would enter his study unannounced, except for her. This was not the first time she had surprised him in his sanctuary for a pleasant diversion from work. The couplings tended to be hurried and hushed in light of the location, but no less stupendous. In fact, for some strange reason, the necessity to remain quiet multiplied the pleasure.

She had not moved, watching his progress with hungry eyes. She reached up as he neared and stroked him, eliciting a groan and whispering, "Do my kisses suffer by comparison, my love?"

"Lord no, Elizabeth! There is no comparison to you." He nestled over her on the narrow couch, reclaiming her mouth ardently. They loved, greedily absorbed in their desire for each other.

Afterwards they lay together for a long while, kissing tenderly and caressing. Lizzy kissed his noble nose, quietly inquiring, "Do you remember where you put the document you searched for?"

He laughed in sudden surprise. "Yes, I do! It is not even in that drawer but in the cabinet."

She grinned pertly. "My diversion worked then! How happy I am to be of assistance to my husband."

Luncheons were taken with Georgiana. Often it was the first time either of the older Darcys had spoken with her that day. Lizzy fretted somewhat at what she feared seemed like abandonment on their part. Darcy assured her that, other than breakfast, he and his sister had rarely seen each other in the morning hours anyway. He had explained to Georgiana that breakfast was an important time for him and his new wife. Nonetheless, Lizzy worried and therefore endeavored to pass as many afternoons as possible with her new sister.

In a matter of days, she realized that she genuinely enjoyed her time with Georgiana. Lizzy marveled at this. It was not that she had in even the slightest way disliked Georgiana; it was simply that she had imagined the gap in their ages would prevent them from becoming true friends. Lizzy was familiar with the foolishness and stupidity of her younger sisters and had erringly assumed Georgiana similar.

Georgiana was timid and shy, a typical Darcy trait taken to extremes by her, yet also intelligent, accomplished, and witty. She was very like her brother actually. Darcy hid his shyness behind a stern and forbidding demeanor, whereas Georgiana was blatantly blushing and anxious; however, they both harbored a dry humor, a keen intellect, and astonishing gentleness and empathy. Lizzy, as she had with her spouse, naturally used her gregarious character to break through Georgiana's reserve. Darcy was elated at the change to his sister through Lizzy's friendship.

Lizzy, on the other hand, flourished in her own way under Georgiana's gentle personality. Both Darcys were inherently peaceful creatures, steady and unflappable. This serenity soothed Lizzy. At the same time, she found herself awestruck by the talent her sister wielded. She could play the pianoforte and harp brilliantly, painted, was extremely creative with paints, spoke three languages fluently, and had a firm grasp of history and literature. Lizzy spent hours on the piano with her, honing her own paltry skills under Georgiana's patient instruction, and happily sat in quiet conversation while they sewed or played cards. Georgiana also loved the outdoors and walking.

Thus, the afternoons periodically found Lizzy and Darcy separated as he attended to business, projects about the estate, visited a nearby gentleman, went on a ride, or, more often, read alone in the library while Lizzy also visited her friends, spent time with Georgiana, took a walk, or volunteered at the orphanage. By mutual necessity their partings were as brief as possible. Despite individual pursuits, Lizzy and Darcy managed to secure a fair amount of time alone together.

By mid-April the snows had melted away from the combined effect of the inexhaustive rains and a mild warming in the temperature. The gardens were budding, the birds were slowly returning, and Lizzy was experiencing an acute period of waspishness and unease. For two weeks she woke every morning to the loving administrations of her husband, yet could not overcome her peevishness. She did not feel unwell, simply restless and constantly annoyed. Darcy, of course, sensed her angst and attempted to talk to her about it, but she snapped at him, highly unusual, so he let it go, surmising that it was mostly a result of the endless dreary weather and forced confinement.

The afternoon of April sixteenth brought all to a head and was the beginning of one of the worst weeks of Darcy's long life.

Lizzy's increasingly surly attitude was seriously disturbing Darcy, even to the point of not being able to comfort her during their lovemaking. Despite his improved intuitiveness and ability to communicate intimately, he was at a loss as to what was causing his wife's distress. This pained him tremendously. He had considered the possibility that she might be with child as a cause. He was aware that she was late on her monthly cycle and had thoroughly searched the medical text for pregnancy symptoms, but nothing was said of irritation as a sign. Whatever the case, he determined to devote the evening after dinner to lovingly and patiently encouraging her to open up to him.

Lizzy, in the meantime, was privately also grievously disquieted with her persistent vexation, but she could not seem to control her emotions. That morning as her amazing, tender, sensual, and gorgeous husband had nuzzled her neck, stroked her body, and whispered his love and devotion, she had felt only irritation, and for the first time ever since their wedding night, she did not reach fulfillment. Later, when alone in her dressing room, she had broken into sobs that she could not halt. She, too, had wondered if she might be pregnant and had also perused the text. Unfortunately, if she was with child, it was far too early to be verified and she could not blame her mood on a possibility.

Darcy and his steward were secreted in his study all afternoon dealing with one of Darcy's more complicated and sensitive investments with a German steel manufacturer. When his wife burst into the room unannounced, it was not a mere irritation but an astoundingly rude, deleterious interruption and a heinous breach of propriety.

"William," she snapped, "what is the meaning of you ordering the stables not to allow me to take the curricle out today?"

"Mr. Keith, will you please excuse us for a moment?"

Lizzy glared at her husband, realizing on some level that she was utterly wrong but not able to stop her fury. "Well?" she demanded once the door shut behind the steward.

"Mrs. Darcy, may I remind you that when I am in my study with my steward, I am not to be disturbed unless it is a matter of extreme import *which*," he raised his deceptively serene tone mildly to halt her retort, "this most decidedly is not. However, as the damage has already been done, I will answer your misplaced and rude inquiry." He paused and took a deep breath to calm his anger, his countenance dour. "The roads are washed out and muddy, and a storm is expected to arrive this afternoon. It is not safe for you to be out, alone or otherwise."

"But… "

"There is nothing further to discuss, Elizabeth. I am sorry for the inconvenience but it cannot be helped."

Tears welled in her eyes and she turned away. Darcy sighed, feeling most of his anger fading, and approached her, touching her arm lightly. "My love, I know you are tired of being cooped up. I assure you the pleasant Derbyshire weather is coming soon. Tonight we must talk about whatever is bothering you. However, right now it is essential that I finish my business with Mr. Keith. I beg of you, please do not barge in here in this manner again. It is unseemly."

She whirled on him, her face enraged, causing him to retreat a step in shock. "Forgive me, Mr. Darcy, for being such a nuisance. I will bow to the Master's demands and trouble you no more." She stalked out of the room, slammed the door, and marched up to her bedchamber, a room in which she had spent less than an hour during her entire four-plus months at Pemberley. Darcy did not see her for the remainder of the night. His exasperation at the entire episode was intense, yet little did he know that their misfortunes were just beginning.

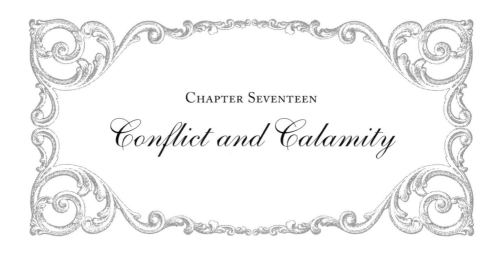

Chapter Seventeen

Conflict and Calamity

Lizzy did not dine with Darcy and Georgiana that evening. A maid informed them that the Mistress was not feeling well and had requested a tray in her chambers. Darcy maintained his mask of serenity in front of his sister, who suspected nothing, but inside he seethed. Throughout the remainder of that wretched afternoon, as he forced himself to focus on the business at hand with Mr. Keith, Darcy had vacillated between boiling anger and nauseating heartache. Somehow he had managed to conclude the arrangements with the steel company in Germany, but he would be hard pressed to articulate how it had transpired. The details had taken so long that Darcy had barely enough time to dress for dinner, so he was unaware of his wife changing residence to her unused bedchamber.

Therefore, when he ascended the staircase immediately after dinner, apologizing to his sister for an aborted evening, he was further shocked to discover his wife absent. He had determined to talk to her, swallowing his ire as best he could—which actually was not too difficult, as his love for her and concern for her well-being were consuming his thoughts.

Initially, upon not finding her in their chambers, he was flooded with panic. *Where could she be?* A storm had struck, as he had predicted, and his worst fear was that she had decided to take a walk. He dashed from the room, encountering Marguerite in the hallway, who informed him of Mrs. Darcy's whereabouts. Darcy was thunderstruck and numbly murmured a *thank you* as he returned to their rooms.

It would require paragraph upon paragraph to list the emotions that assaulted poor Mr. Darcy throughout that evening and night. Mechanically he went through the motions of bathing and shaving and preparing for bed. He wandered about the room, ignoring their warm and inviting bed with the covers turned down in anticipation, until he could take it no more and, in a fit of rage, violently closed the bed curtains on the sight and stalked into their sitting room where he remained.

Once there, he spent the hours pacing and muttering. He vainly attempted to read and write in his journal and attend to correspondence, paced some more, prayed, and drank several glasses of brandy. He walked down the hallway to her door at least a dozen times and knocked twice, but received no answer either time, which vexed him further. Finally, the combined effects of alcohol and sheer exhaustion, both mental and physical, caused him to fall asleep in the chaise around two in the morning.

As for Lizzy, her childish and unfathomable temper tantrum of earlier had left her weary beyond belief and ill. She called for a tray but could not eat. By the time her husband found her missing from their chambers, most of her irritability had evaporated, leaving only profound shame in its wake. She was utterly mortified at her actions. She continued to experience a lingering pique that she could not account for, but mostly she was heartsick. She paced about the unfamiliar and poorly decorated room, wanting nothing more than to be in Darcy's arms, but she was too embarrassed to approach him.

She suspected and hoped he would come to her after dinner. When he did not, she became freshly rankled for a spell but finally buried her foolishness and pride. She peeked into their bedchamber, but her timing was unfortunate. At that precise moment, Darcy was knocking on her door and she was viewing a dark bedchamber with drawn bed curtains. Darcy assumed she was refusing to answer, and she assumed he had peacefully gone to sleep without her. Their erroneous assumptions brought on a renewed rush of acrimony.

Lizzy raged, paced, and sobbed until she was literally sick. Weak and trembling, feverish and cramping, she crawled into the cold bed and fell into a troubled sleep. Therefore, she did not hear her husband's second knock.

Darcy woke at dawn cramped, cold, headachy, and not nearly rested enough. His mind was clouded with excessive drink and sleep deprivation. He could hardly formulate a coherent thought, but he knew one thing for absolute certain: he was lonely and desperate to hold and kiss his wife. Nothing mattered but the incontrovertible fact that he loved her beyond comprehension and was miserable without her. He approached her door but was informed by an exiting chambermaid that the Mistress was fast asleep. Darcy opted to freshen up, a wise choice in light of his disheveled appearance, and come to her over breakfast and mend their argument, no matter what it took to do so.

While Darcy dressed, Lizzy woke and immediately ran to the chamber pot and was sick again. Marguerite drew her bath and Lizzy gratefully sank into the hot water, too queasy even to think about eating. Lizzy felt as if a blanket had fallen over her head. She was fuzzy and sleepy, the now familiar tendrils of irritation whisking over her once again. Mostly she was overwhelmed by woe from what she foolishly perceived was her husband's abandonment.

The next two hours were a chaotic mess of the two despondent lovers narrowly missing each other and therefore continuing to leap to false conclusions. By the time they coincidentally encountered each other in the main foyer, their individual emotions were running rampant. Darcy was rushing out the door to attend to an unexpected and serious occurrence at the wool-shearing shed, his horse and Mr. Keith both stomping in agitation in the courtyard. Lizzy was still feeling unwell and her sadness, confusion, and chagrin were rendering her unfit for civil company, so she was heading to the quiet solitude of the conservatory. For several moments they simply stood there in silence, eyes not meeting, as they both frantically grasped for the proper words to verbalize in a public area with the footman holding Darcy's overcoat within earshot.

"I am on my way out," he eventually offered. "I do not expect I shall return until late afternoon."

Lizzy, of course, had no knowledge of the disaster, continued to believe he had slept unperturbed through the night, and refused to meet his eyes, so she did not witness the naked agony and desire revealed therein. "I see," she murmured. "Well then, until later I suppose. I pray you have a pleasant day, Mr. Darcy."

Darcy was further confused by her flat tone and taken aback by her words. "Pleasant? Elizabeth, I rather doubt… ."

"I thought I would later take a walk about the grounds." She interrupted him, glancing up for the first time as she continued in a heated rush, "Provided, of course, this meets with the approval of the Master?"

The very second the words passed her lips, as she finally saw the yearning and grief in his eyes, mingled with confusion, she knew she had made a dreadful mistake. It was too late. The Darcy mask of aloof indifference and disdain fell over his face and he straightened stiffly, only the thin line of his lips indicative of his anger and wounding. "Whatever you wish, Mrs. Darcy. Good day, Madame." With a curt bow, he spun on his heels and left.

Lizzy stood rooted to the spot for long moments, stunned and so horribly ashamed. Her remorse threatened to bring her to her knees and she struggled to breathe as she lunged toward the door, tears pouring from her eyes so she could barely see. "William!" she screamed.

He was halfway down the drive traveling at a brisk canter, but he turned in his saddle. Their eyes met across the distance for the briefest span, but it was enough. He smiled and waved. Lizzy nearly collapsed in relief as she smiled and waved in return. Then he was gone and she would not see him again for four days.

That one fleeting glance was sufficient to sustain her throughout the morning and afternoon. Last night's storm had passed, leaving the ground boggier than it already was, but the air was clear and sweetly fresh. The sun shone brightly and it promised to be the loveliest day of the spring thus far. Lizzy felt renewed. Her nausea had vanished; her heart was buoyed by her love's smile; and the constant irritation of the past two weeks had dissipated. She was famished and ate a hearty lunch, chatting pleasantly with Georgiana, who remained unaware of the argument and was simply glad that Elizabeth was well.

Two hours elapsed as Elizabeth and Georgiana practiced on the pianoforte together, talking and laughing in sisterly companionship. Lizzy urgently needed to stretch her legs, the sunny day beckoning to her. Georgiana opted to go for a ride, so the women parted for the latter half of the afternoon. Lizzy confiscated a bucket from the kitchen, visiting briefly with Mrs. Langton and the girls, before she set off. On one of her earlier excursions abroad, she had discovered a copse of dewberries approximately a half mile north on the main road. It was perhaps a week or two premature, but in hopes that a few might be ripe and aware that Darcy adored them, Lizzy set off in their direction.

Her route took her along the main Pemberley avenue to the northwest across the bridge, a good mile by itself. There was a path that led diagonally through the woods to the north beside the river, but Darcy had cautioned her to avoid it in the winter, as it was no more than a narrow deer trail and not well maintained. She strolled leisurely, her spirits soaring additionally with each step she took. By the time she was halfway down the drive she was humming and swinging her bucket like a young girl.

She arrived at the berry thicket, delighted to note that although they were mostly green, there was an ample supply of ripe berries. She continued to hum and sing softly as she picked, actually perspiring in the increasing warmth. Her mind wandered to her husband incessantly as she formulated plans for their evening together. The madness of their argument must be put behind them and, as she envisioned all the titillating ways to make up, her flush increased. Feeling slightly light-headed from the unexpectedly balmy day and her licentious musings, Lizzy tucked her partially filled bucket under her arm and set off for home.

She had crossed the road and taken her first steps south when she heard the rattle of carriage wheels and horses from behind her. She moved to the edge and halted, prepared to amiably greet whoever was approaching, but her brilliant smile froze on her face when she beheld the leering visage of the Marquis of Orman.

He reined his chaise to a halt next to her. "Why, Mrs. Darcy, what a delightful surprise this is! May I inquire as to your health this fine afternoon?"

"I am quite well, thank you, Lord Orman. I trust you are the same?"

"Perfectly delightful, I daresay. What errand brings you out here unescorted, Mrs. Darcy?"

"Merely walking on this fine afternoon, as you pointed out, and collecting dewberries for Mr. Darcy."

"What a thoughtful wife you are, Madame. Darcy is a fortunate man indeed."

"We are mutually fortunate. I shall not delay you any further, Marquis. Good day to you." Lizzy curtseyed and turned to resume her walk.

"Mrs. Darcy, may I offer the services of my carriage? It is warm today and you appear quite flushed."

"I assure you I am fine and, if you remember, I revealed to you that I enjoy walking, so thank you, but no." She took several steps before she realized that he was alighting from his vehicle.

"Mrs. Darcy," he called to her and she stopped, "I would like to take this opportunity, if you will allow, to apologize for my behavior at the Masque. It was inexcusable and I am deeply remorseful. Can you find it in your heart to forgive me?"

She glanced at him, flushing at the reference to that horrible event, and extremely uncomfortable. Nonetheless, Lizzy was by nature a forgiving person and, despite Darcy's assertions as to the exact nature of Orman's character, she wanted to believe he was truly repentant. She smiled slightly and again briefly met his eyes. "Let us not speak of that occasion, My Lord. It is best to put such unpleasantness behind us."

"Excellent!" he exclaimed cheerfully, "Then, as all is forgiven, you can accept my offer for a ride. Come, Mrs. Darcy."

"Again, thank you, sir; however, I honestly do prefer to walk. Good day, Marquis."

She curtseyed yet again and began to turn, flabbergasted afresh when he grasped her elbow firmly. "I must insist, dear lady. Your feet are drenched with mud and your face is ruddy and perspiring. You appear unwell. What manner of a gentleman would I be to leave an ailing woman stranded on the roadside?" His smile was lecherous, and Lizzy was seriously apprehensive but also angry.

"Lord Orman, unhand me at once and leave me be. I wish to walk, and Mr. Darcy would certainly not be pleased to hear of your attentions." She shook her arm but he tightened his grip painfully.

"Is Darcy the only man worthy of your attentions, Mrs. Darcy?" He roughly pulled her toward him while leaning into her body and she realized with dawning horror that he intended to kiss her! Without conscious contemplation, Lizzy acted. She resisted forcefully and swung the wooden bucket with astonishing velocity and accuracy, smashing it into his head. He yelled and released her elbow. Lizzy spun and bolted into the woods without a backward glance, dropping her bucket of purple berries on the road.

Lizzy ran in a blind panic for some fifteen minutes as she zigzagged among the trees and heavy underbrush. She wasted no effort on glancing behind her to see if Orman followed, her mind conjuring an image of him capturing her in the emptiness of the wood so terrifying that she was spurred by a burst of energy.

However, as young and athletic as Lizzy was, even she eventually reached the end of her endurance. Gasping and wheezing, she stiffly plastered her body to the rearward side of an enormous pine and cautiously peeked behind her. Nothing.

The wood, except for her panting, was silent. Nonetheless, she remained still for another ten minutes as she caught her breath and slowed her erratic heartbeat.

Only as her terror of Orman subsided was she able to contemplate her current predicament. Lizzy was gifted with an excellent sense of direction, so even though she had careened crazily and the tall trees effectively blotted the sun, she felt fairly certain she had taken a roughly easterly course. This meant she would need to turn to her right, south, to reach the Pemberley thoroughfare. She did not think she had crossed the deer trail in her wild dash, so hopefully she would find it now. It was getting late in the afternoon and, with the thick trees, darkness would fall rapidly in the wood. With a last careful inspection of the area behind her, she set off.

For a half hour she walked. The forest was damp, murky, and far colder. The sweat on her skin cooled and she began to shiver. Just as the edges of panic crept over her, she stumbled upon a deep ravine with a briskly flowing river at the bottom and the straight outlines of a trail running clearly alongside. Lizzy inhaled loudly and closed her eyes in relief.

She stood there for a spell, breathing deeply of the mingled aromas of earth and pine. Her mind now unclouded by panic, she allowed herself to meditate on all that had transpired over the last twenty-four hours. William's treasured face floated before her and she smiled. She ached to hold him. She was humiliated by her actions and comprehended the magnitude of forgiveness she did not deserve from him, yet knew he would grant without hesitation. Such is the love he bore for her.

Tears sprung freshly to her eyes at how blessed she was to have him in her life. She closed her eyes once more and imagined his fingers touching her face and his lips on hers. She could hear his voice in her head and she trembled. Her hands spread over her abdomen and she wondered. *Oh, please, Lord,* she thought, *let the root of my sickness and moodiness be a blessing.* She fleetingly pondered how she would tell him about Orman and then pushed the thought aside. *No unhappy thoughts, Lizzy. Just William.*

Her heavenly reverie was sharply interrupted by a crashing from behind her, accompanied by a hideous warbling sound. She pivoted in fright and involuntarily took a step backward, one foot catching on an exposed tree root at the edge of the ravine while the other slipped in the loose mud. She flailed her arms but there was nothing to grab. Her last conscious thought as she tumbled over the edge of the ravine, her shoe violently wrenched from her foot, was how William would laugh at her being spooked by a turkey.

❦

"Mr. Darcy! Mr. Darcy!"

Darcy glanced up from where he was standing in the yard before the cotton mill and into the frantic face of a young stable boy named Mathais, who was galloping full tilt toward him. He frowned as Mathais reined in, nearly pitching over the head of the horse. He grabbed at the bridle. "Whoa, girl! Steady there. Mathais what is the..."

"Sir, you must return to Pemberley immediately! Mrs. Darcy is missing!"

All the color drained from Darcy's face, and only decades of contending with disasters and grief kept him from collapsing. "What do you mean, 'missing?'" His voice was controlled and only someone who knew him well, like Mr. Keith, would detect the note of hysteria.

Mr. Keith yelled to saddle their horses and a dozen men leapt to comply as Mathais launched into his tale. "According to Miss Darcy and Mrs. Langton, Mrs. Darcy left to take a walk at about half past two. She was going to the berry thicket on the main road." Darcy glanced at his pocket watch; almost five-thirty. Mathais was continuing, "Miss Darcy became concerned after several hours and a groom was sent to the patch. He found the bucket of berries along the road and footprints heading into the woods."

Darcy swore, sensing violent tremors and raging panic threatening to overwhelm him. One hand instinctively moved to the breast pocket where he daily secreted the pouch with her lock of hair. Only movement, action, could prevent him dissolving in a puddle of desolation and anguish. He yelled for his horse, although Parsifal was already saddled and heading his way, and turned again to the boy. "What is being done?"

"Mr. Thurber and Mr. Clark were organizing the stable staff and groundsmen for a search of the woods. I was dispatched to you, so I know nothing else."

Darcy barely heard him. He mounted Parsifal and in a flash was gone.

❦

Dusk was swiftly waning to full darkness by the time Darcy and Parsifal raced into Pemberley's drive. Darcy was hailed instantly by Mr. Thurber, who was supervising the search, pending his master's return.

"Mr. Darcy, we have been searching for three quarters of an hour, thus far to no avail. I directed one group from the road where Mrs. Darcy's footprints were seen entering the wood. Unfortunately, the prints disappeared some hundred feet in where the underbrush and leaves obscured any tracks. Another group set off along the deer trail in hopes that Mrs. Darcy would have happened upon it. I have several other smaller groups spaced at intervals methodically edging their way inwards." He paused and cleared his throat. "Sir, we found this."

He handed Darcy one of Elizabeth's simple cloth bonnets, torn and muddy. Darcy stared at it, tears welling and throat constricting. Mr. Thurber looked away, heartsick for his master, and for all of them, truth be told. The entire staff had grown to admire Mrs. Darcy and the thought of her coming to any harm had them all in varying states of sorrow.

"I... ." Darcy swallowed, tucking the bonnet in his coat pocket, "I need to help. You are in charge here, Mr. Thurber." He remounted Parsifal.

"Mr. Darcy, here is a whistle. It is the established signal."

Darcy nodded and spurred toward the bridge. A knot of men stood at the deer path entry with others spaced along the edge. There was no new information. Darcy nodded solemnly with jaw tightly clenched as he heeled Parsifal into the forest. He questioned every searcher he found as he made his way further along the trail. Several men gathered where the path met up with the ravine rim, carefully examining for any sign and shining their lamps into the deep shadows of the ditch. Suddenly the clear trill of a whistle sounded from further up the path. Darcy dashed to the site of some ten men grouped in a knot and was off Parsifal and over the brink so rapidly it was a miracle he did not break a leg.

Elizabeth's body lay pressed against a fallen log at the edge of the creek. A stable man was gingerly turning her onto her back when Darcy fell to his knees in the mud next to her. "She is alive, sir," he said, gazing at Darcy with watery eyes. "I am so sorry, Mr. Darcy. We passed this spot three times, but the darkness and her position camouflaged her presence. It was only Stan spying her shoe caught above that finally alerted us."

Darcy nodded, unable to speak, as he bent to examine his unconscious wife. He could easily understand why the searchers had not seen her. The log, which had fortuitously prevented her from landing in the water, had also effectively blended with her dark hair and dress, rendering her nearly invisible. Most of her hair had come unpinned during her frantic run and tumble down the twenty-foot slope, and her dress ripped in a dozen places.

Darcy managed to croak out an order for more light and to send for the physician, duties that were hastily executed. Darcy was no stranger to death and maiming. Managing an estate as vast as Pemberley unfortunately included the occasional catastrophe, such as what had occurred at the shearing shed today when a hoist had broken, crushing two men under the plummeting bales of wool. Of course, none of those previous disasters had involved someone precious to him. Horror clutched in his soul—fear tormented—and only years of stringent self-possession and a steely backbone kept him thinking rationally.

He noted first a gash above her right temple where blood had caked with the mud, forming an ugly mess in her hair, but the wound did not appear to be actively oozing. Her skin was cold, the pulse in her neck rapid and thready, but her respirations regular and unlabored. Her bare right foot was swollen and bruised at the ankle. He did not palpate any obvious broken bones or other lacerations. In fact, the primary damage seemed to be to her head. She was wet and shivering, so he called for a blanket. Lifting her carefully into his arms, he navigated, with assistance, up the slippery slope and onto his horse, returning to Pemberley Manor slowly.

The house was a flurry of activity and blazing lights. Darcy carried Elizabeth to their bedchamber, in retrospect a time-consuming inconvenience, but it only seemed fitting. He was firmly but gently pushed away as Mrs. Reynolds and Marguerite took over. He retreated to the foot of the great bed, clasping one pillar for support and watching the women begin the task of cleaning and examining his wife. It was several minutes before he marked the splotch of blood staining the front of his shirt. He puzzled over it for a bit, inventorying his person for a wound of some kind, when his befuddled and agonized mind grasped that it had come from Elizabeth. He must have articulated an exclamation of some sort because all eyes turned to him, Mrs. Reynolds's face grim as she nodded.

Darcy was confused and suddenly felt weak. The outer door opened as the physician and maids with fresh water buckets came in. Voices erupted with inquiries and explanations. Darcy heard "unconscious" and "ankle" and "bleeding" and more, but it all seemed to come from far away and through a fog. He vaguely heard his name called but as if from a million miles away. The room started to spin, his vision blurring as he tightened his grip on the bedpost.

"Master Fitzwilliam!" It was Mrs. Reynolds's authoritative snap, calling him by a title he had not worn since a young boy, that partially restored his clarity. She was right before him, face stern but loving. "Mr. Darcy, you must sit down." She took his elbow and guided him unresistingly to the chair by the fire.

"But…" he began.

"Listen to me! We must attend to Mrs. Darcy. We cannot afford to have another patient on our hands! Do you understand? Stay here and put your head between your legs." She patted his head affectionately, gestured to Samuel who hovered at the door, and returned to the bed. In seconds Samuel was by Darcy's side, pressing a glass of brandy into his slack fingers and ordering him to drink.

After what felt like an eternity of waiting with only sporadic glimpses of Elizabeth, but was in fact only an hour, the doctor approached Darcy where he sat slumped in the chair. He jerked to his feet, swaying slightly, face creased with misery and entire body filthy with dried mud and blood.

"Mr. Darcy, let us speak in the sitting room."

The two men sat facing each other, Darcy deliberately sitting where he could espy his wife through the open door.

"As you undoubtedly noted, your wife suffered a blow to the head, perhaps several as she fell, but one of which lacerated her right temple. The wound itself is superficial, only requiring six stitches. We cleaned it thoroughly so it should not fester. Luckily, it is well into her hairline and will not leave a visible scar. As for the head trauma, sir, the truth is I simply do not know.

"At this early juncture, her unconsciousness is actually a good thing. She would likely be in a great deal of pain, and sleeping through all this allows her body to deal with it and protects her mind. We have found that these states of suspended awareness generally reap no lasting damage if they persist for a few days. Since we have no way of seeing inside her head, I cannot say with any certainty if there is injury internally."

"Can you hazard a guess?" Darcy asked.

The doctor spread his hands. "I hate to do that, Mr. Darcy, as there is so much we do not comprehend about how the brain functions. However, considering her relatively good condition overall for falling down what I am told was a twenty-foot, mud-soaked, and rocky embankment, and recognizing her youth and perfect health in general, my *guess*, and it is only a guess, would be that she would recuperate without deficiency."

Darcy nodded, "Thank you, sir."

The physician continued, "There is more, Mr. Darcy. Mrs. Darcy suffered a sprained ankle. It is not broken, and the muscles and tendons feel to be intact. I have wrapped it and instructed the women to keep it elevated. It should heal nicely, although when she does waken, she will need to stay off it for two weeks at the very least. I have examined her thoroughly and, although bruised and scraped, she has no broken bones or cuts that will scar or likely fester."

He cleared his throat and glanced away briefly, alarming Darcy, before he continued, "The next matter is of a personal, sensitive nature, and I apologize ahead of time…"

Darcy laughed harshly without humor. "In light of all this," he waved his hand vaguely toward his bedchamber, "I rather doubt you could offend me. Speak frankly."

"Had you or Mrs. Darcy suspected that she might be with child?"

Oddly, Darcy was not the least bit surprised. He had not knowingly linked the blood on his shirt with the possibility of a miscarriage, but it suddenly fit. "No… that is, we had not discussed the possibility, but it had occurred to me. She is… was… three weeks or so late for her cycle, and," he sighed deeply and closed his eyes as the turmoil of the past days abruptly crashed over him. "She had said nothing to me, but she has been extremely irritable lately, although I do not know if that means anything."

"Oh yes, it certainly can. My wife was horr…" the doctor paused and flushed slightly and Darcy laughed faintly, surprised at the strange humor of the situation.

"Well, that is good to know, I suppose," he whispered. "So, she has… lost… the baby?"

The physician frowned, "The truth, Mr. Darcy, is that I cannot be sure. She bled, a great deal, but not as much as normally seen with a miscarriage. However, if she was very early in her pregnancy, that may be why. I do not wish to submit her to an examination of that nature at this time. My gentle palpations proved nothing. The bleeding has mostly stopped, also unusual in a miscarriage. I have instructed Mrs. Reynolds in what to watch for. We can pursue the matter in a few weeks when she is fully recovered. In the meantime," he rose, and Darcy rose as well, "the women will care for her needs. I shall return in the morning. You must rest and attend to your own health, Mr. Darcy. Your wife needs you so you cannot allow yourself to become ill."

Darcy returned to their bedchamber where Mrs. Reynolds was covering Elizabeth with a blanket. Everyone had left for the time being except the two of them.

"Mrs. Reynolds, thank you for… Well, for everything."

"Of course, Mr. Darcy. I will leave you two alone for now. Samuel is drawing your bath, sir. I will send a tray up later."

"Thank you. Will you talk to Miss Darcy? She must be frantic. I will see her as soon as I can."

Darcy knew there was so much to say, so much to do, but he could not focus on anything other than his wife. Finally alone, he knelt at the side of the bed, too weary to move a chair, and took her hand. Aside from the bandage over the right side of her head, a marked pallor, and a few lingering drops of mud in her plaited hair, she was beautiful and merely appeared asleep.

The women had lovingly cleaned her head to toe, dressed her in a warm white flannel gown, changed the bed linens, and positioned her body comfortably. Darcy tenderly ran his fingers over her cherished face, whispered her name, ultimately giving in to his crushing agony. His head fell to her bosom and he was wracked with convulsing sobs felt in every fiber of his body.

He must have fallen asleep or into a stupor. He returned to awareness at a light touch on his shoulder and a gentle whisper. "Brother?"

He groggily gazed up at the teary, sympathetic face of his sister. "Georgie," he murmured and held his arms open as she fell into his embrace there by the bed. More tears were shed by both of them, but it was cleansing and nourishing to Darcy to feel his sister's love and share his grief and anxiety with her. They talked in soft tones, prayed together, and eventually Darcy was encouraged to leave to bathe while Georgiana maintained a vigil at Elizabeth's side.

For three days they would take turns as companion to the unconscious Elizabeth. Darcy rarely left, primarily only when forced by his bodily needs. He ate little and slept only when his mind betrayed him by slipping into a fitful doze. Georgiana worried as much for her brother as she did for her sister. They all attempted to reason with him, but he refused to listen, the infamous Darcy stubbornness at full capacity, so they surrendered.

The physician came three times each day. Throughout the first and second day he expressed little concern over Mrs. Darcy's continued unconsciousness. He declared her heart stronger, her breathing regular, her pupils reactive to light, her wounds healing as they should, and her bleeding stopped. She seemed in no outward discomfort. He left a bottle of laudanum, for if she did waken, he assumed that she would be in pain and need relief. This unsettled Darcy but he did not argue. Lord Matlock had sent for his personal physician from London by express messenger; however, it would still take two to three days for him to arrive.

Marguerite bathed her, repositioned her frequently with Darcy's assistance, and washed her hair thoroughly. Mrs. Reynolds regularly provided warm tea and broths, which they fed by careful spoonfuls. Darcy was numb. His mind refused to function beyond his need to be with her. Mr. Keith and Mrs. Reynolds handled everything else.

By the afternoon of the third day, the doctor was evincing some disquiet. Elizabeth's overall status was improving. Her ankle was substantially less swollen; the head laceration was healing well and definitely not infected; the other bruises and scratches were in their proper stages of regeneration; and her vital signs were strong. However, the fact that she manifested no indications toward arousing did not bode well for her mental and neurological recovery. He confessed that his personal experience as a physician was not abundant in the realm of head trauma, so he could only speak from a textbook point of view. Whatever the case, there was nothing any of them could do but wait.

~❦~

When Lizzy opened her eyes she saw... darkness. How long she stared with unseeing eyes was impossible to guess. Eventually, however, two facts seeped into her addled mind: she could see a faint light from somewhere vaguely to her left; and she had a blinding headache. Cautiously and incrementally between stabbing pains, she turned her head to the left, recognizing after a grueling period of chaotic scrutiny that the light came from the fireplace in their bedchamber. Her eyes fuzzily drifted about the familiar room while her mind refused to function and the pain threatened to engulf her. She probably fell asleep for a time, because, next she knew, her eyes opened again to a slightly brighter light that she sluggishly realized was twinges of a sunrise peeping in through the windows.

The pain was there as fierce as ever, but she did seem to be more in control of her thoughts and her eyes focused clearly. As cautiously as before, she turned her head to the right, alighting on the dearest sight imaginable. Her William. He was asleep beside her, clothed, and covered with a light blanket rather than under the comforter with her. She frowned, sending throbs through her skull. *He looks horrendous.* At least three days' growth of beard, dark circles under his eyes, lips chapped and pale, and hair uncombed. It made no sense and hurt too much to try reasoning it out.

"William," she said, aware immediately that no sound had actually passed her lips. She closed her eyes, willing the headache away, licked her incredibly dry lips with a tongue equally dry, and tried again. "William." A vague squeak was all. It took five more whispers to finally rouse him, and then he only stared at her as if paralyzed.

"Elizabeth?" So softly. *Am I dreaming?* He lifted tremulous fingers to her cheek and then her lips as she continued to stare at him. "Elizabeth?" She smiled against his fingertips and kissed them lightly, snapping him out of his stasis. With a guttural cry he rose onto his elbows and brought his mouth to hers, kissing her as tears fell and he moaned, "Elizabeth! Oh God! I… I love you so much!" He ran fingers over her face, kissed her repeatedly, all the while sobbing as hushed endearments fell in a torrent.

Why is he crying? Nothing made any sense and her head was exploding. She weakly reached her left hand up to his cheek and then into his hair, but the effort to do so was colossal. "William, my head hurts."

He recoiled as if stung by a wasp. "Oh, my love! Of course it does. Forgive me!" He launched out of the bed, hastily pulled the servant's cord, and busied himself at something on the bed stand. Before she could manage turning her head fully in his direction, he was beside her on the bed, gently lifting her in his arms to a sitting position. "Here, my love, drink this. It is laudanum. It will ease the pain."

It tasted horrible and Lizzy had heard stories of opium users, but none of that mattered if the agony in her head and, she now discerned, from her right foot, was relieved. Peripherally she was aware of how marvelous it was to have her husband's sturdy arms around her and to be reclining against his firm, warm chest. Her memory was hazy, she was incapable of forming a coherent deduction, and she was assailed with lethargy and drowsiness. As the blanket of sleep fell over her, she struggled to look up into his face. He was smiling at her, blue eyes sparkling with joy.

She tried to smile, unsure if she was able to finagle it, whispering as her eyes fell shut, "William, I was frightened by a turkey. Is that not ridiculous?"

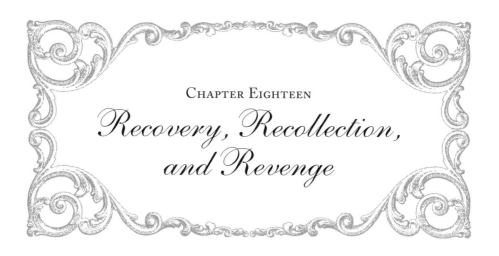

CHAPTER EIGHTEEN

Recovery, Recollection, and Revenge

FOR THE SUBSEQUENT FIVE days, Lizzy slept interminably. When she woke, she was seared with blinding pain that required frequent doses of laudanum to induce sleep. Therefore, it was a cycle of constant slumber with minimal conscious periods used to encourage her to eat and attend to her physical necessities. Darcy was in a barely controlled state of panic the first few times she slept, certain she had slipped into unconsciousness. His relief when she woke up was immeasurable, tears readily springing to his eyes. He undoubtedly told her he loved her more in those five days than in the past four months, and there was hardly a second he was not touching her in some manner.

The doctor assured him the headaches were normal under the circumstances and would lessen in intensity daily. Her other wounds were healing exceeding his expectation. The ankle, although discolored with every hue imaginable, was no longer as swollen and mobility was marginally limited. The numerous other bruises over her body were also in varying shades of yellows, greens, and purples, but rapidly receding. They had not spoken about the possible miscarriage and Darcy, frankly, could not bear to cope with it right now. He only wanted to focus on his wife's recovery and his own bliss at having her with him.

Her recollection of the past two weeks was spotty. When he asked her about the turkey comment, she had no idea what he was talking about. At times she remembered running through the woods and being frightened but she could not recall why or at what, and then she would forget the woods entirely. Attempting to focus on her flight and the circumstances leading to it merely augmented her headache, so Darcy desisted in questioning her. She made no mention of their argument, and he did not bring it up. Aside from her pain and sleepiness, she was her usual self: witty, jovial, and loving. Her appetite improved, although she was frequently nauseous and was ill twice. All of this the physician said was to be expected.

Lord Matlock's private physician was consulted and he concurred, greatly easing Darcy's mind. Lady Matlock arrived two days after the accident and stayed, taking over Lizzy's care from Mrs. Reynolds so the housekeeper could resume her duties. Georgiana and Marguerite were diligent companions as well, allowing Darcy the freedom to attend to his own needs, such as bathing and shaving and eating regularly. Nonetheless, he was never further than the next room. In fact, he did not move past the third-floor landing for more than a week, only traveling that far twice for brief conversations with Mr. Keith.

He wrote to her father, explaining briefly what had transpired and ensuring him that Lizzy was recuperating rapidly. He politely asked him to apprize the Gardiners and Bingleys, pledging to write further once the immediate crisis was alleviated. Col. Fitzwilliam, notified by his father, breezed in five days after the accident, providing support and a bit of light humor and diversion, originally not well appreciated by Darcy but eventually helpful in restoring balance and easing his gloominess. The plethora of flowers and well wishes from the families of the community was truly staggering. Darcy was awed. He scattered the blooms throughout the bedchamber, adding fresh ones from the conservatory and gardens, so the room was a rainbow of color and sweet aromas.

Once Darcy relinquished his anxiety over Lizzy's health, he turned his consideration to the event itself. Her bad temper, resulting in their ridiculous argument, he attributed to possible pregnancy and their mutual stupidity and obstinacy. By what he ascertained from Georgiana and the staff he questioned, Lizzy had been in a cheerful, exuberant mood and perfectly healthy when she set off to pick berries. The groom who had discovered the strewn berries and discarded bucket had little to tell. Her footprints leading into the forest were clear and solitary.

The road itself was one well traveled by both carriages and pedestrians. There were other footprints near Mrs. Darcy's as well as marks from a carriage, the groom said, but there was no way to deduce with confidence if they were related, nor would it help much anyway. When Darcy asked if he had noted turkey tracks, the groom had answered a baffled negative. The mystery of it gnawed at Darcy, but he saw no way to solve it, so he had to abandon the quest for enlightenment for the time being.

By the end of the eleventh day after the accident, Lizzy's headaches were minimal and tolerable; however, her amnesia surrounding the day of the accident persisted. The stitches had been removed from the laceration to her head, her bruises were almost invisible, and her ankle only twinged slightly. She had occasional bouts of nausea, but it appeared to be lessening. She passed most of the daylight hours awake with only short naps, and was beginning to experience the restlessness of her forced confinement in their chambers.

Darcy carried her to the sitting room and window seat with increasing frequency as her headaches diminished. The doctor said she must stay off her foot for at least a week longer but could be moved farther afield, provided she did not overtax herself. Their chambers were unquestionably Lizzy's favorite rooms in all of Pemberley, but she longed to leave them. Darcy promised her that in the morning he would carry her to whichever room she wished to visit. This pleased her and she kissed him gratefully.

He returned the kiss chastely and then pulled away, tucking the blankets around her snugly before retreating. Each evening he did this, sitting near and tenderly caressing her hand as she fell asleep. After that he read or, on occasion, moved to his desk, left the door open, and attended to business, eventually joining her on their massive bed. However, he slept in a nightshirt on top of the down comforter and under his own blanket, and other than holding her hand, avoided any physical contact.

Until the past four nights, Lizzy had been in too much discomfort and far too weary to lament her husband's caution. She understood he fretted over her well-being, but the truth was that his lack of affection was troubling her more than anything. She yearned for his love with a desire that was partially emotional and spiritual but, frankly, was largely lustful.

Her preoccupation and urges invaded her sleep. In the middle of the night she roused fully to the always succulent view of her stunningly alluring husband sprawled beside her deep in slumber. Wasting no time on contemplation, she carefully slipped out from under her blankets and nestled next to his warm body. He sighed and reflexively gathered her into his arms. Lizzy had a clear agenda and it did not include sleep.

Knowing well the form of caresses and kisses arousing to him, she employed them all, the instantaneous response exactly as she anticipated. He moaned, his craving as strong as hers even in sleep. He sought her mouth, kissing her with the pent-up passion of a near fortnight without her, combined with the residual terror of possibly losing her forever. His hands acted of their own accord, pressing her tightly into the hard planes of his body before he snapped awake.

With a gasp he pulled away, grasping her fondling hands in a firm grip, and pleading breathlessly, "Elizabeth, please! We cannot... we must not..."

"It is alright, my love. I am feeling much better and I need you, Fitzwilliam. I want you to love me. I know you will be gentle," she smiled at his worried face, leaning in to kiss him, "although I make no promises that I will be." She teasingly claimed his lips and he groaned, giving in for a moment of utter delight and then shuddering as he again pulled away, rapidly sitting up on the edge of the bed with his back to her.

He cradled his head in his hands and she could see him shaking. "Fitzwilliam, what is it? You are scaring me! I assure you I am fine, and I know you desire me." She rose up and wrapped her arms about his waist, laying her cheek against his back. "Do not try to deny it, beloved; I know you too well."

He clutched her hands against his abdomen, partly to comfort her and partly to prevent her roaming any lower, and spoke shakily. "My heart, my ardor for you has attained a critical level, have no fear of that. It is just... . I have not spoken to the doctor about this..."

"The doctor! What in the world does the doctor have to say about our lovemaking? William, you are being ridiculous, and I cannot fathom why you would contemplate discussing this with a stranger!"

He stood up abruptly and began pacing, not meeting her eyes. "Elizabeth, there is something... we deemed it wise not to... you have been so ill, and I could not bear..." He trailed off and Lizzy identified his extreme distress.

She was terrified but also miffed that they had kept something obviously important from her. "Fitzwilliam Darcy, I insist you sit down this second and tell me what is going on! We promised to harbor no secrets. Whatever it is, I have the right to know and we must deal with it together."

He looked at her with such misery on his lovely face, misery as she had witnessed during the first few days of her recovery. "William, if you do not come to me, I swear I will get up and walk over to you!" To prove her intent she started scooting to the edge of the bed, prompting him to step quickly.

"No, Elizabeth, relax. You are correct. I must tell you." He sat next to her and grasped her hands, gazing into her eyes. "Beloved, when I found you… on the day of your accident… you were bleeding copiously from… Your fall probably resulted in a miscarriage and I…" He swallowed, too overcome to continue as he watched her, and stroked her cheek. "My love, Elizabeth, I am so sorry!"

Lizzy was staring at him, a puzzled frown on her face. She did not reply for several minutes then, "I heard a *probably* in there. What precisely happened and what information did the physician impart?"

Darcy inhaled deeply and closed his eyes, "Your blood had soaked through your skirts and onto my shirt."

"Sorry about that."

He opened his eyes in surprise at her teasing tone, further amazed to see her smiling slightly. He shook his head faintly, "My clothing was ruined already, so it is insignificant. Elizabeth, are you alright?"

"Pray continue, William."

He frowned, "Very well. The physician asked me if we suspected you might be with child, to which I replied it was possible. I informed him that your monthly cycle was late and you were… edgy. He told me that can be a sign." Lizzy nodded and flushed, hanging her head in shamed remembrance. "He said the bleeding may be indicative of a miscarriage, but he could not be certain."

"Why not?"

"The hemorrhaging was not as extensive as usually seen and ceased quickly, although he ruminated that the early stage of your condition could affect that. Of course, you may not have been pregnant at all. He also expected the bleeding to continue but it did not." He halted, sighed greatly, and ran his hand over his face. "I do not know, Elizabeth. I confess to avoiding the topic. It is too painful."

Lizzy cupped his face with her hands and kissed him tenderly. "My sweet love," she whispered, meeting his eyes and smiling, "let me reveal to you what I know. Aside from this bleeding which I do not remember and by the physician's own admission was questionable, I am now approximately six weeks late, and I am never late. There is the craziness of my attitude, for which I profoundly apologize. Madeline shared with me that she suffered the same moodiness with her pregnancies. I am sure your uncle would commiserate."

She laughed softly and kissed him again, lingeringly. "Every morning I wake and am queasy. It may be residual of the head trauma, yet why do I feel ill only in the morning and before I even move? Lastly," she grasped one of his hands and planted it squarely on her breast, "what do you feel?"

Darcy had raptly absorbed her words, his quick intellect and education on the subject nimbly locking the pieces of the puzzle together with heightened excitement. His intimacy with her precious body instantaneously recognized the answer to her query. "You are fuller!"

"Yes, and they are tender, so gently, please," she teased, threading her arms around his neck and shifting so that she was on his lap. "Fitzwilliam, I am not positive. Perhaps the physician will be able to verify. I desperately desire for our baby to be safe inside me, and I think it is. However, none of this can be resolved at one in the morning. Therefore, I propose less discussion and pleasant," light kiss, "arousing," nibbling, "satisfying activities. Oh, William! I have missed you so! At the risk of sounding horribly selfish, all I want now is you. I cannot survive another night without your arms around me. I love you and I need you."

She kissed him ardently, pouring all her yearning and passion into the task, and he responded accordingly. With an aching groan he pushed her back onto the bed, cautiously and carefully showing her how intensively he loved, required, and hungered for her. Cold rationality was sluggish in surfacing.

With a throaty cry reminiscent of true pain, he untangled himself from her, clasping her face in tremulous hands, closing his eyes for a moment, and inhaling deeply. "God in Heaven, help me! My sweet Lizzy, my love, you surely know how fervid my passion for you. It is eating me alive, I need you so! I cannot, please, I beg you... If I hurt you in any way, if I hurt our child, Elizabeth, I... I could not live with that! Please, I promise we will talk to the doctor tomorrow, obtain answers. Tell me you understand, beloved?"

"Shhh... Fitzwilliam, I understand, I do." She wiped his tears, her own pooling in her eyes as her lips trembled. In a small pleading voice, "Please do not make me sleep over there alone. I... I... I want you to hold me! Will you please hold me, William? I promise to behave."

He laughed softly and pulled her into his embrace, nestling her head on his shoulder as he drew the blankets over them. "I will never let you go, Lizzy, never. If ever again you move to my mother's bedchamber, I will batter down the door!"

The physician's appointment was for the afternoon. After breakfast Darcy carried Lizzy to her parlor where she rested and was entertained by Georgiana, Lady Matlock, and Col. Fitzwilliam. She wrote several letters to her family and friends in the neighborhood. She had experienced some thirty minutes of nausea that morning, alleviated by the tea and toast Marguerite had begun bringing her each morning. Darcy had smiled brightly at her discomfort, which normally might have annoyed her, but she understood his emotions and was so blissful herself that she merely smiled in return, if a bit wanly.

He insisted she nap after lunch, a command that no one bothered to counter even though it was abundantly clear she was not the least fatigued. Lady Matlock returned home that afternoon, leaving Georgiana and Richard to amuse themselves, a task they would end up doing until the morrow.

The physician arrived and was momentarily dumbstruck, and Darcy embarrassed, as he had barely entered the room when Lizzy bluntly demanded he examine her feminine regions and tell her husband their marital relations must resume. Darcy nearly choked and hurriedly exited the room, but the doctor recovered quickly. After a thorough investigation of all areas, feminine and otherwise, he called for Darcy. The news was all positive.

Aside from her amnesia, which may never resolve, her head was declared healed. The ankle required another week or so of cautious activity but in a few more days, she could, with assistance, begin tentatively using it. Her feminine regions showed no sign of injury, the bleeding never having resumed. As for pregnancy, it remained too early to assert definitively, although he concurred with the symptoms as those indicative of the state. His gentle palpations had revealed a possibly enlarged womb, but, again, too soon for explicitness. Nonetheless, his cautious diagnosis was that Elizabeth was likely with child.

The affectionate and blatantly amorous glances shared by Darcy and his wife at the news brought an empathetic smile to the doctor's face, and he hastily gathered his instruments. Darcy grinned stunningly at his wife as he escorted the doctor out, mouthing *I love you* as the door shut. He did manage to overcome his natural reticence and mortification for several pointed questions of his own before the physician bid adieu. He then literally ascended the stairs two and three at a time in his eagerness to return to his wife.

Darcy found his wife sitting placidly on their bed after quickly summoning Marguerite to assist changing her into a filmy rose-colored nightgown and brushing her hair. Darcy entered briskly, having shed his coat and waistcoat haphazardly in the sitting room. His eyes locked with Lizzy's the second he crossed the threshold, his pace slowing as his smile broadened, lighting his face with an incandescent jubilance. He sat next to her, merely gazing.

"What took you so long?" she asked with a teasing smile.

He laughed softly, reaching one hand to brush the hair away from her right temple. "I needed to ask the physician a few questions for my own enlightenment and the foyer is a great distance. Even my legs can only take the steps so fast."

She cocked her head to the side and grinned while running one hand up his thigh. "Questions? In the lengthy interval you have forgotten how it is done, beloved?"

He chuckled but deigned not to answer. Instead he leaned toward her, brushing his lips tenderly along the scar at her temple and then to her ear, her jawline, and eventually her mouth as she shuddered and sighed with contentment. "Beautiful wife," he murmured, "I love you, and I adore you, my Lizzy."

They caressed each other dreamily, their yearning intense, yet the thrill in the simple act of touching and kissing mesmerized them for a spell. He moved away eventually only to remove boots and shirt before gathering her tightly into his arms and stretching onto their bed.

Lizzy moaned happily and squeezed him with all her strength. "Fitzwilliam, you are the best man in the world! I love you with all my soul."

Darcy was gentle and tender as promised. Lizzy was consumed with her need for him, but he languidly touched and caressed her satiny skin, his only haste in divesting her of the lovely but obstructive gown. Despite the physician's assurances, he privately worried and had no intention of allowing his pent-up passions to overrule his caution. The end result was a lovemaking session of stupendous proportions as their mutual desire and yearning built slowly and was controlled.

They lay on their sides face to face, each exploring the other's body almost as if for the first time. Darcy kissed each fading bruise and healing laceration and worked his way to her slightly swollen and colorful ankle, kissing and massaging gently. His hands moved over her body delicately, rivers of fire following in their wake. His mouth traveled as well, to each beautifully formed and slightly fuller breast, down her abdomen, dipping into her navel, and in all ways driving her mad with desire.

As he worshipped her body, awakening and spiraling her passionate lust, his heart remembered the agony of almost losing her. It was still so real to him, the torture of those days. Fear continued to clutch his soul and his thankfulness to God for returning her to him was overwhelming. His need to love her, please her, touch her, and unite with her as can only be accomplished through the act of lovemaking drove him to astounding heights of arousal.

As tremendous as his urgency to be joined with her, his thirst to taste and touch and smell every inch of her flesh impelled him to proceed slowly. In consequence, Lizzy had never been so stimulated. Always she was satisfied in their lovemaking, stunned at the intensity of the glorious sensations that throbbed through her body when he masterfully coaxed her to rapture. Perhaps it was the long absence of his touch; perhaps it was the prolonged foreplay, or more likely a combination of both. Whatever the case, she was feverish in her craving for him.

"Fitzwilliam," she sighed in a tone of elation, "I missed you so! I love you… I love you… I love you…" Almost sobbing, she captured his lips in a crushing kiss, and with a deep groan he finally merged with her.

Darcy clenched her firmly against his chest with one arm under her neck and gripping her shoulder, while the other ceaselessly rubbed over her backside. He moaned breathlessly, exalting in the heady aroma of her hair so near his face and her skin as velvet under his hands.

"My love!" he rasped huskily. "Lord, how I wanted you. I need you, my Elizabeth, my precious wife. God… please… do not ever leave me… I cannot live… Beloved!" He pulled her away from his neck and deliriously engulfed her mouth, drowning in her taste, receiving nourishment from her breath. Their respirations came in ragged gasps. Lizzy's nails dug into his flesh with rapacious need.

They rolled and danced in intimate communication, giving as well as receiving, the unimaginable sensations quivering throughout each nerve and cell. When they slipped blissfully over the threshold of rhapsody, the spasms and flutters buffeted over them stupendously, transporting their souls to a place of intense indescribable oneness.

Their eyes met, lips touching as hot breath commingled, and they merged in profound love and belonging. "I love you," they whispered in one accord, "I love you, I love you…" without end, kissing tenderly as their passion crested, cascaded in a prolonged wave, and ebbed slowly. Even after their tremors had ceased, Darcy continued to move within her body, holding her tightly for a long while before finally rotating onto his back with Elizabeth enveloped in his arms.

Darcy sheltered her with a strong embrace, the emotions of the past weeks threatening to overwhelm him as tears welled. Inhaling deeply and kissing the top of her head to avoid bursting into sobs, he squeezed her so tenaciously that she released a small squeak.

"William, I cannot breathe!" she laughed, lifting to look at him. "My love," smoothing his brow, "Are you alright?"

Smiling, he replied, "Yes, beloved, simply overcome with my emotions. I adore you so, Elizabeth, and shudder yet at how close I came to losing you. It haunts me still. I trust you will understand if I cling overly in the weeks to come." His attempt at levity brought a smile to her lips.

"I imagine I can tolerate your presence if I must," she teased, kissing his chest, laying her head over his pounding heart, and hugging firmly.

Contentment, relief, and joy so intensely swathed him that he fell into a doze, his perfect wife stretched on top of him. Her warmth soothed his residual fears.

They had every intention, initially, of joining their family for dinner, but time slipped away in the pleasure of their renewed love. It was well past the dinner hour before either of them felt any sensation other than sheer ecstasy. A tray was called for eventually; both of them needed their strength and Darcy especially worried as, he pointed out smugly, their child needed nourishment. As far as he was concerned, it was a fact and Lizzy was far too joyous to worry over his grief if she was found not to be with child. Besides, she had been convinced for the past week.

As the full moon touched the Peaks with glints of pale light, Lizzy lay gloriously contented in her sleep with her bare backside pressed firmly against Darcy's chest and abdomen, legs entwined, while he embraced her and tickled her neck with his exhalations.

She dreamed.

Like many dreams, hers flowed from page to page without any true coherency. In one scene she was hugely pregnant and her husband was helping her up the stairs while laughing at her waddling gait. Then she was at their wedding, gazing into his sparkling blue eyes as she recited her vows. Next it was Christmas and Darcy was playing the violin as they all listened in amazement. In another, she sat with Harriet, Chloe, Marilyn, and Amelia with at least two dozen children of all ages climbing over the furniture, running amok, giggling, and screaming as their mothers placidly sipped their tea.

Suddenly the pages began to turn in a sequence that struck a chord of disquiet. She was storming shamefully into her husband's study. She lay on a cold lonely bed sobbing and ill. Darcy was riding Parsifal briskly down the drive as he turned and smiled at her, warming her heart. She strolled down the avenue, humming in the bright sunlight with a bucket in her hand. She was lifting her welcoming face to an approaching carriage, freezing in terror upon spying the leering face of the Marquis of Orman.

With a scream she struggled out of Darcy's grip, applying a twisting pressure to her ankle, as she jolted up in bed. "William!" she sobbed, grabbing her pounding head, the pages of her memory flipping rapidly, as she bent over her lap moaning.

"Elizabeth, beloved, I am here! Shhh…" She was in his arms, trembling and gulping for air. "It is merely a dream, my love. Lizzy, look at me," he grasped her chin and she peered at him with glazed eyes, "All is well, dearest, relax on my chest. Breathe slowly. Shhhh. I am here, love, I am here…" He continued to murmur soothing words interspersed with tender kisses as he rocked gently until she calmed. He reclined her onto the pillow, one arm about her as he stroked her cheek and hair.

Her eyes were distant and staring and filled with pain. He could not be certain she was fully awake, so he maintained his calming caresses and mollifying professions until her eyes unclouded and she focused on his face. She shivered still, anguish in her expression when she spoke.

"I remember, William. I recall what happened to me."

"You do? Are you sure, beloved, that you were not dreaming?"

"No, no! I can see it and feel it… I remember running and falling and… the turkey…" she was panting and clutching his arms roughly. Darcy was seriously alarmed at her agitation and tried to console her to no avail. She was frantic. He attempted to move away, intent on mixing laudanum to ease her suffering and distress, but she grasped him tighter. "It was him!"

"Who?"

"Orman! He encountered me on the road and… grabbed me… and tried to… Oh, William! I was so frightened! I hit him and ran. It was so foolish of me and I was so cruel to you before and I have caused you such torment and I may have harmed our baby and…" She was sobbing and hysterical. Darcy was stunned, furious, and despondent.

Elizabeth first, he thought. He poured a generous glass of brandy laced with laudanum, forced her to drink it all, and held her until she drifted into a drugged sleep. Darcy remained wide awake. His burning fury had ebbed, substituted with cold calculation and determination. He may not have all the finer details as yet, but simply the knowledge that Orman was the catalyst to Elizabeth's accident and near death brought graphic images of murder to his mind.

At the first hint of dawn, Darcy slipped out of bed. He sought out Marguerite, informing her that the Mistress had suffered a nightmare requiring a liberal dose of sedative. He instructed Lizzy's maid to stay with her and notify him the instant she roused. He dressed quickly and marched straight to his cousin's door. Richard was ill pleased to be woken so early but quickly overcame his irritation when he heard Darcy's information.

Darcy paced as he spoke, a robed Richard sitting in a chair with an increasingly grim cast to his mien. "She said he grabbed her?" he repeated in shock, "and tried... what do you think?"

"I do not know! Nor does it matter, Richard! He has accosted her, twice now, and she almost died! I insist on justice!"

"Well, of course, cousin! If you did not, I would horsewhip you myself, and then happily deal with the blackguard. All I meant is that you must ascertain the full scope of the charges against him. Orman is a knave, we all know this; however, he is a gentleman and will abide by the rules of engagement once publicly confronted. Especially coming from you since he has loathed you for years."

Darcy continued to pace but his stride slowed as he mused. "I will not allow this to become another Wickham. Orman has run wild for too long, and he must be revealed for the villain he is. If we are fortunate, then I shall succeed in killing him, sparing all of England his offenses. At the very least I will maim him and run him out of Derbyshire."

"How are you to handle Elizabeth? She has been through enough distress and her health is precarious."

Darcy sighed and stopped at the window, staring sightlessly at the glowing Peaks. "More than you are aware, cousin. She may be with child." He turned to the colonel with a delighted smile.

Richard beamed and rushed to clap Darcy on the back. "Congratulations! Watching the two of you, well, let us say I am not surprised." He teased and Darcy blushed faintly, but then turned serious.

"Thank you, however, we are not certain so I beg your discretion. Richard, I abhor secrets and it pains me to even contemplate it, but she must not know until it is over. I am a terrible liar, as you know, so will need your support."

"You have it, naturally."

Darcy nodded. "Once I learn all that transpired, I will tell Elizabeth I am dealing with the matter through legal channels. I will challenge Orman this afternoon, if the coward is still in the vicinity, and I can dispatch him tomorrow."

"Awfully sure of yourself, cousin," Richard grinned.

Darcy looked at him with contempt, "Please, do not insult me! I know never to underestimate one's opponent, but he cannot best me." Col. Fitzwilliam laughed and Darcy had the good grace to smile sheepishly. "With that piece of grandiose braggadocio out of the way, I shall be cautious, never fear. I have far too much to live for."

Marguerite sent for Darcy shortly thereafter. He promptly entered their chambers to discover his wife holed up in her water closet being ill. When she emerged, pale and aquiver, Darcy was there to support her unsteady mobility. They spent most of the morning together in their sitting room.

Lizzy told him everything. His rage at what Orman had said and done was nearly uncontrollable, and once again the famous Darcy self-control and reserve were called into action. As she continued recounting her harrowing dash through the woods, her fear at being lost, and her fright at the turkey that caused her fall, Darcy lived it with her as well as reviving the succeeding week of torment. They held one another close, needing to sense the vibrant life and unwavering love oozing from every pore.

Lizzy was anxious at what Darcy planned in retribution. He tried to conceal his wrath but she knew him too intimately. In the end, he skirted the truth by confessing his overwhelming need to confront Orman and exact physical vengeance by satisfyingly smashing in his nose, but then he would wield his considerable power and influence to have the cur lawfully punished. Lizzy was no fool and perceived that he was evading, but she wisely ruled it was his right to protect his wife as he saw fit.

Of course, she had no suspicion of what he planned.

❧

The next morning, one hour after dawn, Fitzwilliam Darcy of Pemberley confidently stood several feet across from the Marquis of Orman on an open field at Lord Matlock's estate, Rivallain.

After Lizzy's violent resistance and escape into the woods, Orman had driven home rapidly. In part, this haste was due to the significant gash over his left cheekbone, which was bleeding profusely and ultimately required eight stitches to repair, yet largely due to the sober rationality restored along with the whack from Lizzy's bucket.

Orman was a relatively brave man, tough when the situation called, but also a dandy, foolhardy and brash. Elizabeth was not the first woman to receive unwanted advances from the Marquis; however, generally he was wiser in his choices and had, therefore, managed to avoid severe unpleasantries. Electing Elizabeth as the object of his seduction was no doubt primarily prompted by his hatred of Darcy, rather than an overwhelming attraction to her. Darcy's and Orman's mutual discord was not based on any particular incident but was merely one of those loathing-at-first-sight relationships strengthened over time by further revelations of their widely divergent characters and morals.

Orman may have been foolhardy, but he was not a complete imbecile. Sober rationality told him that, without the slightest doubt, Darcy would exact revenge for this recent impropriety. Therefore, as soon as his wound was treated, he departed with alacrity to a friend's manor in Nottingham. When he received the news that Mrs. Darcy had suffered an accident, he trembled in fear.

His spies kept close watch on the situation and although information was nearly impossible to ferret out of the tight-lipped, loyal staff of Pemberley, it soon became clear that, for reasons unknown, Orman's name was not associated with the event. With a false sense of security and atrociously poor timing, the Marquis brazenly returned to his Derbyshire manor the very day that Lizzy's memory was reinstituted.

Thus, when Darcy, along with Col. Fitzwilliam and Lord Matlock, rode up to his house and ordered the butler to summon his master, Orman was utterly unprepared. Nonetheless, when Lord Matlock coldly intoned the charges and Darcy imperiously issued the challenge, Orman bristled and the miniscule amount of honor he possessed impelled him pridefully to accept.

As the challenger, Darcy had set the rules: duel with short swords to incapacitation, at Lord Matlock's estate one hour after dawn on the morrow, and seconds as appointed by each party. So, here they now stood. Their swords had been inspected by their seconds—Col. Fitzwilliam and Mr. Gerald Vernor in Darcy's case, the rules and charges had been reiterated, the ground canvassed for hazards, and coats removed.

Lord Matlock announced the onset of the duel with a loud, "Allez." The combatants studied each other, circling slowly with their swords forward on point. Darcy had well buried his burning rage. He was calm, heart beating normally, and absolutely focused with emotions tightly controlled.

"So, Darcy," Orman taunted, "your foolish wife loses herself in the forest, nearly dies, and you must trump charges against me! Such pride. Darcy of Pemberley would never admit to choosing poorly in the country bumpkin of Hertfordshire!"

Darcy did not flinch, although Col. Fitzwilliam swore, detained by his father from personally running Orman through.

"Esteem her quite highly, do you not, old friend?" Orman sneered, "Favor her so beautiful that all men will fall at her feet? Whom else will you accuse…" He lunged abruptly, sword aimed straight for Darcy's heart.

Darcy had expected this tactic. Not swayed one iota by Orman's blustering, Darcy parried easily, knocking Orman's sword to the left and then nimbly pivoting to the right and rapidly raising his sword upwards. He sunk the edge deeply into Orman's left arm just below the shoulder and then stepped away, sword instantly again at the ready.

Orman was taken by surprise but, to his credit, recovered immediately, sword again on point as the adversaries stalked with eyes locked. Blood soaked his sleeve but he ignored it, face no longer mocking.

The cat and mouse games were finished. Darcy lunged next, deflected by Orman with ease, initiating a round of furious thrusts, parries, and rapid ripostes. They tested each other's strengths and weaknesses, having never fenced together in the past. Darcy scored again with a glancing cut to Orman's neck, promptly followed with another superficial graze across his chest.

Orman howled in fury; Darcy baring his teeth in a snarl, the only show of emotion thus far. Orman attacked with rage, normally not a wise tactic and one that would have proven to be his ultimate undoing, as Darcy was primed. Unfortunately, as he stepped to the left, Darcy's foot landed hard on a sharp stone and he faltered. Orman's sword was averted poorly and, although not reaching its intended location, sunk completely into the flesh along the edge of Darcy's right side, neatly gliding all the way through and exiting the back.

Darcy grunted and grimaced in pain, staggering as he jerked backward with his arm pressed tightly to the bleeding wound. Amazingly, he still somehow managed to score a penetrating stab into Orman's right shoulder. Both men staggered backward a few paces, eyeing each other with rabid hatred and panting harshly.

"Is she honestly worth it, Darcy? A woman?"

"Vermin such as you, Orman, would never comprehend."

"True love, is it? How touching. Never would have suspected you to be the romantic type. Perhaps her gracing me with her lovely smiles was more than you could bear?"

Darcy merely smiled, a chilling smile without humor that unsettled the Marquis, who frowned. His attempts to rouse Darcy's anger and ruffle his composure were failing miserably. Orman began to sweat. He knew Darcy's reputation as a superb fencer and had dwelt on little else all night, in fact. Orman was stouter than Darcy, muscular and potent. However, Darcy had the advantage of height with subsequently longer legs and greater reach. Orman could likely outlast Darcy in a contest requiring endurance, but his skill level with swords did not near Darcy's and he knew it. He must alter his stratagem.

With a plan in mind, he engaged and another round of vicious thrusts and parries ensued. Darcy received a gash across his chest, not terribly deep, but a scar would remain to match the two on his waist. Orman pressed with a steady barrage, driving Darcy back. He applied no particular finesse, trusting to sheer brute force and stamina to wear his opponent down. Darcy landed three more superficial blows, leaving Orman bleeding from several sites.

Despite the fury of his assault, Orman was unable to connect with the nimble Darcy. Both men suffered from loss of blood and pain, but Darcy was a man vastly more familiar with the rigors of hard labor and the trial of persevering with injury after years of training horses. His breathing was only mildly labored and a light sheen of perspiration covered his brow. Orman, on the other hand, was wheezing and sweating liberally.

After a wild thrust, which Darcy parried with his free hand, earning a shallow slice to his palm, he was successful in piercing Orman's thigh scant inches below his groin and less than a fingerbreadth from his femoral vein. Orman screamed and pitched forward, the duelists grabbing each other's sword arms at the wrist, clinched tenaciously nearly nose to nose. They grappled together in a back-and-forth dance of engagement. All of a sudden, Darcy vehemently twisted his right arm free, aggressively smashing his elbow squarely onto Orman's nose, feeling and hearing the satisfying crunch he had promised Elizabeth, followed by a gush of blood and lusty bellow.

In a fit of raging blood lust, Darcy intended to end it there, and would have, but Orman had one last trick up his sleeve. With blood streaming down his face and tears of pain obscuring his vision, he nonetheless had the presence of mind to sweep out with his uninjured leg, knocking Darcy completely off his feet. He landed hard on his back, air escaping his lungs in a loud whoosh. He lay there for a second, stunned and gasping, but saw Orman closing in with an overhand stroke with one purpose only: to kill. Dimly he heard Richard yell a warning.

Drawing from a reserve of strength of unknown origin, he gambled and rolled toward his attacker, lashing out with the sword miraculously still clenched in his hand, and cleanly sliced though the posterior muscles above Orman's left knee. Orman screamed in agony, sword falling from suddenly nerveless fingers as he collapsed in a heap, clutching a now useless, hamstringed leg.

With renewed vigor, Darcy was on top of Orman in a millisecond, knee pressed painfully into his abdomen and left hand choking his throat while the sword point punctured the skin over his erratically pounding heart. Orman's shrieks were cut short by a sharp clench of Darcy's fingers, and he met his victor's blazing eyes with raw fear. The spectators had drawn near.

"Shall I render mercy, Orman?" Darcy inquired frigidly as if merely asking the time of day, "Or should I kill as justice demands? Tell me the truth, swine, and be swift as I judge you have precious minutes before you bleed to death. Did you lay hands on my wife?"

"Yes, but…"

"Did you assault her with the design of enforcing intimacy?" Darcy's sword penetrated through the skin, grazing a rib. Orman writhed but Darcy strengthened the pressure to his belly, twisted the sword minutely, and repeated, "Did you?"

"Yes! I—" gasp "—never meant her harm! Forgive me! Mercy, please!"

Placing the edge of the blade against Orman's throat, Darcy leaned down until he was virtually nose to nose. In a deadly voice he pronounced, "Marquis of Orman, you have been vanquished in a test of honor and have confessed before these witnesses. By tomorrow all of Derbyshire, and then beyond, will know your transgressions. The choice is yours. To live, maimed and a coward, and forsake this region for the rest of your natural life, or to die by my sword. Which will it be?"

"Live," he whispered.

"So be it. Remember your choice, Orman, for I swear that I will offer no mercy in the future."

❦

Lizzy woke that morning some two hours after dawn to an empty bed and fear clutching her heart.

Darcy had effectively evaded her queries the previous night by touching and kissing in all the places and ways that drove her wild with passion. Their lovemaking had been as rapturous and blissful as always, leaving her satiated and sleepy. She fell into a deep slumber immediately with her head on his chest and body nestled snuggly in his arms. If for Darcy their union had been tinged with a vague trepidation and mild nostalgia elicited by the potential for a negative outcome at the duel, it was offset by the exhilaration and overwhelming love he felt for her and the certainty that righteousness was on his side.

Now she sat in their sitting room, attempting unsuccessfully to eat some toast. Nausea and anxiety warred for dominance rendering her appetite nil. Samuel had assisted Marguerite in walking Elizabeth, but all he knew was that his master had left at dawn with Col. Fitzwilliam. It was logical to assume they were simply riding, yet she felt otherwise.

By nine-thirty when Richard knocked at the door, Elizabeth was in a near panic. She stood without thinking, swaying at the sudden pressure to her ankle. He was by her side in an instant.

"Richard! Where is William?"

"Calm down, Elizabeth; he is fine. Here, sit…"

"No! Take me to him now!" She clutched his arm tighter and took a step toward the door.

"Elizabeth, are you insane? If I allow you to walk all the way to the study, your husband will skin me alive. He sent me to assure you he is well and will be up as soon as he…"

"Listen to me, Richard Fitzwilliam," she said in a voice of steel, glaring through narrowed eyes, "I am certain you two were up to no good today. I do not know what, although I imagine it has something to do with Orman. You *will* take me to him this second."

Richard laughed and shook his head. "You two are quite a pair. Never have I seen two more stubborn people."

"Richard!"

"Alright, I concede. I fear you must submit to my carrying you, cousin. I am not brave enough to face the wrath of two Darcys in one morning."

When Lizzy entered her husband's study, it was to find him sitting shirtless on his desk, grimacing and smeared with blood, the physician bent over his right side. He glanced up in surprise at the sight of his wife in his cousin's arms.

Lizzy squealed and struggled frantically, Richard almost dropping her. She tottered to Darcy and he steadied her with a bandaged left hand. "Elizabeth, you are not supposed to be walking!"

"We can discuss that, Mr. Darcy, after you explain all this!" Richard burst out laughing, and even the doctor coughed a suppressed snicker.

Darcy was pale and weary but otherwise in quite good humor, so he too smiled at his wife. "Gentlemen, may we have some privacy?" When they left, he cupped her aggravated, teary face in his hands and kissed her deeply.

She succumbed for a moment and then yanked away angrily. "Fitzwilliam, you will not evade again with kisses!"

He smiled slyly, drawing her gently toward his lips once again, intoning huskily, "Oh, I do believe I could, beloved." He brushed her mouth lightly. "But I shall reveal all first."

He told her everything, dramatizing only moderately, as she examined his wounds. All were superficial except for the stab to his side that luckily had cleanly pierced the flesh, missing all vital organs. He had a nasty bruise between his shoulder blades and a painful bruise on his left instep.

"Are you in pain?"

"Nothing a whiskey and some tender female soothing will not alleviate."

She snorted. "I should spank you rather than succor you!"

He grinned roguishly, "As you deem just, my love. However, we should wait until the physician completes stitching me up."

She laughed, "Impossible!" She hobbled to the side bar and poured him a drink. She studied him as he drank deeply, hand shaking slightly. She ran her fingers through his hair, caressed his face and then kissed his cheek. "You are my hero, Fitzwilliam. I am so proud of you! I wish I could have witnessed Orman's defeat and your chivalry in action." Darcy smiled shyly and mumbled deprecatingly, humbly averting his eyes.

"Nevertheless, a sword duel is rather medieval and fraught with danger. Perhaps, dearest, in the future when you feel the urge to flex your muscles, you can choose a less deadly competition, for my sake and the sake of our child?"

"I shall faithfully endeavor to comply, Mrs. Darcy."

"Good. Later, in our bedchamber, I will administer that spanking so you will not forget." She smiled coquettishly, patting his rosy cheek, before calling the waiting men back in.

CHAPTER NINETEEN

Romantic Interludes

ERE WE ARE, BELOVED. That was not too awful, now was it?" Darcy asked with a smile, as he spanned his wife's waist with strong hands and lifted her from the horse's back. She was a wee bit shaky in the knees, so he held her securely, taking the opportunity to bestow moist kisses along her neck.

"Dearest, if your desire is for me to regain stability, kissing me will only hinder the outcome." She laced her fingers into his hair, tugging his head away from her neck, but claiming his mouth with her own for an enjoyable minute. "Show me your grotto, my love," she whispered huskily.

He took her hand and guided her cautiously up the slope around the backside of the Greek Temple. He had insisted she ride a horse on the long trek from Pemberley, not Parsifal thankfully, but one of the placid, curricle-pulling mares Lizzy had acquainted herself with. Her ankle twinged only slightly on occasion, but was not healed adequately to tackle the uneven grasslands, and she had discovered a heightened photosensitivity that sporadically induced minor headaches.

There remained vast areas of Pemberley's extensive grounds that Lizzy had yet to visit. Sadly, between her extended recuperation and the endless spring rains that consumed most of April, there simply had not been the opportunity. May had ushered in the traditional lovely Derbyshire weather and the last of the clouds had been swept away. The result was a profusion of blooms, greenery, tweeting birds, butterflies, and raging rivers. The ducks had returned to the small pond, placidly paddling amongst the minnows and tadpoles.

Lizzy had regained her strength and mobility by strolling along the array of garden paths closest to the house, sometimes with Darcy but usually with Georgiana as her husband's time was consumed by the demands of planting season and the annual cattle market in early May. There was a tremendous amount of work for him to conclude as next week they would be departing for Hertfordshire and then on to London for six weeks.

Lizzy was overjoyed at the prospect of seeing her family, especially Jane. Yet she could not deny a sense of sadness and homesickness already touching her at the notion of leaving Pemberley. Therefore, she had begged Darcy to devote a day, if possible, to acquainting her with his hidden sanctuary. He was delighted and had made all the arrangements. If riding a horse had not entered her consideration as part of the itinerary, it was worth it to be completely alone with the man she loved more than life.

The forest loomed to the rear of the temple as a seemingly impenetrable wall. Darcy unerringly skirted around the stone wall to a concealed break in the trees. The path was narrow and faint, shrouded by thick brush and overhanging branches so low that several times it was necessary to crouch. Unexpectedly, the tunnel-like path opened onto a glade carpeted in grasses and moss.

Thick trees and flowering shrubs of numerous varieties ringed the entire dell. Scattered glimpses of the pasturelands beyond could be seen through minor gaps in the leaves, but one felt utterly isolated from the outside world. A circle of the azure sky with cottony white clouds and radiant sun opened directly overhead. The pond was calm, transparent, and roughly thirty feet in diameter.

Lizzy halted at Darcy's side, her eyes sweeping the area with increasing enchantment. She looked up at her smiling husband. "William, it is breathtaking! Considerably larger than I imagined, yet every bit as beautiful and tranquil as you described. It is no wonder you sought and found peace here."

He led her to a level area before the pond. "I am not the first to exploit the serene influences inherent here. Darcys for untold generations have retreated to this sanctuary. It is a family secret that I now share with you, my lovely wife, and we will share with our children." He gently rubbed her abdomen and kissed her forehead as he hugged her. "Now, relax and I will return with the blankets and pillows." He kissed her again then left.

Lizzy sighed contentedly, breathing deeply of the clean, fragrant air. She sat on a flat rock and removed her shoes and stockings, worming bare toes into the soft grass and damp earth. Without hesitation, she unbuttoned her dress and stripped to her chemise. The cool air with lightly dappled sunshine contacted her bare skin, raising tiny bumps of tactile bliss. She stepped to the edge of the pool, testing the water with one toe and finding it surprisingly tepid.

Standing with the lukewarm fluid gently lapping about her shins, she released her hair, braiding it loosely in back. Tiny minnows swirled by her ankles, testing her toes for edibility and tickling her in the process. She wiggled her toes and teased with her fingers on the surface, frightening the little fishes momentarily, although they rapidly returned for fresh nibbles, filling her with mirth.

Darcy reentered the grove to find his wife cavorting like a child, practically naked, and belly laughing. He paused unheeded and observed her antics, filled to bursting with an overwhelming sensation of love mingled with felicity and youthful vivacity. No one in all his life, even when he was young, had evoked such a well of joy and unadulterated verve as she did. She sensed his silent presence and turned, eyes vibrant and sparkling, and smile radiant. There was not a moment in Darcy's day, awake or asleep, when her existence in his life was not a cause of awe and thankfulness. Yet, there were those odd moments, such as now, when he nearly fainted from the rapture that washed through his body at the reality that was Elizabeth.

"Remove your boots, my love, and join me. The fish are hungry and your toes are bigger," she teased. He did as she requested, adding his jacket to the pile. A fresh swarm of minnows attacked his feet with relish. "Is the water always so warm?" she asked, "I was surprised. We could bathe! Did you bathe here when you were young?"

"Frequently, yes. The pool is not deep so the water heats quickly. It is rocky though, so tread cautiously, beloved."

Lizzy splashed her way along the shallows, randomly selecting stones. "Oh, look William, this one has red and green swirls! It is lovely." He trailed her happily, taking the collection of unusual rocks for safekeeping. Once his hands were full, she drew close and firmly clasped her wet hands about this neck. He gasped and she giggled, skittering away.

"Unfair advantage!" He laughed, meeting up with her on the grassy clearing where she began busily spreading the blankets. Dropping the rocks, he pulled her onto the blankets, tickling mercilessly until she was breathless from laughter.

"Desist, I beg you! You win." She kissed him and then opened the lunch basket packed by Mrs. Langton. "Hungry, William?"

"Yes," he answered as he ran his hand leisurely up her leg. She turned to see him smiling sensuously with food clearly not on his mind. He kissed her knee, proceeding slowly along her inner thigh with soft kisses as he ran a hand along the other thigh, under the thin chemise, and around her bottom. She sighed happily, fingering silky hair as his head moved over her lap. He kissed her lower belly and then murmured, "Pardon your father, little one, but I must love your mother."

Lizzy laughed. "I do not think he yet has ears to hear you with, beloved."

Darcy kissed her pubis again. "Merely being polite, Elizabeth. Never too early to bestow proper manners." He traveled up her abdomen with kisses and caresses, lingering to peel the chemise away from her shoulders and access her breasts. "Aahh... so beautiful! Divinely appetizing." He nuzzled his face between, kissing languidly over her skin as she moaned in pleasure. Cautiously he licked one nipple, which hardened instantly as Lizzy inhaled sharply.

"Alright, beloved?"

Her breasts and nipples were ultra-sensitive lately, often so tender that they were painful. Other times the heightened tactility led to an increased arousal. Such was the case now, evidenced by how she tightened the grip in his hair and drew his face to her breast, arching impatiently and moaning.

With tantalizing kisses and caresses over every available inch of flesh, they removed their clothing, reveling in the intoxication of sunlight and balmy breezes wafting over their exposed skin. Both of them had dreamed of this for months: the arousing pleasure of making love in the out-of-doors, specifically in Darcy's grotto where many of his most treasured memories began. Their imaginings did not disappoint. Their union was stupendous and fulfilling, leaving them tingling and warmed to their inner souls, blissfully melded as one entity in a consuming love.

Afterwards, Lizzy lay stretched on Darcy's front side, arms crossed over his chest. She rested her chin on one hand, the other stroking feathering fingertips through his wispy hairs while he played with one long tress. They admired each other in serene approval. Darcy smiled and murmured a soft *hmmm* as he brushed her cheeks.

"What are you thinking, my love?" she asked.

"I am watching the sunlight wave over your face and it reminded me of the day I proposed, successfully, that is." He laughed lowly. "Many aspects of that day are rather dreamlike to me, but I vividly remember how the sun illuminated your beautiful face precisely at the instant you accepted me. It was as if God Himself blessed our proclamation."

"William, you are such a romantic and a poet! You ceaselessly astound me." She kissed the skin over his heart. "However, for the sake of clarity I am obligated to point out that your actual proposal occurred several minutes later," she teased, playfully pinching a nipple.

"A technicality, Mrs. Darcy. I do believe, if my memory serves, that you kissed me preceding the sun's caress, thus assenting to my declaration of love and wish to share my life with you."

She laughed. "We should say that you proposed three times! Each one an improvement and the kisses increasing in intensity and delight."

"Do not remind me, beloved. I nearly forfeited my right to the title of gentleman ere we were betrothed an hour!" They both smiled in happy remembrance. He grasped her shoulders tenderly and drew her closer, kissing passionately. "My Lizzy, my lover! It is fortunate I did not comprehend the ecstasy of our love prior to marriage, or I never would have maintained my restraint for those interminable two months. As it is, I was sorely tested. My ardor for you appears to be boundless."

He spoke the truth as decidedly evidenced when she pressed her hips against him. With reciprocated moans of pleasure they gave in to their love again. The memories of the day they at long last proclaimed their love and blissfully shared first kisses augmented their passion.

~❦~

Late September, 1816

"My affections and wishes are unchanged, but one word from you will silence me on this subject forever."

How do you tell a man whom you have rejected and so wounded about your emotions for him? Can they be conveyed in a kiss to the hand? In a mumbled, nonsensical reply? Perhaps to a degree. He stands before her, impossibly handsome, declaring a love and desire for a life commitment that she does not deserve, yet now accepts as what she yearns for with every heartbeat. *It will take all of my life, daily and hourly saying I love you, to wholly express the depth of my sentiments*, she thinks, and by some miracle he has offered her that chance again. She grabs onto it as a drowning man clutches the rope, vowing never to relinquish as he is her salvation from a lifetime of emptiness and despair.

Darcy stands stunned and anxious as she steps close, taking the offered hand and bestowing a gentle kiss and caress. No words are necessary, the gesture a declaration of caring and acceptance. He understands this although the dream-like atmosphere and months of longing despair prevent him from instantly grasping it. His hand is on fire! In fact, his whole body is aflame, jolted by waves of heat emanating from her soft lips and fingers. His soul is renewed, and he knows it is a miracle purely and completely. The beautiful face that has haunted his dreams is now lifted upward. He touches her cheek tentatively and the world ignites.

For a horrifying second he suspects she will flinch or slap him or vanish into the mist. Instead, she closes her lovely eyes and leans minutely into his hand. Nothing in all his eight-and-twenty years has prepared him for the sensation of her velvety warm skin cupped in his palm. It is the most erotic, exhilarating experience of his life! At that instant, the sun lights her glorious face, rendering her mien angelic. *It is a benediction from God Himself!* Only her flesh anchors him to the ground.

Relief overwhelms and, with eyes closed, they surrender to the sublime delight of a tender touch. This is love! A profound heat rushes from their connected skin to the roots of their loneliness, disintegrating forever the walls of misunderstanding.

Time halts. They are dazzled. Enchanted in the rays from Heaven.

"I love you," she whispers.

He inhales sharply and jerks as if stuck by a pin, eyes flying open. "Say it again," he pleads softly.

She smiles, "I love you... Fitzwilliam."

He shuts his eyes briefly, sighing with a sibilant moan. Then he flashes the brilliant smile she has so rarely seen, eyes sparkling and the palest blue. "Elizabeth. Lovely, precious Elizabeth," he breathes as delicate fingertips trace a line of fire across her jaw and chin, finally lingering on her lips.

She holds her breath. *He must kiss me!* Her mind screams, *I will die if he does not and likely die when he does!* She trembles as he gazes at her with heart exposed and raw emotion written on his visage.

Oh, Lord, how I long to kiss her! His well-honed discipline and reserve dangles by the thinnest thread. Years hence he will recall this struggle as one of the harshest of his life; his very soul wars with the agonizing need to crush her to his body as he kisses her thirstily against the desire to show her the honor and respectability that is her due. How he manages to control his urges will remain a mystery. With a visible shudder he withdraws a pace, clasping both her hands securely in his.

"Elizabeth," he begins huskily, pausing to clear his throat, "Elizabeth, there is much to say, much for me to apologize for, although I do not deserve your forgiveness. I did not plan this... rendezvous, and it is not how I intended to proceed in winning your affection. I wanted to court you properly and allot you time to improve your opinion of me and maybe, if I was so blessed, to have you love me. I never entertained the notion, even after my aunt restored my hope, that you felt a fraction of what I do."

She squeezes his fingers, smiling up into his eyes. "I do," she murmurs with a nod.

He exhales a happy sigh and shakes his head slightly in amazement. "Elizabeth, clever phrases and spontaneous conversation are not my forte, as you can attest. Therefore, Fate has gifted me with this adventitious opportunity and, considering how atrociously I botched my well-rehearsed proposal, Fate has proven the wiser." They both smile and laugh faintly. "Simplicity appears to be Fate's recommendation. Therefore, on that note..."

He grips her hands tighter and, without leaving her eyes for a second, he bends onto one knee. She releases a wavering sob as tears well over. Beaming, he asks, "Miss Elizabeth Bennet, I love you fervently and with all that I am. Will you honor me by becoming my wife?"

"Yes! Oh, yes, you know I will!"

Then she is in his arms and it is indescribable. There is no doubt the embrace is vastly more intimate and considerably longer than propriety would dictate. They do not care. Oddly, although perhaps not, there is only a hint of sensual passion; that will come later. Currently they merely delight in the closeness of the other, the engrossing sensation of belonging and unity.

Her face presses against his hard chest as she encircles his waist. A faint voice in her head wonders how she can be so brazen and improper. How can this form of intimacy feel absolutely correct so immediately? His radiating heat, heart pounding powerfully, and sturdy arms that encompass her body and keep her upright, all combine to create a haven of love and protection that surpasses imagination.

He encircles her lissome frame with stunned amazement. She is so small! Nearly from the instant his eyes touched hers at the Meryton Assembly, Elizabeth Bennet has loomed larger than life, to his reckoning. Her vibrancy, sharp intellect, and bold presence offset her svelte physique. As if designed specifically, her head rests perfectly on his breastbone and tucks exquisitely under his chin, while his arms easily surround her, broad hands flattening on her back. With a shock, he recognizes her fragility, coupled with an overwhelming strength. He could snap her bones facilely, yet she grips him with an unbelievably strong clench.

"Elizabeth," he whispers hoarsely, gently pushing her away from his body, "do you think your father is home? I must speak with him and I cannot wait any longer."

She looks up at him. He wipes the tears from her cheeks, eliciting fresh waves of heat so that she laughs shakily. "Yes, he is at home."

He offers his arm, "Come then. We should not linger here any longer."

They walk in silence, arm in arm, and steal glances at each other. Strangely, neither feels shy or uncomfortable, simply suddenly acutely aware of the other's presence and their unchaperoned companionship. She cannot resist focusing on his exposed neck and chest, as well as noting how the damp linen of his shirt clings to his muscles. His eyes betray him by continually resting on her braided hair, her delicate shoulder line, and the flash of an ankle when she lifts her gown.

"Do you prefer to be called 'Fitzwilliam,' or do you have another name?" she inquires abruptly.

"My full name is Fitzwilliam Alexander James Darcy. James was my father's name and Alexander after an ancestor. No one has ever used either. Fitzwilliam was my mother's maiden name. It is the surname of my uncle, the Earl of Matlock. Consequently there are quite a few 'Fitzwilliams' about at family gatherings." He laughs, a sound still startling to her ears but beautiful. She mentally notes to tell him so, but he continues. "My cousins are both often addressed as Fitzwilliam. Col. Fitzwilliam is my cousin. Did you know this?"

She is genuinely surprised, "No, I did not. Nor did I realize you had an earl for an uncle. Mother will be impressed." She laughs and he smiles.

"Richard, Col. Fitzwilliam, is two years my senior, but we grew up together and have always been friends as well as relatives. Anyway, my family all call me William. It is what I prefer, although I rather think you, dearest Elizabeth, could call me anything and I would find it delightful."

She blushes.

"Your family is so illustrious," she says teasingly. "Lords and ladies abounding!"

He flushes and grows somber. "Yes, well, I fear my Aunt Catherine has proven how a title does not indicate worth or an assurance of proper manners. Fortunately, you will discover my uncle and his wife quite different. They will adore you, I am certain." He gazes at her with a bright smile, rendering her breathless. Her steps falter in her rapt adoration of his face, providing the need for him to steady her with one hand to her elbow and the other around her waist, his face then mere inches from hers.

"Are you alright, Elizabeth?" She nods, unable to speak, and neither of them moves. She has always been captivated, even in her annoyance, at how penetrating his gaze is. He has the bluest eyes, fierce as a raptor and brimming with intelligence; yet she notes that they darken somewhat when he stares at her. Previously she had erroneously decided it was disapproval and disdain. Now she understands it is enthrallment, love, and… passion? Desire?

She blushes and tears her eyes away, resuming her steps. Clearing her throat gruffly, she says, "Proper manners or otherwise, having peers of the realm as relatives will win you points with my family! Mother, especially, will likely faint dead away, so be sure you lead with that fact." Her laugh fades when she glances to see him trailing a step behind her, his expression grave. "Mr. Dar… William? Whatever is the matter?"

He meets her eyes and smiles slightly. "I love hearing my name spoken by you, Elizabeth."

"How providential that you do since you will be hearing it so uttered for the rest of my life!" She unthinkingly reaches a finger to the tiny furrows between his brows, rubbing lightly. "What troubles you, William?"

Catching her hand and kissing her fingers, he holds on and resumes walking. After some ten minutes of silent contemplation, he speaks, "I am well aware of the fact that I made a poor impression on the citizens of Hertfordshire, aided partially by Mr. Wickham but primarily due to my own surliness. Your father has no reason to approve of me as a suitor, wealth or family connections notwithstanding. Nor do I wish him to render his approval based on those inconsequentials. It is imperative, Elizabeth, that he knows I love you and deem your happiness of the utmost importance."

They are now within sight of Longbourn so he halts, staring into the empty windows of the manor. She touches his chin with her fingers, drawing his gaze to hers. "William, my father is a reasonable man. Be honest, as I know you only can be, and say to him what you have said to me. He will not refuse you."

He searches her eyes, still frowning mildly. "Does he know about Rosings?"

"No one knows about that but us."

His brows arch in surprise, "Not even Miss Bennet?"

"No, I never told anyone. Did you?"

"Only Georgiana. She extracted the information as only she can." He smiles fondly. "In truth, I was a bit of a wreck after Rosings, and she was worried." He shakes his head and shrugs the unpleasant memories aside. A moment later he laughs.

"What?"

"It is humbling. I manage a vast estate and intricate affairs of business domestic and abroad without flinching, yet I am daunted by the prospect of a confrontation with a country gentleman." He looks at her, eyes sparkling with mirth, and reaches to caress gentle fingertips over one cheek. "Of course, not one of those ventures has ever been as vital to my existence as this one." He squares his shoulders purposefully, squeezes her hand, and turns toward the house, "Come, Miss Elizabeth, my love, destiny awaits!"

Hand in hand, they meet their fate.

"Enough, Mr. Darcy! Release me! I am famished, *your* child begging for food, no doubt. Not surprising if his appetite is like his father's."

He laughed and rolled away from her side, untangling his legs from hers. "Very well, although I believe it patently unfair to blame me for this. *She* could very well have *her* mother's stubbornness and be demanding nourishment without further delay."

Lizzy harrumphed, already busily removing victuals from the basket and tossing them randomly to her husband. She attacked the chicken with relish, thoroughly enjoyed the apple pie, gagged on the honeyed carrots, and flatly demanded Darcy discard the smoked salmon as far away as humanly possible.

She ate quickly, honestly thinking she would perish in seconds if not fed, and then required a half hour of absolute immobility to keep it inside. Darcy stroked her forehead and encouraged her to sip some wine to settle her stomach, speaking soothingly in his resonant voice until she fell into a doze.

He watched her sleep, marveling as he always did at how lovely she was. He laid his hand gently on her still flat abdomen and wondered. The signs of pregnancy were all increasing; however, until she felt the baby quicken, they had judged it best to delay formal announcements. The doctor was scheduled to examine her the day before they departed for Netherfield, Darcy insisting the doctor approve the long trip. In addition, they were hoping he could definitively confirm her state so they could freely share their private joy. Georgiana knew, of course, and Richard, but they had promised to be silent.

Society would dictate that he pray for a boy, an heir to Pemberley. In truth, he wished for a girl. A little angel with chocolate eyes, curly chestnut hair, and a pert nose. Nonetheless, the health of the child and his wife were the principal preoccupation. Lizzy, aside from sporadic nausea and mild lethargy, seemed unaffected thus far. Her appetite, as recently evidenced, was humorously vacillating. One moment she was queasy and literally the next second she was ravenous and weak.

Mrs. Reynolds had ordered to have small trays of eatables placed in nearly every room of the manor so the Mistress could nibble whenever she felt the urge. Lizzy had not actually been ill since the day her memory was restored, so Darcy did not fret overly. Inevitably, she managed to eat enough, and the medical book assured him that all she was experiencing thus far was perfectly normal.

Thankfully, her extreme moodiness had disappeared. Mornings were not her best time; therefore, their romantic interludes had ceased for what he hoped was a temporary duration. Not that he could complain in that quarter as overall her amorousness was unaltered, if not slightly increased. He had quickly reorganized his daily schedule to coordinate with her. Now he rose while she slept, went riding, or worked in the stables or at his desk for several hours before joining her for breakfast. For the bulk of the day he attended to business throughout the estate, rarely coming home for lunch, but returning mid-afternoon to convene for tea, which generally led to a pleasurable liaison before dinner.

He smiled with supreme contentment. No, Mr. Darcy had absolutely no cause for woe regarding the physical expression of their love. He never had. As previously stated, barely had her father given them his blessing when Darcy discovered, to his mingled humiliation and gratification, the sensual response they evoked in each other. Lost in delicious reverie, he lightly ran fingertips over her belly and hips, dipping into her navel, unaware that she had roused and was observing him.

"Have you traveled off to Mars or Jupiter, beloved, or somewhere closer by?"

He started at her voice and then laughed. "I no longer have the yearning to fly to the outer reaches of the heavens, dearest. Heaven is to be found here." He leaned over, kissed her stomach where he imagined their child rested, and then stretched out, gathering her into his arms. He kissed her forehead. "Do you feel well?"

"Yes, thank you. In fact, the remaining muffin smothered in honey is calling to me."

"Perhaps you should rethink that. Honey on the carrots made you retch."

"That was carrots, not a muffin, and quite some time ago. These matters change with the wind!"

He chuckled, lifting up and reaching into the basket to retrieve the desired treat. Pulling off small bites, he fed her, watching carefully for a negative response.

"What were you musing when I woke? You truly appeared a million miles away."

"Not so far as all that. More accurately some one-hundred-fifty miles, as I was revisiting our previous reminiscence of first kisses upon the occasion of your accepting my proposal. I have always been profoundly gratefully that we stood on the only side of Longbourn without windows. I am certain your father would have withdrawn his consent at the least, if not strangled me on the spot."

Lizzy laughed. "No fear of that, William, because he would have keeled over with a heart seizure first at the sight of his innocent daughter behaving so wantonly."

Darcy laughed but flushed brightly, the entire episode still a cause of amusement and embarrassment for him.

⁓❦⁓

Darcy waits in the courtyard and paces... and paces... and paces.

The interview with her father went well, sort of. Mr. Bennet evaded final consent, pending hearing Elizabeth's opinion. Knowing how she feels for him, as stunning as that revelation was, he should not be anxious. Yet he is. What he had not previously comprehended was the deep love Mr. Bennet held for his second daughter. Darcy had erringly regarded Mr. Bennet as rather foolish, lazy, and uninvolved as a parent.

Yet, within minutes of entering the study, Mr. Bennet put him on the defensive and displayed a keen intellect and unswerving devotion to Elizabeth. Realizing that this actually placed them on equal footing, Darcy altered his usual aloof, commanding approach. Instead, he relinquished all pride and bared his soul to the older gentleman. Mr. Bennet listened, nodding occasionally, but displayed little emotion. Then he calmly dismissed Mr. Darcy, giving no answer, and requested to speak with Elizabeth alone.

Her smile and warm pose as she entered her father's study did hearten him, but he could not erase the echo of Mr. Bennet's initial claim, blurted in his surprise, that Lizzy had previously asserted her hatred of Mr. Darcy. Thinking of those words made him flinch anew and pale in terror. Air and space were essential to quiet his irregular heartbeat and frayed nerves.

So now, he paces. She is taking so long! What if Mr. Bennet says no? What if he convinces Elizabeth that Mr. Darcy is unworthy of her, which he is? What if she tells him about Rosings? What if the spell of English mist over a sun-kissed moor is now broken and she realizes she does not love him? What if she does not even *like* him? What if… what if… what if?

Oblivious of all but his own misery, he abruptly hears a sharp giggle and glances up to see four pairs of eyes staring at him from the house. *Oh, this is too much!* Blushing furiously, he keeps walking past the edge of the house to the small garden beyond. He roughly picks a bloom and sinks onto the stone bench, fidgeting until the poor flower is mutilated.

Lizzy kisses her father's forehead, whispers a heartfelt *thank you*, and sprints from the room. She heads toward the parlor, logically deducing he would be there under barrage by her mother. Only imagining what horrors her family is subjecting the poor man to, she dashes in, pulling up short when her rapid scan of the room comes up empty of her betrothed.

"What have you done to him?" she blurts, all four of them pivoting toward her.

"Oh, Lizzy! How wonderful this is! Mr. Darcy! You have saved us all!" Mrs. Bennet is all atwitter, clutching her hand and gasping. Not wasting time, Lizzy glances to Jane, who smiles serenely and inclines her head toward the east garden.

Sprinting again, barely registering her mother's continued praise of her conquest, she flies down the steps, following the recently well-trod path to the garden. She slows only when she sees him. He sits on the bench, hunched over with his elbows on his knees, playing with something in his fingers. Her heart literally skips several beats and butterflies dance in her stomach merely at the sight of him.

He looks up, lurching so rapidly to his feet that she thinks he is attempting to leap to her, but he simply stands there staring at her face. The moment stretches as her smile widens.

"It is official. I am all yours."

The expressions crossing his countenance would be vastly humorous if she did not feel his turmoil. She laughs gaily as they swiftly reduce the gap between them, eventually standing less than a foot apart. He envelops her petite hands with a steadfast grip, face jubilant and awash with liberation. He places her enfolded hands against his throbbing heart and settles his forehead on hers, releasing a mighty sigh.

As delightful as the sensations are, she cannot prevent a giggle escaping. He pulls away a fraction and smiles at her blissful face. "Are you laughing at me?"

"Only a little. Did my frightening father scare you, Mr. Darcy?"

"He can be rather intimidating when he wishes it, Miss Elizabeth, and as he held my entire future happiness in his hands, I am not ashamed to confess being overcome with tremendous fear."

"I shall have to tell him. I doubt my father has frightened anyone in his entire life! He will be amused."

"How pleased I am to be a fount of amusement for the Bennet household. I believe I have also adequately supplied the daily portion of entertainment for your mother and sisters."

She bursts out laughing. "Poor William! Mr. Darcy, who hates to be teased, has received his allotment today."

Releasing one hand to finger the loose strands of hair away from her eyes and smiling unabashedly, he replies, "I suppose I should be chagrined, but I find that teasing does not annoy me as much as it once did. Levity appears to have entered my existence along with you, dear Elizabeth, and it heals me."

She continues to giggle. "So, are you better now? Your heart continues to pound."

"I judge my heart shall forever pound when near you." His voice deepens an octave and tender fingers trace over her features, darkened eyes following. "Elizabeth," in barely a whisper, "you are incredibly beautiful. I so love and adore you. I am the happiest of men."

Giggles cease. She is breathless and mesmerized, captured by his eyes and the renewed thrills racing through her body at his touch. His eyes and fingertips have reached her parted lips, feathering lightly. Panting breathlessly, voice nearly inaudible, she pleads, "William."

"Elizabeth, please, may I kiss you?"

Unable to speak, she only nods faintly. As if in a dream of exquisite beauty with gazes riveted, he lowers his head slowly while cupping her face with his strong yet tender hands. Thumbs caress her cheeks and their eyes slide shut with the gentle pressure of mouths brushing once, then again and again and again.

Are there words adequate to describe what is indescribable? Their kisses are restrained, pure, and delicate; yet the sensations educed are torrential, dynamic, and astonishing. Simultaneous shivers and sighs of pleasure escape their lips and they laugh softly, twinkling eyes meeting.

"Is it supposed to feel so… incredible?"

He smiles and shakes his head minutely. "I would not know, but I believe it should." Without another word he claims her mouth again, kissing with gradually increasing fervor, hands traveling to her neck for soothing strokes.

Of their own volition, her hands begin tentatively exploring the muscular contours of his chest and shoulders, moving up to encircle his bare neck with fingers entwined in his hair. Her lips instinctively part and, in a rush of primal need, he deepens the kiss, moaning faintly when she responds hesitantly in kind. It is sheer ecstasy! The warmth and moisture and intimacy of this manner of kissing beyond anything either of them has ever experienced.

Leaving her luscious mouth, he plants moist kisses all about her face. He kisses the top of her head, inhaling deeply of the lavender scent in her lush hair that he began associating with her months ago. Intoxicated beyond the effect of a fine wine, he rains soft kisses along her scalp to her ear and then to the sensitive flesh behind her lobe. He moans her name, utterly lost to love and rising passion and gently drawing her earlobe between his lips while his hands caress over her arms and then to her upper back, unwittingly pulling her closer to his body. Returning to her open, receptive mouth, he ardently pours his very soul into this rapturous expression of their mutual love and craving. She matches each motion, responding to him with greater boldness that escalates rapidly to a wild abandon.

She groans loudly, unconsciously pressing her entire body tightly against his, arms over his shoulders and clutching his back and head with alarming power. Cold reality crashes over him with the awareness of his marked physical arousal, evident to them both as indicative of the strict line he has allowed himself to cross. Utterly mortified and shamed, he clasps her shoulders and frantically pulls away.

Unable to meet her eyes, agonizing at the reproach and horror he expects and deserves to see there, he hoarsely stammers, "Elizabeth... Miss Elizabeth, I beg your forgiveness! My behavior is ungentlemanly and unforgivable. Please, accept my heartfelt apology."

She is confused and dazed with strange but pleasant currents racing through her, her heart fluttering so alarmingly that she is light-headed. Feeling bereft at the sudden abandonment of his warmth, she stutters, "I... I am so sorry... I thought you wanted to... I should not have..." Shy and insecure for the first time since encountering him that day, tears well in her eyes and she hangs her head to avoid his gaze.

For a few moments they stand there not touching, breathing heavily, and collecting their befuddled thoughts.

"What you must think of me..." she mutters.

"Can you forgive me, my love... ?" he blurts at the same instant.

"Forgive you... what?" she asks in surprise.

"Whatever do you mean, 'think of you?'" again speaking over each other.

"I behaved so wantonly..."

"I lost control of myself..."

Halting mid-sentence, they stare at each other. Slowly she begins to smile and laugh quietly. He watches her in perplexity, flushing and then gradually lifting his lips in amusement as her laugh deepens.

"She is laughing at me again."

"On the contrary, I am laughing at us! Mr. Darcy, let me see if I understand this: you are apologizing for enjoying kissing me, your betrothed, while I am apologizing for responding to said kisses?" He nods, flushing brighter. "Therefore, in effect, we are apologizing for being in love?"

He opens his mouth and then snaps it closed, glancing away from her enchanting face. "It does seem rather ludicrous when you state it thusly." He looks at her, countenance serious, and clasps her hands. "Elizabeth, you surely understand that it is not merely the enjoyment of our love that concerns me, but the appropriateness of its expression before we are wed. It is shockingly improper for us to even discuss these matters, let alone experience them!"

She bites the corner of her lip and averts her gaze. "William, I appreciate your concern, although I submit that little about our relationship has been proper or appropriate, and yet here we are. You are correct, of course, in maintaining decorum until we are married, but…"

"Elizabeth, please, I…" he begins, but she interrupts with a fierce, teary stare.

"Mr. Darcy, I will not apologize for communicating openly with you! Nor will I hide my love for you. We have done far too much of both, nearly losing each other in our stupidity, misconceptions, and pride."

He studies her eyes, grinning happily. "You are amazing, Elizabeth, and I love you ardently." Embracing her comfortingly, he kisses her sweet lips lightly.

"Lizzy!" Jane's voice calls from the corner of the house. "Luncheon is ready. Mr. Darcy is welcome."

"Thank you, Jane. We will be in directly."

Holding each other, he strokes her face and she runs her fingers over his features, smiling happily and wholly content. Another tender kiss and then he pulls away, bringing her hand to his lips. "I shall leave you now, dearest. Extend my gratitude to your mother, but I am not presentable and, frankly, my heightened emotions would render me unfit for polite company. I will return this evening."

He takes a step to leave, but she grips his hand to halt him. In a burst of enthusiasm, she wraps her free hand around his neck, pulling him toward her as she lifts on her tiptoes, kissing him soundly. When she releases him finally, they are breathless and his eyes are smoldering afresh, having so briefly been restored to a state of calm.

"From here on, I promise to behave as I should and not tempt fate. So, remember these kisses, Fitzwilliam Darcy, and do not doubt my love for you!"

He can only nod as she propels him out of the garden. At the back door, they part with formal salutations and proper hand kisses. She watches him until he is out of sight, and then, with a giddy laugh and a twirling dance, she joins her family.

"Perhaps you should not enter the water, William. Your wound is not fully healed."

Darcy looked down at the twin scars on his side, still reddened and puckered, but healing well despite him removing the stitches without the physician's consent and constantly scratching at it. Lizzy was forever slapping his hands and scolding him. The laceration on his chest had mended quickly, a residual fine pale line the only evidence. His bruises had faded rapidly, although his left foot still pained him if he stepped the wrong way. She joked that they were a pair of invalids. He joked that they therefore must each nurse the other with tender loving.

"It is well sealed over and no longer pains me, well, not too terribly that is. Do not fret. Come." Taking her hand, he led her as they cautiously waded over the rocks to the middle of the pond. At its deepest a mere four-and-a-half feet, the temperate water was blissful. Crouching down, the water rising to mid-chest, he held Lizzy in his arms as they floated leisurely about.

"Oh, this is delightful," she sighed, lying backwards to float on top of the water. Darcy firmly clasped her waist and thrilled at the sight of her. "I have not done anything like this since I was a small girl. The lake near Longbourn was a favorite haunt on hot summer days. Sadly, when a girl reaches a certain age, it is considered unseemly to play in the water."

"Yet you did it anyway, am I correct in assuming, Mrs. Darcy?"

She opened her eyes and grinned. "Oh, how well you know me, husband. Of course I did! My mother nearly fainted each time and insisted my father punish me, which he did not do." She laughed. "You might remember this and reweigh any wishes for daughters resembling me, beloved. Two or more of us may prove beyond your endurance."

"Obviously Mrs. Reynolds has been remiss in her duty to regale you with stories of my exploits as a youth, or have not my scars convinced you? My temperament may be serious, but I was reckless. Combine our attributes and, regardless of sex, I imagine we are both doomed to early gray hairs."

She sat up in his lap, winding her wet arms around his shoulders. "I heard past-tense words in that sentence. In light of recent events, I deem not much has changed in respect to your recklessness." She kissed him.

Grinning, he declared, "I have been properly chastised for my mischief, may I remind you, and owing to how well you administer spankings, perhaps our children will not be so intolerable after all."

"Ha! Children, I am to understand, are not supposed to *enjoy* the spanking."

"Maybe you need to practice the discipline further. I will be happy to oblige, for the sake of your increased excellence and our children's upbringing, of course." He nuzzled her neck, delivering tiny bites.

"Incorrigible! Perhaps we should pray for girls after all."

"Oh yes, because you, Mrs. Darcy, are all that is sweetness and light!"

Lizzy laughed gaily, hugging her husband close and resting her head on his shoulder as he gently glided about the pond. They bounced along in silent contentment, Lizzy actually beginning to fall into a doze, while Darcy held her and softly kissed any available skin.

The afternoon continued in much the same manner. They bathed until fingers and toes were wrinkled like summer prunes, drying in the filtered sun as they strolled about the glade. Lizzy snipped flowers while Darcy educated her regarding the unique Derbyshire vegetation. Frequent they retired to the blankets for snacks and sips of wine while Darcy read to her. Mainly they talked about anything and nothing, deliriously content to be completely alone for probably the last extended length of time, considering the hectic weeks to come. As the sun sank far below the tops of the towering trees, plunging the grotto into shadow, they made love again. They nestled and lazily kissed until the sun was nearly spent, the dell dark and chilly when they finally rose and dressed.

Lizzy was hesitant to vacate the grotto. No matter how often they revisited this place, and they frequently did over the years, this interlude would be special. She halted at the edge of the trail for a last look around, moving only when Darcy lightly touched her elbow. "Come away, beloved, it is late. We will return in June and have many months to return here." He kissed her temple and she sighed, finally turning.

Acknowledgments

THERE ARE LITERALLY HUNDREDS OF people I could thank for making this adventure a reality. Naturally Miss Austen for creating these characters, Deborah Moggach for her fabulous screenplay adaptation of *Pride and Prejudice*, and Joe Wright for directing the film so brilliantly.

Personally I thank my own Mr. Darcy, who for more than twenty years has shown me what true love is and has further made me a believer by supporting me in this endeavor, no matter how late dinner was placed on the table. And massive hugs to my two fantastic kids for being so patient when Mom was lost at the laptop!

I thank the plethora of readers from my website (www.darcysaga.net) who have endured, inspired, and encouraged me every step of the way. You have made me believe in myself, and I absolutely do not have the words to convey the depth of my appreciation. I love you all! I also want to thank Deb Werksman and everyone at Sourcebooks for believing in me and this story. Last and most important, I must give all praise, glory, and thanks to my Lord and Savior Jesus Christ. He is my ultimate Rock and the Creator of all good things.

Thank you for taking this journey with me. The Darcys thank you as well!

About the Author

SHARON LATHAN IS A NATIVE Californian currently residing amid the orchards, corn, cotton, and cows in the sunny San Joaquin Valley. She divides her time between being a homemaker nurturing her own Mr. Darcy and two teenage children and working as a registered nurse in a neonatal ICU. Throw in the cat, dog, and a ton of fish to complete the picture. When not at the hospital or attending to the often dreary tasks of homemaking, she is generally found reposing in her comfy recliner with her faithful laptop.

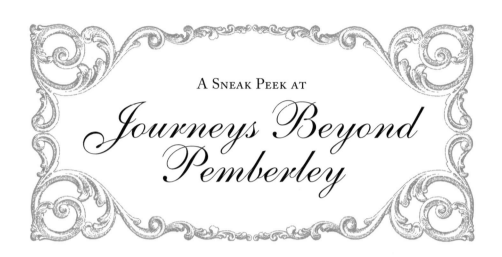

A SNEAK PEEK AT

Journeys Beyond
Pemberley

ELIZABETH DARCY STOOD NEXT to Georgiana on the massive portico before the main doors to Pemberley. They were dressed in their traveling clothes, the grandest and plushest of the Darcy carriages parked in the drive, waiting patiently for the Master of Pemberley who was currently speaking with his steward, Mr. Keith.

The warmth of May in Derbyshire had set in full force, days radiant with bright sunshine until late into the evening. The vast gardens of Pemberley were responding as Mr. Clark and his staff diligently engineered with literally every color of the rainbow bursting in nearly eye piercing splendor. Trees of every species indigenous to England, and many that were not enhanced the landscape with diverse shades of green and leaves in a multitude of shapes and sizes. Lizzy had regained her strength and mobility by traversing the miles of pathways weaving through the varied gardens. The by-product of her wanderings was a familiarity and deepening love of this place that was now her home.

Lizzy dreamily mused at how tremendously she had changed in the nearly five-and-a-half months since she ascended these same stone steps as a nervous bride. Outwardly her entire appearance was drastically altered with gowns and jewels and furs beyond her vaguest imaginings six months ago now normal. Her hair, even in its traveling coif, was superior to anything she had ever fashioned previously. She was largely unaware of it, but there was a serenity and grace to her bearing that had not been present before. She would forever laugh spontaneously and carry a ready quip on her lips, but her character was notably more refined and softened. The minute gestures and vocal intonations associated with the social etiquette of the upper classes had permeated her being unconsciously.

Inwardly she recognized a happiness and contentment that anchored her soul. Although there remained an enormous amount of Pemberley's management and the Darcy business affairs that she did not understand, her role as Mistress of Pemberley was a comfortable and accepted one. Her place in the household and the community was firm, and her confidence was secure. This massive house, which had frankly frightened her to death initially, was now home. She no longer walked through the endless halls with feelings of paralyzing awe and unworthiness. In five short months she had grown to love the manor and its surrounds with a devotion transcending anything she had ever felt for Longbourn. Already she missed the library and bedchamber and sitting room and…well, all of it! The approximately six to seven weeks of their planned absence stretched before her as an empty sadness despite her excitement to see her family, and it was necessary to exert every ounce of self will to not rush inside for one last glance.

At that moment her husband strode out the door with the purposeful and powerful gait uniquely his own, mien intense and serious as he imparted a few last minute instructions to his steward. He paused as Mr. Keith commented about something. Lizzy smiled in admiration at the picture he presented. Commanding all to attention as he stood with shoulders back, masculine six-foot-three-inch frame erect and impeccably dressed, elegant and regal, with sonorant voice authoritative. Pure potent love and incredible pride burst through her as a wave. All that she had become in these past months was due to him. His love for her, his devotion and respect, his loyalty and faith in her capabilities, his steadfastness and latitude, and most importantly his intuitive comprehension of her temperament, perceptions, and requirements collectively encouraged her to blossom into the woman she now was.

He nodded in finality, shook the steward's hand, and turned to his sister and wife. Instantly his face lit with a beaming smile, and although no less noble or masterful, his countenance softened considerably.

"My dears, are you ready?"

"Waiting for you brother."

"Come then," and he offered an arm to each of his two favorite women in the entire world. He assisted Georgiana into the coach first, made sure she settled comfortably, and then turned to Lizzy inquiring with deep concern, "Are you well, beloved?"

"I am fine, William. Do not fuss so." She patted his cheek and took his offered hand.

Leaning close and wholly indifferent to the hovering servants, he kissed her forehead. "I will fuss whether you wish it so or not, Mrs. Darcy. Therefore you may as well own to any discomfort you have immediately to save me perpetually questioning!"

He assisted her into the carriage, following behind, as she laughed. The truth was that she had been increasingly indisposed for the past five days. She had attempted to hide her infirmity from Darcy, but this was a fruitless endeavor. His eagle-eyed scrutiny and intimacy with all matters regarding his wife had penetrated any guile she ventured. The physician had examined her yesterday and confirmed that which they had presumed: she was definitely with child. Despite previously harboring little doubt, the Darcys greeted the validation with jubilance. If her queasiness and extreme fatigue prevented her from literally jumping for joy, her heart was leaping. Darcy was nearly beside himself with euphoria, and only Lizzy pleading with him to enlighten their families first kept him from informing all of Derbyshire.

The doctor had given her a clean bill of health, assuring them both that her symptoms, albeit difficult, were completely standard. He guessed that the worst of her nausea and lethargy would pass in a month or so, at about which time quickening would occur. He had spoken to them both at length and bluntly as to what to expect. As for the trip itself, he saw no reason to postpone or cancel, merely urging to take it slowly. In light of the occasional mild headaches Lizzy suffered as a lingering effect of her trauma coupled now with pregnancy, it was wise and essential to not overextend.

With this in mind Darcy had plotted the normally one day trip to Netherfield as a two-day journey, departure not until mid-morning when Lizzy usually felt better. So here they now were at nearly eleven o'clock and finally wheeling south on the long Pemberley drive. The two carriages with their luggage, Samuel, Marguerite, and Mrs. Annesley had left earlier. A courier had been dispatched to London the week prior to prepare Darcy House and another to Hertfordshire for the Bingleys and Bennets. Lizzy sat close to Darcy, gazing out the open window until Pemberley, with Mr. Keith and Mrs. Reynolds waving their adieus, completely disappeared from view. With a heavy sigh, she nestled under his out-stretched arm and he hugged her tightly. "I miss it already," she said.

"I always feel that way too," Georgiana replied, "until I get to London. There is so much to entertain! The symphony, the plays, the park across from our townhouse, the little paddle boats on the lake…"

"The shopping," Darcy interrupted with a grin.

Georgiana blushed, "Yes, the shopping as well, although it is you, dear brother, who insist I obtain new gowns and the like. In the end, you buy more for me than I acquire for myself!"

Lizzy laughed. "Somehow that does not surprise me."

Darcy was unfazed, "I shall not apologize in providing for and spoiling the women in my life."

"Elizabeth, you will so enjoy the shopping. We can purchase baby items! Oh, how wonderful it will be." Georgiana glowed and clapped her hands in enthusiasm.

The older Darcys smiled indulgently, Lizzy personally too weary and queasy to visualize tromping through the clogged, odiferous streets of London as anything less than horrible. In truth, she was taking this entire excursion one step at a time. Currently she only focused on seeing her family and proudly squiring her handsome husband about. As shameful as the emotion was she experienced fresh surges of vanity at how wonderful he was in every conceivable way as far as she was concerned, and how amazing that he belonged to her. She glanced up at his face as he exchanged pleasant conversation with his sister, his lush voice vibrating through her body where she pressed against his side. Six months ago, she thought her love for him stronger and deeper than her heart could contain, yet it was as a single star in the array of the endless heavens compared to now.

He met her eyes, smiling sweetly as he stroked her cheek then kissed her briefly. He repositioned his body slightly sideways so she could recline onto his chest, long legs stretched completely across the spacious carriage interior. She dozed for short spells throughout the journey, snacking sporadically from the generous provisions provided by Mrs. Langton, while Darcy read.

The trip was uneventful, arriving safely at the inn Darcy had secured near Northampton. Lizzy had a moderate headache from the unrelenting sun and jostling which she had successfully hid from her husband for the past hour. However, when she exited the carriage, Darcy aiding her, a flash of light reflecting off a glass window of the inn pierced her brain as a bolt. She cried in pain, reflexively released Darcy's hand to press palms to throbbing temples, and crumbled to her knees.

"Elizabeth!" She was in his arms within the span of a heartbeat, Darcy barking orders sending servants dashing to obey. It was all rather a daze to Elizabeth, head hammering and stomach churning. In record time, she found herself lying on a plush bed with a cold compress over her face, a frantic Darcy at her shivering side.

"Here, my love, drink this. I do not believe you have consumed enough fluids today. An error of mine that I shall not repeat. Marguerite," he turned to Lizzy's maid standing nearby, "please retrieve Mrs. Darcy's blue gown and robe." He assisted Lizzy with the glass, unbuttoning her dress as she drank.

"Darling, I will be fine in a moment," she began shakily, but he halted her by pushing the half-empty glass against her lips.

"Hush now, Elizabeth. You need to rest. Drink, that is an order, and then you must sleep. I will have dinner brought to us later."

"No, William! I will rest here as you wish, but you go and dine with Georgie. Spend the evening with her as we planned. Marguerite will stay with me." He started to protest but she interrupted, "It is merely a headache from the light. My own stupidity for not shutting the shades. It will fade quickly; they always do. You need to eat a complete meal."

He argued further, but Marguerite assured him she would send for him if needed. As Lizzy was already slipping into a doze, he reluctantly relented. By the time he returned several hours later, she was awake, had eaten a hearty dinner, and the headache had dissipated. She sat on the balcony gazing at the stars when he joined her. She nestled onto his lap, cuddling contentedly, and they talked quietly. She appeared rested and in her usual lively humor, but he remained anxious for her health, internally chastising himself for not lowering the shades.

He kissed the top of her head where it nestled so perfectly under his chin, his arms tightening around her body. "As delightful as it is to stargaze with you I insist we retire. You need your rest for the remainder of our journey, and I will not risk the health of you or our child."

"You worry unnecessarily, my love. The headache has vanished, I slept so am well rested, ate an excellent dinner, and am currently blissfully embraced by my handsome husband. What more could a woman possibly want?" She smiled up at his anxious face, wiggled closer, nestled her face into his neck, and bestowed a light kiss. "Actually," she said, imparting another kiss, "I do have a marvelous idea." She slid one hand under the hem of his shirt, nibbled on one earlobe, and slipped the tip of her tongue into his ear. "A final activity to fully restore my health."

"Elizabeth," he sighed, eyes shutting in pleasure, "we should wait until… settled at Netherfield…please…" Moans interrupted words as she firmly situated his hand on a breast while her lips traveled deliciously along his jaw. "Your headache could return, beloved, listen to me…"

Lizzy stopped his voice by seizing his lower lip and sucking gently. Darcy moaned again, unconsciously rocking a burgeoning arousal into her bottom and rubbing her breast.

"You talk too much, Fitzwilliam."

"No one has ever accused me of that!"

She smiled and began seductively stroking and kissing him. He earnestly struggled to dissuade her, but to no avail. Lizzy's obstinacy was manifest in a myriad of ways, and one was when she desired him. Of course, Darcy never strived to avoid romantic activities with his wife, so he was not well experienced in how to do so!

Lizzy laughed at his stammering opposition. "I want to love you, Fitzwilliam, any way you desire. I crave your touch on my skin and your body on mine. I hunger to bring you pleasure and show you how ardent my love for you." She kissed his eager mouth passionately, overwhelming senses with her breath and insistence. Pulling away finally, she whispered, "Take me to bed, my lover."

He stared into her eyes for a moment longer, searching carefully for any residual pain or fatigue, but only sheer desire and love shone forth. With a sigh, gripping her securely in strong arms, he stood and entered their bedchamber. The inn's bed was not as large as Pemberley's ,or as fine, but it was comfortable. Darcy sat on the edge, lying his wife gently back onto the downy comforter while kissing her lovely mouth.

Pulling back mere inches, he stroked the hair from her face, twining silky tresses about his fingers as he gazed at her. "Elizabeth, you are incredibly beautiful. With each day your loveliness increases. I do not comprehend how it is possible, yet it is true."

In typical Darcy fashion he alternately caressed, kissed, and nibbled over each delicate facial feature, all the while murmuring endearments and praises for the beauty of his wife. Lizzy's eyes were closed, her senses reeling with her husband's words of devotion and heated touch. Darcy paused at her lips, running feathery fingertips over her flesh, observing her rising passion with tremendous satisfaction and indescribable happiness. "Elizabeth," he whispered, "my wife, my lover." He slid his tongue over her lower lip as she sighed. "Mine forever, beloved...Mrs. Darcy."

Elizabeth had long ago succumbed to the amazing reality of her husband, but the magnificence of his physique never failed to overwhelm her. His potent masculinity and virility and stamina continually stunned her. The sensations they roused in each other at the tiniest touch, or even at a look, staggered her still, yet she embraced it as a heaven-gifted expression of the extraordinary bonding love they shared. After nearly six months of marriage, their passion only grew stronger, their lovemaking as necessary as breathing, with rarely a day passing without gratifying release and blissful devotion to the other achieved, often more than once. They occasionally purposed to experiment with some new technique from the books or a fantasy, yet usually their movements simply evolved naturally at the moment. Opportunities arose spontaneously and were latched onto with zeal, neither hesitant to try something new. Trust was unwavering, love unmatched, and desire to please the other first of paramount importance. Selfless giving was the central goal.

Tonight was different only in Darcy's residual apprehension, which induced him to proceed in a reserved manner despite Lizzy's clear desire for a wild interlude. In the end, she would not care, as their mutual rapture was as blissful and blinding as always.

Slowly reality and strength returned to them both. Lizzy moved first, turning in his arms and encircling his shuddering, damp skin, and bestowing a lingering kiss. "I love you," they said concurrently and then chuckled, kissing one another tenderly.

Smoothing the tangled hair off her forehead, he kissed a perfectly arched brow. "Are you well, my love?"

"I am divine but sleepy. Hold me, William?"

"Forever, Elizabeth. Forever."